A low, chuckling laugh rolled out of the mist, and a shadowy form paced up to the very edge of visibility, a gray shadow against the lantern-lit fog. "So you noticed, did you? I told him that his spell wasn't subtle enough." His accent was Aundairian; his tone, cocky.

He paced closer, slowly resolving into a three-dimensional person. He carried a dark shield on one arm, but no weapon in his free hand. Five more vague shadows appeared on both sides of the trio, cutting off any potential escape.

"But we noticed you, too," said the man. "And now it's time for you to pay the full fare for everyone on the *Silver Cygnet*." He snapped his fingers. "Let's go, people."

Brandishing weapons, the five shapes closed on their victims, two next to the speaker at Cimozjen's right, three from his left.

Cimozjen steeled his resolve.

the inquisitives

Bound by Iron

Edward Bolme

BOUND BY IRON

The Inquisitives · Book 1

©2007 Wizards of the Coast, Inc.

Cover art by Michael Komarck
First Printing: April 2007

9 8 7 6 5 4 3 2 1

ISBN: 978-0-7869-4264-0
620-95930740-001-EN

U.S., CANADA,
ASIA, PACIFIC, & LATIN AMERICA
Wizards of the Coast, Inc.
P.O. Box 707
Renton, WA 98057-0707
+1-800-324-6496

EUROPEAN HEADQUARTERS
Hasbro UK Ltd
Caswell Way
Newport, Gwent NP9 0YH
GREAT BRITAIN
Save this address for your records.

Visit our web site at www.wizards.com

Dedication

For my father, Donald Weston Bolme, known affectionately as "Bop" by his grandchildren: You taught me more about morality than pretty much the rest of the world combined.

Acknowledgements

My deepest gratitude to my wife, Sarah, for her patience and support in trying times.

To my editor, Mark, for working with me so hard on this and for being candid enough to say that he hates my outlines.

To Dr. John D. Butts, Chief Medical Examiner, for providing a reality check.

To Rick Sowter, Steven Wilber, and Jack Lee for being available; and to Jeff LaSala, Marcy Rockwell, and Paul Crilley for cross-promotion.

I would also like to thank the many fans who've written me or posted online such nice things about my previous work. I don't do this for the compliments. I do it to bring you entertainment and a few things to think about. But such feedback is the only way I can learn about whether or not I have succeeded.

Table of Contents

Prologue

The world crashed in on him, blinding light surging on waves of chaotic noise.

The warforged raised an arm to shield his eyes as one wall of his home swung open. He stepped out, holding his axe at the ready as he always did, as he did even in the darkness, for the world was an unpredictable beast. It was always there, lurking, waiting to strike. Every noise that dripped from it oozed peril.

He looked about at the surrounding circle of spiteful faces, and he felt awash in bloodthirsty eyes, snarling mouths, and angry fists. He turned slowly, staggering on the slanting floor, searching for the one who would try to kill him. Someone always did. Thus far he had survived the assassins, slain them, every one.

At last the warforged marked him. A human with long, unkempt, salt-and-pepper hair and a stew-matted beard. He carried a round shield in his right hand and a three-headed war flail in his left. A patchwork of scars served as his mail, crisscrossing his pale skin. He wore ragged breeches that came to just below his knees, and simple leather shoes ill suited for combat. An iron band of elegant design encircled his left arm above the biceps. As thin as the

1

human was, it was surprising that the armband didn't slide off.

The human came closer, swinging the spiked heads of his weapon in a small circle. The steady centrifugal pull of the chains allowed the human to sense their position at all times, which reduced the chances that a snap strike might result in an errant flail head.

This human has been trained to kill, he thought, but I have been *forged* for this purpose.

His unblinking magewrought eyes captured every nuance of the human as he closed. The human was skilled, perhaps even had the greater skill, but it was the rare human for whom war was ingrained as tightly as it was for a warforged.

Positioning his large battle-axe defensively, he kept the aging human at bay, dodging the spiked heads of the swinging flail and allowing nothing more than a minor gouge across his expressionless metal face. He backpedaled often, forcing the human to use more energy to close the ground again. As the battle progressed, he found that he was rather familiar with his assailant's battle technique. He had seen it twice before, demonstrated by two other humans similarly aged and armed. They had not been not quite as skilled as this one, but he had learned much from them.

He had killed them. This one he would kill too.

He feinted forward, throwing his assailant off stride, forcing him to begin his assault anew. The warforged made a deliberately errant strike. And, as he had anticipated, it drew the human into a familiar pattern of blows, a five-swing combination that made use of the swinging chains to attack the head and each side of the torso and legs in one smooth series, maximizing the momentum of the flail heads.

It was a dangerous combination. The first time it had nearly undone him. The second time he had been able to evade the worst of it. But the warforged had thought about it for many long hours in the darkness, and he knew that the third time he would prevail.

The human executed the fourth swing, the fifth . . . and the warforged stepped into the blow with his battle-axe held high. He allowed the chain to wrap around his right forearm. The spiked heads smashed into his armor plating. Then he shifted his grip on the haft of his battle-axe to pin the flail heads in place, locking the human's weapon with his.

A look of surprise crossed the human's face. The warforged pulled, and the human reflexively yanked back, not wanting to lose his weapon. The warforged abruptly switched from a pull to a push, and the haft of his axe struck the human squarely across the chest, knocking him down.

The warforged released the grip of his right hand, allowing the human to pull the flail off. With his left, he spun the great axe around and brought it up over his head. Then, with a mighty two-handed swing aimed at the center of his supine opponent, he ended it.

The warforged yanked the heavy blade from the human's breastbone, and took a moment to ensure that the blow had been lethal. Save for a tremor that came and left, the human lay still.

The victorious warforged looked about at the sea of faces. They were exuberant, anguished, relieved, but none were still hateful, none still looked at him.

He turned. He went back home.

And the blissful darkness enclosed him.

Chapter ONE

Dark Meetings
Zol, the 10th day of Sypheros, 998

Clutching her cloak about her, Henya glanced up at the sky. The rain clouds had largely broken up, their energy spent. Somewhere beyond her sight, the sun drew near the horizon, sinking behind the dark evergreen trees that covered the land of Karrnath. Although the sky still shone with pallid autumn sunshine, down in the cobbled streets of Korth all was growing dark. Not only dark but cold. Protected by the quiet embrace of the building's shadows, the damp chill of impending winter crawled out of the alleys to slither through every gap in her cloak, and pry at every loose seam of her clothing. If the sunshine had still reached into the narrow streets she walked, she would have seen her own breath. As it was, she felt it condensing on her hood as she tried to hunker down even further into the folds of her cloak.

She was cold, that much was true, but she had food. One hand extended from the front of her wrappings to hold the handle of a large woven basket, by necessity leaving a drafty opening in her cloak and slowly chilling her fingers through. The basket was filled with a large pork roast and several round loaves of dark rye or, as her father called it, "chamber music." It was simple fare, especially with the weak home-brewed beer her father made, but it was better than the alternative. Her family had suffered deep pangs of hunger during the famine two winters past. They'd been so hungry that they'd barely had the energy to chop wood for the fire, so they'd spent the long winter months cold and famished, chewing on shoe leather to ease their growling stomachs. It had been a miserable way to celebrate the end of the Last War.

That and her younger brother had never come home. She'd helped him learn to walk those many years ago, and now she wondered whether he still could. Could he still walk, or had he been crippled? Or did he lie rotting in some forgotten field somewhere?

She'd asked, of course, as had so many others. Standing in long lines at the Korth military administrative bureau. Stoically awaiting her turn to hear . . . nothing.

Her brother's death she could handle. Through hunger, siege, and battle, the Last War had taken her great-grandfather, two granduncles, and several of her aunts, uncles, and cousins. She'd grown up with stories of martial valor and the last battles of many of her relatives. She'd known all her life the war might take her brother as well. Such sacrifices were necessary for the preservation of the nation and brought glory to the family name. And even dead, a Karrn soldier could still serve the crown as an animate warrior, his body gathered by a royal corpse collector, alchemically preserved and magically ensorcelled to fight for the military even after his life had ended. It was considered an honor to have the king spend such lavish amounts to preserve the service of a common foot soldier.

Her brother's survival would be wonderful, to see his smile again and his clear blue eyes. Even were he crippled, she'd feel no sorrow, delighting in the chance to be able to serve him again.

Not knowing, that was the worst. According to the official records, her brother's unit had fought as a rearguard at Shadukar. The army had been compelled to withdraw and had been unable to scour the field afterwards. There was no way to know his fate. "In all likelihood he was killed in battle," the clerk had said, "but he might have been captured, might have been struck unconscious or disarmed and fallen therewith into the hands of the enemy."

Upon hearing that, Henya had turned up her nose and narrowed her eyes, fighting back the tears.

The clerk had misinterpreted her reaction, and mumbled an apology. "Of course, there's no way a man of such prowess as your brother would have done other than kill the stinking Thranes until his final breath."

Such prowess? He'd been just another soldier to the clerk. Recruit number 992-1-1763. One of the faceless peasants pressed into service, just another body to carry a spear.

She'd held her tears and left. For the last eighteen months, she'd wondered whether or not her brother had been captured, whether he might some day return home, return to his family, return to her and grace her life with his laughter once again. According to the Treaty of Thronehold, all prisoners were to be repatriated. That knowledge had given her hope for the first year, to know that if the Thranes had indeed captured him, they could neither keep him as a slave nor execute him.

Soon, though, that hope gave way to despair, for if he'd been captured, it shouldn't have taken him a year to find his way back to Korth.

The persistent ache in her cold hand pushed her from her dark reverie. She reluctantly unclenched her other hand from where it held her cloak shut, and switched her grip on the basket, losing most of her remaining warmth in the process. She drew her cold hand back into her cloak and did her best to coax her numb fingers to grip the fabric closed as tight as they could manage.

Looking up, she saw that the sky was darkening, the light growing more scant in the narrow backstreets and alleys about her. She had slowed her pace as she'd fretted about her brother, and the evening had waned. Starting to shiver, she hurried forward into the gloom. If only her brother could come back. She'd give so much for just one more chance to hear him say—

"Ho there."

The voice was so masculine, so gravelly, that she stopped in her tracks. She turned to the sound, a hesitant, desperately hopeful smile starting to bloom across her face.

A short figure, likewise in a hooded cloak but with a moderate beard poking out of the hood, stepped out of the shadows. Though he stood no higher than her shoulders, he moved with purpose and, judging by the breadth of his mantle, he was very muscularly built. He drew close to her, shaking one arm loose from the folds of his cloak. He brandished a heavy stick pierced through at the end by cruel spikes.

"Give me your basket, wench," he growled, shaking his club as punctuation.

For a moment, she almost yielded, but the thought of her family fanned her ire. She glanced at his bulk and height, and decided that even burdened with a basket, she should be able to outrun him. She didn't have to get far, just to Angle Road. There'd certainly be someone there who'd defend her against a conscience-less thug.

"Give it," he repeated.

"No!" she spat, and turned and ran as hard as she could, clutching the precious basket with both hands, the chill air forgotten.

She expected to hear him pursue her, but no noise of boots on gritty cobbles dogged her heels. Instead, after a panicked breath or three, she heard a single grunt of exertion. She had barely enough time to register the sound when stars exploded in her vision and she found herself stumbling into a rough, stone wall and falling to the rain-damp ground.

Disoriented, she shook her head, all memory of her plight temporarily forgotten. She started to sit up, but dizziness and a raging ache in the back of her head gave her pause. Footsteps drew near, and she looked up. There, towering over her, stood a broad, cloaked figure with a spiked cudgel. She thought he might help her to rise, until his growl of distaste brought everything back to her.

"Help!" she screamed.

7

He raised the club. "Lock yer jawbone!" he snarled. Then his words slowed to a malevolent cadence. "You don't want to stoke up a member of the Iron Band, do ya, wench?" He pulled up the sleeve of the arm that carried the club and displayed an armband. It glinted in the darkness.

She gasped, raising a trembling fist to her mouth. "I'm sorry," she said. "I didn't know. I mean, you can have—that is, if you'd asked, I'd—well, soldiers like you—"

"Quiet, wench," he said. He looked around at the dirt of the cobbled side street, but in the looming darkness, there was little detail to be seen. "Gone," he harrumphed. "And that was my best throwing rock. Do you know how long I looked for just the right one?"

"Please don't hurt me. You can have my food . . ."

"But now it's all spilled on the ground," he said as to a child. He sighed and tapped his bludgeon lightly on the side of his calf. "You've done given me some trouble tonight, wench. I'm going to have to take something of equal consideration for that rock." He leveled a harsh kick that took her in the meatiest portion of the thigh.

"I can help you find the rock," came a voice from the darkness, a voice quiet yet clear, "if your skull feels empty without it."

The thug turned around with a snarl to see a tall stranger approaching, a long walking-stick in his hand. He was bare headed, but his open longcoat nearly swept the ground. "Shut your beerhole, you," the robber said. "And get out of here, unless you want a portion of what she's got coming."

"Spoken like a rat who hears not the cat," said the interloper, strolling forward, his metal-shod staff tapping quietly on the cobbles in counterpoint to his stride. "Drop your stick and go on home. You've already proven your manhood and courage by assaulting a defenseless woman, armed with only with a large spiked stick to help even the odds."

"You have no idea who you're dealing with, stranger."

"I need not know you. I stand by my god."

"Be careful," urged Henya. "He's one of the Iron Band!"

The newcomer stopped in mid stride. His head canted slightly to the side. "Really?" he said, skepticism bending his voice.

The thug stood as tall as he was able. "It's the sovereign truth," he said, shifting his grip on his makeshift weapon. "And I was the meanest, toughest one of them all. They called me 'The Killer with No Mercy,' and I deserved the title. That's why I lived to tell the tale. So unless you want to go the way of the three hundred Aundairians I slew, I suggest you scat."

"The Iron Band," said the tall man.

"That's right. I heard myself the first go-round."

"Hm. Funny."

"You won't think it's so funny when I beat your carcass so full of holes the corpse collectors'll use you for a whistle."

"No," said the man, raising his free hand as if in benediction. "That's not it. What's funny is that I do not remember any dwarves."

The thug shifted his feet. "What do you mean, you don't remember? Haven't you seen a dwarf before?"

The man shrugged. "Plenty of times. But the commander refused to recruit them. Stubby little legs were simply too slow," he added, fluttering two fingers in a mockery of running.

The dwarf hesitated a moment, then raised his cudgel and started to close, waving it near his ear. "Right, that's enough out of you."

"Indeed," said the human, ignoring the dwarf's threatening posture, "as best I recollect, the Iron Band was made up exclusively of humans and half-orcs. Every last one of us."

The thug stopped. "Us?"

The human nodded. "Oh yes." He sniffed, placing his free hand on his hip. "And I am most displeased that you are trying to set up your stunted little pedestal on the graves of my blood brothers."

With a gravelly bellow, the dwarf charged. Henya crushed her eyes closed.

● ● ● ◉ ● ● ●

Cimozjen hadn't expected his words to provoke the dwarf into an all-out charge, and the spontaneity of the attack caught him off his guard. He raised an arm to ward off the first clumsy overhand blow, and the wood of the cudgel smacked into his unarmored forearm. The dwarf's follow-up came crossways and stripped Cimozjen of his staff.

The dwarf continued his assault—reckless, untrained—with a series of wild swings. The rusty spikes of his club whistled through the deepening darkness as Cimozjen evaded the strikes, gauging his adversary's skill and power.

The lack of a response gave the dwarf more courage. He pushed himself harder and harder, trying to land a blow. Yet as he did so, his breath grew more labored. Cimozjen surmised that a tendency towards lassitude and debauchery had taken its toll on the dwarf's constitution, or, more charitably, that he had perhaps a disease of the lungs that had precluded him from military service.

"Looks like you should have thought to bring a weapon to the fight," panted the dwarf. "You're going to pay for that mistake."

He swung again, and the spikes on his bludgeon caught the edge of Cimozjen's long leather coat, tearing several long rips in it and pulling it off one of his shoulders.

Cimozjen retreated and took a second to inspect the damage. "I just bought this yesterevening," he groused. He slipped one arm out of its sleeve and grabbed his coat near the hem. He started to shuck the other sleeve off.

The dwarf swung again, and Cimozjen dodged, flustering with the coat and getting his hand twisted up in the leather sleeve. The dwarf followed through with a heavy back-handed strike to the midriff, but this time Cimozjen did not give ground. He stepped in, catching the head of the mace in his longcoat. He heard a popping sound as the spikes punctured the thin leather in several places, holding the weapon fast.

Cimozjen whipped his coat around the weapon, swaddling

it in leather padding. A quick jerk yanked the weapon up, and Cimozjen was likewise able to snare the dwarf's weapon hand with one long sleeve, trapping it in place while simultaneously freeing his other hand from his sleeve.

With a gleam in his eye, Cimozjen used his weight and leverage to force the dwarf's arm down, driving the thug slowly to the ground and a position of submission.

"Tell me, lad," said Cimozjen, gazing into the dwarf's grimacing face, "shall we start this conversation anew, and let it take a more hospitable turn?"

"Fine," growled the dwarf, and he threw a heavy roundhouse punch with his sizeable left fist.

Cimozjen had but an eye blink to reflect on the fact that he had used both of his hands to lock up only one of the dwarf's. The next thing he knew, he was lying on the cold, wet ground. He started to rise to a sitting position, one leg curled and the other straight in front of him. There was something in his mouth, so he spit it out. Even as he did so, he realized that it was a piece of one of his front teeth, now lost in the dark of the filthy side street.

The dwarf was frantically trying to unwrap his club from the shroud of Cimozjen's raincoat, but, by the sound of it, the only success he was having was in ripping ever-greater holes in the garment. The tips of the spikes could be seen peeking out through the battered leather. He glanced over at Cimozjen rising, gave one last frantic jerk at the coat, and rushed forward to attack.

Cimozjen didn't even manage to get a knee underneath himself before the dwarf was upon him.

I am so careless, thought Cimozjen, that a dwarf has a height advantage over me.

Chapter
Two

The dwarf struck an overhand blow. Still reeling from the punch, Cimozjen barely raised his shield arm in time. The other arm still propped him upright where he sat. The blow wracked his forearm with pain.

The dwarf swung again, and Cimozjen managed to angle his arm. The club slid down his forearm and off, causing no harm to his body but bringing a new burning pain to the length of his arm bone. In that brief moment, Cimozjen managed to push himself up so that he was sitting on his heel. The other leg was still in front of him, drawn in defensively, and he thanked the Host that the dwarf didn't think of striking his exposed knee.

The dwarf struck again and again—rapid overhand blows— slowly beating down Cimozjen's defense. Every strike made his arm throb all the more. Then one of the blows struck Cimozjen's head, just above the left temple. He felt two or three spikes tear his scalp, and his ears rang from the impact.

Abruptly his opponent changed tactics, and the next attack came with a snapping sidearm swing, catching Cimozjen full in the ribs. With his sagging arm guarding his bleeding head, his side was completely unprotected, and again he felt blunt iron spikes jab into his flesh.

Cimozjen reflexively dropped his arm, and for his troubles he got several more cuts on the inside of his arm as the dwarf pulled the spiked club back.

The dwarf paused, wheezing through his teeth. Cimozjen couldn't quite tell if his panting utterances were an attempt at laughter, or just an expression of extreme exertion.

Now that he was sitting on his heel and, for the moment, stable, Cimozjen whipped up his right arm and snared his fingers through the dwarf's thick beard. He closed his fist around a hefty handful of coarse hairs and pulled, simultaneously pushing up with his leg and whipping his head forward. He aimed the heavy part of his brow at the dwarf's nose, and was rewarded with a loud crunching sound and the spray of the dwarf's spittle in his eyes.

The dwarf flailed at him, succeeding only in hitting Cimozjen weakly on the back of the head with the handle of his club.

Cimozjen dropped back to a sitting position, then yanked the dwarf forward and head butted each of the dwarf's cheekbones. He paused for a second to ensure the dwarf's nose was bleeding profusely, then he butted it once more for good measure. The grinding sound was at once appalling and satisfying.

Cimozjen sat back, whipped the dwarf's head to the left and right to disorient him, then twisted to the side and yanked the dwarf forward by the beard, throwing him over his shoulder. The dwarf landed flat on his back with a heavy, meaty thud. The club skittered along the ground with a string of hollow-sounding thunks and dull metal pings.

"So be it," panted Cimozjen, wincing at his pain, "I gave you the chance to walk free. But now I must tell the town watch. And then your nose will be the least of your troubles." He paused as he inspected the dwarf's damaged face. "Well, perhaps not. But look on the bright side. You can fall on your face with impunity now."

He rose to his feet and lurched over to the young woman. He kneeled beside her, wincing as he did so.

"Are you badly hurt?" she asked in a trembling voice.

"I am well enough, I suppose," grumbled Cimozjen. He hissed an intake of breath. "Though I wrenched my neck butting his face. Not as limber as I used to be." He rubbed the base of his neck and grumbled. "Nor as fleet. How do you fare, miss?" he asked at last, looking down at her with longsuffering eyes.

"He struck my head," she said. "And my basket of food . . ."

"I cannot help your groceries," said Cimozjen, "save to help you find them before the rats do. But let me see to your head." He reached out his left hand and gingerly ran it along her scalp, at last settling on a knot on the back of her skull. "Right, that's a good one. Feels as large as a wood nut."

"Don't you worry about that," she said bravely. "I'll be fine."

"I tell you the truth, you'll be better than fine. Allow me." He cupped his hand over the bruise, bowed his head, and held his right hand fisted to his breast. Whispered words flew from his tongue, a barely audible litany.

She gasped. "It tingles . . . it . . ." Then her tone turned sour. "What are you doing? You didn't use a leech, did you? I don't want one of those things in my hair!" She put her hand to the back of her head and felt around. "Where—hey, where did—" She paused, looking at Cimozjen in confusion. "Magic?" She smiled in amazement, then her look faltered. "But . . . but I've no coin, good man. I can't afford . . ."

"Do not trouble your heart, young miss," said Cimozjen. He bowed his head. "I am sworn by oaths to Dol Dorn, the Puissant and Powerful. The Sovereign Host rewards my faith and humble service with a few blessings to share with others, and for that I am grateful."

"An acolyte of Dol Dorn, eh?" said the woman, as if she fully understood the deeper secrets that implied. "Still, I am surprised that you could defeat a member of the Iron Band. They're said to be the best warriors we've ever fielded. Outside of the Order of Rekkenmark, of course."

"You're sure you're well enough now?" asked Cimozjen, trying to change the subject. "You're not injured elsewhere?"

The young woman pulled her hood back over her head and started to rise. "What I mean to say is, well, over the years I've seen their sigil armband in a place of honor on several family mantles, and the tales they told . . . well, I suppose maybe those stories were exaggerated. But I hope not overmuch."

Cimozjen smiled as he, too, stood. "Rest assured, young miss, he was not a fellow of the Iron Band."

Confusion clouded her brow. "But he showed me the armband. There's nothing else quite like them."

"Whatever he may—pardon me, young miss, would you repeat that?"

"He showed me the armband."

Cimozjen held up one finger and marshaled his thoughts. "I must beg you to forgive me my poor manners, if you please, young miss," he said.

He turned to the dwarf, who lay on his back, rocking back and forth with both hands over his nose. The unfortunate thief groaned more or less constantly, the sound muffled by his callused palms.

Cimozjen stalked over, kneeled down, and felt along the dwarf's left arm, then along the other. Just above his right elbow he felt a metal ring. Gripping the dwarf's ragged cuff in both hands, he roughly tore the shirt to expose the armband. It glinted slightly.

"Ass!" yelled Cimozjen. He punched the dwarf solidly in the stomach. "It's worn on the left arm!"

He grabbed the dwarf's scalp and yanked, raising him to a sitting position. The dwarf whimpered behind his hands, keeping his eyes squeezed shut. Cimozjen reached one hand beneath the rear of his tunic and drew a long, heavy dagger. The keen blade sang as he freed it from the scabbard.

The dwarf's eyes popped open.

Cimozjen held up his blade and turned it side to side. "Remove that band from your wrist, or I'll pull it off the stump of your shoulder," he hissed.

The dwarf pulled his hands away from his ruined face and, fumbling, took the armband off. He tried to offer it to Cimozjen, but his hands, bloody and trembling, let it drop to the damp ground.

Keeping tight hold of the thief's hair, Cimozjen picked up the armband using the blade of his dagger. He inspected it closely in what little light remained. He turned back to the dwarf. The pain he felt twisting his neck added gravity to his stare.

He smiled mirthlessly. "Perhaps you'd care to show me where you found this?" he said. His cold tone carried the dire consequences of the dwarf's alternative.

"H-happy to," stammered the dwarf through his hands.

"Good." He used his blade to open the flap of his haversack. He let the armband slide off the dagger and into safekeeping, then spun his weapon expertly. "Otherwise, to find out, I would have to resort to measures that I find . . . distasteful. And if you were to cause me to break my vows like that—"

"You don't need to be getting into explanations now, if'n that's fine by you." The thief rummaged one hand around inside his cloak and found a rag, which he put to his nose.

"I am glad that we agree on this," said Cimozjen. He stood, his injuries protesting every motion. "Let's bid the good woman a fair evening, shall we?"

"Of course," the dwarf said, his tone rather nasal. "Good night, woman."

Cimozjen twisted his hair and whispered something in his ear.

"I, uh, I'm sorry for, uh, what I did, you know," said the dwarf in a voice pitched rather higher.

The woman stamped her foot. "I should give you a good whacking for what you did," she said. She picked up the dwarf's spiked club and began unwrapping it.

"Here now, there'll be none of that, miss," said Cimozjen.

"Oh, no," said the woman. "Just words. Though I thought you might want your coat back, brave man."

"Of course. My thanks," said Cimozjen as he took the proffered garment. "Please forgive our abrupt departure," he added, touching his dagger to his brow, "but we've some business to attend to immediately. May you find your basket and goods, and make it home safely. I shall pray for you." Cimozjen looked back at the dwarf. "Well?"

"Hm? Oh, uh, King's Bay. The, uh, piers. At the west end of the Low District."

"We're off, then," said Cimozjen with feigned joviality. He recovered his staff, holding it in his hand with his dagger, and the two left the young woman behind.

"If you don't mind my asking," said the dwarf as they walked along, "where in the woods did you pull that dagger from?"

"This? My father—Sovereigns keep his soul—gave it to me when I was thirteen. I always carry it."

"Don't take this as a complaint, because it's not, I mean I'd just as soon not have got myself stabbed dead back there, but why didn't you pull it out in, um, you know . . ."

"Why did I not knife you?" Cimozjen clucked his tongue. "I've taken enough lives in my nigh-on fifty years that I prefer to work things out peaceably when I can. I feel no need to notch my reputation with further bloodshed. I stopped your crime. We both lived. That's a fine enough outcome for me, and hopefully one to please the Sovereigns, as well."

The two walked through the darkened streets for some time before the dwarf finally broke the silence.

"Begging your pardon, and not that I want to be contrary, but you don't really need to keep hold of the hair on my head any more. Truly you don't."

"Yes, I'm afraid I do," said Cimozjen wearily.

"And why would that be?"

"Just in case I need to yank your head back and slit your throat."

"I thought you said you didn't need any more bloodshed."

"I'm willing to make an exception tonight."

The dwarf tried to think of a reply, but failed. Then, several blocks later, he said, "If you think you might see such an exception coming upon us, I'd be very grateful if you'd be sure and let me know beforehand, right?"

＊ ＊ ＊ ＊ ＊ ＊ ＊

The two walked the cobbled streets. The cold had turned bitter after sunset, and those few others still in the streets were only too happy to ignore the pair. Cimozjen, his ruined longcoat draped over his shoulders, marked the paces with the clacking of his metal-shod staff, his dagger held concealed against the wood, just in case. His other hand seemed to rest easily on the dwarf's shoulder, but was tightly wound into his hair. Just in case.

The dwarf led Cimozjen through the Community Ward to King's Bay, an elongated backwater carved ages ago from the banks of the Karrn River. It was one of the few operable portages along that stretch of the river. For dozens of miles in each direction steep bluffs prevented any craft larger than a canoe from making a decent landing.

King's Bay was also cold and very, very deep, which gave cause for some to wonder whether or not it had been formed by a sinkhole that went all the way down to Khyber. Superstitious sailors would make an offering to the Devourer every year that the whole of the port would not drop into the abyss, at least not while they were sailing on it.

The piers that reached into the bay were by and large the same—aged, weatherworn planks strung between pilings made of heavy Karrnathi pine trunks. A few piers were new, rebuilt or in the process thereof with the arrival of peace, and one, the King's Pier, was a veritable causeway made of stone that reached farther into the dark waters than any other.

Though the wharfs remained largely unchanged as one walked the length of King's Bay, the surroundings most certainly did not. Cimozjen and his guide turned left as they reached the bayside, and as they walked, the buildings gradually became smaller, denser, and less presentable. Bawdy dockside alehouses and brothels plied a steady trade in the cold weather, offering warmth and companionship, or at least the illusion of it. Gambling houses and the so-called smokehouses found other, more direct means to part people from their silver.

Together Cimozjen and his prisoner paced the length of the waterfront, coming at last to the westernmost of the piers, sited in the lee of a bluff that rose rather abruptly from the ground just to the west. There, the dwarf stopped.

"I trust that you did not find this armband lying here dockside in this ramshackle ward," said Cimozjen.

"No," said the dwarf, a tremor in his voice. "I got it from that man, over there." He pointed to a small pale patch that lay at the water's edge, barely visible from the wan glow of a nearby establishment. "I hoped maybe he'd have a small purse or something, but that was all he had on him. Weren't 'til I got somewhere private and had a chance to look it over careful that I figured out what it really was."

"You mean to tell me that driftwood is a body?"

"It's the sovereign truth."

"Show me."

"You're the one with the dagger."

They stepped off the edge of the cobbled waterfront and made their way down a weed-infested slope to the water's edge. The dwarf slipped on the wet ground, and, because Cimozjen still held his hair, he lost his balance and landed heavily on one hip. This in turn pulled Cimozjen after him. He stumbled into the dwarf and knocked him further, forcing the thief to slide into the water, though by some miracle he recovered his feet as he splashed in.

"Blunted, that's cold!" cursed the dwarf. "Could you please let go of my hair now? Argh, I can't see a cursed thing!"

Cimozjen released his locks. With a miserable whine, the dwarf climbed up the bank a bit, plopped down, and started removing his dripping footwear with one hand. The other continued to staunch the bleeding remnants of his nose.

Cimozjen looked at the water's edge. The dim shape was definitely a body, the shoulders apparently run aground in the shallows. Little more could be seen, as the rest of the body was submerged. Cimozjen pulled a braided leather necklace from beneath his collar and grasped the holy Octogram that hung from it. "Dol Arrah, favor your brother's servant this day," he intoned, and the symbol began to glow with a radiance of ethereal beauty, "and grant my prayer that you make your perfect face to shine upon my duty."

"All that, and he orders the gods around, too," said the dwarf, tittering nervously. A glare from Cimozjen killed his joviality, and he mumbled an apology.

Cimozjen sheathed his blade and set his staff down. Stepping into the cold water, he gently pulled the body out and laid it to rest on the sloping shore. He bent down to inspect it.

The corpse was tall and unnaturally thin. His bones spoke that he'd once been a more robust man. He was pale blue, but how pale he'd been before dying and being left in frigid water, Cimozjen couldn't tell. He had long, scraggly hair and an unkempt beard, originally brown, but both shot through with strands of white and gray. His dilated pupils were surrounded by a corona of ice blue, unnaturally suited to his newfound skin tone. And his scant attire—pants and a vest—was, at best, ratty and filthy.

The cause of death was obvious. A heavy blow across the chest had broken ribs and split his breastbone.

"Did you kill him?" asked Cimozjen.

"No, I didn't," said the dwarf. "Even if I had an axe, which I don't, I don't think I could hit a man like he's done been hit."

"Go on."

"I found him like that this afternoon. Well, he was just kind of under the water, like a dead fish. I used a stick to pull him to shore. Figured drifting in the water like that odds were he hadn't been picked over yet. That's the sovereign truth, the whole of it, I swear."

"And he stayed here undisturbed all day?"

"Well, it looks like he kind of slid back in, because I left him half ashore. Or maybe someone else picked him over and gave him a shove. But sure, no one has really bothered with him since. In this part of town, that's no surprise. When the watch comes down here, which don't happen overmuch, they're mostly concerned about them as still moves."

Cimozjen nodded. "I thank you for your assistance. And you should thank the Host that I only broke your nose. If the city watch had caught you, you'd find the Code of Kaius a lot less compassionate than I have been. Instead, you're getting a second chance this night. Make the most of it. Now go."

Cimozjen turned his attention back to the corpse, ignoring the scuffling and grunting as the dwarf tugged on his sodden shoes and beat a hasty retreat. Cimozjen pulled the hair out of the dead man's face, trying to recognize his features. The arc of the dimpled chin, the angled eyes, the exaggerated curve of his upper lip—they were hauntingly familiar, yet unrecognizable, inanimate and emaciated as they were.

He started scanning the rest of the body, looking for telltale marks, scars . . .

And then he saw the tattoo.

Twenty-nine years earlier:

"Do you like it?" The soldier—a tall, robust man with dark, oiled hair and a well-muscled torso—threw his tunic aside and proudly displayed the intricate tattoo on his bare chest. The skin it covered was raw and sore, and glistened with an ointment to speed healing.

Several others around made approving grunts and murmurs, so Cimozjen could hardly resist interfering. He sauntered over and neatly sliced his way through the small knot of soldiers.

Cimozjen leaned forward and peered at the tattoo closely. It was exquisitely rendered, with excellent detail and a good depth of color. "Mm. It's a bit off center," he said in an underwhelmed tone of voice.

"It's drawn over the heart!" snapped the soldier.

"Ah, I see. In that case, it's right on target." He straightened and held out a hand. "Cimozjen Hellekanus at your service. Welcome to the Iron Band."

The soldier took his hand in a grip as tight as sailor's knot. "Torval Ellinger, recruited out of the Rekkenmark."

"Truly?" said Cimozjen. "I spent two years there myself, before I volunteered to go to battle."

"Tired of mucking the stables, were you?" asked Torval. The others snickered.

"No," said Cimozjen. "Tired of mucking your bunk."

The other soldiers hooted at his riposte.

"But I have a question, good Torval. If you've been to the Academy, why did you feel the need for a chipmunk tattoo?"

"It's a wolf!" snarled Torval, irritated. Then, with a calm pride, he added, "It's rendered in the old heraldry style, a wolf rampant—the traditional symbol of our land."

"Eating an acorn?"

"Grabbing the crown of Galifar!" roared Torval.

"Ah. Well, it's a very nice tattoo, now that you've explained it," said Cimozjen suppressing a wry smile.

"You may not think it's much, but you're the lone arrow on that. Right, boys?" He looked at the other soldiers, hands out, and the others murmured their assent. "They'll be even more impressed when they see this," he bellowed. He flexed his muscles, hunching forward and bowing his arms to display his entire upper body to best advantage.

"Perhaps I'm missing the point," said Cimozjen. "They'll be even more impressed when you're constipated?"

Torval drew himself up and stalked slowly over to Cimozjen, until the latter found his nose all but touching the top of Torval's breastbone. "Look me in the eyes and say that," he growled.

"I would look up," said Cimozjen, "but think the view would be underwhelming."

"Coward," said Torval. "All talk until a real threat comes, hm?" He chest-bumped Cimozjen, knocking him a step back, and closed the distance to loom over him once more. "So are you going to fight me like a man, or run crying to the commander?"

Cimozjen looked up to lock eyes with Torval. "I *am* your commander," he said.

Torval's face did not merely fall. It collapsed. "Uhh . . ." he said.

Cimozjen thumped him on the chest. "And if a soldier like you falls for that feint, maybe I should try it against the Thranes, hm? What do you think?"

"What?" roared Torval. "You—you—" Anger flushing his face, he cocked his fists, ready to smash down on Cimozjen like a sledge. His torso once more knotted into a rock-hard formation more reminiscent of masonry than muscle.

Cimozjen raised his eyebrows in appreciation. "Wow," he said as he thumped Torval's chest again. "Never mind that. When the Thranes come, I'll just take cover behind you and your chipmunk."

Chapter
THREE

A Cold and Joyless Homecoming
Zol, the 10th day of Sypheros, 998

Tears stinging his eyes, Cimozjen carefully spread his torn long-coat on the ground. He picked up Torval's corpse—a body far lighter and more frail than it had been when he'd carried the injured soldier to the healers so many years ago—and laid him out as best he could on the tattered leather. The cold, damp skin and unresponsive flesh seemed unreal, warring in Cimozjen's mind with the memories of a sanguine, vibrant man.

He folded the coat respectfully about the body, and used the buckled straps to secure it as best he could. "You deserve far better, my friend," said Cimozjen. "I know not what you've gone through all these years, but you deserved far better then, and you do so now." He gently closed the man's eyes. "I'm sorry."

He hefted the limp bundle and slung it over one shoulder, then grabbed his staff and climbed carefully back up the slope to the boardwalk. As he walked back toward the better parts of town, he could feel the eyes of the dockside revelers watching his progress. Even if the size and shape of the leather-wrapped corpse had not given away its true nature, the two feet that stuck out of the end made it painfully clear. It bothered Cimozjen that

Torval's corpse only had one shoe on. It seemed the final insult.

He trudged through the cold night with his burden. His arm throbbed from its heavy bruising, his side pained him as his tunic chafed against the wounds left by the mace, and the strained muscles in his neck grew tighter as he walked. Yet his thoughts were not on his own travails, for he had suffered far worse before, and knew he would survive these. Instead, he ruminated about his friend and cohort, a brother closer to his heart than his own family, bound there by the oaths they'd shared and blood they had spilled and shed together. How he wished he could have called upon the Sovereign Host for Torval's healing.

At the first major road he turned away from the waterfront and headed into the city.

As he passed beneath a magical wisplight, a slender gentleman paused in his own errand and looked at the unlikely pair. "Need some help, friend?" he asked gently.

Cimozjen slowed. The stranger was well dressed in a green coat and a wide tricorn hat. He had neither the look of a corpse collector nor the bearing of a thug, but seemed to have genuine concern. It was a rare thing. Simple civility was one of the many casualties of the Last War.

Cimozjen smiled sadly. "I fear not," he said, continuing on his way. "He's already dead. I thank you, though."

Yet as he walked, Cimozjen realized that the stranger had helped, after all. Somehow giving voice to the obvious helped to clear his mind of its melancholy musings. He could do nothing to help Torval anymore, but perhaps he could find justice for his suffering and death. He set his intellect to the task, to discern what series of unfortunate events might have led Torval away from being honored as a hero of the Last War to being a piece of forgotten detritus scavenged from the waters of a benighted bay.

He could think of nothing, but the more he tried, the more determined he became to find the answer, come what may.

After several long blocks he took a right at Low Dock Lane. The well-cobbled road rose steadily upward, carved across the face of a steep river bluff. Oft called Low Decline by residents, it connected the worst part of the docks directly to the less fashionable Westgate end of the Hightower Ward, and as a result, the upper portions were duly patrolled by the city watch.

By the time he had topped the bluff, Cimozjen was breathing hard and his knees ached from the strenuous climb. He felt he might not have made it without the extra support his staff gave him.

As he had hoped, a squad of White Lions stood apathetic watch over the road, huddled in their cloaks and chatting by the light of a single lantern. Their apathy vanished as Cimozjen and Torval drew closer, the corpse's two feet bobbing with every heavy step Cimozjen took.

Cimozjen saw one of the guards extend his hand out of his cloak and give the guard next to him a sharp shove on the shoulder. That soldier and another moved to intercept Cimozjen as he came closer.

"Halt," the guard said as he drew close, hand resting on the hilt of his weapon. The second guard moved into a flanking position to Cimozjen's right, where Cimozjen was unable to track him thanks to Torval's hips blocking his vision.

Cimozjen stopped and shifted Torval on his shoulder. "White Lion," he said respectfully. "I wish to—"

"Explain yourself," snapped the guard. "What are you up to here?"

Cimozjen took a deep breath before answering. Not only was he rather winded, but doing so helped ensure he did not launch a sarcastic remark that would cause him more trouble. "I am bringing a body in for evidence," he said. "I wish to see the captain of the watch or the investigator on duty."

The guard glanced at his partner. Cimozjen heard a noise that he surmised was the guard shrugging.

"Fair enough," said the guard. "I was going to take you to the Old Man anyway. You don't have the look of a corpse collector."

The other guard chuckled. "Never mind that he's collected a corpse."

"Stuff your mouth," snapped the first. Then he looked back at Cimozjen and jerked his thumb to the north. "Come on, you. Give me your stick and let's get going."

"If you'd be so kind as to help me with my burden . . ." said Cimozjen.

"I get paid to make dead bodies, not carry them. Move."

❋ ❋ ❋ ❋ ❋ ❋ ❋

The White Lions served as both town watch and military garrison for the City of Korth, and they had barracks near each of the major gates into the city. The barracks served as housing, armory, hospital, and headquarters, and, with their grandiose design and plethora of banners and memorabilia, as a blatant symbol of the executors of authority in the city. Naturally, the Westgate barracks had been built fairly near Low Dock Lane, a fact in which Cimozjen found no small measure of relief.

He followed the first guard into the front room of the barracks. The second guard followed behind him. A fire blazing in a large stone hearth lighted the spacious front room of the headquarters. A sizeable iron stewpot hung over the fire, and the pungent aroma of venison stew filled the room. As soon as the scent caught his nose, Cimozjen's stomach rumbled and his mouth started watering. It was hearty fare, ideal for a cold, damp night.

The room had a few tables scattered about, with chairs and guards here and there. A large beautifully rendered map of the city hung on one wall, and the pelt of some alarmingly huge beast covered another.

"Halt there," said the guard, scowling at Cimozjen as he gestured. Then he turned. "Lads, someone wants to see the Old Man." He tossed Cimozjen's staff in the corner of the room and went over to the fire to warm himself.

Cimozjen moved over to one of the chairs, kneeled, and divested himself of Torval, setting the corpse to recline in the chair as best he could.

"Hey," said a grizzled old guard, "get that filthy maggot farm off the chair!"

Cimozjen straightened up and tried to stretch, but his wounds and knotted muscles prevented him. "I've given him my chair," he said. "I shall stand in his place."

"He don't care none where he sets," said the guard.

Cimozjen fixed the old man with a gaze. "I do."

The old guard held the look for a moment, then dropped his eyes. "Well at least move him away from the fire, will you? Don't want him to fester and start stinking up the place."

Cimozjen sighed heavily, then slowly pulled the chair, Torval still in it, across the room. He made it seem more of an effort than it truly was, just to irritate the guard with the unreasonableness of his demand.

Just before Cimozjen finished his task, a short man strode into the room. As he entered, the other guards all stood and touched their brow in salute, but then began sitting back down. Cimozjen straightened, inclined his head respectfully, then looked the captain of the guard up and down.

It was a Karrnathi tradition to call the leader of one's unit "the Old Man," a habit born of the nation's culture of respect for one's elders. Thus Cimozjen, the aging veteran, had difficulty stifling a sardonic laugh when the captain of the guard appeared to be a young lad no older than his own youngest son.

"You find something amusing?" asked the captain, stopping several paces away from Cimozjen.

"No, not at all," said Cimozjen. It was very true. He found the captain's youth disappointing at best. He wiped his nose, adding, "It's a hard night on the sinuses."

Once he had mastered himself, he noted that the captain had the unmistakable features of one whose veins flowed with a blend of elf and human blood—smaller, slighter build, more angular face, and large eyes the color of the summer forest canopy. He was doubtless a decade or more older than he appeared, but nonetheless easily remained Cimozjen's junior in years.

He wore a fine suit of leather armor, obviously tailor-made to his physique. Cimozjen noted that it looked like it could double as padding beneath a suit of chain mail, yet, judging by its immaculate polish, it never had.

And he had the elven arrogance. He wore it like a bull elk wore antlers. Despite the fact that Cimozjen stood a good eight inches taller, the captain somehow managed to look upon on him with an air of superiority.

Looking down while looking up, thought Cimozjen, that's a good trick.

"I am Yorin Thauram II, Captain of the Watch. I am told you begged to see me?"

Cimozjen licked his lips. "I asked to see you, yes. Cimozjen Hellekanus, at your service."

"Does this have anything to do with that . . . thing sitting in the chair here?"

"You refer to my friend?" asked Cimozjen, stressing the word slightly to put the situation in its proper light. "Yes it does. His name is Torval Ellinger." Cimozjen pulled Torval's armband from his haversack and handed it to Yorin. "He was one of the Iron Band, and by the looks of it, he has been murdered. I bring him to you in hopes that you might be able to help me find his murderer."

Yorin looked at the armband. "It appears authentic," he said, after some inspection. "But why isn't he wearing it?"

"Because he's dead," said Cimozjen, as if that should explain everything. He nodded his head toward Torval "See for yourself."

The captain tossed the armband to the old guard by the fire then walked over to Torval's body. He snapped his finger. "Unwrap it," he said.

Another one of the guards rose, walked over to Torval, undid the buckles that held the leather around him, then held one end of the coat and pushed Torval out of the chair, sending him unceremoniously tumbling to the floor.

"Here now," yelled Cimozjen, "have some respect!"

Seeing the sodden, unkempt mess that now lay sprawled on the floor at Cimozjen's feet, a couple of the guards sniggered at Cimozjen's outburst. Torval's limbs lay splayed about, and his damp hair lay in a tattered veil across his face and shoulders.

"I'll have some respect when he starts swinging a weapon again," said Thauram. He held out one hand. "Spear," he demanded.

"Spear, Captain Thauram," said a guard, handing his weapon over.

The half-elf took the butt end of the spear and pushed Torval over to lie on his back. One arm remained trapped beneath him. The open wound on his chest looked vile and black against his death-blue skin.

"*That,*" said Yorin, poking at the dead man's chin to turn his head, "was in the Iron Band?"

Cimozjen exhaled hard. "Yes, he was, captain."

"And I'm King Kaius."

Several guards chuckled at the captain's wit.

Cimozjen shook his head and sniffed. He folded his arms across his chest. "Do you impugn my honesty, captain?"

Yorin turned and appraised Cimozjen anew. He stepped up to him, grasped Cimozjen's chin, and turned his head side to side. "Looks like you've had an eventful evening as well, *civilian.* You've a trail of blood down your cheek. Where'd you get it?"

"It has nothing to do with Torval's murder."

The captain walked around Cimozjen, who stood fuming. "What's this, more blood?" Yorin poked Cimozjen in the ribs with the butt of the spear, causing him to grunt involuntarily. "Yes indeed, you've had an active night, haven't you? What have you been up to?"

"I defended a young woman from being robbed by a would-be thief, if you must know," said Cimozjen. "For my troubles, I received some pains." And now, he thought, looking darkly at Torval's corpse, *for my pains, I am receiving new troubles.*

Yorin tilted his fine-featured head back to look even more arrogant. "You realize that under the Code of Kaius, all thieves must be turned over to the White Lions, elsewise one may be considered an accessory to the crime."

Cimozjen favored the young half-elf with a weary look. "I prevented the robbery," he said, "hence no crime was committed."

"You said he was a thief."

"The captain will recall that I said he was a would-be thief," said Cimozjen. "I am always careful to say what I intend to say."

"Mm," said Yorin, refusing to acknowledge Cimozjen's minor victory.

"Be that as it may," continued Cimozjen, "the would-be thief received due measure for his plot. You can trust me on that. He will not look at himself the same way again."

"And where is this woman, that she might be able to corroborate your tale?"

"I gave her leave. She had a family awaiting her return, I am certain, and she was cold and fearful. I had no further need of her presence, so I released her to return to her family."

"I see," said Yorin. "We can send a detail to fetch her easily enough."

"The captain must understand that I had never seen her before this evening. Given the dim light and the circumstance under which we met, I doubt I would be able to identify her should we ever cross paths again. I presume she lives somewhere toward the south end of the Community Ward, but that is all the better I can say."

Yorin turned away before Cimozjen had even finished speaking. He walked halfway across the room, then back over to Torval and stood over the body, studying it. "That he was killed, perhaps even murdered, none can deny," he said. He inspected the body some more. "It took a powerful arm to strike that blow," he said, looking askance at Cimozjen. "And you're a strong man. I am told that you carried this corpse up Low Decline, all the way from the docks or thereabouts."

"Do you think I murdered him?" asked Cimozjen.

"You first said the words," replied Yorin by way of answer, "not

I. Perhaps you killed him yourself, and brought the body here, seeking to absolve your involvement by pandering to us with a play at cooperation." He turned to face Cimozjen, hands clasped behind his back. "Of course, if this vagrant were to have been killed in the act of robbery—or an *attempt* to rob, even—then by the Code of Kaius anyone would deem that you slew him defending your life, and for taking a life in that manner no crime would have been committed." He paused. "Was this vagrant the one who attempted to rob your mysterious vanishing woman?"

"Torval would never stoop to such an act."

"Such an *act,*" echoed the captain, nodding. "That was a curious choice of words."

"Robbing unarmed womenfolk does not merit the word 'deed.' Deeds should be great, or noble. Those endeavors that are vile are 'acts.' "

Yorin gave Cimozjen a dubious glance and snorted. He turned his back and paced over to the fire. "Let me understand this properly. You were walking along, this very night, alone, mindful of nothing but your own business. You . . . chanced upon a thief robbing a young lady, and intervened—this itself a *deed* quite brimming with nobility and valor, to say nothing of good fortune for yourself. You battled the thief—the *would-be* thief that is—defeating him, and then quite mysteriously set him free despite his nefarious intent. Likewise the mysterious maiden you peremptorily excused from your presence. Do I have this . . . rendition of events accurately stated?"

"That is an over-brief but essentially accurate understanding, yes."

Yorin laughed, a choppy and supercilious snigger. He turned, his lips pursed in a mocking grin and one eyebrow raised as he gestured toward the body at Cimozjen's feet. "Then tell me why this . . . this derelict mess appears nowhere in your tale!"

Cimozjen sucked on his lips for a moment to compose himself before answering.

"Torval Ellinger had nothing at all to do with the attempted robbery, nor with the woman," he said, speaking as clearly as he could. "However, the knave that I defeated had Torval's armband in his possession. I prevailed upon his better judgment to lead me to the place where he'd acquired the armband. Thereat he led me to Torval's body, which lay at the water's edge past the westernmost dock of King's Bay. I wrapped the body in my coat and brought it here."

There was a brief pause, broken only by the popping of the fire.

"Oh, that was spectacular," said Yorin at last.

"Excuse me, captain?" said Cimozjen.

"Did you see that, lads?" said Yorin, arms spread, turning slowly about to gather all the assembled White Lions in his gaze. "Did you see that? A pause, the briefest of pauses, one so brief that only a trained observer like myself would have noticed, and in that fleeting breath he spun the essential strands of this new embellishment! Then, did you also note the ponderous cadence of his reply, the slow nature of which was designed to give us the illusion of clarity, but in which he was able to embroider his tale with detail to give it that . . . that clear sound of truth? I tell you, this man is a master orator!"

He clapped his hands and chortled, then raised one admonishing finger. "Ah, but what gives it away? For one, the mixture of ambivalence and superlatives. Note that the body was at the water's edge—floating or ashore, he does not commit himself to the one or the other—and yet he clearly avows that the body was past the end of the westernmost dock! Such juxtaposition is a clear sign of fabrication!"

"Hold there—" interjected Cimozjen.

"Note also that this thread leads in a new and entirely different direction from everything else he has mentioned!"

"Captain, that is because that's all you asked me about!" snapped Cimozjen.

Yorin turned back to face Cimozjen, a supercilious smirk twisting his youthful face. "You try to foist your error on me? Ha!

It's everything you talked about! And now what do we have? The only thread connecting this whole sorry account is the *would-be* thief." He chortled. "Indeed, gone are the robbery, the maiden and, with them, civilian, your credulity."

Cimozjen stared at him in disbelief for a moment. "The word," he said at last, "is credibility."

Several of the guards snickered.

"Silence!" barked the captain. He looked back at Cimozjen and snapped his fingers. "Papers."

Cimozjen pulled a small hinged brass folder dulled with tarnish from his haversack. Opening it, he removed a neatly folded parchment, opened it, and handed it to the White Lion.

Captain Thauram raised his eyebrows and pushed out his lower lip. "Provisional papers?" he said. "I see."

"It's a complicated story," said Cimozjen, "and one that has no bearing on Torval's murder."

"Of course," said Yorin. "All manner of vagrants and deserters have gotten provisional papers since the war." He looked at the papers again. "You claim a home a few leagues east of . . . where in the depths is Vurgenslye? Lads? Anyone?"

There were shrugs all around.

"So a person whose home and citizenship that cannot be proved, hailing from somewhere near a hamlet no one has ever heard of. Indeed." He tossed the paper back at Cimozjen, and it fluttered to the floor. He took a few steps, turned, and sat on the corner of a table to address his guards, completely ignoring Cimozjen. "What I see here is simple. This man is a stranger in town. Possibly a blacksmith by trade, or more likely a deserter, either of which explains his musculature, his lack of scars, and his rather subservient bearing.

"So tonight this timid, if robust, old man is wandering the streets of a strange city, whereupon he gets set upon by a vagrant, who, wracked by hunger and soaked by the afternoon's rain, was in dire need of food and fresh clothing to survive the night. By some stroke of luck, or perhaps because the vagrant was too weakened by starvation to be able to strike a telling blow, this old man manages to overcome the vagrant, and, in a moment of panicked frenzy, actually slays him. Now, those who have never known the bravery or discipline of the army can be undone by the act of taking a life. This being the case, he brings the body here with a carefully woven tapestry of events that accentuates his own heroism in the matter. It is a simple case of self-protection on one hand and fear of discovery on the other."

He looked over at Cimozjen and drummed his fingers on his knee. "Still, I could be wrong. This may indeed be an actual murder. Hold him here, and send a rider to the other wards to see if there are any reports of trouble that might involve this man. And toss that . . . thing out in the street. I don't want to see it any more. Let the corpse collectors fetch it in the morning."

Two guards grabbed Torval by the ankles and started dragging him to the door.

Cimozjen shook his head in disbelief. "You . . ." he began, but managed to hold his tongue before he shared any more of his thoughts.

The half-elf slid off the table and glided over to where Cimozjen stood. He placed his hands on his hips, looked at Cimozjen and said, "You hate me now that I've uncovered your fear, don't you?"

Cimozjen noted that although the half-elf looked *at* Cimozjen's eyes, he didn't actually look *in* them, hence he saw only what he wished to see.

"I tell you the truth, you know not what I think," said Cimozjen.

"Ooooh," said Yorin, in a sing-song taunt. "I'll bet I do. Right now you wish you had the courage to strike me, don't you? But you're too unsettled by the blood on your hands, and you're too afraid of what will happen to your precious skin. But you'd love to fight me."

Cimozjen smiled. "I cannot harm you, captain," he said, so quietly that only he and the half-elf could hear, "for I am sworn to *protect* the weak and the foolish."

The captain's countenance flared into a snarl, and he swung a backhanded slap at Cimozjen face. It was a slow-developing strike as Yorin cranked his arm back for maximum force, and Cimozjen saw the blow coming. He ducked his head and turned into the blow, so that the back of the elf's hand landed on the heaviest portion of Cimozjen's skull.

Cimozjen looked at the captain. The young soldier's face twisted as he contained the pain without a sound, but his left hand massaged the back of his right.

He'll be wearing gloves for a week to cover that bruise, thought Cimozjen.

After a few quiet moments, Yorin pointed to a corner. "Hold him there," he commanded. "If he tries to escape before the rider returns, kill him." Then he quickly exited the common room.

"Move it," said one of the guards with a gesture, and Cimozjen complied.

As he walked over to the corner where he would spend the next hour or more, Cimozjen passed a small person swathed in a dark cloak and apparently napping. As he passed, the figure stirred, and he heard a short but welcome whisper.

"I believe you."

Chapter Four

Minrah studied the human as the guards escorted him over to the corner of the common room. He bore, as the captain had pointed out, a trickle of blood running from his scalp down to his cheekbone where it had been smeared away, and the left side of his tunic was torn and stained with small patches of blood. His boots and trousers were wet and smeared with dirt or mud. Yet he moved with more dignity and bearing than did the two guards that ushered him along. And his face . . .

Humans did not age nearly as elegantly as elves did. Neither did they age as slowly, lasting barely a century at best. Yet when they aged, their looks became so much more compelling. She couldn't explain it, but she felt her heart thrilled by the narrow wrinkles that spread above his cheeks, the strands of silver that had overrun his temples, the rugged set to his jaw. It was like humans combined the right parts of a dwarf's durability and an elf's elegance. And she had no idea how their eyes could be so deep. Maybe it was because they lived each day facing their own imminent death, knowing from birth that their heart was inexorably slowing.

She studied him as he sat there. He looked to be an experienced warrior, for he walked with his left shoulder held slightly forward, a habit common to those who'd carried a shield into combat for years. His eyes scanned the room, never idling at the ceiling or floor. In this way, he remained aware of all potential threats. And he never placed his hands in a position where they would be constrained, as if he expected he might have to use the weapons that should have been at his side.

She traced one fingernail along her jaw line as she studied him, her face concealed beneath an overhanging black hood. His eyes looked over at her, trying to penetrate the shadows of her hood. She saw a twinkle of curiosity in his eyes, wondering why she had spoken to him. Then he looked away again, gauging her to be no threat.

Oh, how wrong he was.

The captain of the watch re-entered the room, and the human's eyes flared. His predatory gaze followed the pathetic young Thauram around the room, but the White Lion did not acknowledge his existence. Then Minrah saw a slight flush suddenly color the captain's cheeks, and she realized that he was afraid of the human. In that moment, Minrah made her decision.

She waited until the captain left the room, then she uncurled herself from her chair and walked over to one of the soldiers who leaned against the wall near the fire. Stepping close and touching one hand to his chest, she softly asked, "Would you mind overmuch were I to speak with the prisoner?"

❋ ❋ ❋ ❋ ❋ ❋ ❋

The cloaked figure walked over to Cimozjen, pulled over a chair, and sat, tucking one foot under the other knee.

"You believe me, do you?" said Cimozjen, never taking his eyes off the guards.

"Yes, I do," said a decidedly feminine voice.

Cimozjen inclined his head with renewed curiosity.

"Any fool can see that the death-blow was several bells old at the soonest. A fresher wound would still have been oozing, and his skin had lost all color."

"I fear that our Watch Captain Thauram is not just any fool," said Cimozjen. He turned to look at her. "My name is—"

"Cimozjen Hellekanus. I heard. I'm Minrah."

"That's it? No family name?"

"Never had one." She pulled back her hood and shook out her hair.

Cimozjen blinked several times. "You're an elf!" he said, taken aback.

Minrah looked at him, her large, almond-shaped eyes twinkling with bemusement. Long ears, the longest Cimozjen had ever seen on an elf, swept elegantly back, hinting at a crown by their shape. "Yes," she said, eyeing him curiously, "what did you expect?"

"I—to be honest, I know not precisely what I expected, but in truth, an attr—er, supportive elf-maiden was not even on the roster."

She giggled, a sound like water trickling over rocks in the sunshine, a sound far removed from the cold, dark, and painful night of the last two hours. "Well, Cimozjen, I'd say your luck is a far cry better than your imagination."

Cimozjen looked away to study the guards again. "I see. And what is it that I can do for you this evening, Minrah?" he asked.

Minrah leaned forward. "Now that's an interesting question. I would have expected you to ask what I could do for you. After all, I said I believed your account of events. That itself implies that I am willing to help you out."

Cimozjen took a deep breath and let it out. "It has been my experience that there are few in this world who will help a stranger without asking for something in return. As you have offered to help, you must see value for yourself in doing so. I object neither to your company nor to your assistance, for you have a pleasant voice, but I will not be held liable for a debt that I cannot repay.

So whatever your price may be for your assistance, let it be known, that we have no misunderstanding between us."

Minrah giggled again, and the sound brought a smile to twitch at the corner of Cimozjen's mouth. "You consider yourself one of those few selfless and generous people, do you?" she asked.

"No," said Cimozjen after a brief pause, "but I try. And I aspire to be a far better man than I am."

"I think you're probably more kind than you care to admit," said Minrah. "But as a matter of fact, my suspicious acquaintance, I do have a price. My price for helping you is simply this. That you let me help you. As in me, and not someone else."

Cimozjen turned toward her fully, his curiosity piqued. He started to say something, then rethought and said, "I'm not entirely certain that that makes any sense."

"Simple. I am an independent researcher. I look for interesting things. If possible I make those things more interesting or more intriguing, and then I write about them. That done, I bring them to the offices of the *Korranberg Chronicle,* the *Sharn Inquisitive,* or whichever chronicle I think might purchase the story from me. I guess you could call me a bard of the broadsheet.

"This story, your story, it intrigues me. A veteran soldier like you—you are a veteran soldier, right?"

Cimozjen nodded.

"I knew it. A veteran soldier finds an old compatriot dead on the streets, murdered. He seeks justice in his native land, but the keepers of the law betray the respect that he and his friend should have earned through their years of service. That is a compelling tale of woe, and done properly I could sell it for ten, maybe fifteen crowns to the right buyer.

"But"—she reached out and gripped his forearm for empha- sis—"what if that soldier were able to unravel the secrets that his dead friend had to tell? What if, despite being spurned by those whom his society entrusted for their safety, what if that man were able to overcome the difficulties, find his friend's murderer, and bring that craven brigand to justice? Now that, my good man, would be a story! I'd write it in sections, sell each of the sections for a sovereign or two each, then, just as we approach the heroic climax, the final chapter, the desperate final act that everyone awaits . . . I hold out for a galifar or more! I could easily make ten, twenty times as much with a story like that! That's why I am willing to help you. I want that story to have a bloody, vengeful climax every bit as much as you do. And, I might add, by being a voice in the narrative I would make a name for myself, a name known to the common people."

Cimozjen furrowed his brow. "The common folk? I mean no disrespect, for they are the bone and muscle of the land, but I think you would find the ear of a noble to be far more valuable than the fawning of a farmer."

"For one such as you, a great warrior, that is surely true," said Minrah. "But for us bards, who live by our wit—more or less honestly, that is—the acclaim of the crowd is a golden sound. A noble may gift you with gold, but a crowd can shower you with a cloudburst of copper, and they are far less fickle a patron. The day that the people look through a chronicle for a story written by me, or dare I say that they even demand one, that, ohhh, *that* my friend, is the day I become a true bard of the pen!"

Cimozjen leaned back and laughed, a genuine, warm laugh that resounded in the otherwise quiet room. He swiped his knuckle across the bottom of his nose. "If it brings Torval justice," he said with a wry smile, "who am I to complain if all of Khorvaire knows his story? Very well, Minrah of no family name, we have ourselves an understanding, and a deal."

"Here now, what's all this?" said a guard, stepping closer and squashing the mood that had developed.

"It's nothing, White Lion," said Cimozjen, "simply—"

"I'm just telling him the story about the ogress, the duckling, and the justicar of the Silver Flame," said Minrah, nudging Cimozjen surreptitiously with her foot. She turned back to Cimozjen. "Here's another one for you. What did King Kaius the First say when he executed his court jester?"

"Truly I cannot say," said Cimozjen, caught unprepared by Minrah's ploy.

"I'm at my wit's end!"

Cimozjen laughed as realistically as he could.

"Or this. How many Darguun halberdiers would you need to take Cyre?"

"I'm sure I have no idea," said Cimozjen.

"We'll never know," said Minrah, starting to laugh. "Even they don't want it anymore."

Cimozjen tried to laugh again, but found he couldn't force out much more than a wheeze, so instead he doubled over and thumped the table to conceal his mediocre emoting.

The guard rolled his eyes and walked away.

"My apologies, Cimozjen," said Minrah, leaning in close, "if you loiter here long enough, you'll learn every tired and terrible joke in town. I can't tell you how many new recruits I've seen try to impress the old hands with that last one."

Cimozjen laughed, and this time it was genuine, for there were many such painful jokes from his time in the military, as well.

She leaned forward. "So let's begin. I'm curious. Why didn't you just tell the captain that you were of the Iron Band? Wouldn't that make him want to help you?"

"How do you know I'm of the Iron Band?"

Minrah grinned. "By the way you treated your friend, you had to have served in the Last War together. I made a guess, and you've just confirmed it. So why not tell him?"

Cimozjen rolled his eyes. "I've seen enough of his kind. Garrison gargoyles. I wanted to know if he would help me because it was right. If not, then by revealing my service, all I could truly garner would be the illusion of help as he tried to curry favor."

"You're absolutely right on that one."

Cimozjen cocked his head. "You seem to know these people rather well," he said. "Do you come here often?"

Minrah shrugged. "Whenever I'm in town, yes."

"And our preening cockerel puts up with you?"

Minrah held up her palms helplessly. "I wrote a work once that cast young Thauram in a good light—I make things up when I have to, no surprise—and as a result, he tolerates my presence. This is the worst of the White Lion troops, the most pathetic soldiers guarding the least desirable location, so this is where the best stories come." She punched him playfully on the arm. "And you're my proof of that tonight!"

At that reminder, Cimozjen's heart became somber again. He felt his face fall, and a part of him was sad to see what was left of the jovial mood pass away as had his friend. "Tell me how you can help me find justice, Minrah."

"Simple," said Minrah, picking up the conversation with a businesslike tone. "I'd start now, but your friend—Torval was it? He's much too big for me to drag around by myself, so we'll have to leave him in the street for the moment." Minrah pulled her knees up and hugged them to her, a strangely girlish act for such a mature conversation. "We just wait here until the rider gets back. When he does, Yorin Thauram the Second-Rate will let you go, and you can take me somewhere private." She smiled knowingly. "Where I can find out what your friend has to say, that is."

"I fear he has little to say anymore," said Cimozjen.

"Not to the casual acquaintance, no. But I'll get him to talk to me. See, I look for things. And when I look, I find them. Little things—threads, marks . . . clues. Then I—well, this time you and I together, we piece together what we know from those clues, and then we look for more clues based on that. It's kind of like untying a tangled spool of thread. And at times, it's just as frustrating." She reached out and gave his hand a reassuring squeeze. "But I believe we can do it. You and me, together."

Cimozjen glanced at the door that led outside. "I do hope you are right, else my heart will never be settled again." He blew out a heavy sigh, puffing his cheeks. Memories stung his eyes. "Would that you had known him the way I knew him. He—" Cimozjen stopped for fear his voice might crack, and roughly rubbed his free hand across his mouth and chin to regain control.

"I know," said Minrah, gripping his hand tighter. "Believe me, I know."

❀ ❀ ❀ ◉ ❀ ❀ ❀

It was nearing midnight before Yorin Thauram II, with a mix of reluctance and relief, let Cimozjen leave. Cimozjen tenderly rewrapped his friend's body, gathered it up, and hoisted it over his right shoulder. Minrah picked up a small pack, a bag, and Cimozjen's staff, and then, without asking, slipped her hand into the crook of his left elbow and snuggled into his arm. Together, the two of them walked through the darkened streets of Korth.

A heavy autumn mist had set in, making the world seem ethereal. The few other pedestrians they passed in the cold night were but shades in the hazy dreamscape. The only color in the gray-on-gray nighttime city came from the rainbow halos that surrounded the magical lanterns that illuminated the intersections of major streets.

"Let's talk about our first step, then," said Minrah. "Shall we start by finding a necromancer that might be able to get Torval to talk?"

"No," said Cimozjen flatly.

"Why not? I know it's pricey, but a veteran like you should be able to—"

"I'll not entrust Torval to the mercies of the Cult of Vol," spat Cimozjen with startling vehemence, "nor to anyone else who practices their vile rites. I've had . . . poor experiences with their ilk in times past, and I'd trust their assistance even less than I'd trust Thauram and his kind."

In response to his outburst, Minrah just gave his arm a reassuring squeeze. They walked in silence together for a dozen blocks or so before she spoke again.

"They still amaze me, after all these years," she said.

"The White Lions?"

"These lights." Minrah pointed to one of the lanterns as they passed. "They never stop shining. Ever. I think it's amazing that magewrights can do that, spend a relatively short amount of time on a project and leave an indelible mark on the world like that. That's what I want to do. Write a story that will be read over and over again for a thousand years. It's a kind of immortality to have your name remembered forever."

They walked in silence for another block. At the next intersection, she spoke again. "Did you know that the name 'everbright lanterns' originated in Thrane?" she asked.

"No, I did not. I thought that's just what most people call them."

"A lot of them do, I think, especially in the cities, but the nickname is most prevalent in Thrane over every other nation in Khorvaire. It spread everywhere with their missionaries, I suppose, so now it's more of a Khorvairian word than anything. Kind of lost its roots. I think the phrase originally had to do with their obsession with the Silver Flame, their holy eternal fire, burning all the time in its cathedral. A true believer is always supposed to have the light of the Silver Flame burning bright in their souls, or so they say. So I've always thought that they used that name as kind of a reminder to themselves of what they ought to be doing. Bringing their light to the world."

Cimozjen mulled the idea over for a moment. "Sounds reasonable."

"And the Brelish often as not call them cold fire lanterns," she said. "I think that's because they appreciate the irony of the phrase 'cold fire,' the inherent magical implications of the name. I mean, their capital, Sharn, is replete with magic, built as it is right there on a manifest zone with all those huge towers. If the magic faded from the area, the whole city would collapse. But in the meantime, they revel in it."

"I see," said Cimozjen. "And in a like manner Karrns call them wisplights because they're so faint compared to the sun. Wispy sunlight—wisplight. It seems the most realistic label."

"No, silly man," said Minrah. "I'd wager it's because of the

Karrnathi obsession with mystery, death, and undeath. You're a superstitious and moody people, probably because you grew up with all these large, dark pine forests encroaching on your towns. I think they're named because they're faint and round and can only be seen at night, like will-o'-wisps. That's why in the small towns, folks only call them 'wisplights.' They're closer to their superstitions than city folk."

Cimozjen pursed his lips. "I'd not thought of it that way," he said, "but I do suppose you could be right."

"There's no 'could be' about it," said Minrah with a confident laugh.

"Up there," said Cimozjen, "that's where I'm staying. The Walking Wounded."

"I see it. Charming picture of a one-armed zombie on the sign. Do you have a private room?"

"No."

"Why not?"

"I find them a needless indulgence," said Cimozjen.

"I should have expected a veteran to say as much. You've probably spent most of your life bunking with other solders, haven't you?"

"Yes, and trust me, one learns to sleep lightly."

Minrah paused in her step, her hand slipping from Cimozjen's elbow. "Do soldiers actually steal from each other? That's pathetic!"

Cimozjen chuckled. "No, they do not. At least not in the Karrnathi army. Well, maybe once in a great while one will try, though I dare say that losing a right hand in the center of camp tends to discourage such activities. Yet soldiers will play pranks."

Minrah giggled as she caught back up and took his arm again. "Do they?"

"Oh yes. Snoring, that's the killer. It shows you're heavily asleep. Plus at night, it can give away the location of your camp to an enemy scout, so no one ever truly regrets taking advantage of a snoring man while in the field. I remember one night w—uh, one or two soldiers shaved a general bald as he lay snoring in his bed. Head and beard, cut to stubble. Left him with nothing but an X for his forelock."

"Did you ever get found out?"

"Minrah, whatever makes you think it was me?"

She laughed and tilted her head on his arm. "You said you remembered, not that someone told you. And I heard your little stutter. It was you and Torval, wasn't it?"

Cimozjen grinned. "In truth, it was. And, according to the general's orderly, every night afterward he tied a strip of cloth around his head to hold his jaw closed." He stopped and turned to impel her subtly toward the front door of the inn. "Here we are."

Minrah walked up to open the door but paused with her hand on the latch. "You understand that we'll need a private room tonight. We shouldn't have others poking around our affairs." She drew in a breath through her nose. "Don't carry him like a cord of wood, all right? Cradle him in your arms, and let his head rest on your shoulder. So which side of the door is the owner's desk on?"

"I do not remember," said Cimozjen. "Does it matter?"

"Of course," said Minrah. "If it didn't, I wouldn't have asked." She looked at Cimozjen, and he waited patiently for her to explain. "Look, we don't want the innkeeper to see Torval's face. Even a stone-cold drunk has more life in his face than he does. Hmm. Just hold him whichever way is more comfortable, and I'll square him away. Whatever you do, don't let him shift, or his head might flop down."

Cimozjen maneuvered Torval's body into position, wincing as his wounds and knotted muscles protested the additional abuse. Minrah arranged Cimozjen's longcoat about Torval's body, unveiling his head, smoothing his hair somewhat but leaving his dead face concealed.

"Right," she said, "just head in and keep walking. Don't stop. I'll handle the rest, and I'll be right behind you."

Minrah opened the door and Cimozjen stepped through. She scooted in right behind him, walking straight up to the owner. "I don't mean to be rude, but our friend here pickled himself in a jug and decided he wanted to drink the river as a chaser. We'll need a private room, a basin of hot water, and a pail as quickly as you can." Even as she finished, she pressed a coin into the flustering innkeeper's palm. "Let's be quick about it, now, unless you want him to share what he's been eating and drinking all evening!"

She grabbed the lantern that sat on the desk with one hand and the innkeeper's wrist with the other, pulling him along, following Cimozjen to the staircase that led to the rooms. "Quick, quick, which is the closest private room? The longer he's carried around doubled up like that, the more likely it is that we'll be squeezing everything out of him. Drunk as he is, that might mean both ends!"

"The, uh, th-th-the, um, second door—third door! Third door on the left!"

"Thank you!" said Minrah. She quickly ducked beneath Cimozjen's elbow to the door and opened it for him. "A pail then!" she said. "Quickly! Maybe two!"

The innkeeper rushed back downstairs as Cimozjen stepped into the room. Minrah followed, placed her bags and his staff in the corner, and closed the door behind them. "Set him down there, on the floor," she said, pointing to the area of the room that would be most concealed from the hallway were the door to be opened. She remained by the door while Cimozjen caringly laid his friend out.

The door opened, banging loudly into the foot that Minrah had planted in its path. She immediately poked her head back around and saw the nervous innkeeper. "A pail! Excellent!" she said, taking it and the towel stuffed inside. "I think we're fine, now that we have him lying down. Some hot water, maybe, and a plate of sausages—yes, if you could get us those, that would be good. No need to rush though. I think we're good here with the bucket now. Thank you ever so much!"

She eased the door back closed to cut off the innkeeper's questions.

"I think we're safe now," she said.

"You lied!" said Cimozjen, turning his head toward her.

"Of course. I wanted to keep things as easy for us as possible."

"It was totally unnecessary!"

"Keep your voice down, or you'll get us thrown out!"

Cimozjen fumed. "That was not necessary. He caters to veterans, and he and I have a good rapport. You betrayed his trust in me."

Minrah shrugged. "Maybe so, but most innkeepers prefer their guests to be breathing. Anyway, it worked."

Cimozjen stared at her, letting his eyes channel the anger and betrayal he felt.

At last she held up her hands in concession. "Fine, I'm sorry. It was just the easiest, quickest thing to do."

"That is the bull's-eye," said Cimozjen. "The road of lies and deceit is very easy, but it leads ever downhill. And, judging by how quickly you turned down that path—"

"Hold your tongue right there," snapped Minrah. "I'm doing whatever I can to help you, and this is the gratitude I get? You couldn't do a thing out there on the streets, and you know it, but I got us safely up here. So there's no reason to think the less of me. I'm not dishonest."

"I pray that all lies do not come so easily to you," said Cimozjen quietly, "or as quickly."

Minrah looked like she wanted to answer, but the words no longer escaped her puckered mouth. Instead, she dropped her eyes and fiddled with her fingers, then went over to the door and sat down. "So much for chivalry," she spat. "I guess maybe you're used to a more commercial relationship with your women."

Cimozjen clenched his teeth and stared at Torval's lifeless face. At last he broke the silence. "Well, then. We've managed to wound each other, and cruelly as well. I propose we accept our hurts, forgive the trespasses, and move forward, because the only one who's not been offensive this evening is the one being slighted by our inactivity. So shall we?"

Minrah nodded without looking up. "I suppose," she murmured.

Chapter
Five

A pot of tea and a couple sausages later, Minrah had regained her focus. She moved over to Torval's corpse and extended the wick in the lamp for better light.

"Right," she said. "This is exactly how he was when you found him? Aside from the fact that you've ported him over half the city, of course."

"Yes."

She pulled out an iron armband from her bag. "And you're sure this is his?"

"Where'd you get that?" asked Cimozjen. "I'd thought the guards had kept it."

Minrah shrugged. "They left it on one of the tables. I figured we had more need of it than they did."

"And you saw no need to ask, either. Still, it is his. Let me have it." Cimozjen turned it over in his hand. "See, right here? If you look carefully and angle it to the flame, you'll see his name is engraved on the inside."

"That's his name? They just look like scratches to me."

"It's an ancient script, and hard to read even if you've

had practice."

"And you're sure this is him?"

Cimozjen tilted his head and gave her a look.

"I had to ask. So let's see what your friend has to say. Hopefully it will be a lot, because he hasn't been dead for very long. No decomposition—no surprise if he's been submerged in King's Bay—and no evidence that the fish have been at him much. He's got some water-pruning in the fingers here, which one expects with a body in the water. Sort of like when you take a bath. You've taken a bath, right?"

"Once or twice."

Minrah gripped Torval's head and began looking it over carefully. "Right. Hasn't looked after his hair in years. No headband, nor did he wear one as near as I can tell."

"How can you tell that?"

"If you wear something on a regular basis, your skin adjusts to its presence. Typically it's a little smoother, a little paler, and there's a kind of border at the edge of where the item goes. Look here," she said, holding up her index finger. "Feel this. See how I have a small dent on the side? That's because I use a pen a lot. Same thing goes for people who wear headbands, rings, things like that."

"Fine. But I could have told you he wore no headband."

"When was the last time you saw him?"

Cimozjen darkened. He cleared his throat. "A long time," he said, his voice husky. "Twenty-two years ago."

"Things change over the course of twenty-two years," Minrah said. "For one, I'll wager his hair and beard were not this long, or as gray. It's odd, wouldn't you say, that a veteran soldier not only grew his hair so long, but also that he wore nothing to keep it out of his eyes? I've always thought warriors wanted a clear field of vision."

Cimozjen nodded. "That is true. We were also taught to keep our chins clean-shaven. Beards offer the enemy the chance to grab your hair and direct the motion of your head, and that's a billet to the casualty lists. And look at this matting."

"So there's our first clue," said Minrah. "We don't yet know what it means, but it's a clue, because it's something out of the ordinary."

She ran her hands down his face. "Nose broken several times, it seems." She turned his head from side to side. "Looks like he's missing part of his left ear." She pulled the hair back to reveal the ear. The lobe was missing from where it joined the head to about halfway up the curve. She ran her finger gently down the injury. "Looks like magical healing was used. There's no sign of any scarring. Yet if you were going to use magical healing, why not regrow the lobe?"

"Such services are more costly," said Cimozjen. "It's far less expensive just to have one's bleeding stopped or to reattach something that's been severed than it is to regenerate what's no longer there. Given what we can see of his wellbeing, perhaps he could not afford it."

"But the ear isn't a crucial injury," said Minrah. "It wouldn't even bleed overmuch. So if he were so poor, why not just bandage the ear and save his coin for food?"

"That I do not have an answer for," said Cimozjen. "Perhaps a healer was feeling charitable?"

"Perhaps," said Minrah. She leaned forward and scowled. "You know, this wound is a smooth cut. It was made by a blade." She guided her hand sideways toward his head like an axe. "To cut the lobe off, it would have to come in like this. But look at what else it would hit."

"If the blade were to sever the lobe," said Cimozjen, "it would have to strike the base of the head, the jaw, or the neck, depending on its angle of attack."

"And that would be a more serious injury," said Minrah.

"Wound," said Cimozjen. "An injury is when you fall off your horse."

"Sorry," said Minrah absently. She straightened up. "So someone healed his bleeding, but didn't take enough care to restore his ear. They cared about his life, but not his looks."

"Based on his attire, I'd say that was a given."

"But it's important," said Minrah. "A pattern is forming here, if only we can figure out what that pattern is."

She worked her way down the body, pausing to wet a cloth and scrub away the grime and blood from the massive wound on his chest. "Death was clearly caused by this hit. If you look inside, you can see the breastbone was cleft. That took power. Probably the impact itself slew him, not the bleeding. Though there would have been a lot of that. And the wound is balanced, see? Deepest in the center, thinning out evenly to either side. That means it was done by an axe with a curved blade, not a sword or a scimitar."

"How so?"

"A sword blade is straight. It would either leave a flat wound if it happened to hit straight on, or more likely a hack, a wound that's heavier to one end. A scimitar leaves a longer, slicing mark. This is a chopping mark."

After a few more moments' study, she spoke again. "He wore the armband on his left arm, right? The skin's smoother there."

"That's where it's worn," said Cimozjen, "so that it remains close to the heart."

"And here," she said. "Look at this." She turned the inside of Torval's forearm to the light. There were scars there, shaped like the letters S and I. "These aren't like his other scars. He made these deliberately. See how raised these are? That means he rubbed sand or something into the cuts after he made them. He wanted these scars here, and he wanted them to be visible."

"S-I," said Cimozjen. "What would that mean?"

"I was going to ask you," said Minrah. "Is it someone's initials? A military term?"

Cimozjen shook his head slowly. "I can think of nothing. Perhaps he was unable to finish the scarring before he died?"

"I'll keep that in mind, though I doubt that's the answer," said Minrah. "The scars aren't that fresh." She continued to study Torval's corpse, slowly moving down his torso. "He's got a lot of scars," she said, "but I'd expect that from a soldier. Hmm. Hoy!

Look at that. Tell me, did he have both shoes when you found him?"

"No, just the one. I remember being irritated about that. Why?"

She held up Torval's leg and waggled his unshod foot. "This ankle's broken."

"Is that so unusual? If my ankle were broken, I'd want no shoe placed on my foot either."

"But there's no swelling and hardly any bruising," said Minrah. "His ankle was broken after he died."

"I guess that rules out a dancing injury," said Cimozjen lamely. "Another clue, then?"

Ignoring his comments, Minrah scrutinized the area, bringing the lantern very close to his ankle and heel and using a small hand mirror from her bag to illuminate the skin more evenly. "Aha, I thought as much," she said at last. "There are scrapes at the back of his heel and along the top of his foot. Bloodless scrapes."

"What does that mean?"

"Again, they happened after he died, or shortly before. Given even a short amount of time, they would have scabbed over. These didn't." She sat back on her heels and looked at Cimozjen. "You said you found him in the water, right?"

Cimozjen nodded.

Minrah ran her knuckle back and forth across her chin and gazed sightlessly at the shadows of the room. "So he died, and afterward he got these injuries on his foot and lost a shoe. Sounds to me like he was dumped in the water after his death, and weighted down with a rope and a stone."

"Well, whoever did it probably wanted him not to float around."

"Dead bodies don't float," said Minrah.

"Sure they do," said Cimozjen. "Everybody knows that—"

Minrah held up her hand. "Let me explain. Bodies float while they have air in their lungs. But when you die, the air goes out, and you sink. It's not until the corpse begins to putrefy that it floats back to the surface. Now the water in King's Bay is probably cold enough that he'd stay down all winter and not come up until late spring, but they still weighted him with a rock. They wanted him to stay down. Forever."

"So no one would ever know his fate."

"Right. But say his ankle broke, maybe when they threw him in. They might have thrown the stone in first, you know, because you'd want a pretty heavy stone to weigh down a large body. His ankle broke, and the rope slid off his foot, taking his shoe with it." She glanced at the other shoe. "If he had a matched pair, then the missing shoe also went over his ankle. That might have made it easier for the rope to slip off."

"That rings of the truth, I suppose," said Cimozjen. "But what does it really tell us?"

"Quite a lot. He was probably killed by people who are primarily sailors, because they tried to bury him in the water and not in the dirt or in the sewers. It also means that they took pains to hide his body. This isn't a case of him getting into a fight on the docks and falling in or getting shoved off. Still, he may have been dropped off the end of a dock, or he may have been thrown off a ship."

"Or just a rowboat," said Cimozjen. "It would be easy enough to steal one for an hour or two after dark."

"Not a rowboat," said Minrah, shaking her head. "It would be too awkward to throw a body off a dinghy with a heavy rock tied to him. It'd be liable to tip, and that's dangerous in cold weather like this, because you're likely wearing heavy clothing that'll drag you down."

"He could easily have been killed elsewhere, and brought to the water," said Cimozjen, "so I see not how this gets us anywhere."

"That's possible, yes, although we can't forget that they also used a large rock. Maybe they dragged one of those across town with them, but it seems unlikely." She looked back at the body. "Now let's take a look at those clothes, shall we? Help me get them off."

"Over my dead body," snapped Cimozjen.

Minrah shrugged. "He is your dead body."

"Show him some respect."

"I am. I'm trying to solve his murder."

Cimozjen sighed in frustration. "With the Host as my witnesses," he said, "I'll not have a young woman looking at my friend's naked body. It's just—it's not right. I'll not dishonor his body like that. It's been dishonored enough for one lifetime."

He stared at her for a moment, scowling. She returned a blank gaze.

Finally he raised one hand to rub his forehead. "It's been a long day. We should rest, the both of us. Come the morning, I'll buy some attire more suitable for him, and then you can have a look at those rags. Does that sound equitable?"

"If that will make you happy," said Minrah with an understanding smile. Then she looked at Torval once more. "Listen, not to be cruel, because I don't want to, but aren't you concerned about the smell if we just leave him here until morning?"

Cimozjen laughed darkly. "I'm a soldier." He looked at her pointedly. "There is nothing worse than the smell of a battlefield, with the blood, and the filth, and the slaughterhouse smell of savaged bodies. And all through it is the stink of fear. One small corpse will bother me not at all. Over so many years, I've grown used to the smell."

"Sure, but his chest is opened up, and I don't want anyone else to think maybe we're butchering chickens up here."

Cimozjen took a deep breath and sucked on his lips. "Open the window. The cold and the fresh air will help in that respect."

"I'll burn a candle," said Minrah, and she turned to fish through her bag.

Cimozjen looked around. "Er, Minrah, you can have the bed if you wish a comfortable seat tonight; I'll just—"

"I don't need the padding to meditate," said Minrah. She crossed her legs, settled her back against the wall, and folded her hands in her lap. "No, please, you go ahead. I'll be just fine right here."

"You're sure of this?"

"Absolutely."

"Because the bed would be more comfortable than the floor, and—"

Minrah gave him an odd sideways look and smiled. "Now's not the time. If we're to work things out together, I need you at your best. Lie down. Sleep." So saying, she closed her eyes and breathed deeply.

"As you wish," said Cimozjen uncertainly. "If you'd rather I moved to a separate room, I—"

"Sleep," Minrah insisted.

"Aye," said Cimozjen. Flapping his hands on his thighs uncomfortably, he stepped over to the mattress, sat down, and kicked off his boots. He left all his other clothes on and wrapped himself in a blanket. Then he drew his dagger and, holding it in one hand, curled up to go to sleep.

He prayed that if he dreamt of Torval, that it would be Torval alive.

Chapter
Six

By the time the slanting rays of the morning sun reached into the room, Minrah was already gone. She'd roused herself from her meditations, stretched, and broken her fast with some dried fruit from her bag.

She walked through the streets of Korth, which were just starting to fill with the day's industry. The aroma of a bread shop caught her nose, and she stopped in and purchased a loaf of hot wheat bread. The bread steamed as she tore it apart and ate it.

She passed by Crownhome, the massive fortified palace of King Kaius III, just as one of the royal trumpeters of the Conqueror's Host sounded the hour. Turning north, she soon reached the top of the bluff that separated Crownhome and the South Gate from the so-called bottom districts—the Low District and the Community Ward, where the poorest and hardest-working Karrns made their homes. She paused for a moment to look at the serene cityscape of the morning.

From this vantage it was clear why Korth was also known as "the Crucible of Karrnath." Aside from being the largest settlement in the nation, the city looked rather like a vast shallow bowl, with the dross collected at the bottom. Tall bluffs, cut by only a handful of steep roads, divided the poorest sections of town that existed by the river's edge from the merchant and noble areas of town that rested atop the fertile landscape.

With the morning sun at such a low angle, the bluffs and towers still cast their long shadows west and north across several neighborhoods. Crownhome itself carved a large swath of gloom all the way to King's Bay. The bay lay still and dark. A number of merchant and transport craft moored at the city's docks. Two rocky stacks separated the bay from the Karrn River, where mists peeled from the water's surface, coaxed away by the sun's rays.

Minrah smiled. She always smiled when she was working on a mystery. Writing snippets of her story in her head, she walked down to the docks. She spent over an hour watching the sailors and tossing chips of wood into the bay, and even tried her hand dangling a line from a pier for a short while. Then she sauntered back to the Walking Wounded to see if Cimozjen had yet risen.

She rapped twice on the door to the room. Hearing nothing but an indeterminate grumble, she opened it up and peered inside. Cimozjen lay on his side, facing the wall.

"Hoy, look at that," said Minrah, softly but with exaggerated cheerfulness. "The sunlight is reflecting off your bald spot! That must mean it's a new day! Time to rise, soldier boy!"

Cimozjen growled something unintelligible, then rolled onto his back. "I feel terrible," he said. He winced in pain and reached his right hand to his left side. "Bother, I think it's stuck to my skin." He started to roll out of bed. "I need some hot water to—" He suddenly grunted in pain and flopped back onto the mattress, a grimace twisting his face.

"Hoy, are you ill?" asked Minrah, rushing over to his side.

"No," gasped Cimozjen. "My muscles are all knotted up. In truth, I doubt I can move my neck." He started to reach for his head, but when his hand had only gotten two thirds of the way there, he winced again and let it flop. "And it's beyond my reach. Oh my."

"Has this ever happened before?" asked Minrah, panic edging her voice. "Do I need to call a healer?"

"It's a mix of age and overexertion," said Cimozjen wearily, his eyes squeezed shut. "I tell you, I'm not as young as I once was. I strained my muscles during the fight last night . . . was that only last night? By the Host, it seems like it's been days. And carrying Torval around, I tried to ignore the pain. I used to be able to do it. Persevere through the hurt, that is. But my body's simply unable to take the abuse any more, and my mind's not willing to accept that fact." He chuckled. "Look at me. I'm out of the fight, and yet even talking about it, I still refuse to believe it's the truth."

"So what can I do?" asked Minrah, gently placing her hand over his heart.

Cimozjen paused before answering, breathing heavily as he tried to will the pain from his body. "Were you Torval, you'd lift me out of bed and set me in the biggest hottest bath we could find in the city. Or maybe a steam bath or a hot stone massage. After my body was thoroughly boiled, you'd stretch me out mercilessly until my muscles surrendered and loosened up. Unfortunately, you're not as big as Torval, nor as strong."

"But fortunately," countered Minrah, "I am a lot more alive, and a far sight prettier too."

Cimozjen laughed. "Right you are, and a true joy that is." He sighed. "Gods, would that I had neither my stubbornness nor my selfishness. Sadly, Minrah, there's only one way I'm getting off this bed today. " Cimozjen snorted. "Although I should count my blessings, for I have one more option for rising than Torval does.

"Would you kindly move my left hand to rest on my neck? It shall hurt, thanks to my strains and the blood that has stuck my tunic to my ribs, but do not let that stop you, do you understand? Keep my hand there until I tell you otherwise." He moved his right fist to rest over his heart. "If you're ready, you may proceed."

Minrah nodded, despite the fact that he couldn't see her with his eyes closed. Gently she took his hand and started to raise it up. Halfway up, she started to feel resistance; she saw the material of his tunic pulling taut across his arm and down his side. Holding her breath, she pushed harder, forcing his arm up. It started to tremble. She wasn't sure if it was because of the injuries or a reflex action of his strained muscles. Then, in the quiet of the room, she heard the moist sound of his tunic peeling away from his injuries.

Cimozjen grunted deep in his throat, and Minrah immediately eased off. "Keep moving," he said through his clenched teeth.

She pushed harder, and his muscles resisted more. She forced her weight on his arm and guided his left hand to the base of his neck. She saw his fingers almost convulsively spread open to grip his own flesh.

"Faithful Arawai and Fortunate Olladra," he said, forcing the words through clenched teeth, "by the courage imbued in me by Dol Dorn, I dare to implore you humbly, divine ladies, to infuse this your servant with health, wholeness, and vigor."

A warm aura began to coalesce from between his fingers, almost as if the source of light were the tense muscles themselves. Minrah stared in amazement as the glow intensified, then slowly it began to fade again. She realized when it had all but gone that she was no longer holding Cimozjen's arm in place. He was moving it himself and massaging his neck and shoulders.

With a pained grunt, Cimozjen maneuvered his left hand to rest over his injured ribs. He repeated his murmured prayer, and the glow appeared once more, this time illuminating his bloodstained tunic from behind. Once that glow had also faded, he let himself flop limply and drew a long deep breath.

Minrah put her fingers through the largest hole in his tunic and ran her fingers across his flesh. It was healed, whole. "That's amazing!" she said. "Here I thought you were just a soldier, but you can work magic too!"

"I am an oathbound, sworn to the service of Dol Dorn, my nation, and my king. By virtue of my obedience and honor, the Master of Swords favors me with the gift of healing wounds by laying my left hand upon them. I hope someday to merit more of his favor."

"So if you've got the good fortune to have a gift like that, why didn't you use it last night, and save yourself the trouble?"

"I have my reasons." Cimozjen took a few more deep breaths, then sat up, facing away from Minrah. "I need another tunic," he said. "And Torval needs a suitable outfit."

"What are you going to do with him?" asked Minrah. "We can't exactly carry him along with us."

"I'll make arrangements with the innkeeper. Beginning with telling him the truth of last night," he added, looking pointedly at Minrah, who refused to show the slightest shame. "He'll see to it that Torval is quietly buried and his armband returned to his kin."

"Wouldn't you rather put him back in the service of the king?" asked Minrah. "I thought that was the Karrnathi tradition. Don't they use alchemy and magic to make your dead into—"

"An animate warrior?" Cimozjen snorted. "No, I have no stomach for seeing false honor draped on walking carcasses. Nor am I at peace with the concept of having the dead fight for the nation, able to receive neither honor, nor glory, nor even the satisfaction of a battle well fought." He sighed darkly. "We— especially us in the Iron Band, but all the Karrn soldiers—we knew no rest during the war, and it seems he's had none since. I wish him to have some peace while it is mine to give him."

Minrah rose and gave Cimozjen a hug from behind. "As you wish," she said.

After a pause, Cimozjen extricated himself from her arms. "I must go."

"Here," said Minrah, "here's half a loaf that I saved for you. Go get what you need. I'll stay here and watch over him."

Cimozjen looked at her and smiled. "I thank you," he said, then he grabbed his tattered longcoat and left.

❖ ❖ ❖ ❖ ❖ ❖ ❖

When Cimozjen returned to the room, Minrah was pacing the floor. "Hoy!" she said with a bright smile and a bounce. "Zjennie's back at last!"

Cimozjen scowled and held up one admonishing finger. "Do *not* call me by that name."

"Why·not?"

"Because you sound like my mother," he said.

"Eww, don't want that. I'll call you Cimmo instead."

"Must you?" asked Cimozjen. "I don't like that any more than Zjennie."

"My, so formal from someone who just spent the night with me."

Cimozjen fumbled for words, then said, "Only in a purely literal sense!"

"So far," grinned Minrah.

"Minrah—"

"No time for that now, Cimmo" she said. "We've got lots to do today. Did you get what you needed?"

Cimozjen's shoulders sagged as he resigned himself to his fate. "Yes, new tunic for me, a decent outfit for him," he said. "Got a tailormage to repair my coat." He walked over to Torval. Folding his arms, he stared down at the dead man and nodded to himself. "The proprietor understands my situation. He promised he'd see to Torval's disposition without the collectors finding out. So that gives us our own rein, I suppose."

Minrah went over and sat on the windowsill. She hugged her knees and looked at Cimozjen, rocking back and forth in eagerness. "So how much are you willing to pay to see your friend find justice?"

"Whatever it takes," said Cimozjen. Then his brow darkened and he looked up. "You're not demanding payment now, are you? We had an agreement—"

Minrah laughed. "Of course not! But I don't have a lot of coin, and I needed to know if you had enough to pay for me while we pursue this."

"I can make good on your expenses," he said, "so long as they are not lavish." He paused and scratched his scalp self-consciously. "Nonetheless, I must ask you to leave while I change his clothes."

"That's fine," said Minrah. "But do it quickly. We have a boat to catch."

"What do you mean?"

"I took a look at Torval's shoe while you were gone," she said, holding it aloft. "I figured that wouldn't count as undressing him, right? I mean, one was already off. And if you look right here, there's a craftsman's mark. See it?"

"Looks like a quill and a plow."

"The one on top, that's not a quill. That's a dragonhawk feather."

"Which means?"

"Which means this was made in Aundair," said Minrah. "Our trail leads across Scions Sound, oathbound, and there's a ship weighing anchor at noon."

❋ ❋ ❋ ❋ ❋ ❋ ❋

The trumpeter atop Crownhome sounded the time, one hour before midday, his klaxon barely audible above the hubbub of the city. Cimozjen walked resolutely to the docks. Minrah, holding onto his arm, trotted to keep up with his stride.

"Hoy, big man, no need to rush," she panted. She tried to adjust her pack, but doing so made her bag slide off her shoulder. She did her best to wrestle that back into place, while not letting go of the paladin's arm. "We'll be there in plenty of time. Hoy, slow down!"

"There will be plenty of time to rest and recover our wind once we board ship," Cimozjen said, "I'll squander none of it now."

"Listen, I've been looking to travel to Aundair for some time—there's some special research the *Korranberg Chronicle* wants done—but you don't see me galloping along, do you?"

He didn't answer, but kept a brisk military cadence, with

strides neither too long nor too short. His leather longcoat billowed about his legs. His kit bounced at his hip, the coins chinking with every pace, and his chain mail hauberk shushed beneath his new tunic. He'd also recovered his backpack from the inn's safekeeping room, and he wore it on his back with his broadsword lashed across the top. In his left hand he held his metal-shod walking staff, thick and stout, and it ticked against the cobbles in time with Cimozjen's boots.

The bay water was smooth. Only the tiniest ripples against the shore or near the hull of a ship reflected the sun's rays. Minrah pointed past the cogs, longships, and scows to one of the few seaworthy vessels in the harbor, an elegant wide-beamed two-masted brigantine. The Aundairian civilian naval jack hung limpidly from the pole at the stern.

"Hoy, look at her!" exclaimed Minrah as they drew close. "Shallow draft for a river run, and the beam of a fat mare. That'll be a smooth ride across the Sound. I hope they have hammocks!"

"May it not be so," said Cimozjen. "Hammocks give me backaches. Hurry up, you're flagging."

Minrah upped her pace. "I love the feel of rocking back and forth in them, especially when the ship puts them to swaying. Reminds me of my childhood, riding with my folks. I can lie there and rock, and my mind just empties away to nothing."

The twosome walked down the pier, passing a few others who, like Cimozjen, also had a military bearing. One younger elf honed his rapier and watched the river, while an aging man dropped his oilcloth bundle and sat on it to catch his breath. Cimozjen nodded to each of them as they passed, and received curt nods in return.

The pair climbed up the steep gangway to the ship. The long planked walkway flexed with each step that Cimozjen took, and Minrah, giggling, used the motion to put an extra bounce in her step.

They reached the ship's deck, abustle with activity as longshoremen loaded cargo and sailors prepared the vessel for the journey. They were immediately greeted by a trio of crewmen. Two ship's officers—a dwarf female with long, thick braids, and a human male with wide-set eyes, a shaved head and a severe black goatee—backed by a large, sunbeaten deck hand with a scarf wrapped around his head and his hand wrapped around a naked cutlass.

The human, a quillboard tucked under his arm, held up a hand, his quill pen still clutched in his ink-stained fingers. "Ahoy, and welcome aboard the *Silver Cygnet*," he said wearily. "My name is Pomindras. What's your business here today?"

"We are told you sail this day for Aundair, and wish to procure passage," said Cimozjen.

"With hammocks!" added Minrah, panting.

Pomindras looked from one to the other and back again, studying their faces and their stances. "We should be able to accommodate you," he said at last. "Is it just the two of you?"

"Just us," said Minrah, hugging Cimozjen's arm tightly.

"We have no baggage beyond what we carry," added Cimozjen.

"Fare is fifty galifars for the both of you."

Cimozjen opened his haversack, fished around, then offered up five small platinum pieces. Pomindras gestured with his quillboard to the other ship's officer. Cimozjen gave his coins to the dwarf, pouring them into her outstretched palm.

"I'll need your names," said Pomindras listlessly.

"Cimozjen Hellekanus, at your service," he said, reaching into his kit. He pulled out his brass case, casually let the sailor see the national seal embossed on its surface, and then pulled out his provisional papers.

"The Army Clerk's Office still hasn't squared you away yet, eh?" said Pomindras. "Very well."

"Minrah of Eastgate. Korth, that is." She pulled stained identification papers from her bag. They had no case to protect them, and bore creases both intentional and accidental.

Pomindras opened her papers with a slight look of distaste. "These are barely legible," he grumbled. "Well, it does at least say your name is Minrah. But if the Aundairian authorities don't like this, that's your problem, not mine, and if you've not the coin for the return, your port of call will be the starboard rail." He gave the paper back and waved with his quillboard. "Aboard."

The dwarf, having pocketed Cimozjen's coins through a slot in the locked iron strongbox she carried on her belt, gestured the two onboard. "I am called Erami d'Kundarak. I'm the purser and the steward of the *Silver Cygnet*. Berths are belowdecks, just aft of yon companionway. There's four to a cuddy, so lay claim to yours now. If you're lucky, the other two berths might not fill. The mess is amidships, but you can eat topside if the weather is fair and you don't interfere with the ship's business. If there's anything else you need whilst aboard, let me know. We may not be able to do anything about it," she said with a wink, "but at least I'll know."

"Thank you very much, Erami d'Kundarak," said Cimozjen, placing his hand over his heart. "May the Host bless this ship with the Sovereigns' speed."

Erami smiled. "The Host bless you, Master Hellekanus, and you, Minrah."

"That would be remarkable, wouldn't it?" murmured Minrah.

Cimozjen started to lead the way toward the ladder, skirting around a large coil of rope on the deck, but just as they stepped away from the ship's officers, a well-dressed man rose from leaning against the gunwale and intercepted them.

"Brightness be," he said, with a rich Aundairian accent. "Chain mail, a sword, and a metal-shod staff?" He crossed his arms and ran an appraising eye down Cimozjen's body and up again. "And those look to be military hobnailed boots, if my eyes don't deceive."

He looked Cimozjen in the eye. "So, Karrn, you're here to fight?"

Twenty-six years earlier:

"Tell me, Cimozjen, are you here to fight?"

Behind them, the chaos of battle resounded—horns, war cries, the terrified whinnies of horses, the howl of the wounded and dying. Overhead, the whistling of the arrows vied against the rippling pops of flaming catapult missiles for the right to quail the hardest heart.

"We're here to conquer, general," said Cimozjen confidently.

"Excellent!" said General Kraal. Karrnathi war banners formed a veritable curtain behind the general, backlit by the early morning sun. The sight alone instilled martial ardor in Cimozjen, as did the respect "Horseshoe" Kraal had for Cimozjen's unit.

The general leaned forward on his horse. "The barrage from those catapults is killing us," he said. "We've drawn their lines thin. Your job is to charge the pikes. The cavalry will be right behind you to trample the cowardly archers flat!"

"Sir!" said Cimozjen.

Cimozjen secured his helmet and ran back the long two hundred yards to his unit. It was awkward going. The dewy ground had been churned to a bloody, sticky muck by armored feet.

The opposing army stood deployed across acres of wrecked farmland in Aundair. It was good defensive ground. Stone walls divided each parcel of land, giving the Aundairian army a decent redoubt every hundred yards or so. Nevertheless, the Karrnathi army, trying to force the Daskara Pass toward Fairhaven, had made solid headway throughout the misty early morning hours, grinding their way through the Aundairian defenses. On the river flank, the Iron Band had broken through, and rather than pursue the nigh-defenseless archers that had stood before them, they'd turned and flanked the next Aundairian unit in the line, cracking the entire left side of the line open. The Aundairian army had broken and fled, retreating rapidly into the mists, and the Karrns had reorganized rather than risk becoming separated in the fog and defeated piecemeal.

But then the Aundairian mages had at last persuaded the fog to lift, and with that, General Kraal's decision to reorganize turned from prudent action to a grave mistake.

The Aundairian general had rallied his remaining forces around a full regiment of longbowmen, a formation of deadly missile mages, and a half dozen catapults all located on a hill a half mile away. To close the gap with the enemy, the Karrns had had to climb over wall after wall while the skies punished the troops with arrows, flaming missiles, and deadly blasts of magic.

The Aundairian foot soldiers held their position at the base of the hill, reinforced by two hundred Deneith pikemen, stretched thin but determined and dug in. Karrnathi infantry kept the line preoccupied with skirmish tactics. General Kraal had sent the Rekkenmark-trained cavalry to harass one flank of the Aundairian line and Talenta mercenaries with their clawfoot mounts to harry the other. Confident in the tenacity of the Deneith pikemen, the Aundairians had stripped away their supporting units to bolster the flanks and extend the line to a full circle around their missile troops, leaving the Deneith mercenaries to hold their section of the arc by themselves.

The general was happy. He planned to launch a full infantry assault to lock up the Aundairian flanks, then to send the Iron Band to smite the Deneith pike and thrust his cavalry through the breach to crush the archers and catapult crew beneath their hooves and claws.

The Iron Band was formed up in a "soldier's tent," a defensive arrangement. The whole unit kneeled. The front rank held their shields to the fore, while the other ranks held them up at an angle to deflect the arrows. Cimozjen reached his unit just as another squall of arrows fell, and he dived under the protective cover of his comrades. The iron-tipped arrows sounded like hail as they struck the shields, and somewhere in the group a soldier cried in pain as an arrow slipped a gap and struck him.

"We're taking it to them, boys!" yelled Cimozjen. "We're charging the pikes. Front two ranks, shield yourselves up as soon as the next volley hits, then charge on my command!"

"Here it comes!" yelled Kraavel from the front of the formation.

Another clatter of iron hail fell upon the roof of the soldier's tent, and as it relented Cimozjen yelled, "Up!"

The unit rose as one, and the soldiers in the front two ranks dropped their weapons and grabbed shields from the soldiers of the next two ranks.

"Horseshoe says the cavalry will be right behind us!" yelled Cimozjen as he moved to the front. Torval handed over his shield, and took Cimozjen's flail. "I say they'll be too late! *Charge!*"

The Iron Band surged forward as a pack. As they drew close to the Aundairian line, the Band let loose a thunder of war cries. Cimozjen ran near the van of the charge, along with a few others. He pulled the shields into a wedge, angled with one slightly overlapping the other, then he hit the pikes.

The impact jammed his arms into his chest, but he felt the massed pikes sliding to one side or the other. One tore a hole in his shield and forced its way painfully between his left arm and the shield strap. Another pike, cleverly held low, ripped into his leg just below the knee. He felt another of the Iron Band slam into his back, shoving him forward. The extra inertia pushed the head of the pike completely through his shield strap, breaking it.

Cimozjen hoisted the shield in his right hand and flopped himself hard to the left. The weight of his body and the shields pressed the pikes to the left and down, forcing a breach in what had been a thicket of iron spearheads. He felt the soldier behind him shove him further to widen the breach, then step on the small of his back. The sudden pressure wrenched his spine, trapped as he was between the pikes—including one still through his shield—and the soldier's foot. He grunted in discomfort, though he was proud to be serving his purpose.

The soldier jumped to the fray, yelling a mighty war cry. Cimozjen managed to raise his head and saw that it was Torval, each of his flails already trailing droplets of bright red blood. Another soldier charged over Cimozjen, striking him in the back of the head and stunning him momentarily.

He shook his head to clear it, uncertain how much time had passed. He lay on a mattress of abandoned and broken pikes, the sounds of battle still around him. He shucked the damaged shield on his left arm, then found a broken pike nearby to use as a spear.

He saw that the Deneith pike formation had been disrupted. Faced with ruthless Iron Band warriors close at hand, they'd had to abandon their long pikes in favor of the small axes they carried as secondary weapons. The axes were ill suited to cleave the Iron Band's armor, and without shields to protect themselves, the Deneith warriors were easy prey for the Iron Band's heavy weapons.

Scattered groups of the Deneith warriors still fought. Cimozjen had expected no less, and he respected them for it. Some of the Iron Band contained them, distracted them, while others charged headlong for the vulnerable archers and engine crew.

Cimozjen ran unevenly for the nearest knot of Deneith resistance, intending to add his spear to the fray. As he ran, he heard rolling thunder approaching him from behind, and then the cavalry stampeded past him, havoc and fury and flashing blades.

Cimozjen laughed as he ran. "Too late!" he yelled. "We'll get them first!"

Then, limping on his wounded leg, he laid into the remaining resistance. It was grim, exhausting work, chopping the hopeless, but it had to be done.

Chapter
SEVEN

Cimozjen shook his head to clear it. "No, of course not. As I told someone just last night, I have seen more than enough fighting to last me the rest of my life." He waved a hand dismissively and started to continue aft, then paused and looked at the man again. "Why do you ask?"

The man smiled. He was a large man, over a hand's span taller than Cimozjen and robust bordering on the rotund, with bags under his eyes and a slight jowl to his chin. His facial features were shaped pleasantly enough, however it seemed that they had never acquired the same size as the rest of his body. They were slightly too small, grouped just a tad too close to look agreeable on a head his size, thus his smile, too, looked constrained. A thick red surcoat embroidered with gold only added to his apparent size. It broadened his shoulders and swept the deck as he walked.

"My apologies," said the man, running a hand through his mouse-brown hair. "I speak without considering my manners. My name is Rophis Raanel's Son, of Fairhaven, though most call me Rophis the Winemonger." He extended his hand.

"Cimozjen Hellekanus, at your service," he said, shaking Rophis's large palm with a firm grip.

"And is this lovely creature your wife?" Rophis asked, gently taking Minrah's hand and bowing deeply.

"Minrah, and pleased to meet you," she said, blushing and nestling up against Cimozjen's arm.

"She's not my wife," added Cimozjen. Then he felt a sudden sharp pinch in the crook of his elbow, just under the hem of his chain mail shirt. He drew a sharp breath between his teeth, but managed to avoid vocalizing the unexpected pain. He glanced down at Minrah, who gazed back up at him, her face beaming.

"Not yet," she said, looking back to Rophis. "But a girl can always hope."

"Indeed," said Rophis. "With a radiant face like yours, I would think that your hope would be enough to spur any suitor to the chase. Be that as it may, uh, Cimozjen, again let me offer my apologies. I spoke thusly only because, well, it took me aback to see someone wearing chain aboard ship. It's a dangerous gambit to wear heavy mail on the water, even when sailing the relatively calm waters of Scions Sound. Were you to fall overboard, you'd find those extra pounds to be a very unwelcome weight."

Cimozjen looked down at his mail hauberk, largely concealed by his tunic. "I had not considered that possibility," he said. "I wear it only because I find the weight easier to bear when the chain's on my body rather than in my pack."

Rophis rubbed his nose. "At the risk of seeming improper, good warrior, I would also suggest that you not wear your pack strapped to your back in such a manner, especially with a heavy sword lashed to the very top. Again, were you to fall overboard, you'd be dragged down by your shoulders. A very difficult situation in any waters. You'll take heed that most tars carry their bag slung over one shoulder, so that it can be readily shucked. I only bring this to your attention because the seas can be dangerous, and it would grieve me to see ill befall you or your lovely . . . companion."

"How do you know so much about sailing?" asked Minrah. "You don't have the build of a sailor."

"Minrah!" scolded Cimozjen.

"Well, he doesn't."

Rophis laughed. "It's all true, of course," he said. "You'd not catch me climbing the ropes, not on your life. Not unless the ship had sunk that far beneath the waves, eh?" He laughed again. "But I have done a lot of sailing, my dear, from here, where I can buy Nightwood pale, to Fairhaven for Windshire rainbow wine, to Flamekeep for their thrakel-and-berry brandy. Once in a while, I'll even go to Droaam. The Droaamites have this . . . this . . . I don't know what to call it. It's heavily distilled, and they won't tell me what it's made from, but their name for it translates roughly as Brain Sledge."

"So you buy and sell spirits."

Rophis shrugged. "It keeps me in coin. There are a lot of veteran soldiers these days who seem to think they have nothing better to do than duel a bottle of spirits to see who'll come out the victor. Although it seems you've managed to avoid that fate thus far."

"I've more important things to do," said Cimozjen. "And when I complete them, I may take a single glass for celebration."

"Just one glass?" asked Minrah. "Then we'd best keep you away from the Brain Sledge. Come, let's go find our room."

"If you will excuse us, Rophis," said Cimozjen with a slight bow.

"We'll be aboard several days," Rophis said with a wave. "I'm sure we'll speak again."

❖ ❖ ❖ ❖ ❖ ❖ ❖

They found a suitable cabin belowdecks. Like all the others available to them, it was equipped with four berths, several squat candles, and a door with a latch but no lock.

"Hammocks!" squealed Minrah, happily hopping into one and setting it swinging.

Cimozjen grumbled deep in his throat.

Minrah slung her pack across the small room to land in another hammock. "We're here, and on the trail," she said triumphantly, crossing her legs and smoothing her skirt.

Cimozjen peered out into the narrow hallway to ensure there were no others within earshot, then closed the door. "We are," he said.

"So let's take stock of what we know."

"First, I think it would be best for us to clear up some misconceptions before they bring us more difficulties," said Cimozjen. "For starters, you need to understand that you cannot be my wife. You see—"

"Of course I can!" said Minrah. "I assure you my parents wouldn't object."

"No, you cannot," insisted Cimozjen, "for—"

"Am I too young for you?" asked Minrah. "I'm not as young as I look, you know. I'll bet I outpace you by a good twenty, thirty years."

"Wh—what?" asked Cimozjen.

"I've seen over eighty winters now," she said. "More than you, isn't it?"

"But you—you look—"

"Elves grow slowly," she said. "I won't be considered an adult until I start my one hundred and eleventh year."

"An adult has to be one hundred and eleven years old?"

"No, silly man, one hundred and ten."

"But you just said—"

"I said you're an adult when you *start* your one hundred and eleventh year. Think about it. How old are you when you start your first year of life?"

"Just born," said Cimozjen.

"Right. So you're zero years old, and at the end of your first year, you're one year old, right? So when you turn one hundred and ten, you start your one hundred and eleventh year of life. And that's when you become an adult."

"It seems an odd number . . ."

"It has something to do with Aerenal numerology," said Minrah with a shrug. "That's all my father ever told me about it. I don't think he ever knew any more than that, to be candid."

Cimozjen nodded and marshaled his thoughts. "I understand. However, you've run off with our conversation here. Your age has nothing to do with—"

"You don't care about how old I am?"

"No," said Cimozjen, chopping the air with his hand. "I mean yes, but—"

"Wonderful!" said Minrah. She rocked happily in the hammock, swaying back and forth.

Cimozjen let out an exasperated sigh. "Minrah, I have my vows."

"I know you do, Cimmo, you're an oathbound. And that's fine. So are we going to talk about Torval, and draw up a plan of action, or are we going to spend the whole voyage mincing up our pasts? I've got the frayed end of a great story here, and I want to start tugging at it!"

Cimozjen threw up his hands, resigning hope of being able to direct the course of the conversation. Dealing with people had been so much easier in the Iron Band. If they were Karrns, the military hierarchy made communication easy. If they weren't Karrns, you killed them. Simple. "As you wish. Let's review what we know."

"Torval was killed by an axe blow from a powerful strike. That means whoever killed him was strong."

"And carried an axe. This is not new to me, Minrah."

"Let me finish. Once he was killed, someone tied a rock to his foot and dumped him off a ship."

"Or off the end of a dock."

"No, not off a dock. Off a ship."

"Perhaps you could explain to me how we know that."

"I went to King's Bay while you slept, and borrowed a fishing line. I weighted the line and measured the water depth at each of the docks. It's not deep enough to be certain of hiding a body. I mean, Torval was over six feet tall, add another foot or two for the rope and the rock, and another foot for his arms floating upward once he started to . . . well, add all that together and we come up with, say nine feet of water for Torval to be fully submerged, with his fingertips barely below the surface. But the deepest water off one of the docks isn't even ten feet deep, and the water is fairly clear. People would see him down there. And if you're going to take all that trouble to hide a body in the water and keep it down, you're going to ensure that it can't be found by the first person who saunters by."

Cimozjen nodded. "In contrast, if he were dumped off a ship in the deeper waters away from the shore . . ."

"He wouldn't be found. Except of course that the rock slipped off his ankle, and put him to drifting. Lucky, that. So do you know where he was dropped into the water?"

"How could I know that?"

"I also tossed wood chips into the bay, so see how the current flows. It moves against the sundial, did you know that? The river flows east to west across the north side of the bay, and as a result, the water in the bay moves slowly around from the north end to the west to the south, then back up the east to the river. It's slow, but definite. Which, since he was dropped at night and found in the day, means that the most likely place for him to have been dropped is the west end of King's Bay."

Cimozjen grunted as he considered this, pushing out his lower lip. "That's the section of the bay that lies farthest from any of the docks," he said. "The water has carved out the bluffs, so it's not particularly useable for much of anything."

"Correct," said Minrah. "So the ship that dumped him moved away from everyone else to do it."

"Might he have been tossed off the top of the bluff?"

"Not without a catapult," said Minrah. "The only fresh scrapes on his skin were on his naked foot. The bluffs aren't so steep that one could hurl him and a heavy rock into the water without the body tumbling down the slope."

"Did you perhaps check if there was a ship in the harbor that had moved out there? If we find that ship, then we can find the murderer, or at least know that the captain abetted the deed by going to the best place to dump Torval's body."

"I did check," said Minrah. "And three vessels did. The long-shoremen told me it's not that uncommon in the spring or fall when shipping is heavy. If a ship is waiting on cargo, she may move over there to vacate a dock for another ship. That means that the captain might not even have known about Torval—and that the killer took advantage of a good opportunity. However," she added, "I can tell you that this very ship is one of the ones that did move over there, and of those three, this is the largest."

"Thus the odds are good that the murderer was on this ship," Cimozjen said.

"He may be still. This looks to be primarily a merchant ship. They take on some passengers, of course, but I'd wager they don't take on too many. I mean, there's not that many cabins here and that Kundarak woman said we might keep this room to ourselves."

"Why—" Cimozjen yelled, then lowered his voice to a murmur again. "Why did you not inform me of this earlier?"

"I didn't want you to pick a fight with the first person to look at us crosswise. If you came onboard actively stalking a killer, your attitude might have prevented us from being let aboard. Or you might have dueled the Winemonger on the spot."

"I suppose that's true. The first part, at least. Torval once told me I had the face of Khyber himself when it came to injustice."

"There are easier ways," said Minrah. "We'll have to ask the captain to share the passenger list with us. And we'll have to watch the crew." She opened her bag and pulled out Torval's shoe. "Why don't you take off your chain mail and take a look around the ship. I'm going to see if this has anything left to tell us."

Cimozjen looked at Minrah with frank appreciation. "I give you my profound thanks for your help in this matter," he said. "However this turns out, you've been of great assistance."

Minrah grinned and blushed. "You can thank me later, when we've untangled the knot," she said with a wink.

❈ ❈ ❈ ❈ ❈ ❈ ❈

The evening meal found the two sitting on a hawser on deck. Although the weather was cold, the striated clouds in the sky were spattered with reds, golds, and purples, and well worth braving the chill. Cimozjen wolfed his meal in a militarily efficient fashion, while Minrah dipped her hard bread into her stew before each bite.

"Did you find anything?" murmured Cimozjen.

"Of course," said Minrah. "Torval's pale skin implies that he spent most or all of his time indoors, which, given his past experiences, his size and frame, is very unusual. His shoe confirms it. There are no grass strains on it, and the wear on the sole is even and doesn't show the typical pits or marks from walking over rocky ground. There's some dust on the sole, like he walked in white sand, perhaps. It does, however, show some unusual wear on the top, which I haven't yet figured out. Best of all, Cimmo, there was this." She proffered a small item in her fingers.

Cimozjen took it and looked at it. "It's a chunk of wood."

"It's a sliver of wood. From the sole of his shoe. You can see that the wood is weathered on one side, and clean of the other. Like as not, he picked it up in the moments before his death, because the clean side was exposed, yet never got dirty. I know it's a stretch, but if we can find some wood that matches the weathering, we might have an idea of where it was he died. So far, all I can say is that it doesn't match anything on deck."

"You want us to look for weathered wood on a ship."

"Like I said, it's a stretch. Did you have any luck?"

"First, I must say that there are an inordinate number of passengers on this ship, despite what you said earlier. Mostly soldiers, it seems, and a few merchants. In fact, I think we have the only cabin that's not full."

"Really?" asked Minrah. "That's odd. I wonder if it was something you said."

"Me?"

"Yes, you, Cimmo. I draw suitors like dung draws flies, no matter what I say."

"That is not precisely the simile I would use for you, Minrah," said Cimozjen.

Minrah grinned, hugged her knees, and leaned her head on Cimozjen's shoulder. "What about the crew?"

"The sailors are a hardy lot, but they all seem more wiry than bulky. None of them seem to have the weight, the sheer power one would need to inflict a wound like Torval's. And they all bear smaller weapons: hatchets, knives, hammers, that sort." He looked at the sails. "I suppose they need to keep a hand free to grab the rigging."

"And those weapons all have two uses," said Minrah. "Chop a rope that's tangled one day, chop a pirate's neck the next."

"True enough."

"Nothing in their cabins?"

"Not that I could see from the hall. They all have small sea chests, though."

"You didn't look through them?"

"I'll not stoop to that, Minrah, that's—"

"You have a lot to learn about unraveling stories, Cimmo." Minrah took another bite of her dinner. "So what you're telling me is that the only person on this ship big enough to have killed Torval is our friend Rophis the Winemonger."

"It looks that way."

"We'll have to make a point to sup with him."

Chapter Eight

Zor, the 12th day of Sypheros, 998

It was fully dark outside, just past midnight, and the ship lay at anchor in the Karrn River. Most of the passengers and crew were asleep. Cimozjen and Minrah had easily evaded the few sailors on watch. They stood at the door leading to the cargo area. Belowdecks without a light, the darkness was so pressing that Cimozjen couldn't see his hand in front of his face. The lack of light made every other sense more acute. The rough feel of the iron handle of the lantern borrowed from the mess as it warmed to his touch, the particular smells of the ship's wood and Minrah's hair blending, the subtle slow sway of the deck beneath his feet as it shifted with the river's current.

Fortunately, Minrah's eyes pierced the dark like an owl's. She worked at the simple latch that secured the cargo hold, making small tinking noises. The only other sounds were an occasional creak of the ship's wood and the distant steady pacing of a sailor on deck.

"This is wrong."

"Cimmo," whispered Minrah, "we're searching the ship."

"We're entering places where we're not allowed to go, and if they catch me with this naked sword, they'll think we're up to something nefarious. Piracy is a hanging offense, Minrah."

"Well, of course we're not supposed to be here," said Minrah. "We're trying to find the place that Torval was killed. You think he'd be killed somewhere any old lackey could visit?" She rolled her eyes. "What if someone asked you to swear you'd keep a secret, and then confessed to murdering Torval? Would you keep the secret?"

"I'd challenge him to a duel."

"And if he refused?" She paused as Cimozjen wrestled with the conundrum. "We may be breaking the captain's rules, but it's not like we're breaking them for our own advantage. We're trying to find justice for Torval. Surely that reason is good enough for you."

"Why do I feel like you're eroding my oaths away?"

"It's good for you," said Minrah. "Your bow's strung too tight."

Cimozjen just scowled.

"There," whispered Minrah. She slowly let the door creak open.

The two slipped in, Minrah gently guiding Cimozjen in the dark. She shut the door. Once it was secured, her hands reached out in the darkness and took Cimozjen's hand, gently prying the lantern from his grasp. Cimozjen heard a tick-tick sound as she struck flint to steel, creating sparks that flashed like lightning in the dark hold. At last the wick of the oil lantern took to life. Although the wick was trimmed low, the newborn light seemed almost as bright as day.

The hold was as wide as the ship, some thirty-five feet from side to side, and ran eighty or so feet fore-to-aft. Where they entered, the hold was a mere six feet high, but an atrium of sorts opened in the center of the hold, rising all the way to the main deck some twelve feet over their head. The short end of the hold was densely packed with cargo, and a sizeable supply of casks and foodstuffs hung from the rafters near the door that Minrah had just picked. In the atrium area, the hold was less than one quarter full. Large crates dominated the aft portion, and smaller boxes and bales lined the sides.

The two pushed their way through the netting, their noses filled with the scent of sausage and pungent cheese.

"Look at all this empty space in the center," whispered Minrah as she handed the lantern back to Cimozjen. "I would have thought a merchant ship would wait for more cargo before casting off, or if leaving half full, to have stored the cargo nearer the hatch."

"Mm," said Cimozjen. He poked at the netting. "It appears that our fare will include a robust amount of cabbage between here and Aundair. There will be some ill winds blowing, of that I am sure."

Minrah giggled. "I'm going to take a look over there," she said, pointing to the port side.

Cimozjen started to work his way around to the starboard. "Nightwood pale," he mumbled to himself, tapping absently on a cask. "And again. Hm. And that'll be Karlak port. That's a good evening glass, I tell you truly."

A loud creak sounded in the hold. "Hoy," said Minrah. "Cimmo, take a look at this."

He turned to see the shadow of Minrah kneeling in the center of the hold. As he walked closer, he saw that she had opened a trapdoor in the floor.

He peered in. "A secret storage? For rocks?"

"That's the bilge. Don't you know anything about ships?"

"I know farming, soldiering, and raising children right."

"It's the bilge. Any water that leaks into the ship or washes over the deck ends up here. And the rocks are the ballast, to help keep the ship upright."

"Rocks? Hmm. I guess that makes sense. One would need something below the waterline to offset the weight of the tall masts."

"Notice anything unusual?"

"The rocks are wet," he said, "so we're sinking, if slowly."

"No, there's always water down in the bilge. What I mean is that there's a gap in the rocks. Look around. It's like someone took out a bunch of the rocks right here, next to this hatch. All around, they're piled up higher."

"You're right," said Cimozjen, holding the lantern into the hatch. "And I do believe that one of those would weigh down a man like Torval well enough."

"Do you know what this means?" hissed Minrah.

Cimozjen nodded slowly. "That his killer knows his way around a ship. A veteran sailor."

"Cimozjen," said Minrah, "I didn't say a rock was missing. I said rocks. It looks like it might be a dozen gone."

"A dozen—"

"This is bad," said Minrah, looking all about. "We need to get out of here." She rose abruptly and pushed the hatch, and it fell shut with a bang. "I'm sorry!" she said.

"Hss!" said Cimozjen, holding up his sword hand to silence her.

In dark quiet of the hold, they heard the slow creaking of the hull, the shuffled pacing of a sailor on deck and a quiet snuffling sound.

"Do you hear that?" whispered Minrah.

At the sound of her whisper, the snuffling grew more insistent, then shifted to a panting noise occasionally broken with a few whines.

"That sounds like a dog," said Minrah.

"If indeed it's a dog, then it's a six-times big one," said Cimozjen.

They heard the sound of something shifting, and claws scratching on wood.

"Oh, poor dog, all shut up down here," said Minrah. Pointing to the large crates aft, she added, "Sounds like it's in one of those over there."

"And doubtless for good cause," said Cimozjen.

"Sure, so it wouldn't foul the deck. Sailors are nothing if not tidy." She whistled softly. "Where are you, puppy?" She found a large wooden crate, over six feet in each dimension, and the sniffing and eager panting renewed with even more insistence.

"Do not open that crate," said Cimozjen.

"He wants out," she said. "Listen to him. What a big baby. Just for a few moments." She held her hand up to a small knothole that pierced one of the wide, heavy planks, and was rewarded by the sudden arrival of a wet nose that sniffed eagerly, pausing only to whine insistently. "Ohh, did those mean sailors lock you up so you wouldn't make a mess?" She moved around to the front of the crate.

"Or else because they're training it to be a killer. That is perhaps why they needed to dispose of a dozen bodies."

"Don't be silly, Cimmo. Dogs don't swing big axes." So saying, she pulled the pin from the solid iron latch and flipped it open.

The door crashed open, tossing Minrah aside. A huge, shaggy creature stepped out on stout canine legs. It had a broad, muscular torso with three long arms, two mounted at its shoulders and the third jutting from below one thick pectoral muscle. It was so top-heavy that as it exited the crate its third arm served duty as an additional leg. It had two long muzzles, fused into one where they met at the face and filled with long, strong teeth. Three piggish eyes, haphazardly scattered above the snouts, glared in hatred as it scented the air.

It turned its grotesque head to the dim lantern and saw Cimozjen, standing in a martial crouch with his sword held defensively in front.

"What in Khyber are you?" asked Cimozjen, awe and disgust in his voice. "Not that I expect an answer . . ."

The creature rose off of its third arm, standing upright to its full seven feet of height. It reached one large, misshapen paw over the top of the crate, and drew it back holding a cruel-looking weapon with a double-bitted axe blade at each end.

Cimozjen exhaled, readying himself. "That's as good an answer as any," he muttered. He extended his sword, holding the lantern to the rear, protecting his precious light as best he could.

Cimozjen saw a shadow flit along the hull as the creature closed, snarling. "Minrah," warned Cimozjen, "stay behind me, and I—" His words died as he heard the door to the hold open and slam shut again.

The creature hunched down, ready to spring. Its meaty paws worked the rough wooden haft of its weapon. It bared its irregular teeth, lips curled so far back that a dribble of thick saliva slid from its jaw to splat on the deck.

Looking at the beast's tensed muscles, the sheer size and power of its build, Cimozjen wished he'd had the foresight to set the lantern somewhere safe. But of course, he realized, if the creature were clever enough to douse his light, such a move would assuredly prove fatal.

The creature snuffled loudly, then lunged, a straightforward charge at Cimozjen, whipping the heavy axe around in a short but powerful downward chop. Cimozjen spun to the side, flailing his lantern in one direction as he dodged the other. The beast reflexively followed the path of the light, only to see it career away at the last moment, and its blow chopped solidly into the wood of the deck.

Cimozjen used his momentum to spin around and swing at the beast, but the darkness and the fast spin had disoriented him slightly, and the angle of his blade was too steep. He watched his sword glance off the beast's ribs, shearing away a portion of its dense fur. If the blade had drawn blood beneath the shaggy coat, Cimozjen could not see it.

The creature turned with amazing speed, wrenching its axe from the wood. It snarled and hacked at the ground in frustration. A grotesque split purple tongue lolled out of its butterfly-shaped maw and licked at its nostrils. Small red eyes stared malevolently at Cimozjen as it appraised him.

The two circled each other warily, Cimozjen casting quick side glances to determine which, if any, of the surroundings he could use to his advantage. To keep the creature's attention away from his darting eyes, he spun his sword rapidly through the Rekkenmark Sword Drill. He also hoped the flashy sequence might unnerve the creature. He was quite uncertain whether he'd survive the next few moments with no armor, shield, or helmet, and any advantage would help.

The creature snorted like a bull, and waved its weapon back and forth. Then it took one long step forward and swatted crudely at Cimozjen's weapon with its own.

Cimozjen yanked his sword out of the way in a circular swing, then brought it back down, striking the wooden haft of the monstrosity's axe. The blow, though solid, did not go clean through the beast's weapon. Rather Cimozjen's blade buried itself in the wood.

The two combatants stared at the locked weapons in surprise. Then the creature hoisted the double-headed axe into the air, taking Cimozjen's sword and arm with it. Cimozjen desperately tried to yank his weapon free, but while his arm was still raised, the creature punched him solidly with its third arm. The impact knocked the Karrn off his feet, but also wrenched his sword free from the wooden haft. Cimozjen stumbled and fell, rolling to the right to keep the lantern from shattering on the deck.

The beast charged, swinging a wild, two-handed chop at the supine man. Cimozjen rolled toward the swing and in. The axe blade whistled as it passed his ear, drawing a gash across his cheek, and he felt the wood shake beneath him as the blade took another chunk out of the decking.

As Cimozjen rose, hoping to hamstring his foe, the lantern guttered. His heart caved in his chest, and he aborted his attack to pull all his focus into holding the oil lamp steady. He knew he had no chance of surviving against the twisted creature in pitch darkness. He backed away quickly, heading for the center of the open area, knowing that he stood no chance of backing into a crate. He kept the beast in his peripheral vision until at last the wick's flame rose tall and steady once more.

Thus relieved, he turned to look at his shaggy foe again. It had crept up upon him while his attention had been diverted by the lantern, and took another wild swing at his sword. This time it caught Cimozjen unprepared, and with a loud metallic clang, it struck his wrist and the blade. The impact sent his sword from his grasp, tumbling along the floor to come to rest against the wine casks, and nearly severed his thumb from his hand.

Cimozjen stared at the creature, turning his hand palm-down to hide the injury. He felt hot blood trickle down his fingers to drip upon the deck. The creature's horrid maw twisted into an unnatural asymmetric grin. It let out a juicy, humming growl, which Cimozjen instinctively knew was a sound of cruel mirth.

Cimozjen lunged hard for his weapon, but the abomination was expecting such a move. It leapt with stunning alacrity to defend the sword, using three of its five limbs to propel it in a low, powerful leap. It arced through the air and landed, claws scrabbling on the wood, bifurcated maw open to tear into Cimozjen's flesh—

Except he wasn't there. He'd thrown the hard feint to draw the creature into such a move, trusting its larger weight to impede it from recovering from its error in judgment. He ran to the center of the open area and kneeled, as if ready to spring upon the creature himself.

The thing roared its frustration, a howling burbling messy sound. It grabbed its weapon with two of its hands, preparing to swing it like a club, and closed on Cimozjen in a reckless charge.

"Dol Dorn save me!" Cimozjen snatched the iron ring of the bilge hatch in his ruined hand. Ignoring the pain as he stretched the severed muscles and ligaments, he flipped the hatch open and leaped backwards.

Too consumed with bloodlust, the beast paid no attention to Cimozjen's ploy. It charged forward, raising the heavy axe for a killing blow, but then its foot stepped into the open hatch. Its great inertia impelled it forward, and Cimozjen saw the sudden lurch as its knee struck the edge of the open hatch. A strangely liquid pop sounded as its knee broke against the rim of the hatch, and the creature flopped to the deck, landing heavily on its chest, its arms extended.

Pain and rage filled its piggy eyes, and it roared its wrath. It moved to gather itself up, but Cimozjen stepped forward onto the haft of its cruel weapon. With a practiced move, he snatched his dirk from its hidden sheath at the small of his back, gripping its hilt between his middle and ring finger. Bracing the dagger's butt against the heel of his palm, he stepped forward and plunged the steel blade through one of the creature's red eyes, driving it deep into its brain. The hideous beast grunted, twitched, then sagged into nothingness, the last stinking breath hissing away through its slobbery jowls.

Chapter
NINE

Questions and Lies
Zor, the 12th day of Sypheros, 998

Erami d'Kundarak kneeled near the top of the ladder. Pulling her well-worn robe tighter about her nightshift, she called down into the lower deck, "Report!"

"Cargo bay's locked, it is!" came the reply. "We'll need us the key if'n you want us to go see."

"Or we could just let well enough alone, leastaways until daylight, that is," came a second reply. This suggestion was welcomed with a murmur of affirmation from several sailors.

"Belay your tongues!" snapped Erami. "I'll not have troubles in my cargo hold! You lot stand fast! I'll be right back!"

She rose and stomped back to her cabin, her short but muscular legs moving her quickly across the deck. The whole while she cursed all sailors, a cowardly and superstitious lot if ever there were.

Back in her cabin, she quickly changed into something more officious than a faded robe and a satin nightshift that was weary with age. She also took the chance to jam boots on her feet. The clomping noise they made when she stomped gave her stride more presence.

Once dressed, she grabbed her ring of keys and her heavy hammer and made for the ladder once more. She made sure to stomp as she crossed over the heads of the sailors the next deck down. Once down the ladder, she paused to scowl at the eight sailors, armed and gathered at the door to the cargo hold.

"What's with all the long faces?" she barked. "You think you'd all been buggered by Lazhaarites!"

"We just don't rightly know what's going on in there," mumbled someone safely to the rear of the corridor.

"That's right. And I aim to find out," said Erami. She flipped her key ring around and held one of the keys up. "Here," she said, passing it to one of the sailors. "Open it up. Let's get to work."

"Why don't you open it?" said a sailor, again one safely hidden from her view.

Her countenance darkened. Sometimes she wished humans were shorter. It would make such crass insubordination a lot harder to get away with. "Because you're paid to keep this vessel on course, shipshape and free from danger. There's something inside there that might be a danger. You mongrels are to find it, kill it, and tell me what it is. In that order. I, on the other hand, am paid to count money and, in case you've forgotten, pay your wages. And if you tell the commander that I cheated you out of two weeks' pay when we get back to Fairhaven, whom do you think he's liable to believe, hmm?"

The sailors stared at her for a moment, then the one holding the keys grimaced and said, "Ahoy, boys, let me through to open the door. Let's have this over and done with."

They pushed their way into the room, lanterns and weapons held high. Slowly they inched their way in, murmuring to each other as they progressed. Erami followed them in, her hammer resting on her shoulder.

"Avast there!" shouted someone. "Amidships!"

"Stand to!"

"Careful, lads!"

A pause, and then, "How in the storm did it get out?"

Erami pushed her way through the netting that hung from the rafters filled with larder, and approached the nearest sailor. "What is it?" she asked.

"There's your answer," said a sailor, pointing to a hulking pile of fur that lay near the middle of the cargo bay.

Erami stepped forward. Whatever the twisted and malformed heap was, it was alive—or at least it once had been. It lay unmoving, its head resting in a quiescent pool of blood. "That, sailor," said Erami, "is not my answer. It raises more questions. What in Siberys is it? And more important, what killed it?"

There was a short silence, and then one of the sailors offered an answer. "The cabbage stew?"

❀ ❀ ❀ ❀ ❀ ❀ ❀

Pomindras looked at his steward, his hands steepled over his nose and his eyes devoid of emotion. "I know of the beast. It was an exotic animal that was being transported for a very wealthy client."

"Then why was it not on the cargo manifest, commander?" asked Erami, her anger seeping out with every syllable.

"It is. It's the 'large crate, taxidermist's trophy.' We thought it best to keep you in the dark about its true nature."

"Commander," snapped Erami, "if I am to be your purser and steward, I need to know—"

"You need to know what I think you need to know! And you would do well to keep in mind who the commander of this ship is."

"Yes, commander," answered Erami, her ire, for the moment, controlled.

"You say it was dead?"

"Yes, commander," said Erami. "It was nigh exactly in the center of the hold, lying almost atop the bilge hatch. One of the legs was ugly broken, and one ear lopped off, but what undid it was a strike to one eye. Perhaps a sling stone, a spear, or something else of the like. And there was a large weapon in one of its hands, a double-ended battle-axe sort of thing."

"And what of the hold?"

"Blood, commander, and not just that of the creature. Whoever killed it, the beast got one or two chops in. Blood on its weapon, trails of blood circling here and there. Looks like it scored a bleeder. That and a few chunks taken out of the decking is the extent of the wreckage. I'm happy to report the cargo was undamaged."

"Any idea how it got out?" asked Pomindras.

"No, commander. Either it worked the pin out by itself, or someone deliberately let it loose."

"Thank you, Erami," said Pomindras. "However, next time the ship is endangered, I want you to wake me."

"I tried to, commander, but you were out cold with the drink."

"Then prod me with the rim of my shield until I rouse myself!" He rubbed his temples before turning to the boatswain. "What of the passengers and crew?"

"Most were awakened. Some were in the halls, some adeck. We did spot one of them armed, on the first deck below, and thought to hold him for you."

"And who would that be?"

"Cimozjen Hellekanus, commander, a veteran of Karrnath. Provisional papers."

"I remember him." Pomindras rubbed the corners of his eyes then ran his hand roughly across his shaven scalp. "Bring him in."

The first mate opened the cabin door and gestured. Two sailors escorted Cimozjen into the cabin, and a third followed, holding the Karrn's sword and scabbard. The sailors guided Cimozjen to stand in front of Pomindras.

"You wished to see me, captain?" said Cimozjen respectfully.

"Commander."

"Pardon me?"

"I am not the captain. The one who owns this ship wishes me to remember my station, so I am the ship's commander."

"My apologies. I did not—"

"I am told that you were stalking about the corridors with your weapon in hand."

"You were misinformed. My weapon was sheathed." The sailor behind Cimozjen nodded his confirmation.

"I see," said the commander. "And why were you stalking my ship armed?"

"You heard that terrible noise, did you not? It sounded as if it were some nightmare from the Mournland. As there was no trouble on deck, I thought to go below and investigate. There I met your crew, returning from below."

"Any blood on his weapon?" asked the commander.

The sailor drew Cimozjen's sword halfway out from its sheath. "No, commander."

"Blood?" asked Cimozjen. "Why would there be blood on my sword?"

"Because there is a killer aboard, and I need to ensure that it is not you."

Cimozjen lowered his head. "Would that I might truly say that I was free of innocent blood, commander, but I cannot. However, I can avow that I have not killed a single person since the end of the Last War."

"What about this evening?"

"Commander, surely this evening is still after the Last War, is it not?"

"Did you kill any—anyone this evening?"

"Commander, upon my honor, my sword has spilled no blood upon this vessel, nor has it done so upon this evening. My soul be forfeit if I lie." Inside he winced at how quickly he had adopted Minrah's method of misdirection.

"Did you enter the cargo hold tonight?"

Cimozjen spread his hands. "I have no cargo beyond my bags, commander. Why would I enter the hold? And besides, I would have thought it to be locked."

"Yes it is," said the commander, leaning forward. "Did you open the lock?"

"No, commander. I did not, and I would not."

"But what of magic?"

"I have no magic to see me past a secured door, commander."

The commander exhaled. "One other item. The, um, deceased has had an ear severed. Did you do that?"

"Surely the commander can see that such an act would draw blood, and I swore my sword free of it." Inside, his stomach curdled.

"Answer my question! Do you have the severed ear?"

"No, commander. I possess no one's ear, nor would I wish to own such a trophy. You are free to search my person and my billet."

"So I shall," said the commander, "Strip off your tunic."

Cimozjen complied without hesitation, shaking out his tunic once it was off. Pomindras looked the man over. He was built like an old soldier. The powerful muscles were still apparent, though now they labored beneath a veneer of age—a slight paunch about the middle, a sag to the once-taunt skin. Cimozjen turned in place, arms held out to the side.

There was not a fresh mark on him. Scars, certainly, but no wounds, nothing that would spatter blood on his ship.

"You may go," said Pomindras, "but mark that my eye will be upon you." He growled. "Erami, fetch me Rophis Raanel's Son."

❂ ❂ ❂ ❂ ❂ ❂ ❂

Cimozjen leaned against the railing at the stern of the boat, his hands folded and drooping. He stared at the water, gazing sightlessly at the crescent reflections of several of Eberron's moons as his brain retraced the events of the past two days.

He had not besmirched his honor by avowing a lie. But he had made statements out of context, arranged facts out of chronological order, claimed his worn weapon as the sum of his threat, and presented questions as answers. All this with the intent to deceive. He had abetted someone in breaking into a locked area, and killed a creature that had been held harmless in a cage. He had selfishly looked after his own safety, abusing the blessing of the Host and spurning their promise of deliverance. And yet . . .

And yet his friend still lay dead, murdered and unavenged, calling to his soul. He had gathered information that might lead to Torval's murderer, and thence to justice. And if he had not been deceitful, then would he not have broken his vows to his blood brothers, to his fellow soldiers of the Iron Band? They had sworn eternal vigilance and loyalty.

He could no longer think, which was a blessing, as he had no idea what to think. His mind had circled the same thoughts for hours, dodging between guilt and vindication so many times that it was dizzy, exhausted, curled up upon itself like a dog, ready to sleep.

He heard a soft step padding up behind, then a slender hand reached out of the darkness and gently touched his arm just below the elbow.

"What troubles you, Cimmo?" asked Minrah, her lyric voice seeming to be the moons' wavering reflections given life.

Cimozjen did not answer.

"I was worried."

"Then why did you run?"

"Fight that thing?" asked Minrah. "Me?" She pulled him around to face her, reached out one soft hand and placed it on his unshaven face. "Are you insane? We didn't have to fight it, and I sure as spit didn't want to. That wasn't our problem. All you had to do was get to the door, and we could have locked it in the hold and run back to bed." She paused, giggling uncertainly. "That's as sure as rain. Running was the only smart thing to do. So why didn't you?"

Cimozjen nodded, deciding to speak. "I stayed to protect you."

"Well, that's just—you—hoy now, you did?" Her face split in a wide smile, visible even in the faint moonlight. "You love me," she said happily.

"I have sworn to protect the weak and the foolish," said Cimozjen. "Down there, you were both."

Minrah sobered up, but her eyes were still alight. "That's what chance dealt me," she said. "I'm no fighter. But I also don't have all these oaths. They nigh killed you, Cimmo."

He turned back to the railing and lowered his gaze. "At least my motives would have been clear."

"That's a fine reason to die."

"It's better than the alternative."

She watched him for a moment, then slid her arm into his and looked at the water as well. "What's eating at you?"

Cimozjen sighed. "This whole situation. It's . . . unclean."

"Murder is not a pleasant subject."

"I find my oaths and vows at odds with my conscience, and my desires at odds with the laws. I fear that if I spend too much time in this situation, that it may consume me."

"What do you mean?" asked Minrah.

Cimozjen drew a deep breath in through his nose, his lips pressed tightly together. "Consider the dwarf, the one who led me to Torval. Would that I had healed him, but bitterness clouded my vision. I could have given him the gift of forgiveness, shown him a better path, been the reflection of Dol Dorn, the illustration of restraint and honor to inspire him. I could perhaps have turned him from his base path to a higher one. Yet I did not. And I know not his name, so it may well be impossible for me to rectify my error."

"You think a thief is so easily turned into a day laborer?" Minrah said. "You're deluded."

"Whether or not my efforts would have been in vain, the very fact that I did not try reflects badly upon my heart. I find my soul clouded." He turned around and leaned back upon the railing, head turned to the sky to gaze at Siberys's ring. "During the Last War, I found myself in a similar bind," he said. "I prayed for the Sovereigns' intercession. And they gave it, though in a way I would never have foreseen." He snorted in black humor. "I fear to ask them again, for their answer might stand athwart the path to Torval's justice."

"Then don't. We'll do it ourselves. We don't need them." She shrugged. "So I guess you killed the thing that murdered Torval, hm? It had the build and the axe."

"Not here," murmured Cimozjen, "the night and the water may carry our words to unwanted ears."

"Oh, don't worry about that," said Minrah. "I started about five or six different rumors among the passengers and crew. People all over the ship are talking."

At that, Cimozjen bowed his head and pinched the bridge of his nose. He had had enough dishonesty for one night.

❀ ❀ ❀ ❀ ❀ ❀ ❀

The undercurrent of discussion rose anew with the dawn, and most of the people on the ship spoke of the events of the previous night while breaking their fast. The crew generally tried to disprove any wild theories that were presented to them—or, at times, within earshot—and this activity itself incited the passengers to even wilder theories.

Based on Cimozjen's interview with commander Pomindras, Minrah insisted they make the opportunity to chat with Rophis, to see how his questioning had gone. By virtue of Minrah's unquestioned talent at flirting, they managed to sit alone with the large merchant.

"You were questioned, too?" asked Rophis. "Then at least I am in a good company. I spoke with the commander. It seems there was some sort of fight in the cargo hold. A slaughter of some sort. The commander asked if I were involved. He seems to think I've the size and temper to risk my life in such a manner." He chuckled. "For my part, I feared it might have been someone out to thieve my goods, but I am assured that everything remains in good order. I understand someone's hunting hound got loose, and one of the crew was forced to put it down, as the mad disease had seized it."

"The mad disease?" asked Minrah.

"A distemper of the blood. It makes the brain go savage, and the corruption foams up from the animal's bowels and out of the mouth."

"That's what the crew are all saying," said Minrah, "though I daresay that the howling was like no cur I've ever heard. Do you believe them, or do you think they're covering something up?"

"Why should I not believe them?" asked Rophis. "They've nothing to hide, do they? Had it been a savage beast, they'd be crowing their bravery for all the passengers to hear."

"If it were someone's hound, then where is the body?" asked Cimozjen.

"They weighted it with a stone and cast it overboard last night," said Rophis. "Didn't you hear the splash? To leave it to lie would risk spoiling the foodstuffs and perhaps even turning the rats mad. However, it is all done and done with, so there's no need to speak any more of it. Continued talk of dead curs and foaming rats will put me off my appetite." Rophis patted his ample belly and rose. Bowing genteelly, he took his bread and cup to a different table.

Minrah watched him as he struck up a conversation with another group of passengers, a smile jumping quickly to his face.

"Fascinating," she murmured.

"What?"

"Merchants lie to each other for a living," said Minrah, "and no merchant I've ever met would pull the crew's wagon so readily. Chances are the sailors have something on him." She sipped from her cup. "Or he on them."

❋ ❋ ❋ ❋ ❋ ❋ ❋

The *Silver Cygnet* sailed down the Karrn River through the day. A cold northerly wind blew without respite, and the crew used both sail and oars to make excellent speed. Cimozjen stood near the bow, wrapped in his longcoat and watching the banks for any sign that the horrid thing from the cargo hold might have floated downstream and hung up on a snag or rock.

The day passed slowly and uneventfully, and the rumors of the morning faded into nothing as the story of a foaming wolfhound gradually won the field.

That evening, as Cimozjen and Minrah dined again on cabbage stew and hardbread, Rophis came and seated himself next to them, plunking a dark bottle and three tin cups in the center of the table.

"Allow me to apologize, my friends," he said. "I imagine that the manner in which I ended our conversation this morning was on the wrong side of abrupt. It was plainly rude. In recompense, I've brought you a gift that we might share a drink together."

Cimozjen turned the bottle to look at the label. "Soldier's Gruel, eh?"

"What's that?" asked Minrah.

"Stout that's been distilled," said Rophis, "then aged in oak casks. They've reused the same casks for centuries, so it has a slight earthy taste. But it's thick with a kick, a meal in a tankard. Not that we have a tankard, of course, so these cups will have to suffice."

"I've made do with far worse," said Minrah, "and with far less savory gentlemen. I'll pour!"

As she busied herself with serving, Rophis asked, "So tell me, young woman—"

"Minrah is her name," said Cimozjen, taking his cup.

"Of course it is. My apologies; I am not the best with names." He took a healthy swig from his cup. "Tell me, Minrah, what do you do when not sailing with valiant warriors?"

"I write. And I sell my work to the chronicles."

"Is that so?" Rophis said, leaning forward. "And you earn your keep just writing? You must be very good."

Minrah blushed and raised her cup. She took a small sip, keeping the cup at her lips as an unconscious shield. "I do my best, and I sell enough to keep me in coin. Sometimes I have to do something boring like write a saga of some noble's inflated self-image to make ends meet, but mostly I just write stories about things that I see."

Rophis sat back and stroked his chin, a lopsided grin on his face. "Tell me then, what sort of things do you see?"

She giggled behind the rim of her cup. "I see more than you think."

"Show me. What sort of things do you see when you look at me?"

Minrah smiled, took a deep drink from her cup, set it down, and then reached out and took Rophis's hand. He leaned forward, watching as her hands glided up and down his palm, then turned his wrist this way and that.

"I see that you are a very wealthy man," she said, "one who earns enough to pay his own scribe. You certainly don't perform your own manual labor. You enjoy using the power you have. You've had extensive training in the use of martial weapons, but have not been in the position to practice the art in the streets or on the battlefield. You're used to the companionship of women. You want to keep certain details of your identity a secret. And although you claim to be from Fairhaven, you just as likely hail from Karrnath."

Rophis shifted and pulled his hand away. "That's—you saw— are you a seer, that you read all that in the palm of my hand?"

"Of course not," said Minrah. "When I said I see things, I meant just normal items that everyone else looks at but doesn't really notice. I look at details, and I think about them and what they could mean. My father taught me how, and I practice it every day of my life." She shrugged. "It helps me put my stories together."

Rophis stroked his chin. "Indeed? So how did you determine what you just said?"

Minrah picked her cup back up, speaking between small sips. "Well, for starters, you have neither a notch for a quill nor ink stains upon your finger, hence someone does your scribing. You also have someone clean and polish your fingernails, although it's been a week or so since that's been done. Your hands are not calloused, so you don't do hard work. But they are strong, which can be explained by regular exercise with swords and the like. And you usually wear a ring on your right middle finger, which is often where a signet would go. Since you brought neither that ring nor your servant with you, you're hiding your identity."

Rophis smiled wryly. "And what of your comment regarding women? Not that I object, nor should I boast."

"You didn't flinch or tense when I stroked your hand." Minrah giggled. "You should have seen Cimmo here when I first took his arm."

Cimozjen grumbled. "Minrah, I—"

"Don't make it worse for yourself," said Rophis with a hearty laugh. "Such a pretty young creature is sure to put most men off their stride. No, my dear Minrah, your skill at observation is very good, but your conclusions are, unfortunately, off the mark."

"Are they?" said Minrah with a pout. "Bad luck, then. Would you care to point out my errors?"

Rophis leaned back in his chair and ran his hands up and down his belly for a few moments, then said, "Very well, I shall, for your face delights me." He took a moment to gather his thoughts. "My hands are strong not from weapons, for I've had no formal training. Rather they have been strengthened from carrying heavy bottles by the neck and pouring drinks for those who purchase my wares. While bottles are not as heavy as a sack of potatoes, they are heavy and they do not leave the sort of calluses that one gets when moving crates. As for my ring and nails," he said wearily, "I indulged myself rather too deeply in luxury last month in Fairhaven, following which a deal in Korth unfortunately went sour. As a result, I had to sell my sapphire ring to fund the purchases I needed to make this trip a profitable venture. It is shameful for a merchant to run his hoard dry, as one needs wealth to make wealth, but this I have unfortunately done." He smacked his lips. "And now you know my failings. I trust the candor of my confession will attest to its truth."

He drained his cup, reached for the bottle, refilled it, and drained it once more. He patted his belly again, then looked up at her and smiled warmly. "Well. Thank you both for your time," he said. "It has been most diverting. And Minrah, your play at perception and deduction has given me a new hand of tales with which to regale my customers." He rose, bowed politely, and sauntered off, chuckling to himself, "Me, a warrior? Oh, what an idea!"

Cimozjen watched the merchant until he left the dining area. "Well," he said, tilting his head toward Minrah, "I suppose one cannot be correct all of the time."

Minrah glowered at Rophis's back. "Yes, I can."

Chapter
TEN

Darkness had long since covered the sky, leaving the Ring of Siberys to shine like a trail of scattered silver dust. A few moons paraded slowly along the ring's argent path, illuminating the Karrn River, the ship that lay at anchor, and the furtive figure that skulked through the darkness, evading the two sailors that paced the watch.

Carrying an unsheathed sword close to his side, he moved slowly, carefully, slipping by the watch to the ladder that led down to the foredeck cabins. He descended the ladder into the darkness below decks. At the bottom he looked about, then allowed himself a deep breath to steady his nerves.

He reached one hand into a pouch that hung at his belt and pulled out a small ceramic bead, aglow with a faint blue light. It was enough to navigate by, yet still so dim that it was unlikely to attract attention.

With this light, the figure shuffled down the corridor. He held the light close to each cabin door to see which number might be carved into the wood. At last he found the cabin he sought. He readied his sword and, with his hand still palming the bead, he slowly opened the door. The sound of steady glottal breathing spilled out of the room.

As the door swung open, he clenched his hand about the bead until only the faintest blush of light still shone. He slid in, angling toward the hammock where a bulky shape lay unmoving.

He leveled his sword, turning the blade's angle to the vertical so that it would slide between the ribs, and thrust as hard as he could. The blade struck true, and for an instant he thought he had accomplished his goal, until he heard the unmistakable sound of steel striking against chain mail.

Then he heard a scream.

❂ ❂ ❂ ❂ ❂ ❂ ❂

Minrah, sitting cross-legged in her billet, snapped out of her meditations at the sound of an impact. She saw the intruder in their cabin, saw the blade in his hands, saw him pull the weapon back from Cimozjen's hammock.

Fear seized her, fear for her life ending abruptly with the sensation of assassin's cold blade in her vitals. She shrieked and pushed herself away from the killer, mindless of the fact that she sat in a hammock. She backed into the wall, but her feet kept pedaling, pushing the hammock's netting out from under her, and she tumbled backward, crying out again in surprise as she flopped into the lower bunk and then thumped to the floor.

Startled by her scream, the intruder scrambled away from her, striking his heel against Cimozjen, who'd been sleeping on the floor. The intruder fell backward, dropping his sword and his bead just as Cimozjen raised his arms to protect himself.

❂ ❂ ❂ ❂ ❂ ❂ ❂

Hearing the clang of metal against the deck and an earthy curse from an unknown voice, Cimozjen pushed himself free of the stranger, rising to his hands and knees. He grabbed for his scabbard, but it was trapped beneath the stranger's weight. In the dim blue light he saw the man grab his own sword again.

Cimozjen flopped onto his back, crab-walking to distance himself as the assassin took two wild swings. As the killer closed, Cimozjen thrust out with his feet and connected, slamming the assassin into the far wall of the small cabin. Cimozjen rolled and grabbed for his scabbard again, snatching it up and raising it just in time to block a downward chop. The intruder raised his blade for another strike, and Cimozjen shoved the scabbard upward, smiting the man in the loins. As he doubled over from the blow, Cimozjen thrust his scabbarded sword into the man's gut, and then jammed his knee with a thrust of his foot.

Because he lay on the floor, his kick lacked the extra impetus of his weight behind it. His efforts were not rewarded with the sound of breaking bones, but he did manage to send the killer to the floor. Cimozjen rolled to his feet and drew his sword, holding his scabbard in his left hand as a potential shield.

"Why are you doing this?" asked Cimozjen.

The stranger likewise rose, though rather more slowly than Cimozjen. His face twisted with an unreadable mix of emotion. "Sorry," he panted. "I can't let you stop us!"

He charged again, whipping his blade through a pattern that, even in the dim light of the glowing bead, Cimozjen recognized as the Queen's Best Sword Drill, or, as the Karrns mockingly called it, the Cyran Spin.

Cimozjen feinted an opening, then brought his sword around to parry the expected blow. Sparks flashed in the dimly lit cabin as the two weapons collided. Cimozjen struck with his scabbard, taking the intruder in the temple with the metal-reinforced sheath, then he spun and drew his sword across the man's belly, taking a terrible slash. Spinning completely around, he lanced the stranger through the ribs with his sword, and the would-be assassin arched his back and slumped to the floor as Cimozjen yanked out his sword and took a few precautionary steps back.

"Who are you?" Cimozjen asked, his voice spurred by anger, indignation, and adrenaline.

Lying on his side on the floor, the man coughed wetly, and drew in a burbling breath. "Jewel of Khorvaire," he gasped, "I can't even kill an unarmed man anymore."

Cimozjen grasped the Octogram pendant that hung from his neck. "Dol Arrah, favor your brother's servant this day, and grant my prayer that you make your perfect face to shine upon my duty," he said beneath his breath. The warm glow of the holy symbol suffused the room, its radiance drowning the pitiable blue light of the old man's bead. Cimozjen kicked the man's sword away from his twitching fingers and kneeled beside him.

The man's breathing was labored and wheezy. Cimozjen turned him over, to find himself staring at the visage of a scarred human some six or seven decades of age. Blood colored his lips crimson, and his eyes stared at Cimozjen, filled with a heavy weight of regret and shame.

"My last . . . chance . . ." gasped the intruder. He clutched and pulled at his tunic with a hand tattooed with a crown and bell. A wretched slurping sound marked each breath he took. As Cimozjen watched, he could see the man's voice box sliding a little to the left with each labored breath. As it moved, the old man's breaths became shallower and shallower. He started to thrash and kick.

"Hang on, soldier. I'll take care of you," said Cimozjen, and he set to working his healing powers upon the man, a task made more difficult by the Cyran's struggles. Gritting his teeth as he worked his way through his supplication, he forced the wounded man to lie flat on his back and clamped his hand over the man's heart. A warm glow lit the room from within the man's chest. It erupted out of his wounded abdomen, casting a reddish hue to everything. Nevertheless, the man's esophagus continued to move to the side, displaced by over an inch and getting worse with each liquid breath. Cimozjen increased the speed of his litany and placed his hand over the man's throat, trying to understand the injury.

The intruder moved his hand to touch Cimozjen's wrist, interrupting his prayer of supplication. He tried to smile, but the expression was twisted by pain into a pastiche of camaraderie. He coughed once more, wetly, and bloodstained saliva covered his chin. "No," he wheezed. He labored to draw a few last shallow breaths, then closed his eyes and whispered, "Seems I'd . . . just . . . embarrass myself." He drew a last shallow, gasping breath, his legs kicking weakly, then he stretched his neck like a drowning man, his tongue protruding. His fingers clutched at Cimozjen's wrist, the nails digging into his flesh.

"Hang on," said Cimozjen through clenched teeth. He rattled off another prayer, speeding through the supplication as fast as years of repetition allowed.

With the second infusion of divine power, the man finally stopped struggling for air and relaxed. Then his tattooed hand slid slowly from his tunic to the floor.

Cimozjen sped through another prayer and pressed his hand on the man's chest at the base of the neck, firmly, but this time the warm healing glow merely spread across the surface of the skin.

"Traveler's treachery!" gasped Minrah, huddled into a small ball on the floor.

Cimozjen pulled the man's clenched hand from his wrist. He stared at the dead man for a long moment. "What was that all about?" he asked quietly.

"I—that is, maybe—he was trying to kill us!" stammered Minrah. She unconsciously adopted Cimozjen's furtive tone.

Cimozjen turned to look at her. "Your powers of observation are as acute as ever, Minrah."

She pointed. "I saw—he stabbed you in your hammock."

"At least he tried," whispered Cimozjen. "Thank the Host I stashed our bags in my hammock. The question we need to figure out now is why he wanted to kill me." He sat back on his heels. "Did you hurt yourself when you fell?"

"No, I don't think so. No, I'm fine. Dash of luck, that."

"Good."

Minrah crawled out from beneath the hammocks and looked at the man, still clearly nervous. "So what's that tattoo on the back of his hand?"

"The crown and bell? That's the Queen's Favor. Marks him as a twenty-year veteran of the Cyran army."

"A Cyran? True enough, he talked like one." She looked at his face. She glanced from side to side and whispered, "I've seen him around the ship, but he always seemed to keep to himself. You think maybe he owned that monster that you killed last night? That is, it looked like it might have come from the Mournland."

Cimozjen tilted his head and scratched the back of his neck. "I rather doubt it," he murmured. "If he did own it, I think he would have mentioned it. But he said he'd not let me stop him, and something about his last chance."

"And that he'd have embarrassed himself," added Minrah.

"What an odd thing to say," said Cimozjen quietly. "Embarrassed? And he apologized. That's strange."

"You know what's even stranger?" asked Minrah looking around. "No one's coming to see what the ruckus was."

Cimozjen cocked an ear. "True, but they are a rough lot, each mother's son of them, and it was a fairly quiet combat, as combats go. Maybe they're used to the sounds of fighting, or they think you just fell out of bed. Which, I might add, you did do."

Minrah smiled sardonically. "I do believe you're being far too generous with our fellow passengers."

"Personally, I believe that an excess of generosity is not within the realm of possibility," he said. "Still . . . what do you think?"

"I think maybe they're all in on it," she said, spinning her finger in a circle. "They're all after us."

Cimozjen narrowed his eyes. "If they were," he murmured, "they'd have all come together. No need for secrecy. But it does appear that some of our fellow passengers have no concern for our wellbeing."

He looked at the dead man. "Maybe lack of curiosity will work to our advantage, though. His body is healed of all visible injury.

If no one's about, we should be able to move it somewhere else, on deck or in another hallway. With the blood on his lips, maybe folks will think he died of consumption. I have an ill feeling of what might result should I be forced to answer to the commander for killing someone in my cabin, regardless of my innocence in the matter."

"That's a plan, then," said Minrah. "Strip off his tunic. I'll wipe up what I can of the blood and throw it in the river."

"Right. The blood and sword holes would make folks suspicious." Cimozjen stripped the man's shirt off and handed it to Minrah, then, hoisting the man under one arm, slipped out into the hallway.

Minrah stared at the closed door. "And, uh, I'll sit watch for the rest of the night, all right? Right." She set to cleaning up, pausing to pick up the faintly glowing bead. She rolled it between her finger and thumb. "Well, that's a fun trinket," she said.

"Wake up, Cimmo." Minrah nudged her companion with her foot. "A new day has dawned, and we're on the Sound."

"Mm?" Cimozjen rolled onto his back and groaned. "I'll be glad to be off this ship," he grumbled. "I know not what's worse— sleeping in a hammock and ruining my back, or sleeping on the floor and having my shoulders be too sore to move."

"Oh, quit your bellyaching and heal yourself up."

"I'll not do that," he said. He pushed himself into a sitting position and roughly scratched his scalp.

"Why not?"

"First, it's wrong to abuse the blessing of the Sovereign Host."

"Oh, what do they care?" said Minrah. "You've got it, use it. You think they'd even notice?"

"Second," said Cimozjen, "one never knows when a dire need might arise. Suppose I healed my shoulders, my stubbed toe, and a canker in my mouth, and then you were to fall down a ladder and break your leg? Hm? I bear my pain for you, Minrah, and the others whom the Sovereigns may send to me for help." With a grunt, he pushed himself up and arose.

"Well, you need not bear it alone much longer, dear heart, for I just heard we're going to dock at Throneport."

"Throneport?" Cimozjen snorted. "Throneport may have mattered before the Last War. Now it's nothing but a derelict township that feigns to bend its knee to an empty throne."

"Oh, silly Cimmo, that's not all it is," said Minrah. "While there's no longer a great king, Jarot's hand remains. Throneport is a stronghold for the Sentinel Marshals."

Cimozjen's eyes brightened. "You're right, it is," he said. He ran one hand across his stubbly chin. "I'm sure they'd be interested to hear that the *Silver Cygnet* was smuggling dangerous beasts."

Chapter
ELEVEN

First Taste of Freedom
Far, the 13th day of Sypheros, 998

Sunset colored the chilly autumn sky as the *Silver Cygnet* hove to. Sailors threw lines to the stevedores and ran out the gangway.

Cimozjen and Minrah gazed at the island before debarking. It thrust steeply skyward from Scions Sound. Farms graced the few tracts of arable land that nestled between the rocks, and the mercantile town of Throneport waited at the water's edge. At the crest of the island stood the castle for which the island was named—Thronehold, the ancient seat of the Galifar kings, an elegant structure that looked both graceful and martial against the sky.

"That's it? That's the whole island?" Minrah snorted. "It's smaller than I would have thought."

"Let's go," said Cimozjen.

The ancient dock was one of several piers built from living coral by Vadalis bathymancers almost a thousand years before. During the days of the Kingdom of Galifar it had been crisply squared and rose-colored, well maintained by the servants of the throne. However, during the Last War the dock had suffered a century of neglect and was now worn, cracked in places, festooned with seaweed and limpets, and heavily stained by the seawaters. It was an unfortunately accurate allegory for the isle of Thronehold and its vacant throne, once the crown jewel of the continent.

"It's a wonder no one ever tried to take it over," said Minrah. "You'd think that with the Five Nations fighting for the throne, an obvious first strategy would be to seize Thronehold."

"The true king need not seize his own throne," said Cimozjen. "The very act of using military power to take the castle would demonstrate that one was a usurper, and would probably unite the rest of the nations against him."

"Politics," said Minrah. "Yech."

"So where do you think we might find the Sentinel Marshals?"

"I've heard their headquarters are in the castle," said Minrah. "If so, we'll have to ask the Thronewardens, who look after the place."

"We should go straight there. Sovereigns willing, we'll get there before the sun is completely down."

They moved briskly through the streets of Throneport. Once, a hundred years earlier, it would have been a bustling center of open-handed commerce. In the post-war times, even with the arrival of a new ship, the town seemed suspicious, furtive. The people were still there, but in the absence of a uniting king most of those residing in Throneport worked for personal interests, be those the goals of their home nation or some other affiliation. It gave the town a corrupt feeling, like a city of thieves and assassins.

The pair wound their way toward the castle, panting with exertion as they ascended the steep streets. As they passed one of the lower baileys of the castle—a fortified outbuilding connected to the main castle by a high, arcing bridge that soared high overhead—a soldier hailed them from a shadowed portcullis.

"Pardon me, good folks," he said, "but that street is the road to the castle gate."

"Yes," panted Cimozjen, "we know. How much farther is it to the castle?"

"It's still a bit of a climb," he said, "and I fear you'll find your effort wasted. They seal the gate at dusk."

"What?" said Minrah. "Why would they do that?"

"It's been the tradition since the start of the Last War. While there is a threat to Thronehold, the Thronewardens seal the castle during the hours of darkness. And so long as there is no king, there is, by definition, a threat."

"But it's the Thronewardens we want to see," said Minrah.

"For what purpose?"

"We were hoping they'd be able to admit us to the headquarters of the Sentinel Marshals," said Cimozjen. "We have some information we believe they'd be interested in."

"Is that so?" asked the soldier. He stepped out from the portcullis, and pulled off his helmet. Silvery hair spilled out onto his shoulders, framing an aged, kindly face. His slanting eyes and thin features showed him to be of mixed human and elven heritage. His weathered face bore wrinkles of care and cast a sad appearance over him despite his strong, piercing eyes. "It just so happens I've been a guard here since shortly after the start of the Last War. I know the Sentinel Marshals." He extended a hand. "My name is Theyedir Deneith. Tell me what you have for them, and if the information is worthy, I'll show you to them, be the castle sealed or not."

❧ ❧ ❧ ❧ ❧ ❧ ❧

It was the last watch before dawn, but the sailor standing watch was far from sleepy.

Having a squad of thirty armed and armored soldiers suddenly appear on the dock carrying lanterns aimed at you tends to have a rousing effect.

"No one's allowed aboard from midnight until first light," the sailor called out, "Commander's orders."

Focused as he was upon the armed throng, he neglected to notice the soft pad of approaching footsteps behind him. He did feel a hard blow strike the back of his head, though only briefly, before he slumped to the deck.

Cimozjen lowered the gangplank and let the Sentinel Marshals aboard. Several of them secured the ladders and the corridors leading to the cabins, the rest Cimozjen and Minrah led directly to the cargo hold.

The Marshals had a wizard with them, who ensorcelled the door such that it unlocked and opened of its own accord. "Now's your chance, Karrn," he said to Cimozjen. "Show us we were right to trust you on this."

"You don't believe him?" asked Minrah.

The wizard smiled, lopsided but genuine. "Personally, I put more stake in Theyedir's good feelings about you than in the story you two told. Daft as that old tinhorn is, he seems to have a good instinct about these things."

Cimozjen led the way in, whispering a prayer, Minrah huddled close behind him. He kissed his amulet, and divine light shone forth in the room. "The large crates are in the back," he said, gesturing as he worked his way through the cargo, "but I have no idea what might be in them. The beast was held in that, the largest of the crates. Down here's the only evidence I have of its existence." He stopped in the center of the cargo area, kneeled, and pulled up the trap door to the ballast hatch. Then he lay on the deck and lowered his head and shoulders into the hatch. After a moment's grunting and reaching in the cramped area, he pulled up two items.

"This is my father's dagger, given to me, and to him by his father before him. It bears the Hellekanus family crest on the hilt. And here," he added, proffering a blue-gray piece of hairy flesh the size of a shovel's blade, "is the ear of the creature that I killed with it. These are testimony to the truth of my tale, which I swear upon my honor, my bones, and my sovereign patron of arms."

He tossed the ear to the nearest soldier, then rolled to a sitting position on the side of the trapdoor hatch and twirled the dagger.

"I missed you, old friend," he said, then lifted the rear of his tunic and slid the blade back into its place.

Minrah walked over and put a reassuring hand on the back of Cimozjen's neck.

Behind them, the sergeant of the Sentinel Marshals inspected the ear. "Look here," he said. "It's been tattooed. '17.' That's very odd. What do you think?" He handed it to the wizard.

"Very odd indeed," said the wizard. "I'd think it a gnoll, were it not so abyssally large. I'd pay a high price for the chance to inspect this creature, living or dead. Perhaps we should find out if there are any others."

The sergeant waved a hand. "Check the other crates, but use caution."

The Sentinel Marshals started moving among the crates, looking.

"What's that smell?" said one, sniffing. "Smells like . . . cockroaches." He peered into the slats of a crate. A squeaking, chittering noise carried through the bay. "Oh, good gods! Bring that light here, will you?"

Cimozjen moved over to the soldier, his sacred amulet glowing by Dol Arrah's pleasure. As he drew closer to the soldier, the man drew away from the crate, for a large, insectile leg the length of a javelin extended between a pair of slats and rested its clawed appendage on a nearby box.

"Sergeant," called the soldier, "we've got 'em, we do. This makes dockside rats look like fleas!"

"I—I—I'm going to go back upstairs and wait on the dock until this is all over," said Minrah, a tremble in her voice. She turned and exited the cargo bay at not quite a run.

"Sergeant," called another Marshal, "you'll want to see this."

The sergeant walked over to the Marshal. Cimozjen moved to join him. The sergeant stood near a smaller crate, one that was marginally larger than an upright coffin, watching as the Sentinel Marshal worked at the locked hasp with a crowbar. The sergeant held one hand elegantly behind his back, clutching a long, thin rapier concealed behind him.

"So you see what I spoke of, sergeant," said Cimozjen. "This is a ship of nightmares. Twisted daelkyr creatures, monstrous insects, smuggling these must break a number of laws, does it not?"

The latch flew open with a loud snap, sending splinters flying through the air. The soldier pulled the door open, stepping well away.

"Bugs, perhaps," said the sergeant. "But this, this is against all the laws of Galifar—and the Treaty of Thronehold besides." He turned his head. "Seal the ship. Arrest all the crew. Hold all the passengers for interrogation."

Then he appraised the warforged that tentatively emerged from the crate, a battle-axe in its hands, head turning to look at each of them in turn.

❀ ❀ ❀ ❀ ❀ ❀ ❀

"I do not understand," he said. The open area was abustle with activity. People opened crates, counted coin, and hauled material hither and yon. Yet the crowd was not all staring at him, no one was yelling, nor was anyone trying to kill him, at least no one that he could determine.

"I already told you, 'forged," said the man without looking up. He was seated behind a table with a large sheet of parchment emblazoned with intricate filigreed sigils. "Slavery is illegal. We've seized what assets we can, and here's your share." He shoved a canvas bag across the table to the warforged.

"What am I to do with this bag?"

"Take it."

"Take it where?"

The man sighed and looked the warforged in the eye for the first time. "This bag and everything in it is yours now. It's valuable coin, so place it somewhere safe. Do you understand?"

"I will do as you wish," said the warforged. He picked up

117

the bag and looped the thick twine drawstring around his neck, leaving the bag to hang pendulously across his chest.

"Fine," said the man. He turned the parchment around and pointed. "Make your mark here."

"My what?"

"Your mark," said the man. "Your signature, if you can write." He paused and stared at the warforged for a moment. "You're quite the work, aren't you? The mark you make to show that you've been here."

The warforged considered this for a moment, then nodded his comprehension. In one powerful motion, he swung his battle-axe over his head and struck the parchment exactly where the man had indicated. The man shrieked and flopped over backward, and the small table split in half under the impact.

"Khyber's codpiece!" bellowed the man. "Get that—that thing out of here before he kills someone!"

Two guards hustled over and gently escorted the warforged out of the bowels of the ship.

"I'm not going back home?" asked the warforged.

"You can go wherever you want, now," said one of the guards. "You've been emancipated."

"What am I to do?"

"Whatever you like," said the guard.

"What would that be?" asked the warforged.

"I don't know. Join a group of adventurers or something. Isn't that what your kind usually does?"

And with that they ushered the warforged up a ladder and out onto an open deck. He raised one hand to protect his artificial eyes as the sun rose before him.

❋ ❋ ❋ ❋ ❋ ❋ ❋

Minrah and Cimozjen leaned against the aft railing, breaking their fast with food Minrah had taken from the ship's larder. It had seemed unlikely that the ship's cook would provide anything else. Cooking was difficult when one's hands were manacled.

As the *Silver Cygnet* would be sailing no farther in the foreseeable future, the Sentinel Marshals had reimbursed the pair with half of their paid passage, taken from the ship's strongbox.

"So what did they do with that bug?" asked Minrah with a shudder.

"They confiscated it," said Cimozjen with a shrug. "I understand the wizard will be rendering it into its various parts for arcane research and alchemic ingredients. There were a few other oddities, as well." He shook his head. "I am confused, though. What did smuggling a monstrous arachnid have to do with Torval's death?"

"Gambling," said Minrah.

"What?"

"I took a good look at the cargo hold, now that the open hatch is letting the sunlight in. Remember how there was that white coloration on the sole of Torval's shoe? That was chalk. There's a ring of chalk all around the edges of the open area. It was an arena, Cimmo. I'd wager anything they were holding matches between slaves and beasts. Think of it: the creature you killed had a 17 tattooed on its ear. Maybe Torval's scar wasn't SI at all, but rather a number: 51."

"I doubt it," said Cimozjen. "I'd think it odd that one would have an ear tattoo and the other would have a scar on his arm."

"I wish we still had it with us to be sure, though. We just assumed it was letters and not numbers."

"You wish we were still lugging Torval's arm around?" said Cimozjen incredulously. "Or did you just wish to skin him before burial?"

Minrah shook her head as if from a daze. "I'm sorry. I wasn't thinking."

Cimozjen nodded. "I understand. Still, the Treaty of Thronehold stipulated that all prisoners would be repatriated."

"Maybe he crossed the law. Got arrested."

Just then a warforged walked up to them. His armor plating

looked to be made of thin sheets of rough-hammered iron bolted together. Stretched between the gaps, thick strands of some smooth, organic white material stood in stark contrast. The 'forged held one hand shading his eyes from the dawning sun. The other held a huge axe, the heavy double-bitted head dangling near the ground.

"Are you adventurers?" he asked without preamble.

"No, good 'forged, we're not," said Cimozjen.

"Of course we are!" said Minrah almost at the same time. Then she turned to Cimozjen and shot him a questioning look. "What do you think we're doing here, Cimmo? This is a great adventure! Mystery, murder, revenge, what more could you ask for?"

"Good. Then I am now part of your group," said the warforged.

"Wonderful!" said Minrah with a bright smile.

"What?" asked Cimozjen. He held up one hand in a vain attempt to stop the conversation so he could catch up.

"I have been cast out from my home," said the warforged. "I am therefore to join a group of adventurers. That is what my kind usually does."

"Glad to have you!" said Minrah, clapping her hands together. "Hoy, what's in your bag?"

"Wh—now wait just a moment," said Cimozjen. "We know not why he even wants to—"

"He's been thrown out of his home," said Minrah, as if that should explain everything. "Don't you turn your back on him. He's one of us now!"

Befuddled, Cimozjen tilted his head and asked, "Where exactly is your home, 'forged?"

"My home is down there," said the construct, pointing to the open hatch to the cargo hold. "I stay in my home until they open it up and someone tries to kill me. Home is very small, but it I find that a comfort."

Cimozjen narrowed his eyes. "You're the one from the crate?"

Minrah blinked several times. "A crate? A crate was your home? But—how long did you, um, live there?"

"All my life," said the warforged, "though I do not know how long that has been."

"Do you know when you were made?" asked Cimozjen.

"Yes. I have always known that. It is a part of my functional specifications."

Cimozjen and Minrah waited, until finally Minrah said, "So when was that?"

"I was brought forth from the creation forge on the third day of the month of Eyre in the year 996."

"Over two years . . ." whispered Minrah.

Cimozjen dropped his head and rubbed his hand through his hair. "Oh, my," he said.

Chapter
Twelve

So do you have a name, friend?" asked Minrah as she popped into her mouth a piece of warm bread heavily laden with berry preserves.

The fresh loaf and jar of preserves were both gifts. The streets of Throneport were abuzz with talk of the raid on the *Silver Cygnet*, the strange creatures being smuggled within her bowels, and the warforged that had, apparently, been kept as a fighting cock for over two years. Cimozjen and Minrah were small celebrities, while the warforged was an oddity that the crowd couldn't leave alone. As the dawn passed, the warforged grew increasingly tense until Minrah and Cimozjen managed to extricate themselves from public attention.

The trio loitered outside a grocer's store a block off the main thoroughfare that led from the port to the castle of Thronehold, Minrah leaning against Cimozjen and he leaning against the store's wall. The warforged likewise stood with his back to a wall, but looked not at all relaxed, and held his battle-axe at the ready. In an attempt to ease his mood, Minrah had persuaded the warforged to remove the pendulous bag of coin from around his neck and allow her to keep it in her bag, where it would be less of a temptation for thieves. It hadn't abated the construct's tension in the slightest.

"Name?" the warforged asked.

"Of course. Your name." Minrah paused. "What do folks call you?"

"I am sure they called me all sorts of things, but I was never able to attend to what they were yelling. Someone was always trying to kill me."

"They still might," said Cimozjen with a snort. "Especially with a bag of coin dangling like a lure around your neck."

"What?"

"It's a great and terrible world out there, my friend," said Minrah. "Yes, there are people who'd just as soon kill you, but there are also some truly sweet people, like Cimozjen here. Isn't he just as handsome a side of beef as you've ever seen?"

"I have never seen a side of beef," said the warforged. "But something you said confuses me. How can something be both great and terrible? Is not 'great' a superlative of good, and 'terrible' a superlative of bad?"

Minrah giggled. "Words can have more than one meaning. Great can mean good, or it can mean vast, like the Great Talenta Plains. Or it can mean powerful, like a great king. Or it can mean all of those at once. And terrible, well, it means something that can inspire terror and awe. Bad things do, but so do huge things. There can be a terrible storm, for example. Or sometimes terrible can mean extreme, like that poem that says, ' 'Twas terrible a price to pay / In blood for them to win the day.' "

"I think I understand. The world is large, and it is filled with extremes. A great and terrible place."

"Right. And it's a damned sight larger than that crate you called 'home.' "

"But I liked my home. It was comforting."

Minrah shrugged. "For a long time, my home was in a caravan. And I felt it was safe and comfortable, until"—she dropped her eyes—"well, until I found out differently." She sucked on her lips for a moment. "But you get used to it."

Cimozjen downed the last of his bread, and said, "I tell you the truth, if you want things around you to give you peace and security, you'll have neither. Your, uh, home was comforting, but you never knew when they'd open it up and you'd have to fight. Am I right? So even when you were snug in your home, you lived with a sense of dread, did you not?"

The warforged nodded.

"I thought as much. Listen. If you want to have both freedom and safety, you will never achieve your goal. Before you can have true freedom you must have confidence in your own abilities, and set your sights on ideals that are higher than you. You'll find faith in the Sovereign Host invaluable."

Minrah rolled her eyes.

"Take my advice for what's it's worth," Cimozjen said. "And, if you would be so kind, give us a name."

"You are Cimozjen, and you are Minrah."

Minrah laughed, and Cimozjen smiled in spite of himself. "What I mean is, please tell us your name."

The warforged considered for a moment. "I have none."

"Sure you do," said Minrah.

"Perhaps not, Minrah," said Cimozjen, "Remember, he's probably been kept in a crate since he was made."

"But they had to call him something, didn't they?" said Minrah. She thought about it for a moment, then asked, "Did you hear anything right before they opened your cr—er, home? Something consistent all the time?"

"I did," said the warforged. "It sounded like this." His voice buzzed with a roar like an ocean, and within the noise a voice yelled out, crying "Fferrrrdurrrahnn!"

"Could you repeat that?" asked Cimozjen.

The warforged did.

"That's an impressive imitation," said Minrah. "But what does it mean? I couldn't make it out."

"Fighter N?" offered Cimozjen.

"The last part sounded like 'drawn,' " said Minrah, "but that doesn't make any sense."

"Perhaps it was 'thirty-one,' another number in the manner of that creature's ear."

"Perhaps, but that sound rather put me in mind of someone calling out to a crowd, and calling out numbers just doesn't seem compelling." The elf grumped, deep in her throat. "Well, we'll just call you Durn for now. Is that all right?"

"No, it's not," said Cimozjen. "You're not going to use even a mild expletive as a name. We'll call him Fighter for now. At least that's an accurate description of his skills."

"Oh, you're no fun," groused Minrah.

She looked up. "Hoy there, Cimmo," she said, having espied a procession that made its way along the thoroughfare to the castle. "I'll wager those are the Marshals' prisoners now."

"So that's where the crowd went off to," said Cimozjen. "Come on, then, uh, Fighter. Let's show you one of the better aspects to this world—justice. The sergeant of the Sentinel Marshals said we could attend the questioning of the ship's officers and the other passengers."

"That's terrible," said the warforged.

"What?" said Cimozjen. "No it's not. I should think it will be very interesting."

"The projection of authority upon those in bondage is sure to evoke awe and terror, is it not?"

"Of course it does, Fighter," said Minrah, "but—oh, right. You know the definitions, but we'll have to work on the application of your language skills."

By the time they reached the main road, the procession had already passed by. It was a long, single line of people shackled together. One long chain ran from cuff to cuff on their left ankles, and another ran from right wrist to right wrist. The shuffling of feet and chinking of chains made for a very depressing sound, even to the normally ebullient Minrah. Sentinel Marshals paced along both sides of the line, barking at the prisoners and occasionally jabbing at slow ones with the butt of a spear.

Unburdened by either chains or dread, the trio set a faster pace and gradually began to pass the line as the guards urged it forward. Every time they passed a prisoner, the three would turn their heads to look at his or her face.

"That looks like just about everyone on the ship, agreed?" said Cimozjen as they perused the line, his face showing a mixture of satisfaction and compassion. "Well, I suppose the innocent will be free of this whole situation soon enough."

"It's not the innocent that I'm concerned about," said Minrah, looking toward the head of the line.

"The Sentinel Marshals will sniff out the guilty, I assure you."

"Then explain this, Cimmo," said Minrah. "Why isn't the commander among the prisoners?"

"Excuse me?"

"Everyone we've passed so far has been a passenger, have they not? Look, there's that old man from Breland, and there's that pair of brothers from Aundair. The one in the rear came from Flamekeep, if I remember right."

"How is it that you know so much about these people?" asked Fighter.

"I haven't sequestered myself in our cabin like Cimmo or been caged like you have, friend," said Minrah. "I've spent hours and hours on a ship with them, and I try to talk to a lot of people. You never know when you might find an interesting story." Minrah pointed. "See, Cimmo? Look there. There's that dwarf lass, Erami d'Kundarak. Why is she in the line and not commander Pomindras?"

"I'm sure I have no idea," said Cimozjen, his voice edging.

"Let's get to the head of the line. I want to see if there's anyone else that's been lucky enough to avoid the chains."

The trio picked up their pace and quickly moved to the head of the line, taking note of every face they saw.

"You know who else we're missing?" asked Minrah.

Cimozjen stroked his chin. "Rophis the Winemonger."

"That's right. Him and the commander. Judging by the number of prisoners, that's a complete accounting of those missing."

"That's a grave concern. Sergeant!" he called. He trotted over to the Sentinel Marshal that headed the procession. "Sergeant!"

The Sentinel Marshal ignored him until Cimozjen tapped him on the shoulder. "What?" he snapped.

"I am wondering, my good man, where the ship's commander is, as well as a certain passenger—"

"They have been taken care of," said the Marshal.

"Do you mean executed?" asked Cimozjen. "But we had—"

"They have been taken care of," repeated the Marshal.

Cimozjen looked at him oddly. "Perhaps you mean they were brought up to the castle earlier, and quietly so. I can certainly understand your desire for discretion, but as you should well recall, I am the one who exposed their smuggling and slavery to you. May I ask, then, when and where the prisoners will be questioned?"

"That is none of your concern."

"Indeed it is my concern, sergeant, for not only am I the accuser in this case, but I also believe that these selfsame slavers held a friend of mine in their thrall until he was murdered."

"The questioning will be private," said the sergeant.

"But you told me that we could attend. We have questions we'd like to have answered, and our unique perspective, having been on the vessel in question, would pro—"

The sergeant stopped in his tracks and turned to face Cimozjen. "I'd rather not arrest the day's hero for hindering a Sentinel Marshal pursuing his duties," he said, "but you're testing my patience. Now leave!"

"Arrest me? But I've done nothing wrong! By the Code of Galifar—"

The sergeant abruptly stepped back, a broad smile beaming from his face. "Isn't this a true hero?" he shouted, sweeping one arm out to engage the crowd. "Not only does he risk his life to uncover the blaggards who were violating countless articles of the Code of Galifar, but he declines any personal reward for his daring deeds! Let's hear a cheer for him! Khooooot!"

The crowd of onlookers cheered.

The sergeant motioned the crowd to silence again. "Sad to say, my troop and I have much to do yet this day, and will be busy interrogating these prisoners until well after sundown. However, I see that the Crown and King is opening their doors early this day, and while this fine man refuses any personal payment for his deeds, I am certain that he'd be happy to spend the reward money buying drinks for the good people of Throneport!" With that, he drew a small leather coin pouch from his belt and slung it to Cimozjen, arcing it high so that everyone within the area would mark its flight.

Cimozjen caught the bag easily, giving the sergeant a look mixed of grudging respect for his cleverness and bitter disappointment at his evasion.

The sergeant whipped one hand into the air. "He's dying to tell the tale of his escapades, folks. You need only beg him to do it! If this is how he starts his morning, think of the wild and glorious tales he has to share!"

The crowd cheered again, and rather more loudly this time. Following the grand gesture of the sergeant, they crowded around Cimozjen, gently badgering him and his companions toward the Crown and King.

Behind the waving hands of the excited peasantry, Cimozjen saw the Sentinel Marshals brutally urging their charges onward.

❀ ❀ ❀ ❀ ❀ ❀ ❀

The tavern had the musky and pervasive odor of spilled beer gone rancid and tobacco smoked days or even months prior, and was thus much akin to most taverns spread across the Five Nations. The sergeant's coin purse had been long depleted, and the drinks it had purchased already forgotten. While Cimozjen's early tales had held the crowd in thrall, those he'd told more recently had been carefully chosen for minimal effect and told with deliberate ponderousness. Thus he had driven the locals to their own tables and tales told with rather more excitement and considerably less honesty, leaving him and his companions alone. Cimozjen and Minrah sat. Fighter stood in the corner, his battle-axe at the ready.

Minrah sighed in disgust, resting her chin on the heel of her hand. "I can't believe you let him get away with that."

Cimozjen stretched, gave Fighter a reassuring pat on the arm, and slouched down in his chair. "With what?" he asked.

"With manipulating you into coming in here and wasting your time buying drinks for ingrates."

"I did no such thing," said Cimozjen.

"Did you come in here? Yes. Did you buy drinks? Yes. Did you waste a lot of time? Yes. Aside from that, you did yourself proud, Cimmo."

"I did not allow him to manipulate me," he said. "I chose to do as I was bidden."

"What? You chose to—gah! That was just—that was not smart. Not smart at all."

"Perhaps. But it was kind."

"Kind? Kind to whom?"

"All of the people in this tavern."

Minrah sat back and folded her arms across her breast. "I'd rather be smart than kind."

Fighter stirred. "I concur. When they opened my home, there was always someone who intended to attack me. I needed to use my intellect to figure out which it was. Kindness would not have availed me any. Therefore Minrah's preference is the correct one."

"There is much you have to learn about the world, Fighter. Did you not think about things while you were in the—uh, your home?"

"No. I waited. Sometimes I waited for long periods of time, but during those times I had no need to think, for I was not being attacked. Sometimes there were noises outside my home, but as I could not reach those noises, nor could they reach me, I ignored them. I find it considerably more taxing being without my home, for I must always be alert for whoever will next attack me."

"Alas, your education is sorely lacking, good warforged. To begin with, intelligence is a trait, while kindness is a virtue."

"Sure, and I'd rather be lucky enough to be smart," said Minrah.

"Intellect is a gift the Sovereigns give you," said Cimozjen, ignoring her outburst, "while kindness is a gift you give others. The world would be a far better place if people thought more of others than of themselves."

"Like that's ever going to come to pass," muttered Minrah.

"Someone's coming," said Fighter. "He's armed."

Cimozjen looked up and saw a guard approaching, marking his paces by using a spear as a walking stick. The guard was silhouetted against the windows, and Cimozjen couldn't make out the face. "Is the sergeant checking up on us?" he asked quietly.

"It's Theyedir," said Minrah. "The old soldier from the lower bailey."

Theyedir approached their table. Cimozjen stood, his hand straying to the sword at his side. Seeing this, Minrah stood and moved quickly to the far side of Fighter. Fighter edged along the wall to cover Cimozjen's flank.

"Have you come to question us, now?" asked Cimozjen.

Theyedir slowed his pace, a look of timid concern on his face. He leaned his spear against the wall and held up his hands peacefully. "I am sorry if I have disconcerted you. It was not my intent."

"Then what is your intent?" asked Cimozjen.

"I have heard some disturbing rumors about my beloved Marshals," he said. An apologetic smile reorganized the wrinkles on his face into a more pleasant arrangement. "May I sit, please? I would hear what you have to say about the matter, in hopes that you might shed some light."

Cimozjen nodded. Theyedir sat. Cimozjen and Minrah followed his lead, and Fighter moved back into the corner, keeping a wary eye on the old half-elf.

Theyedir laced his fingers together and leaned forward. "I have loyally served the Sentinel Marshals all of my years," he said. "As a boy, in the early stages of the Last War, I cleaned their offices and ran errands. I became a guard as soon as they let me hold a weapon. I even got myself adopted into their house when I came of age. All this I did because I believed in their ideals, trusted that they would uphold the Code of Galifar and strive to preserve the Kingdom of Galifar even as the fighting over the succession became more intense. I find it gravely unsettling, given such an incident as this, that the Marshals seem intent on sidestepping justice." He paused then leaned his head into one hand, his thumb at his chin and two fingers extended to his temple. "Please, tell me everything."

"How do we know you're not just trying to spy on us, pry out our knowledge to carry back to your superiors back at the castle?" asked Minrah.

"You are bitter and suspicious, young woman, for those you entrusted with justice have, from what I have heard, betrayed their duty," said Theyedir. "I cannot offer you any proof beyond my own word and honor that I am being forthright with you, and the actions of those I serve have baffled me as much as you."

"We trusted the Marshals once, and look where it got us," said Minrah. "Nowhere. So I don't trust you, either."

Cimozjen reached for the hand that Theyedir had left on the table. He gripped it firmly and stared hard into Theyedir's eyes. The old Marshal stared back at him, moving nothing but his eyes. After several long moments, Cimozjen released his grip.

"I do."

"You trust him? After all this? Cimmo, you can't be serious."

"I am. And remember, I'm chasing blood here. You're chasing ink."

"That's why I'm the only one keeping a clear head."

Cimozjen started to say something but held his tongue.

"What?" asked Minrah.

"Being oathbound, I will not allow what so regretfully crossed my mind to cross my tongue. Therefore I will simply beg you to indulge me here, Minrah. He did support our case to the Marshals, and I will not hold him accountable for what they did with it."

Cimozjen proceeded to tell his entire tale, starting from his encounter with the dwarf thief and continuing to the events of the morning. Theyedir stared at him, never moving, never letting his eyes wander. Minrah, at first reluctant even to acknowledge the aging guard's presence at their table, could not restrain herself from embellishing those points at which she had firsthand knowledge. Even Fighter shifted closer as the tale unfolded, although the warforged still kept his back to the wall.

Cimozjen told his tale with the succinct clarity that comes with extensive military service. At the end of his narrative, Theyedir nodded. "That's a fascinating tale, Cimozjen. And you're doing all this . . ."

"Because it's the right thing to do," he said.

"Do you still carry Torval's armband?"

"No, I do not," said Cimozjen. "I entrusted it to an acquaintance, an old veteran like myself. He swore that he would see it delivered to his family. It's a tradition. But I do have my own, if you'd like to see it."

"I would," said Theyedir, holding out his hand.

Cimozjen rolled up his sleeve to bare the ornate armband. However, instead of taking it off and handing it over, he simply leaned forward. "It cannot be removed," he said. "Not until I'm dead."

Theyedir peered at the graven armband, then recoiled. "The Iron Band." He put his hand to his forehead. "What—what was your purpose there?"

Cimozjen tilted his head defensively. "A recruiter came to Tanar Rath while we were garrisoned there, holed up for winter. I was selected for training, and I managed to pass. Later I learned that the Iron Band was being created as an elite unit. I eventually came to command a talon, until, well, until the course of the War turned in other directions." He paused. "It's nothing to concern yourself over, Marshal. The Last War is over, and I've no grievances held against those who fought for the other side, let alone those who stood aside to guard the ancient seat of Galifar."

Theyedir calmed himself. "I suppose you're right. The Last War is over, and the Iron Band fights on only in tales told by the fireside." He drummed his fingers on the table. "But—well. Never mind. As for your problem, I am afraid I know nothing at the moment, but I will see if I can uncover anything to help you. Rophis Raanel's son, you said, and Commander Pomindras—those were the only ones who were not in chains?"

"As near as we can tell, that is the truth of it," said Cimozjen.

"I don't make mistakes," said Minrah.

The conversation hung silent for a long moment, until Minrah spoke up again. "Might the commander have bribed his way out of trouble? With Rophis's wealth and his station, he—"

"No," said Theyedir. "The Sentinel Marshals have the honor and reputation of a dragonmarked house to uphold. For a Sentinel Marshal to accept a bribe for any reason, no matter how small the crime, is punishable by public execution."

"Oh," said Minrah. "Well, that's about the only idea I had."

"Very well," said Theyedir, rising. "I suggest you stay at the Crownshadow. It's a good guesthouse. I'll send word to you there if I manage to uncover anything about this." He turned to go.

"So what's your stake in this?" asked Minrah. "What reason do you have to do anything to help us when your fellow Marshals would just as soon spit in our eye?"

He looked back over his shoulder at the recalcitrant elf. "My reason is the same as Cimozjen's," he said, "and the same as the Marshals' should be."

Chapter
Thirteen

They boarded at the Crownshadow as Theyedir had suggested. Cimozjen booked a suite. He stayed in one room, and insisted that Minrah take the other. Fighter stepped into the freestanding wardrobe in the common area, even though it was easily too small for his frame. However, he didn't like the feeling of dread that returned to him when he was inside with the door closed, so he opted to sit inside the open wardrobe, facing the suite's door.

The *Silver Cygnet* remained docked at the pier, her helm chained hard over to immobilize her. The trio waited helplessly for a way off the island and searched for any sign of Rophis or Pomindras, or any of the prisoners. Each day, two or three ships docked at Throneport, though most were simple fishing boats, and the rest were headed for destinations other than Aundair.

It was their third day of waiting. Minrah slouched against the wall of the common area, while Cimozjen paced back and forth, pausing to look out the window of his room and scowl at the hobbled ship. Fighter remained as still as a statue, both hands gripping his axe.

"Cimmo," said Minrah, "we need to find Rophis. He's hiding something."

Cimozjen gave a noncommittal grunt. "Many people have secrets. Some because they scheme, others because they're embarrassed about their vices. I pray he's just a down-on-his-fortunes merchant who got on the wrong vessel."

"You're being deliberately obtuse. Rophis tries to pass himself off as an Aundairian, and he's no such thing. He's spent a lot of time in Karrnath, was probably even raised there, but when I pointed that out, he tried to tell me I was wrong. Why?"

Cimozjen shrugged. "Why do you think he's Karrn?"

"He has a slight accent he tries to hide. And he uses Karrn phrases. He said, 'I'm in a good company,' as in 'I am in a good military unit.' That's a distinctly Karrn turn of phrase." She paused. "In case you don't know, the rest of the continent says, 'I'm in good company,' like folks have come over to visit. He also called it Nightwood Pale, not Nightwood Ale. Again, that's a very Karrn label. And with the soldier's gruel, when he talked about how the casks get reused for that earthy flavor, he talked about how 'they' did it, not about how 'we' did it, and it's a deeply rooted Aundairian tradition. Even isolated farmers do that for their home brew."

"Did he say those things? I'd not noticed."

"Of course not. You're a Karrn. You don't hear Karrn phrases." Cimozjen chuckled. "So what's your blind spot?"

"I don't have one. I'm a child of the continent."

Footsteps ran up the hall outside the door, and the door to their room burst open. Fighter lunged to his feet and took a long stride to cross the floor, bringing his huge battle-axe around in an arc, the blade whistling as it cleft the air. A small boy ran into the room, breathless. At the last moment his eyes went wide as a full moon. He tried to stop, but his momentum tripped him up. He flopped to the floor just as Fighter's axe whooshed over his scalp, slicing a swath of black hair from the back of his head and lodging firmly into the doorframe with a heavy thunk.

Minrah shrieked.

The boy screamed and scampered away on all fours, leaving a crumpled roll of parchment wobbling back and forth on the floor.

"Fighter!" snapped Cimozjen. "Hold!"

The warforged yanked his axe out of the woodwork and rounded on the Karrn, raising the axe for a deadly blow. Cimozjen stood still and folded his hands in front of him.

Fighter took a step and swung, but the movement slowed to a stop in mid-strike, then Fighter lowered his axe to the floor. "That was great," he said.

Minrah tittered nervously.

Cimozjen thought about it for a moment, and said, "Well, Fighter, it seems that your definition of 'home' has expanded somewhat over the last few days. I think that's probably a good thing. Now if you'll excuse me"—Cimozjen bent down to pick up the parchment the boy had abandoned and gave it a quick read. "Hmm. Right, people, let's go. Now!"

Minrah hopped to her feet. "What does it say?" She snatched the paper from Cimozjen. " 'NORTH DOCK NOW FIRE FLIGHT —T.' What does that mean?"

"The answer's at the docks," said Cimozjen as he ushered his companions out the door. Then he paused, one hand tugging on the door's latch. "Um, Fighter? The door cannot close, um, any more. Could you wait here, inside, just for a short while, and make sure no one but us enters the rooms?"

"Waiting is what I know best," said Fighter.

"Many thanks."

"Back in a trice!" said Minrah as she and Cimozjen dashed down the hall.

❧ ❧ ❧ ❧ ❧ ❧ ❧

The two made their way quickly to the quays, thence to cut north along the docks. As they ran down the central thoroughfare, they sensed an excitement humming in the populace, and when they left the streets for the open waterfront, they discovered why. A large airship hung in the sky over the outcropping that demarked the north end of the docks, hovering near the airship tower. She had sleek lines, curved and graceful as a swan. Her hull shone with a fresh coat of ivory paint, and the ship's rails and other trim were colored a royal blue. Delicate spars curled out from amidships to twine like ivy around a horizontal oval of fire that encircled the hull. Though the fires of the ring burned low, they still reflected in the seawater of Throneport, adding a splash of color to the otherwise steely sea.

"That's the north dock," said Cimozjen, "and we're seeing fire in flight right now."

As they gazed at the beautiful ship, they saw a scarlet tendril reach down from the deck to the airship tower that stood atop the rocky promontory. The end of the tendril held a wide wooden disk, and the fluid motion and image combined to remind Cimozjen of a servant offering a plate of sweetmeats at a posh function.

Minrah pointed. "Looks like they're boarding passengers. We need to see who's going on that ship." She put her fingers to her mouth and whistled loudly. "Hansom!"

A small two-wheeled open carriage rattled over to them, and as Minrah sprang aboard, she cried out, "To the airship, and quickly! They're loading the first batch now!"

Cimozjen swung himself on as the driver swatted the single horse with his crop.

As the hansom rattled across the cobbles of the waterfront, Minrah leaned over and said, "I hope you brought your coin, Cimmo."

Fortunately for Cimozjen's self-respect, he had, and he paid the driver generously for the speedy trip to the airship dock. Only one more diskload of passengers had boarded by the time they arrived. Cimozjen and Minrah ran to the end of the queue that led to the magnificent vessel.

Cimozjen shoved his way— with excuses made and pardons begged—to the ship's crew who were taking the vouchers and admitting people to be boarded. "Begging your pardon," he began.

"My apologies, good man," said the crewman by way of reply, "but the *Fire Flight*'s billets are already filled. You'll have to await the next vessel."

"Already?" said Cimozjen. "But she seems such a large ship."

"Not as large as she looks from here, I assure you," said the crewman as he checked someone's paper and voucher. "We just made a brief stop to engage supplies and drop some parcels. And to let our passengers off for a short respite. We only had a half dozen billets free, and those have long since been sold."

Cimozjen considered. "Perchance was one of those billets sold to a man by name of Rophis, Raanel's son? I had hoped to see him ere he left Throneport."

The crewman shook his head. "No, I recall no such name. We sold four to various house members, and two to nobles." He checked another passenger for voucher and papers. "Ah, yes, Lady d'Medani, any luck finding suitable earrings? No? I'm sorry to hear that, although I did warn that your chances would be slim in a small town like this. You'll have better fortune in Fairhaven. It's full of the finest artisans, and the Queen keeps them well employed, I assure you. Now if you please, we will be departing as soon as everyone is aboard." He turned back to face Cimozjen. "If you please, good man, I have passengers and luggage to attend to."

"Of course," said Cimozjen. "Forgive the intrusion." He turned around to depart, and saw that his companion had vanished. "Minrah?" He looked about briefly, calling her name, and finally spotted her on the second floor of a guesthouse, leaning over the balcony railing and staring intently at the airship's activity. "Minrah!" he called.

Without turning her head, she pointed. "There he is, Cimmo. There's no mistaking that frame."

Cimozjen followed her arm to where the airship's curious red tendril—by all appearances, a huge silken ribbon—was raising another disk's worth of passengers and cargo to the ship. A small cluster of people stood on the wooden disk, some waving to those below. And at one side stood a large man, both tall and wide, with a rich red surcoat that near trailed the ground.

❀ ❀ ❀ ◉ ❀ ❀ ❀

Cimozjen walked up to the aged half-elf and shook his hand firmly. "I thank you for your timely note, Theyedir," he said. "It gave us the information we needed."

"Thanks to the note? How about thanks to me?" interjected Minrah. "While you were diddling about in that crowd, I was actually looking."

Theyedir chuckled. "I did nothing, friends, that any right-hearted person would not have done. So you found something?"

"In truth, we did," said Cimozjen. "We also found a transport. Our ship leaves with the morning tide for Daskaran, and thence we take the rail to Fairhaven to see what else we might find. But before we left, I wanted to convey our gratitude."

"Those are indeed excellent tidings. But if you truly wish to thank me, send me a message with news of your progress. It would be good to see that my trifling help might make a difference for the better in the world."

"Would that not be dangerous for you?" asked Cimozjen. "Might not your officers read your post?"

Theyedir shook his head. "I am an old gaffer, considered an odd goblin amongst those of my House. I have been here my whole life, thus getting letters from afar is one of my eccentricities. They expect such quirks from me with my age, and leave me well enough alone so long as I guard this door when I am told."

"As you wish," said Cimozjen, and he clasped Theyedir's hand. "Fare well, and thank you for affirming my beliefs in House Deneith's standards."

Minrah stepped forward and gave him a hug. "You're cute."

The two turned for the dock, inadvertently leaving Fighter

standing there. The warforged shifted for a moment, then said, "Thank you for not attacking me."

Theyedir laughed. "It was the least I could do. Literally."

❧ ❧ ❧ ❧ ❧ ❧ ❧

"It's not like he knows anything," said Minrah. "He's a warforged. He doesn't know anything about it at all. But if his presence bothers you, we can always send him out into the hall."

Cimozjen stepped over to the window. Grasping the top of the frame with one hand, he leaned his head against the glass and stared out at the Aundairian countryside as it flew past the window of the lightning rail. "That's not the point, Minrah," he said.

"Then why couldn't we get a nice stateroom with a big soft bed, instead of two separate cubby holes?" she asked, patting the cots that were built into wall of the sleeper cabin. "The rail has staterooms like that, right?"

"Minrah," said Cimozjen, "I am a married man."

"So? I'm not asking you to marry me, Cimmo. I just want to bunk you."

Cimozjen looked toward the heavens and growled. "That's not the point."

"Don't you find me attractive?"

Cimozjen closed his eyes and sighed. "I do find you attractive, Minrah, quite so. Your zeal and your energy are as beautiful as your smile. At times, you confound me greatly, which is annoying and yet also compelling. But I have sworn a vow to my wife before the Sovereign Host, and that vow is binding. Thus, no matter how attractive I find you, what you suggest cannot be." He turned away from the window to look her in the eye. "On top of that, Minrah, you should look to yourself. You sell your dearest touch too cheaply if you would yield it up freely to a broken-down old soldier like myself."

Minrah giggled. "I just want to see what you're like under the blankets. You've got to be better than those young boys who are always trying to loose their arrows. So it's not like I don't know what I'm asking."

Cimozjen kept his face a mask. "It is said that the act creates a bond between the souls forever, and I must wonder what impact it will have on you to find your soul stretched between men scattered across Khorvaire."

Minrah shrugged. "It doesn't bother me."

"I think, Minrah, that *that* is the point." He paused. "They say that a fruit that has been squeezed too often is garbage."

"I'll wager that if you give me a squeeze you'll find out otherwise."

"I think higher of you than that, Minrah, and you should too. I am my wife's, and she is mine. That is the way of it, and that is the end of it." He turned to look back out the window.

Fighter, standing in the corner, looked back and forth between the two, as a long silence hung in the air.

Finally a smile crossed Minrah's face. "Cimmoooo . . ." she said liltingly.

He turned to find her slowly untying the knot at the top of her blouse. "Enough!" he barked with a chop of his hand.

"Look at that, the old man's a pot ready to boil over," Minrah pouted. Then she giggled. "I think I'll call you Cimmer."

"I have a question," said Fighter. "Minrah said we were on a grand adventure, but all we have done is wait and argue. Is that what an adventure is, sitting and bickering?"

Cimozjen sighed. "There has been a lot of that, but there always is among people. We are imperfect, after all, but do not let these minor troubles divert you from the greater issues."

"Issues like what?" asked the warforged.

"Vengeance, Fighter. That's what it's all about," said Minrah. "A lone soldier hunting down those who killed his friend. Quite a story, and we're all a part of it."

"And bringing them before the proper authorities," said Cimozjen. "Unfortunately, we lack all the pertinent facts. We're hunting down clues, which takes time, as does all this travel. And while traveling, that is when there can be friction, because we have nothing to do and—"

"I had an idea of something we could do," grumped Minrah.

"—*and* there's no way to know how long we'll have to wait before we get results," concluded Cimozjen with a sharp look at his companion.

Fighter nodded, then inspected the blade of his battle-axe. "I can wait," he said. "Even with the time we have spent waiting, I have done more adventuring with you than I had known could be possible."

"And as you'll recall, Fighter, I said we were not adventurers," said Cimozjen. "We're just people."

"That is true. You said we were seeking people to bring them to justice," said Fighter. "Justice means equitable treatment for the crimes committed. Do you therefore mean to kill them for their murder?"

Cimozjen shook his head. "Not if I have a choice," he said. "It's never easy just to kill someone."

"Actually, it is," said Fighter. "A solid blow to the top or side of the head crushes the skull, destroying the brain. Strikes at the neck, armpit, or inner thigh cause unstoppable bleeding. Eviscerating the bowels causes them to—"

"Ewww!" said Minrah, plugging her ears. "Stop!"

Chapter
Fourteen

The Foul Airs of Fairhaven
Sul, the 22nd day of Sypheros, 998

Well, Cimozjen, allow me to be the first to welcome you to Fairhaven," said Minrah as they stepped off the lightning rail.

Cimozjen looked up at the clouds that covered the sky, heavy with the promise of rain. "I've been here before," he said.

"Have you?" she asked. "I didn't think the Karrn armies pressed this far into the country."

Cimozjen clenched his jaw. "You're right. I was a prisoner."

"You were? How come you didn't end up like Torval?"

"I could better answer if I knew what had happened to him. As for me, when the Aundairians found out that I was sworn by oath to Dol Dorn, they put me to work in one of their temples, healing those in need."

"They let you tend their sick and wounded? Weren't they afraid you'd secretly kill them?"

"Of course not. I am sworn to do no harm to the helpless."

"But surely you were doing harm by helping the enemy, weren't you?" asked Minrah.

"I told them I'd heal women, children, and those too badly injured to return to the field of battle. Those who'd lost a limb, for example, or were too old." He sniffed sharply. "They plied on my vows, though, for they brought their own oathbound to me. I am bound by honor to help those of my calling, and I had to do my duty to my brethren even though I knew they'd be returning to fight against my own people. I have long tried to forgive them for abusing my oaths in that fashion." He nodded with the grim memories. "Be careful what you ask for," he added, "because there's more than one way to answer a prayer."

"Consider yourself lucky that your prayer was answered with a surprise rather than not answered at all."

"The Host answers prayers," said Cimozjen.

"No they don't," said Minrah darkly. "Or if they do, it's all capricious. They don't care about us at all. They're the gods and as long as we keep worshipping them, they're fine just sitting around being gods. I mean, they completely abandoned us in the Last War. How else do you explain a hundred years of war, untold slaughter, and the complete destruction of one of the Five Kingdoms?"

"Explain?" Cimozjen snorted. "Do you think we need the gods' permission to go to war? We did it ourselves." He rubbed his chin. "We fought over a throne. We were divided by the very symbol of our unity. And we continued fighting for fifty, sixty years after the original claimants were all dead, instead of just putting an end to it and restoring order. The gods did not abandon us, Minrah. We abandoned them, prayed for them to destroy their other worshippers for our own selfish sakes. If they turned their backs on us, it's because we first were insolent and threw their own ideals into their faces."

"You think so?" asked Minrah, her dander raised. "Then why do they keep letting their priests perform miracles, no matter how corrupt the priests are?"

"Because the Sovereigns keep their promises, even when we break ours, just as a parent will continue to feed a child even when the child misbehaves."

"I have been here before, as well," said Fighter, his battle-axe, as always, at the ready.

Minrah and Cimozjen looked at him. "What was that?" said Minrah.

"Fairhaven. That is what you called this place, correct? I have been before. There is something in the air that is familiar. I think I did a lot of fighting here." He looked around. "Not in this exact spot, but in this general area. Deep inside a building, or perhaps underground." He looked around. "It is upsetting. It reminds me that someone may attack me at any time. This is a violent place."

"Fairhaven?" said Minrah. "It's one of the most peaceful places in Khorvaire!"

"Need I remind you of Torval's boot, or the marks of imprisonment upon him?" said Cimozjen.

Minrah shrugged. "No place is perfect, I suppose."

"At least this lets us know that we're on the right path. First you noticed that Torval's shoe was made here, then we saw Rophis board the *Fire Flight,* which was headed here. And now Fighter remembers this place from his past."

"Like I said, no place is perfect," Minrah said. She looked around. "You go find us a place to stay before it starts raining, then meet me at the Dragon's Flagons. It's by the docks. We have a lot to do."

❦ ❦ ❦ ❦ ❦ ❦ ❦

The sound of heavy rain washed into the hubbub of the Dragon's Flagons as the front door opened, admitting Cimozjen, Fighter, and a gust of cold, fresh air before closing and sealing the sound of rain outside once more.

Within, the crackling of the fire and the clank of tin plates and drinking mugs battled for dominance with the babble of rowdy conversation. Those gathered were a rough lot, even more so than might be expected for a tavern sited outside the city walls. They took up but a half of the room's capacity, but made noise and song enough for a group twice their size.

"Hey!" bellowed an angry voice as the two of them entered.

"What is *that* doing here?" A tall, lithe woman stood, her hand resting on the pommel of the long sword at her hip. She might have been beautiful with her athletic build and long auburn hair folded into a loose braid, but for two items that marred her beauty—the repulsed sneer that crossed her mouth, and the fact that the tip of her nose had been cut off, presumably during the Last War, leaving its scarred remnant looking piggish.

She stalked up to Cimozjen and looked him up and down, her tongue held between her teeth. "Just what in Khyber's curses do you think that is?" she asked, jerking her thumb toward the warforged.

"Fighter," said Cimozjen, inclining his head at his companion.

"Fight her?" yelled the woman. "Aundair dares, bastard progeny of Cannith!" She stepped back and drew her sword, and within an eyeblink the warforged began sweeping his battle-axe into an attack position.

"No!" yelled Cimozjen. He jumped between the two of them, one hand held out to the Aundairian, the other raised toward Fighter's face. The warforged surged forward, trying to push through the paladin to get to his target. Cimozjen's feet stumbled, but he managed to retain his balance. Desperate to save blood from being wrongly shed, and despite the fear of receiving an Aundairian sword in his kidney, he reached up and grabbed Fighter's wrists as the construct started his attack.

The powerful arms of the warforged drove the aging Karrn to his knees, but Cimozjen's resistance robbed the attack of all its momentum.

"Stop!" grunted the paladin through clenched teeth, but Fighter took no heed. He swung his torso to the left, and then raised one foot, planted it on Cimozjen's chest, and shoved him away. He took a wide, sweeping wind-up with his battle-axe, and raised it high as he stepped toward the supine warrior.

A flash of insight told Cimozjen that Fighter's paranoid reflexes were in complete control. Two years of being attacked at unexpected times had honed him to react violently to any threat, and

Cimozjen had just become such a threat. So, as Fighter stepped over him and his deadly axe began arcing down, Cimozjen did nothing but look the warforged in the eye and pray the Host for deliverance.

But Fighter's blade came, not slowing in the slightest.

❋ ❋ ❋ ❋ ❋ ❋ ❋

Minrah shrieked as Fighter's battle-axe struck. She shut her eyes and heard a heavy crack as the double-bitted blade impacted.

"Fighter, no!" cried Minrah. She pried one eye open to see the axe buried in the floor just above Cimozjen's shoulders, where his head would normally be. Just beyond—and safely out of weapon's reach—the Aundairian woman waved her sword uncertainly.

"Dear gods, no—" Minrah gasped, averting her eyes.

"Stop!" bellowed Cimozjen.

Minrah gaped at the man. He propped himself up on one elbow, his head making an appearance from where it had been hidden behind Fighter's huge axe blade.

Cimozjen swiveled his head to face the other way, and pointed at the Aundairian. "Stop!"

"I am stopped now," said Fighter. "I could not cease earlier, only divert the angle of my weapon."

"I meant her," said Cimozjen as he rose. His limbs trembled as he took his feet. "His name, fair woman, is 'Fighter.' That's what he is, and that's who he is." He ran one hand through his hair and took a very deep breath. "Although when viewed in the light of these past few moments, I am inclined to think that it is not a very good name. I apologize most deeply and humbly that you misunderstood me." He held one hand up to examine its quivering fingers.

The woman sneered. "I'm not afraid of that travesty."

Cimozjen hung his head briefly, and then looked at the woman again. "I am not asking you to be afraid of him. I am asking that you leave him be. So if you would please grant me that, I would be most appreciative, for I suddenly find myself in need of a stiff drink." He ran one trembling finger along his ear and drew it back to find it adorned with a small blossom of blood.

One of the woman's associates walked up to her and put his hands on her shoulders. "Let it go, Jolieni. He wasn't involved." He looked up to Cimozjen. "My thanks for your ease, stranger. I trust you'll not hold this against her. She lost one of her friends to a 'forged just last—"

"That and a whole bag of—" shouted someone from across the common room.

"Shut your bung!" snapped Jolieni, raising her sword at the heckler. Nonetheless, she allowed her friend to lead her back to her chair and accepted a new tankard of drink. And although she drank, she did not take her eyes off Fighter.

Cimozjen spotted Minrah sitting at the bar, and walked over to join her, Fighter at his heels watching the crowd very carefully.

"Nice place," said Cimozjen, wiping spilled ale from the seat of a stool before he sat. He clenched and unclenched his trembling hands.

Fighter stood with his back to the bar, his axe at the ready.

"Don't ever do that to me again," said Minrah, her voice fraught with emotion.

"Do what?"

"Get your head cut off. I thought you were dead."

Cimozjen chuckled, and it came out much higher pitched than normal. "I have no intention of leaving this mortal plane at someone else's behest, make no mistake." He looked to the barkeep and raised two fingers together.

The barkeep noted his gesture, nodded and slid him a mug of strong ale. Cimozjen took a long pull and asked, "Whatever made you choose to meet here? It hardly seems to be your style."

"I'd heard of it, but never been here before," said Minrah. "It's the only place along the docks that the river elves avoid. I figured any place that rough would be a good place to start looking for folks heartless enough to watch horrid giant dogs or oversized bugs eat prisoners, or else for someone who might know something about such fights." She looked over her shoulder. "And it is rough. I got challenged to a fight almost as soon as I walked in, and once they figured out I wasn't a fighter—not that that's a hard deduction—I had to promise the proprietor special favors to earn the right to stay here."

"Special favors," said Cimozjen.

"I know what you're thinking, but he's not nearly as enticing as you are, Cimmer." She took a swig of her drink. "Besides, I didn't mention anything specific. I was rather thinking of favoring him with a free mention in my next story. Get the name of this fine establishment known across Khorvaire." She snickered. "I don't think he actually expects me to warm his bed, but I guess he thinks it's a worthy enough gamble. Nothing to lose and me to gain. And he isn't making me pay for my drinks. Maybe he hopes each glass betters his chances. Foolish man."

They sat in silence for a while.

"Do you think they'll attack me again?" asked Fighter.

"Them? No," said Cimozjen, not even looking up from his ale. "I think you showed them enough of your power and skill that they'll leave you alone. At least for now. Speaking of which, we need a better name for you. What did you say you heard? You know, for your name?"

"Fferrrrdurrrahnn!" said Fighter. It sounded a little like he was roaring into a mug through clenched teeth.

"Hmm," said Minrah. "Maybe it's a number, like the one that was tattooed into the, um, that . . . thing's ear."

"Four . . . something?" said Cimozjen. "I suppose Four is as good a name as any, and a lot less likely to get us into fights."

"So I am to respond to the name 'Four' from now on?"

"That's right."

"I accept that. It is as good a label as the other."

"Well, if you come up with a name you like better, Forty, let us know," said Minrah.

"Which is it, then? Four or Forty?"

"Forty-four forty or more!" giggled Minrah.

Cimozjen shook his head. "Just indulge her; it's easier that way."

"Damned right," said Minrah as she took another sip of her drink. They sat in silence a while longer. "Still, it was an interesting conversation, wasn't it?"

"Maybe your ear caught more than mine," said Cimozjen. He dipped his finger in the ale and traced it along his ear. It stung. "I had other things on my mind."

"She's a veteran, that's clear," said Minrah.

"Aye," agreed Cimozjen. "I heard that chant more times than I care to think about."

"And she's grieving. That means the wound to her heart is fresh, unlike the wound to her nose."

"Why is she not bleeding, then, or dead?" asked Four.

"Let us finish, Forty-boy, all right? That man said she lost her friend 'just last' something. Could be just last night or just last week. But just last month sounds awkward. And she'd have had some time to get her grief under control."

"But she's been drinking." said Cimozjen.

"But her stance was assured and speech was clear. She is not drunk," said Minrah. "At least not yet. Then whoever that was across the way said she lost a bag of something, as well. So which do you think she lost? A bag of sweet rolls, a bag of night linens, or a bag of coin?"

"Coin," said Cimozjen.

"Right. And whatever coin she lost was hers. If it were someone else's, say if she'd been guarding some lord's wealth, I guarantee that the loss would likely not sting her as badly as it does." Minrah took a sip, then ordered a pickle from the proprietor. "So we have this. A warforged killed her friend recently. That alone I'd dismiss as the result of a duel or perhaps criminal activity. But she lost a bag of coin or something equally valuable at the same time.

"Now a formal duel is not something people of her station would take to. She looks like she'd just take her grievances out on the spot, and fight to the death. And by the looks of her and her friends, if she'd been robbed, she'd be spouting for revenge, and they'd all be dragging the alleys for the culprit. But she's acting powerless. So it makes me wonder. What if it were an arranged fight, like her friend was a prisoner, too? Did she wager all her wealth on her friend, hoping to buy him free, and lose everything all at once? For that matter, say the other was her betrothed or her husband. She might have lost her entire future in one foolish wager.

"Mark my words, Cimozjen, I was right. This is the place to be. I bet this is all knotted together, and she's a part of it, however peripherally. We just have to ingratiate ourselves here, and start to belong."

Cimozjen glanced over at Four, then down at his armband, hidden beneath the sleeve of his tunic. "That may not be as easy as it sounds."

❦ ❦ ❦ ❦ ❦ ❦ ❦

"Time to wake up, Cimmer," said a musical voice.

Cimozjen's eyes fluttered open, and he groaned with relief. "My, but the sun is bright," he said.

"It's overcast."

"It's beautiful," he said, rubbing his face. He groaned. "All night long I dreamed of falling axe blades chopping me up. It's nice to wake up in one piece." He rose, walked to the window, opened it, and leaned out to take a breath of autumn air.

"I'm glad you're happy," said Minrah.

"I am happy that I did not sever your head," said Four.

"Enough," said Cimozjen. "Believe me, I have already thought enough of such things for this day." He stood and stretched his back. "Very well, here we are. We've found a tavern that might be a source of information. But until it opens, what's on the top of your minds?"

"I'd like to catch up on the *Chronicle*," said Minrah, "see if there's anything that might help me. I mean, us. Plus I want to see if we can find Torval's shoemaker."

"And I want to find out what happened to Torval from the last time I saw him during the War."

After a short pause, Four said, "I want no one to attack me."

Minrah laughed, and Cimozjen turned from the window and said, "That, friend Four, is why I like you."

● ● ● ● ● ● ●

The streets were still wet from the previous night's rain, and much of the urban grit had been washed from the cobbles. The autumn air was brisk, though not quite so cold that plumes of breath could be seen.

Cimozjen, Minrah, and Four stood at the foot of the stairs that led to the Military Bureau, a massive edifice between Castle Fairhold and Chalice Center that served as the central administration for the crown's army. The main double doors sat nestled between thick fluted columns, which in turn supported a huge marble slab that bore the army's crest, as well as beautiful bas-relief sculptures of half-nude Aundairian heroes from the past, all carved in the flowing, elegant style for which Aundair had become famous during the Golden Age of Galifar.

Minrah pointed as they climbed the steps. "Hoy, look at that hunk of humanity up there," she said. "Is your torso muscled as tough as that? He looks about your age."

"My muscles are not quite so hard as his," said Cimozjen. "His are made of pure marble. Mine just look that way." He winked as he and Four pulled open the massive doors of the bureau.

Minrah walked in, her laughter echoing in the large wood-paneled main hall of the building. Cimozjen entered and walked over to one of the doors, waving off the offer of assistance from a greeter.

"You seem to know your way around here," said Minrah.

"I have seen it often enough."

He led the three of them to a smaller office off the main hall and ushered them in. Inside a room brightly lit by everbright lanterns, several clerks worked at desks. Fine wood shelving covered the entire back wall, parsed by dividers into small slots. Carefully marked scrolls filled each of the cubbyholes. Two open arches on the back wall led to more scroll storage.

Cimozjen stood in front of one clerk, an older man missing the majority of his left forearm. With his stump he held a scroll open, and with his other hand he copied the contents onto a new scroll. Cimozjen noted that he was copying only those names that had been crossed out.

The clerk neither looked up nor stopped writing on the scroll he had before him. "Do you have an appointment?" he asked as the nib of his pen scratched across the parchment.

"Please forgive me, but I do not. I wish to inquire after the disposition of foreign prisoners."

The clerk grumped. "You'll need an appointment."

"If you please, I have just last night arrived from Karrnath, seeking to discover the fate of one of our soldiers. I have reason to believe that he was taken prisoner, and I hope to find out what happened to him after that."

"Mm. I see. And you're not going to go away until I help you, are you?"

"If I lived closer," said Cimozjen, "I would make an appointment and await my turn. But it's rather a long trip back home."

The clerk growled. He set down his quill and began laboriously rolling up his reference scroll with his one good hand. "Fine. I'll see if we have anything. But chances are like as not we don't. Our records on our own troops aren't even complete, and the records of enemy prisoners even less so."

"I only ask that you do what you can," said Cimozjen. "Shall I roll up this other scroll for you?"

"No, the ink must dry. But I appreciate the offer." He finished rolling up the scroll, then, with his one hand, expertly tied it shut with a length of twine. "So. This soldier of yours. When would this soldier have been captured?"

"Most likely around the tenth of Lharvion, 976," said Cimozjen, "at the edge of Scions Sound east of Silvercliff Castle."

The clerk froze. "The Iron Band?"

"Yes."

The clerk nodded and looked up for the first time. His face was as rough as a weather-beaten chunk of granite. "Relative of yours?"

Cimozjen cleared his throat, hoping that he wasn't about to dash any chance he had of cooperation by claiming membership in an elite enemy unit. "Comrade," he said.

A flurry of emotions crossed the man's hard face. He set down the pen and pushed his stool back from his desk. Then he rose slowly to his feet, stood fierce and erect, and saluted.

Twenty-two years earlier:

"I don't understand," said Kraavel. "How could the regent do this to us?"

"Easily," answered Cimozjen, staring at the embers of the campfire. "All it takes is a wave of her hand. Her word is law."

"But why would she?" persisted Kraavel, his voice filled with righteous indignation mixed with just enough of a whine that his tone fell short of outright treason.

"Regent Moranna is not required to explain herself to us," said Cimozjen. "In fact, for her to do so would imply that she needs our approval, and that runs counter to her divine mandate. Moranna speaks with the authority of King Kaius III until he comes of age, and if she no longer desires the service of the Iron Band, she is not required to have it."

The mood in the camp was grim, for the Karrnathi army was in full retreat, the Aundairians hot on their heels. The order had come from on high that the Iron Band, among other units, was to be disbanded, and its members were to report immediately to the High Command at Korth for debriefing and reassignment. With three units suddenly swept from his command, General Kraal had been forced to abort his campaign to take Daskaran and turn back to the east. The Iron Band had retreated through the Silver Wood toward Scions Sound, where a temporary bridge had been erected to span the channel between Karrnath and Aundair. The supporting invasion fleet and their troops had been recalled to Karrlakton. The Aundairians, seeing the threat of invasion suddenly evaporate, had sallied forth against the smaller overland force and harried the Karrnathi army in their flight.

The Karrns were camped near the cliffs at the edge of Scions Sound, near the Aundairian edge of the ruins of the White Arch Bridge. An architectural wonder, the White Arch Bridge had reached across the treacherous waters of the channel until its midsection had been destroyed some years earlier. To support the overland forces of the invasion, the Karrnathi military had erected a rope bridge to span the gap, a swaying lifeline several miles long and just wide enough to pass a laden horse, held secure by enchantments emplaced and sustained by the magewrights at either end. When pitching camp for the night, the general had deployed the Iron Band nearest the span to ensure that he abided by the regent's edict to return them to Korth. This way, they could cross the bridge first and be sent on to the capital at first light.

Cimozjen turned away to see his best friend pacing back and forth in the darkness, barely visible in the light of the embers of the campfire. "Speak your mind, Torval," he said.

Torval executed a sharp about-face and kept on stomping his path.

"Torval!"

The bullish man rounded on Cimozjen. "What do you think is on my mind, Mozji?" he yelled. "This is inexcusable!"

"Watch your tongue, Torval," warned Kraavel. " 'Tis treason to—"

"To what?" bellowed Torval. "To proclaim my loyalty to my king and country? To swear that I serve Karrnath with every dram of blood in my body? To boast that we are the finest unit in the whole of Khorvaire? To bemoan the cruel gods that the regent throws away the strongest weapon in the young king's arsenal? What have we done to deserve this?" He raised his arms to the sky. *"Nothing!"*

Several people started to talk, but Torval held his hands out to each side, silencing them. He stalked over to Cimozjen. "And do you know what will happen on the morrow, Mozji? We will be marched across the bridge at dawn, sent first like women and children. The Aundairians will attack, and, if you've heard the same dispatches I have, with overwhelming numbers. They'll break the line, they'll push through to the bridge, and they'll kill the magewrights and cut the ropes. Everyone on the bridge will die, Mozji, falling to their death without ever facing Aundairian iron, and everyone trapped on this side will be slaughtered like pigs." His voice reached a crescendo. "And where will we be?" He stabbed the air. "Over there, *watching! Them! Die!"*

"Torval—" began Cimozjen.

"Shut your beerhole!" yelled Torval, his spittle flying in Cimozjen's face, his hands gesticulating wildly. "You know what I think? I think if the regent wants us to disperse, we do it our way! I say we stand between the Aundairians and the army. You know we could hold them off, all day long and the next, if need be, until the rest of the army is safe! Let us be dispersed on the steel of our foes, dying like men instead of running like rats! And if Moranna wants us sent back to Korth, let our bloodied armbands be returned to the foot of the throne as a testament to the world that no one, not even the voice of Kaius, can sunder the Iron Band!"

There was utter silence in the camp, the warriors' hearts caught between the proud bombast of Torval's words and the rebellion they represented.

Cimozjen looked at his friend, who quivered with rage. "Torval," he said, "you speak of defying a royal mandate." He turned to the surrounding soldiers. "You heard his words, every one of you, did you not?"

The gathered soldiers murmured and dropped their eyes.

Cimozjen began to walk around the campfire as he spoke, his words evenly paced and full of gravity as he glared at the other members of the Iron Band. "Let every one of you understand that this, disobeying the command of the king, this is the very definition of high treason, and every single one who follows Torval down this path will be burned at the stake like a criminal upon their return to Karrnath."

His small circle led him back to face Torval.

"Mozji," said Torval, his voice almost at a whisper. "You are the best of us, but even—"

Cimozjen turned and raised his voice. "But since I'll *die* before I yield even a yard of sod to those muck-eating Aundairians, I do not give a damn what awaits me back home! I say the Iron Band shall make its last stand *here*, right here and right now, in this forsaken land! Let us give not only our blood and our bones, but even our sacred honor in the cause of our country, and let the rest of the army carry our legend back to the king! I will let no one break my vows and take my courage!"

He grabbed Torval's arm and raised it with his own. "Who stands with us?"

The answering roar carried like thunder.

Chapter
Fifteen

Brothers in Arms
Mol, the 23rd day of Sypheros, 998

You know of the Iron Band?" asked Minrah.

"I was there," said the clerk. "Gods-cursedest most beautiful and horrible thing I ever saw. We tried all day to break you boys. I—" He caught his breath and wiped his eye with the heel of his hand. "They pulled us out for a rest, and then threw us back in again." He looked down as he twitched the stump of his arm. "At the end I couldn't hardly even hold my shield up, and you boys, you hadn't had any rest the whole gods-cursed day. And you—you taunted us!" He wiped his other eye with the back of his wrist and stood without speaking for several long moments. "Before we went in again, I told the men next to me, 'Boys,' I said, 'them there is as real of soldiers as you'll ever see in this life or the next, and curse us all for bein' the ones to kill 'em.' " He sniffed wetly. "That was my last battle. And I thank the Host that it were a real one, you know, a real fight against real soldiers. Could've been a lot worse, you know, like fighting those gods-cursed Eldeen druids and getting shot one day all alone in the woods when you're just off watering the weeds. I'm thankful I earned my discharge with honor."

Cimozjen scowled. "You were fortunate," he said huskily.

158

He reached out to shake Cimozjen's hand. "Yes, I was. And I'm glad to know that someone made it through, truly I am. You boys did the Great Sword's own job there. I swear you did. So let's see what we can find for you. Happy to help, I am. Anything I can do for one of you boys." He turned and went into one of the back rooms, muttering to himself, "Gods-cursedest thing I ever saw."

Four took a step closer to Cimozjen. "I do not understand," he said. "During the War he was trying to kill you, and now he acts as your friend."

Cimozjen chewed his lip. "It's rather hard to describe, Four, unless you've served as a soldier."

"I have fought. Many times."

"Your style of fighting was different. It was an arranged duel—more of a brawl, really—where you and the other person were trying to kill each other. In war, one tries to defeat the other side, and there is no personal animosity between the actual soldiers. You can respect your foe, even admire him, and still fight to defeat him. That's a part of what is called chivalry. You fight with honor and courage, but the fight is about the battle, not the other person."

"Chivalry?" said Minrah. "I never saw any."

"It is true, there were undisciplined troops, levees and the like, and more of them took the field as the War dragged on. I dare say the only way their officers could get them to fight was to make them hate the other side, rather than fighting out of a sense of duty or honor. And that's where the shameful things started to happen, like massacring villages and killing the wounded. That is purely and simply wrong—it is evil, in fact—but the more it happened, the more it progressed from the levees to the soldiers to the leaders." He snorted. "Sometimes I wonder if that's why the kings and queens finally agreed to the peace. They feared that if captured, they'd no longer get the respect that nobles are due."

"Your answer does not make me understand any better," said Four.

Cimozjen took a deep breath as he considered this. "Your

style of fighting, what you did, was to win that fight against that person. You had to kill or be killed. If you won, you lived, and if you lost, you died. War is different. For one side, say those of us in Karrnath, for us to win, we had no need to eliminate every other living thing on the continent. Likewise, as soldiers our goal was for our side to win, and not necessarily for us as individuals to survive. Sometimes, by sacrificing his own life, a soldier helps his side to win. And that, Four, is a part of what honor is, to sacrifice one's selfish needs to serve the needs of others."

"Sounds like stupidity to me," said Minrah. "If you're dead, how can you help them later?"

"Sometimes one can accomplish more in one's death than one could in the rest of one's life," said Cimozjen.

Minrah snorted, but said no more as the one-handed clerk returned to the desk carrying several scrolls tucked under his crippled arm.

"These should have what you're looking for," he said.

Together he and Cimozjen looked over the parchments, locating the quartermaster's master list of manifests of the campaign in question. Then the clerk unrolled a second scroll, and they poured over the lists on it. "Here you are," he said at last, pointing triumphantly. "List of those captured."

"We're looking for Torval Ellinger, of Irontown."

"Here he is," said the clerk, stabbing the parchment. "Ellinger, T., head, F."

"Head?" asked Minrah. "F?"

"Heads wounds, you see a lot of them among prisoners," said the clerk. "Someone gets himself whacked hard and either knocked out cold or driven too confused to fight, then they get rounded up after the battle is won. The other common wound you see is when they take a debilitating wound that doesn't cause them to bleed to death. Maybe an arrow in the joint of their shoulder, say, or . . ." he gestured vaguely with his ruined arm. "The F means he was rated as fit. H means they needed a healer, C means crippled and, well, on down the line."

"I'm surprised they even bothered to list them by name," said Minrah. "I'd have expected something like, 'Twenty-seven accursed usurpers, slain where they stood.'"

The clerk and Cimozjen both gave the young elf withering looks. "Fair and equitable treatment of prisoners of civil strife, regardless of station, is required by the Code of Galifar," said the clerk.

"Allow me to apologize on her behalf, friend," said Cimozjen. "She knows not of what she speaks."

"Cimmer—" she huffed.

"Silence!" snapped Cimozjen.

"No apology is necessary," the clerk said to Cimozjen. "I long since learned to ignore the darts and arrows of those who never fought." He unrolled the scroll further. "Aha. A detail was assigned to march the able-bodied prisoners to the Daskaran command."

He returned to the back room for a moment and came out with a large ledger. He flipped through pages and pages of entries before finding the right date.

"Good. Here it says that he was given over to the stewardship of the Custodians at Areksul. Looks like they put him on a timbering gang. That's good work, you know. Beats being sent to the mines or digging graves."

"So at the end of the War," asked Cimozjen, "what happened to those in his timbering gang?"

"I don't know, my friend. You'd have to ask the Custodians."

"And they are . . .?"

"The Custodians of the Fire and Forge. They're an order of Monks of who revere Onatar. Early on in the war they agreed to handle guarding prisoners and putting them to useful work. It actually worked out for the best for probably everyone. The monks refused to fight, and soldiers hate to stand guard, so the order got to avoid combat, and our boys got to do what they were trained to do. And the prisoners, well, I'd rather be guarded by the friars than a group of bored recruits keen for notching their blades."

"Very well," said Cimozjen. "I thank you for your time."

The clerk smiled, a jagged affair that forced its way across his weather-beaten face. "It was an honor. Dol Dorn bless on your search."

"Too late for that," muttered Minrah as they left the office.

⊕ ⊕ ⊕ ⊕ ⊕ ⊕ ⊕

From the Military Bureau, the group traveled to the main plaza of the University of Wyrnarn, where Minrah intended to catch herself up on the contents of the *Korranberg Chronicle* that had been published over the last week.

They moved easily through the streets until Cimozjen caught an aroma wafting on the cool autumn breeze. "Ohh," he murmured, "sweet cremfels. Oh, how I've missed that!" His nose led them to a side street, where a cook leaned out a small window with heavy shutters and watched the street traffic going by.

Cimozjen placed a copper piece on the windowsill. "Cremfels still a crown?" he asked.

"Indeed they are," said the matronly cook with a smile. "Will you be having cinnamon or preserves on that?"

"Just butter, please." He watched as the woman pocketed the coin, then ladled batter into a cast-iron fry pan. A new burst of the sweetbread scent washed over him. "It's been two years, Four. Two years since I've had the pleasure of these." He swallowed hungrily.

"What of your wife?" asked Four. "Do you not miss her as you miss your sweet cremfel?"

"I do indeed. I have searched across Karrnath for her since the War ended, and spent not a lick of time thinking of this. Yet the cremfel is here, and she is not, so I can at least allow myself this small indulgence."

"I'm here," said Minrah, "but I don't see a lot of indulging coming my way."

Cimozjen shook his head. "I swore a vow, that for good and for ill, we would remain together."

"And yet you are not together," said Four. "Have you not broken your vow?"

"In truth, we are together, Four, because I treasure her memory in my heart and behave in all ways as if she were right here with me." He glanced pointedly at Minrah. "She swore the same, and wherever she is, she is doing the same. Thus her memory holds my hand, and mine hers."

Minrah snorted. "You must not want to hold her all that much, if you haven't found her in two whole years."

Cimozjen gave her another meaningful look. "Before the end of the Last War, I had not set foot on Karrnathi soil for twenty years. During a war, a lot can change in twenty years. Just look at Cyre. I searched our homestead. I searched the neighboring villages. I've—" His voice broke and he took a moment to recover. "That's why I was in Korth, you know. Do you know how long it takes to search a city of eighty-odd thousand for a single woman?"

"So you don't even know if she's still alive, and you still won't bunk me?" asked Minrah with a touch of a whine.

"Host, I pray she is alive. The alternative is too terrible to contemplate. Until I know otherwise, my vows remain unchanged." He licked the last of the melted butter from his fingers, then placed another crown on the sill. "One more, please," he said. "I'll indulge myself a bit more as we walk to the University."

❧ ❧ ❧ ❧ ❧ ❧ ❧

"Did you find anything interesting?" asked Cimozjen as Minrah exited the University's chronicle repository.

"Yes, I did," she said with a smile. "No one has yet claimed the gnomes' reward."

"Why would someone want gnomes as a reward?" asked Four.

"No, silly, the gnomes are *giving* a reward. A few months ago, they spread the word that they wanted information on some sort of Aundairian monastic secret society or something. And I intend to collect it. Oh," she added, handing Cimozjen a folded broadsheet, "I grabbed this for you. Some Brelish hero saved his dwarf servant and a bunch of orphans from a nasty beast in the Cogs of Sharn. Thought you might like to read it. Like you, he looks to be one of those dashing save-the-children hero types that chroniclers love. Kind of an old story, but if you've been spending all your time chasing your wife, you might have missed it. Thought it might keep your spirits up as we go about our business."

They spent the rest of the afternoon trying to track down the Custodians of the Fire and Forge, only to find out that their monastery was hundreds of miles to the southwest, between Passage and Arcanix. For the five-score years of struggle that had been the Last War, the order had produced simple but utilitarian weapons for battle, and to meet their needs, they'd had groups of monks deployed across the country gathering materials. During this time, they had all but lost their ability to produce the masterful goods that reflected their spiritual growth. With the advent of peace, many of the monks had returned to their monastery, and were only too happy to begin restoring the art in their handicraft to its antebellum quality.

The information was rather dispiriting. "We'll have to shelve a trip to the monastery," said Cimozjen. He scratched the back of his head. "For now, in any event. It's probably a good day's ride by rail to Passage, another day to visit the order, and another back, and I'll not waste three days when I feel like we might be close to our goal right here in Fairhaven."

"Agreed," said Four. "This is the place. The air is right."

Cimozjen turned his head. "Do you mean it smells right?"

"I do not understand."

"No," said Cimozjen, "I guess you'd not, after all. Well, it's getting dark. Shall we head back to the Flagons?"

Minrah grinned. "I was hoping you'd say that."

They arrived at the Dragon's Flagons earlier than most. Four stood, holding his battle-axe at the ready if not quite—thanks to Minrah's supplications—in a position of being ready to strike. In consideration of this, Cimozjen and Minrah took seats at the end of the long bar, where Four could have his back to the wall and be as far removed from the public view as was possible.

They supped on boiled meat with an onion-wine sauce and baked potatoes with coarsely diced chives and butter, but unlike the previous night, the tavern was largely empty until shortly after ten bells, when a group of four rough and rowdy customers burst through the door.

"Wham! Whack! That was great!" said the first. "But that shield . . . can you believe that shield? I've never seen anything that black. On my sword, I don't think anything could touch him!"

"Serves me right for betting against him," said the second. "You're buying tonight. Again. I don't know how much more of this I can handle."

"Now that sounds interesting," said Minrah. She watched the group as one of them bought a round of drinks and ordered some food, then followed them as they made their way to a table.

Their talk silenced as she drew close and pulled up a chair. "Hoy there," she said with her most winning smile. "Do you big strong men mind if I just take this one little chair?"

One of them looked her up and down, a potential sneer of contempt shading his features, just waiting to erupt on the surface of his expression. He turned to his friends. "Bar whore," he said.

"I most certainly am not!" snapped Minrah. "I just thought you were rather—"

"Don't see them around here much," said the man's friend.

"That's because there's no reason to treat them as well as we treated the camp followers," said a third. "At least they'd wash the blood out of your clothes."

"And sew up the rips," agreed the second.

"If I'm intruding—" said Minrah.

"I'd say that those that eavesdropped on private conversations of the Regent's Halberdiers would have to be a spy, wouldn't you agree?"

The third nodded. "Aye, preparing to renew the war for one of the other kingdoms, I'd say."

"Spies are killed, aren't they?" asked the second. "Drawn and quartered?"

"We ain't got horses," said the fourth, the biggest of the group, with a heavy gravelly voice to match. "We'd have to do it ourselves, after we were done, of course."

By the time he had finished his sentence, Minrah was already making her way back to Cimozjen, her nose in the air and trying to carry herself in such a manner that she did not appear to be afraid. She reclaimed her stool, safely sited between Cimozjen and Four's ever-watchful glare. "They're not my type," she said.

Cimozjen tried to suppress a laugh, and failed.

"They're tight as a flock of cannibal stirges," she said, "all feeding on each other. They might as well be one foul man with eight armpits."

"Brothers in arms," Cimozjen said. "No woman can draw them apart."

"You mean they're . . . ?"

Cimozjen shook his head. "No, that's not what I mean."

"But then—"

"Forget it. You'll never understand."

They looked up as another assortment of rowdies entered the tavern, grinning widely. They talked quietly amongst each other, their conversation punctuated by shoves, punches, and head butts.

"This looks like it may turn out to be an interesting night," said Cimozjen.

"But why now?" asked Minrah as the door opened yet again to admit another half dozen locals. "Why suddenly now?" She leaned forward to get a better look around Cimozjen. "Hoy there," she said in quiet but urgent tone. "That's the one from the ship. The commander, what's his name? Pomindras. That's him, Cimozjen, isn't that him?"

Cimozjen turned to look, hiding his face by pretending to take a deep draw on his drink. "Sovereigns, it is," said Cimozjen. "Those wide-set eyes are a giveaway. Now we know that some of them are here in town. Do you see him, Four?"

"Yes. Do you wish me to kill him?"

"No, do not kill him."

"But that is the goal of our adventure, is it not?"

"I want justice, not revenge," said Cimozjen. "Also, if we kill him now, we probably lose any chance of running down any of the others who might be involved in this. Given how he was let free, we have to assume Rophis and maybe some of the other crew could be involved, too. Just keep an eye on him for us, will you? All things considered, you'll be the least conspicuous doing it."

Minrah adjusted herself so that her back faced the room. "Let's just cross our fingers that he doesn't recognize us."

❧ ❧ ❧ ❧ ❧ ❧ ❧

Minrah and Cimozjen nursed their drinks and resisted the agonizing urge to turn around and check up on their quarry. Finally, Minrah turned and sat sideways at the bar, leaning back against Four.

Cimozjen glanced at her, and saw that her eyes were elsewhere. "Careful, Minrah," said Cimozjen. "Let him not catch you staring."

"I'm looking at his reflection in the window over there," said Minrah, her face aimed at her companion, but her eyes turned away. "He'll think I'm talking to you. He's speaking with those stirges. He's handing them something, leaning over their table. Hoy, and look who just walked in."

"Who?" asked Cimozjen, not wanting to turn around.

Minrah never answered his question, although she didn't need to. Cimozjen heard someone stomp across the floor and slap the bar so hard he felt the tremor at the other end. "Bottle of Orla-un brandy, barkeep," snarled an unmistakably bitter voice.

"But that'll cost your whole take," said a second, gentler voice.

"I don't care," came the clipped answer. Then her voice rose to a shout. "Death beware, for Aundair dares!"

Cimozjen turned around. The woman was demanding attention, and it would be conspicuous not to give it to her. He turned slowly on his stool to see the angry, truncated face of Jolieni snarling across the tavern floor.

"The unholy Cannith beast is dead," she said, fist in the air. "Vengeance is mine."

The proprietor set a bottle of brandy on the bar beside her and walked down the bar to fetch some glassware. She slid her hand across the wood and let fly a gold coin, sending it scooting across the stained wood to the bartender. She grabbed the brandy by the neck, ignoring his offer of glasses. She started to stalk across the floor to her table, but her eye caught Four standing in the corner with Cimozjen and Minrah. Slowly she raised the hand holding the brandy, to point menacingly at Four.

"You're lucky it wasn't you," she called. She held the gesture and didn't break eye contact with Four until after she had seated herself and taken her first pull at the bottle.

Minrah turned away. "She's awfully excited for winning a bet over a warforged."

"It did kill her friend," said Cimozjen, "and she is a woman of great anger. Still . . . ." As Cimozjen tore his gaze away from her, he saw Pomindras saunter out of the establishment. "And there he goes."

"Who?" asked Minrah.

"Pomindras."

"Should we follow him?" asked Four.

"No. If we do, we increase the chance he'll recognize us. We dare not make him nervy, or we might be facing down a whole tavern full of his friends."

Within a half bell of the commander's departure, the Dragon's Flagons was galloping full tilt, every table packed with rowdy and violent people, most of whom Cimozjen noted bore the marks of those who'd fought in the War.

As the number of Aundairian veterans grew, the quantity of alcohol remaining in the establishment shrank and the atmosphere became more and more unstable. Minrah edged closer to Cimozjen, intimidated by the raucous noise and coarse language. For his part, Cimozjen tried to ignore the vulnerable feminine bundle pressed to his side so he could keep his attention on the potential threat of everyone else in the tavern. Beside him, Four raised the battle-axe slowly to an ever more threatening position.

"This is what it sounded like when someone tried to kill me," he said. "Only now I might not be able to tell when it starts. That was an advantage my home provided me. It opened whenever trouble arrived."

"Let's get ourselves out of here," said Cimozjen, praying for an opportunity. And, shortly afterwards, one came. Jolieni's friend, the one who had calmed her down from the fight only the night before, came to the bar to order another small cask of wine.

"Evening," said Cimozjen over the noise of the crowd and showing a smile that said he was genuinely pleased to see the man.

The Aundairian looked at him. "It is a good evening indeed," he said. "For you?"

"Always!" Cimozjen took a chug from his glass and leaned closer. "Tell me, I'm trying to remember this Aundairian drinking song. I'm hoping that you know it."

"Most of the songs I know have to do with barmaids," said the Aundairian.

"The words run something like: Fine wine, drink mine till I'm blind . . . but I'm unable to recall what might come next," said Cimozjen, straining his voice against the background noise.

The man's face brightened immediately. "Hey, yeah, that's a fun one!" he started sing the song at a full, throaty shout.

"Fine wine,
Drink mine till I'm blind!
This cask is my task and I'll not waste my time!"

Cimozjen joined in and the two belted out the rest of the verse together, very loudly.

> *"From the tap to the dregs*
> *Keep on rolling the kegs*
> *For this soldier he begs for more wine!"*

As Cimozjen had hoped, the song quickly caught fire in the general atmosphere of inebriation, and when the chorus had taken hold of the collective attention, he and his companions exited the tavern into the chill autumn air and made their way by moonlight back to their boardinghouse.

Chapter
Sixteen

The morning dawned steely gray and dismal, with heavy clouds overhead dimming the light. After Minrah and Cimozjen had broken their fast, the three companions took an easy walk to the University of Wyrnarn to read the latest in the *Korranberg Chronicle*.

Afterwards, they worked their way from the upscale Distant Exchange markets to the merchants in Chalice Center and around the University, and then through the questionable Whiteroof ward all the way to the area known as Eastbank, asking tanners, leatherworkers, toolmakers, and traders of all sorts if they were familiar with the markings on Torval's shoe.

"It's not a good sign that no one knows it," said Minrah. "That means his mark isn't famous, and therefore neither is the cobbler."

"In that case, we should look in the poorer sections of town," said Cimozjen.

"We are, in case you hadn't noticed," said Minrah, casting a look at the houses and shacks jammed together on the streets, and the makeshift tents that filled the alleys.

"Of course I noticed. It was my way of pointing out to you that we are undertaking the right approach at this time."

Minrah sighed in despair. "This might all be a rabid goblin chase, anyways. The cobbler might have been an apprentice that couldn't earn enough, and went on to another line of work."

"Pray that is not the case," said Cimozjen.

"Not likely, I will," said Minrah. "The gods'd kill the cobbler off just to spite me."

"The Host bless you, miss, if'n you please," came a tremulous voice from a nearby alley.

Minrah stopped and sneered at the beggar. "Pardon me?"

"The Host bless you," the old man said, holding out a weather-beaten hat at the end of a skinny and underclad arm.

"Were you eavesdropping on our conversation?" she asked.

"No, miss, I just only asked for the Host to bless you, that's all. I need me a new coat for the winter, afore it gets too cold, if'n you please, miss."

"Well, you can keep your prayers and see if the gods' blessings keep you warm this winter," said Minrah. "See how much they care for your piety."

Cimozjen stepped forward, fishing in his coin pouch. He took a pair of copper crowns but did not drop them in the man's hat. Rather he kneeled, set the man's hat back on his head and placed the coins in his open palm. "Winter's coming soon, good man."

"Yes it is. Host bless you."

"Still, you've a decent enough hat and"—Cimozjen paused to draw in a sharp breath—"and you have a pair of good shoes."

"They'll do with the right stockings, yes they will, Host bless you."

Cimozjen stood up, hands clasped behind his back. "Minrah, you agree that these are excellent shoes, right?"

"Mm. Beggars' shoes."

"Minrah," said Cimozjen. "Look at these shoes. Are. They. Not. Excellent."

Minrah rolled her eyes and moped her way over to the beggar.

Her eyes went wide, but only for a moment. "Yes, I guess I'd have to say they are," she said, then turned and walked back to stand near Four, her back to Cimozjen.

"Tell me, old man," said Cimozjen, kneeling down. He pulled a sovereign from his coin pouch and toyed with it idly. "Where did you get those shoes?"

"Outside of town, if you please. There's a farmer's family, the Valleaus, and his second son, he's good with the leather, you see. Sometimes I do work for them, bring them things, or carry something into town for them, and one day he gave me these. He said he din't need them."

Cimozjen moved his hand toward the coin pouch, ready to drop the coin back in. "And how might I find the Valleau farm?"

"Easy, sir, biggest farm out the Galifar Gate, it is. Follow the road down the river for about two hours 'til you get to the burned stump of a giant oak tree. That marks the corner of his property, and you'll see a rock wall. Take that road inland for about a half mile to the gate. It's got two whitewashed pieces of wood on it that form a V when it's closed. The path to the right gets to their house."

Cimozjen flipped the coin to the old man. "Our thanks, old man. Stay warm this winter. And the Sovereign Host bless you, too."

The man clutched the coin in both hands, rocking back and forth in glee. "They already have," he said, "They already have!"

Cimozjen walked back over to Minrah and Four. He looked at each of them in turn and smiled with quiet satisfaction.

"Host bless you ag'in!" called the old man after him.

Cimozjen nodded at Minrah.

"Coincidence!" she snapped, and stomped off in the direction of the Dragon's Flagons.

❋ ❋ ❋ ❋ ❋ ❋ ❋

On their third day of visiting the Flagons, they finally convinced Four to sit, but they could not get him to let go of his battle-axe. They sat at a corner table of the tavern, with Four occupying the seat right in the corner. Cimozjen sat to the right of the warforged, keeping a good eye on the tavern, while Minrah sat across from them, comfortable that they would keep her safe.

"We're not going to have an easy time getting to know these people if we keep sitting in the corner with an axe-carrying warrior," said Minrah.

"That is true," said Cimozjen, "but at least he no longer comes across as actively looking for a fight. And if you and I were to sit in the middle of the room away from him . . . well, I'd rather we stuck close by each other. Especially here."

They picked at the bones of half of a poorly cooked chicken. Not only did it have no seasoning, but the skin was burnt and the deepest meat barely cooked.

"It appears that I am impeding your progress," said Four. "You should have talked to that person you recognized yesterday, instead of staying with me."

"Pomindras from the *Silver Cygnet?*" said Cimozjen. "No, I still think it would not have been a good idea."

"Absolutely," said Minrah. "Whatever is going on with all this, he knows about it. He's probably hoping we're still ignorant. If we'd shown that we remembered him from the ship, he might abandon any pretense of secrecy and take more direct measures to preserve his little diversion, and that would be bad for us."

"Because he'd want to put me back in my home."

"That's right," said Cimozjen.

"So instead, we watch and wait," added Minrah. "If he comes back tonight, maybe we can find out what they're up to."

Four continued to scan the crowd, as was a habit for him. "But he has not returned," he said.

"Not yet, no," said Cimozjen. "But the night is not over. He may return. Or better yet, some other people from the ship, who'd be less inclined to recognize us. So pray that we may yet spot someone through whom we can unravel this knot."

"And cross your fingers," said Minrah.

"What good would that do?" asked Four. "It would lessen the strength of my grip on my weapon."

Minrah patted his arm. "That's right, my warforged warrior Four, it would. I'll take care of the finger crossing for all of us, right?"

"Ho there," said Cimozjen. "That friend of Jolieni just walked in, and he's coming over."

"Here?" asked Minrah.

"That's right. Walked in, took a look around, and here he is."

The Aundairian walked up, grasped the empty chair at the table, turned it around, and sat, draping his arms across the backrest. "Evening," he said. He extended a hand to Cimozjen. "They call me Boniam."

"Cimozjen Hellekanus, at your service," he said, gripping the proffered hand firmly.

Boniam turned to Minrah. "And you are . . .?"

"Minrah the Drover," she said. "Pleased to meet you . . . in a more congenial manner." She batted her eyes.

"Well. Yes. That's uh, that's quite a warforged you have there, Hellekanus," said Boniam.

"Friend Boniam," said Cimozjen, "he is not mine. He is his own person, per the Accords of Thronehold."

Boniam shook his head as if to clear it. "Of course. I am sorry. Fifteen years in the army gave me some bad habits regarding the 'forged, I'm afraid. And what is your name?" he asked, extending one hand. "Fighter, was it?"

"Yes, it was," said the construct without moving.

"Be kind, and shake the man's hand," said Minrah. "It's a greeting custom among equals. And introduce yourself."

Four looked at her, then at Boniam's hand. He took one hand off his axe, reached out, and shook. "My name now is Four. It may change again if it is shown to be troublesome."

Boniam clenched his jaw, and his face slowly turned red. "Four," he grunted. "Right. You can let go now." As soon as his hand was freed, Boniam exhaled explosively. He took it back to his lap and massaged and flexed it. "That's quite a grip."

"It is my hand," said Four. "It grips things."

"Yes, yes it does." He nodded to signal the serving girl, and ordered a loaf of bread, some butter and salt, and a round of drinks. He gave his hand one final spidery flex and leaned on the chair's backrest again. "So tell me, what brought you three here?"

"The lightning rail," said Four.

Boniam laughed. "That's not what I meant. What I mean to ask is: this is hardly a place that people seek out, especially fair young women. *Why* are you here?"

"To—" started Four, but Minrah put her hand over his mouth and he silenced himself.

"We're not exactly sure, I suppose," said Cimozjen. "The standard diversions of the city, they . . . they're just lacking. At least here you see real life being played out. So I guess you could say we're here looking for excitement. Visceral excitement."

The serving girl arrived with the bread and drinks, placing her tray on the table and distributing the food. Boniam reached for his leather pouch, but Cimozjen blithely tossed a few crowns on the serving girl's tray.

"Allow me, Boniam," he said, "in gratitude for your company this evening."

Boniam picked up one of the coins. "Now what's this?" he said.

"It's from Karrnath," said Cimozjen.

Boniam tossed it back onto the tray. "Things are so different now that the war's ended. It used to be that all you saw were the Galifar-style coins, but now we've got our own style, you Karrns have your own . . ." he shook his head.

"I assume that once no one could claim the throne, every nation chose to assert its own independence," said Cimozjen.

"So you're from Karrnath, then?"

Cimozjen nodded.

"He is," said Minrah. "I'm from Cragwar originally, but I travel a lot."

"Then well met, Hellekanus of Karrnath and the Drover from Cragwar," said Boniam. He raised his drink. "Here's to the peace, that we can spill each other's beer instead of blood."

"I'll rise to that toast," said Cimozjen, clanking their tankards and taking a pull. He set his drink down. "Still . . ."

Boniam laughed. "I know what you mean," he said. "You can't get soldiering out of the blood, can you?" He shook his head. "I still wake up an hour before dawn, every morning. And I've got my armor and my sword, but no commanders to follow and no enemies to slay. I miss it, especially the big battles. Those were something." He sighed. "Still, I have a good life."

He took a piece of bread, buttered and salted it, and took a big bite. "So," he said, pushing the bread into his cheek. "You came in on the rail? Did you take the long way around?"

"No," said Cimozjen, settling into his chair. He considered for half a breath, then added, "We came across the Sound." He drummed his fingers on the table, then, as Boniam was about to ask another question, he interjected one of his own. "How's your friend doing? Jolieni, I believe her name was."

"Jolieni," said Boniam. "It's hard to tell. Either she's wrestling her sadness into submission, or she's just hiding it in her breast. Killien was the only person she truly talked to about matters of her heart. And it was so sudden, they couldn't do anything . . ." He took another bite of his bread and chewed it slowly, staring at the tabletop. "We've taken her in, of course, but . . . well, I think that's just as hard for her. She's pretty fierce about doing things her own way, and . . . well, it's probably her part to tell you the whole of it. But there it is. Thank you for asking after her."

He looked up. "Listen, things start at eight bells, so I have to go. But I just wanted to take a little time to find you folks, get to know you a bit, and to say thank you once more for not allowing that whole situation to get out of control the other night. She was letting her temper get the better of her, and I am thankful that you chose the peaceable path, this time, at least. A fight in a tavern is not the right way to do things." He shoved the last of his piece of bread in his mouth and stood. "Well, I have to go meet some people, but thank you for breaking bread with me." He started to salute, thought better of it, and waved in farewell as he turned and left.

The three of them watched him depart.

"That was odd," said Cimozjen. "He seemed genuinely friendly, yet . . ."

"Yet much of what he said, and more importantly what he asked, seemed forced," said Minrah.

Four stirred. "Do you mean someone was forcing him to talk, as I was forced to fight?"

"No," said Minrah, "it was more like he had someone's list in his head."

"That must have hurt," said Four.

Chapter
SEVENTEEN

Another Coincidence
Zol, the 24th day of Sypheros, 998

At the tenth bell, they decided to call it an evening. Outside the Flagons, the moons shone brightly in a clear sky, and a mist lurked upon the waters of the Aundair River, glowing eerily in the moons' light.

Breath misting in the air—with the exception of Four, who had no need to breathe—the trio wended their way in tired silence through the nighttime streets to their lodgings. The only noise they made was the steady tread of their footsteps and the regular clack of Cimozjen's metal-shod staff on the cobbles.

"I admit that I have not spent much time outside of my home," said Four as they made their way through Whiteroof, "but I thought that the mist usually congregated at the river. How is it that some has made its way up here?"

Minrah looked around. Mist swirled around the everbright lanterns that cast scattered patches of light down the street they walked. "That is odd," she said. She stopped. "More than that, the air is still. The fog shouldn't be swirling like that."

Cimozjen gripped his walking staff all the tighter. "Trouble's brewing."

"Around us?" asked Minrah.

"Probably."

"We should leave the area quickly," said Four, turning in a circle to scout the street. The mist grew ever thicker, encroaching upon their vision and smoothly wiping away distant noises.

"No," said Cimozjen. "If someone is stalking us, they've set up an ambush. Running will send us into their arms."

"By which you mean weapons," said Four.

"Not intentionally, but yes," said Cimozjen. "And if this strange mist is meant for someone else, we may cause ourselves grief by stumbling into the midst of it."

Minrah grabbed Cimozjen's arm and pulled herself close, glancing at every shadow she could. "So what do we do?"

"Best to keep our heads and stay here. The fog hides us just as much as anyone else."

"Keeping our heads is a sound goal," said Four.

"Also, Minrah," said Cimozjen, "let go of my arm so I can swing a weapon."

"Cimmerrr . . ."

He shrugged her off none too gently. "Finally, we choose our ground." He pointed with his staff. "Fighter—"

"Four."

"Apologies. Let's move over there. It looks a sturdy storefront, and it has no wisplight. With our backs to the wall, they'll be unable to surround us, and we'll be less visible in the dark."

The trio quickly moved toward the wall, a rough-hewn but solid affair that boasted a large painted sign that none took the time to read. Cimozjen drew his sword in his right hand, holding his staff in the left to work as a shield. Minrah pressed close behind Cimozjen, to his annoyance, for her huddling forced him to adjust his balance to compensate. Four stood at Cimozjen's left shoulder, his battle-axe at the ready.

"Keep an eye looking up, Minrah," whispered Cimozjen.

"How thick do you think this fog will get?"

"I'm sure I have no idea," said Cimozjen.

They waited, ready. The unnatural fog slowly erased the world around them until all that lingered was a swath of misty cobbled street some thirty feet across. Whatever had caused the effect seemed to content itself, and if the fog grew thicker from that point, it did not do so visibly.

"Do you hear anything?" Minrah asked.

"No," said the warforged. "Nothing other than your breathing." They waited.

A low, chuckling laugh rolled out of the mist, and a shadowy form paced up to the very edge of visibility, a gray shadow against the lantern-lit fog. "So you noticed, did you? I told him that his spell wasn't subtle enough." His accent was Aundairian, his tone cocky.

He paced closer, slowly resolving into a three-dimensional person. He carried a dark shield on one arm, but no weapon in his free hand. Five more vague shadows appeared on both sides of the trio, cutting off any potential escape.

"But we noticed you, too," said the man. "And now it's time for you to pay the full fare for everyone on the *Silver Cygnet*." He snapped his fingers. "Let's go, people."

Brandishing weapons, the five shapes closed on their victims, two next to the speaker at Cimozjen's right, three from Four's left.

Cimozjen planted the butt of his staff next to the outside edge of his left foot, and held his sword raised in his right hand as it if were also holding the haft of his staff. He trusted the darkness to make the juxtaposition of his weapons look like a heavy-bladed pole arm. He noted with no small relief that the attackers each carried different weapons, and that they moved as individuals, not as a unit. He doubted very much that Four and he would be able to withstand a concerted attack by veteran troopers, but a group of hooligans, even if they were seasoned fighters, could be defeated in detail.

"Get your body away from mine if you want both of them to stay in one piece," Cimozjen growled to Minrah. He heard her whimper, but thankfully she did pull away from him.

He smiled when he saw that one of the thugs that accompanied the mysterious enemy swung a flail—back and forth, not in a gentle circle. Cimozjen stepped closer to him and again planted the butt of his staff against his foot. He turned his torso away slightly, angling the staff. "Do you think you know how to handle that thing, son?" he asked.

The man rattled the chains. "You watch as I tear you apart."

"Are you sure you said that right?" asked Cimozjen. "Your face looks like you've hit yourself more often than your target."

The flail-wielding man twitched, but held his composure.

Cimozjen added, "But maybe it's just that you've been having trouble learning to eat with a fork."

The other shadowy attacker snickered at the jibe, and the combination of insult and laughter proved too much for the affronted man. He yelled and charged, swinging his flail in a powerful two-handed blow.

Cimozjen steeled his resolve.

❃ ❃ ❃ ❁ ❃ ❃ ❃

Four wondered how best to handle the situation. In all the times the world had broken open his home, he had never had more than one person attack him at once. This was a new experience.

He had, somewhere in the foundation of his consciousness, some basic predispositions and concepts, but he had never explored these—he'd spent his time in his home in a quiet contented emptiness of no-thought—let alone put them to use.

On the other hand, it was a pleasant change of pace to have an upcoming combat unleashed slowly, giving him time to identify the attackers and begin to formulate a plan. It was far better than being surrounded by a hundred screaming people and wondering where the threat was.

He faced three attackers. He had to assume that the one named Hellekanus would handle the other two. The one named Minrah was of no immediate tactical use, save possibly to throw in the path of an oncoming attacker.

As they closed on him, one of the three held back. Four could tell that it was because there was not enough space for all three to attack at once, and for that, he was grateful to Cimozjen and his tactical expertise. All of Four's previous fights had been in the open, and he would not have thought of using a building as a defensive weapon.

Four decided the best approach would be to focus on the destruction of the attackers one at a time. That way, if they tried to use clever team tactics to divide his attacks and defenses, he would not be fooled. The danger that this focused approach required was a risk that he considered acceptable. He knew he would be repaired.

The one on the left was the size and shape of a human, and held a spear. He closed the gap, crouched low, spear at the ready. The one on the right was small like a halfling. He wielded a short sword, and he hung back a bit, perhaps fearful of the superior reach of Four's weapon. The spearman would come first. The swordling would make the follow-through attack. That conclusion made Four's priorities obvious.

Four held his weapon high, keeping his eye on the one with the spear. The human would likely try to get a quick jab in before the warforged's powerful arms could bring his heavy axe-head to bear. Four knew that the spearman could jab quickly and either retreat or roll to one side. The inertia of Four's heavier weapon meant that he would miss an overhand counterattack two thirds of the time.

Four primed himself to strike back.

The spearman lunged, pushing off with his rear leg and thrusting with his arms. Even as he closed, Four thrust with the haft of his battle-axe, a straight-on shot to the face. Inertia was much easier to overcome in a linear fashion than with an arcing swing. The spear plunged through the tightly-strung tendons of Four's torso, severing many of those that helped manipulate his left hip, but Four's counterstroke smote the man at the very top of his cheekbone, and Four heard the bone crack beneath the impact.

Staggered, the man lurched back, left hand rising to his face. He sensed the danger and kept himself low, slashing blindly about with his spear as he backpedaled.

Four cocked his arm and stepped forward, hoisting his battle-axe for a slower but much more powerful centrifugal overhand swing. The blade bit into the back of the man's shoulder, breaking that bone as well. The man hit the ground on the seat of his pants, bent over almost double.

Four stepped to the side and swung the axe.

Minrah wanted to run, but pressed against the storefront there was no place to go. Only her two acquaintances stood between her and the six unknown attackers. She looked at Cimozjen through wincing eyes, her heart caving within her breast. She saw the first attacker take a swing at him, and she gasped, near to a scream— and Cimozjen managed to get his staff in the way of the strike, although the flail's chains wrapped around its haft, and now the two weapons were sorely tangled.

She heard a heavy, meaty thunk. Unable to stop herself, she glanced at Four. One of the attackers sat at the feet of the war-forged, head dangling grotesquely between his knees as blood pumped from the nearly severed neck.

She screamed. Her hands covered her face and her fingers obscured her eyes, but for a long, horrid moment she could not tear her gaze away from the decapitation.

She didn't fully hide her face until the halfling stepped in behind Four and plunged a short sword into the soft, organic wrappings of his back.

Cimozjen glanced at his staff. Held high and braced against the outside of his foot, it had held against the attack. The flail's spiked heads, whipping around the staff at the end of their chains, had entangled his makeshift shield entirely.

Just as he had hoped. Cimozjen knew a thing or two about fighting with flails.

He yanked his left arm to the outside, pulling the flail, complete with the attacker's hands. The unfortunate man was surprised that his flail had tangled so badly, and as Cimozjen pulled it aside, the attacker instinctively—and foolishly—held his grip, leaving his startled expression with nothing to guard it. With a powerful punch, Cimozjen slammed the pommel of his sword into the man's face. "Inept novice," he mumbled as the man stumbled and fell to the ground.

The leader snapped his fingers again, the sound sharp and crisp against the hazy background of magical fog. "Take him down."

Cimozjen looked over and saw the second of the thugs hesitate and pull back toward the leader. He held a rapier, judging by the silhouette of the weapon against the faintly lit fog.

The rapier waggled up and down. "But I—he's a soldier, and I've just—"

The leader smacked the other across the back of the head. "Then smite him with your magic, dolt. Gods, how you managed to avoid frying what little brain you have is beyond me."

Cimozjen charged.

❦ ❦ ❦ ❦ ❦ ❦ ❦

Four staggered. The arcane currents that maintained his existence eddied and swirled within him. It felt as if his legs and hips were changing shape, and the chaos within him worsened as the halfling twisted the blade, shearing away more of the tendons that held his bone-and-metal frame together.

He heard Cimozjen mutter something as the sound of combat continued to his right, and he knew that Minrah was not created in such a manner that she might provide him aid. He was on his own, and his target was small and behind him, away from the functional threat area dominated by his arms and the blade of his battle-axe.

The sword twisted again, and Four twitched as the flow within him changed once more. After all this time, he thought, I shall fall to an attack from the rear, a strike to the back. His mind echoed the phrase—*strike to the back*. He wished he could do that. In that moment of clarity, he realized that the head of his weapon was double-bitted, front and rear, and it, too, could strike to the back. With a mighty heave, he swung the weapon high in the air, giving it as much momentum as he could. When it reached the apex of its arc, he yanked the hilt forward, snapping the heavy blade into a fast swing.

Four felt the blade of the short sword press deeper into his interior, but he was satisfied with the sensation. The long haft of his battle-axe trembled with the heavy chop as he hit his assailant squarely in the back. The warforged backpedaled, knocking the halfling down with his bulk. The short sword remained stuck in Four's body.

Four turned and stomped on the halfling's neck as hard as he could. He was rewarded with the sound of a wet, pained gag, and he trusted that the halfling would be out of the fight for a while at the minimum. Regrettably, the disruption within his flow caused the warforged to stagger as he tried to recover his feet.

That was when the third attacker's mace hit him squarely on the temple.

* * * * * * *

Sensing that the mage was uncomfortable in martial situations, Cimozjen tossed his staff at him, spinning it through the air, and charged the leader. The leader gave ground quickly, raising his shield for protection while drawing his own weapon.

Cimozjen slashed his sword low, hoping to catch the leader's knee beneath his shield, but the man was too fast, skipping his leg up as Cimozjen's blade passed. Cimozjen lunged forward and thrust, but inexplicably hit nothing as the man raised his shield to block.

"Curse this mist," growled Cimozjen. He thrust again, once more missing both the man and his dark shield.

The leader spun around, keeping his shield toward Cimozjen, and struck a backhand blow at Cimozjen's unprotected right side.

Cimozjen felt the blade bite deep into his flesh, then slice as it was withdrawn from the wound it had just made. The edge of the sword felt hot as it cut into his muscle, and he felt the weave of his tunic being pulled along through the wound like little barbs.

The leader's momentum carried him around to face Cimozjen again, but the veteran soldier charged in hopes of getting a strike in before his foe could raise the shield anew. With a roar he struck a heavy downward chop toward the man's collarbone, but the enemy had anticipated such a move. He came around with his shield raised high, and in that brief moment before impact, Cimozjen saw his face.

Pomindras, the erstwhile commander of the *Silver Cygnet*.

Cimozjen's sword bashed into the man's shield, and at the same time he felt a bolt of electricity course through his body. The impact and jolt nearly caused his sword to drop from his enervated fingers. He cried out in surprise and nausea as the shock trembled in his joints and curdled his stomach.

He stepped back from the leader and lunged hard and fast toward the mage.

❃ ❃ ❃ ❃ ❃ ❃ ❃

Deep within the folds of his criss-crossing tendons, Four felt his neck crack.

His head flopped to the side, resting on his shoulder.

But he didn't fall.

He didn't think he could fight effectively while viewing the world on its side, so Four stepped back from his attacker, who was startled into immobility over the warforged's resilience. Once at a safe distance, Four reached over with his left arm and pulled his head back upright once more. It was unstable but serviceable, and it kept his perspective the way he was used to.

Thus satisfied, he again gripped his battle-axe with both hands and moved toward the mace-wielding foe.

The attacker promptly dropped his weapon and ran into the misty night.

Four turned to Minrah and gestured with one hand in the direction of his retreating foe. "Can they do that?" he asked. "I did not think that was allowed."

❦ ❦ ❦ ❦ ❦ ❦ ❦

Half-blinded by pain, Cimozjen surged forward. The mage stood, slightly hunched, his eyes and mouth forming nearly perfect O's of surprise and fear. Cimozjen ran him through the gut without breaking stride, ramming his broadsword so deep that the hilt slammed into the unmoving wizard's floating rib.

Simultaneously Cimozjen's shoulder struck the man in the breastbone, and the double impact knocked the mage over. He fell, sliding off Cimozjen's weapon. Years of training and practice kicked in, and Cimozjen drew his sword back out of the man as he stepped past him and spun to face the leader again. Turning his head, he saw that the leader was not charging him, so he took an extra vicious strike at the downed mage. The wounded man grunted, but said no more.

Cimozjen readied his sword.

A shadow in the mist, commander Pomindras turned his head back and forth between Cimozjen and Four, then fled into the night.

Cimozjen listened to his footsteps depart, but then the fading sound was suddenly overwhelmed by a gruesome crunch behind him. Cimozjen turned to see Four just pulling his axe out of the sundered body of a halfling. The warforged looked carefully around, turning his entire body instead of just his head. He spotted the first attacker Cimozjen had felled, the flail-wielder with the broken face, and walked over to him, raising his battle-axe.

"Four!" called Cimozjen. "Stop!"

"Why?" asked Four, stopping.

"Because we won," said Cimozjen.

"We did?" came a quiet voice.

"Yes, we did, Minrah," said Cimozjen. "You can get up now."

Keeping his weapon out, he moved toward his companions, scanning the darkness for any new threats. In the nighttime mist, the blood-splashed cobbles looked colorless and rather ordinary. Even the bodies of the fallen were not particularly loathsome when stripped of detail by the haze. The mage lay splayed out on his back, while behind Four two other bodies, one large and one small, lay crumpled. In contrast to the sights, or perhaps because of it, the mist served to enhance the horrid odor of internal organs.

"Um, you have . . . a sword in your back," said Cimozjen.

"Please remove it," said Four. "It is causing me difficulties. My neck is damaged, too."

"Your neck?" asked Cimozjen, withdrawing the blade from Four's organic wrappings. "Do you need attention?"

"I am in functional condition," said Four. "However, we should avoid further combat."

Cimozjen leaned his staff against the wall and ran his fingers along the wound in his side. "I can agree with that," he said. He walked over to the man he'd first struck and looked down at him. He was still alive, his pained breath hissing in and out through his teeth. Cimozjen nudged him with his boot. "Get up."

The man slowly rose, weaving back and forth as he struggled to maintain his balance. He kept his hand held protectively over the left side of his face.

"Who sent you?" asked Cimozjen. "I know your commander, but were you also on the *Silver Cygnet*?"

"What are you talking about?"

"Who are you with? Whom does Pomindras serve?"

The man shook his head.

"Listen," said Cimozjen, "I hold nothing against you. You did as you were told, or perhaps as you were hired to do."

As he spoke, he pulled out his holy talisman from beneath his tunic and gripped it. He said a brief prayer, and it began to glow. The divine light starkly showed the massive bruising that marred the man's face. Murmuring another prayer, Cimozjen reached out with his left hand and gently ran one finger along the edge of the bruising, and the unsettling sound of bone knitting whispered in the quiet of the night. The man gasped at the discomfiting sensation.

"There," said Cimozjen. "It'll still be sore, but it'll not keep you up all night. So. Who sent you?"

"Not likely. If I tell you, they'll kill me."

"Tell me who you're with."

The man sneered. "You have no idea who you're dealing with, do you? We were just going to teach you a little lesson, send you packing back to Karrnath with your hands covering your backside. But now, now you're in real trouble. Pomindras will find you."

"I healed your cheek," said Cimozjen sternly, "and I can retract that service if you have no gratitude for the Host's blessing."

"I'm not afraid of you."

Cimozjen hit him with the hilt of his sword again, a hard blow right where he'd broken the cheek a few moments earlier. The man went down with a cry. Cimozjen hauled the man up by his collar and kneed him hard in the stomach twice, then let him drop again. He hauled him up a third time and pressed the tip of his bloody sword against the man's jugular vein.

"Hoy," whispered Minrah, "Cimmer is boiling over."

"Listen, Aundairian, I'm going to spare your life, and you're going to show me some gratitude. Do you understand?"

The man nodded.

He pressed the sword even more firmly into the man's skin.

"Neither you nor any of your friends is going to attack us again, or I will not be so merciful. Do you understand?"

The man nodded again, more emphatically.

"And you tell your masters that we want the one responsible for the death of Torval Ellinger of the Iron Band. If they turn him over to me, we'll leave. Understand?'

The man nodded once more. "Torval Ellinger."

"It's not good enough, Cimmer," said Minrah. "I know his type. He's a thug. Brave when in control, weak when threatened."

"Do you swear it?" shouted Cimozjen.

"Swear!" said the man. "Yes, I swear, we'll let you be. Torval Ellinger."

"Not enough, Cimozjen," said Minrah. "The instant he's away from your sword, he'll be plotting to kill us—and with more people. You have to kill him."

"He swore. By the soldier's code—"

"He lied, Cimmer. He's no soldier. You can't trust those like him. My folks, they did, and—! Just do it, Cimmer."

Cimozjen released his grip on the man's clothes and took a step back, lowering his sword. "I'll not kill a defenseless man, Minrah."

"You have to!"

"No," said Cimozjen. "It's not right."

"He knows you won't. That's why he'll swear anything to get you to let him leave. Cimozjen, you have to kill him!"

"I can not."

Four stepped forward and swung, cleaving the man's skull where he stood.

"I can," he said.

Chapter
Eighteen

Idyllic, Not Peaceful
Zol, the 24th day of Sypheros, 998

Cimozjen stared at the warforged, aghast. "What was that for?"

"Minrah said it had to be done, and you said you could not do it."

"But there was no reason to kill him!"

"Yes, there was," said Minrah, who nonetheless shielded her eyes from the carnage. "People like that are like rabid rats. You can't let a single one of them get away. If you do, they only—"

"One of them did get away, Minrah," said Cimozjen. "Pomindras? Commander of the *Silver Cygnet*? Perhaps you remember meeting him once or twice. He ran off when he saw he was the last one standing."

"So did the third one I faced," said Four. "If I had known that fleeing was an option, I would have tried it once or twice during my battles. It is probably better that I did not know, for I did win all of my fights."

"See?" said Cimozjen. "Two of the six already ran off! Here I had a chance to send a message back to them, but no, you had to get bloody handed! Not even you—you left it to him," he added, jerking a thumb at Four.

"I'd rather be bloody handed than a pristine snob who can't do what needs to be done! I swear, Cimmer, you'd let a troll eat your legs if it were using proper table manners!"

Cimozjen rolled his jaw for a moment, then wiped his sword on the cloak of one of the fallen and grabbed his staff. "Clean your axe, Four. Let's move."

He led them on their way, and after a short block or two, they left the zone where the magical fog held sway. Seeing only one or two other civilians in the distance, Cimozjen sheathed his sword.

"I tell you the truth, your perception is fundamentally flawed, Minrah," he said. "You see my oaths as chains. You think they restrict me from doing things that I would otherwise normally do. Now I can understand that to a point. Even the name 'oathbound' brings to mind the trappings of slavery. But my oaths are not a fetter around my limbs, nor a yoke upon my neck. My oaths protect me, uphold me, and assist me to prevail. They are not a noose. Rather they are the straps that hold the armor of virtuous ideals securely in place, protecting my heart, my mind, and my soul. They are the firmly embedded nails that hold me together. They keep me upright, defend me against doing that which is indefensible, and they shield me from shame and self-loathing. Just like armor halts the blade that one fails to deflect, so do my vows halt me from the evils I might perpetrate when my guard is down.

"In short, Minrah, any warrior's fury can get the better of him in the midst of battle. My oaths bind my highest ideals to me so that in the midst of rage or self-pity or bitter vengeance, I, unlike a certain other person, do not end up with my undergarments around my ankles."

Minrah clucked her tongue. "Are you insinuating something?"

"I have no need to."

"You'd better strap your lips, Cimmer."

After a pause, Cimozjen nodded. "That was uncivil of me, and for that, I apologize."

Minrah giggled. "Besides," she said, waggling her eyebrows, "dropping my straps is my best weapon."

Cimozjen shook his head and sighed. "You are a very beautiful young woman, Minrah, intelligent and energetic. So sad it is that when the day of your wedding comes, you'll have nothing special left to offer your husband."

"I'm special."

"Your own actions speak otherwise of you."

"I'm not going to get married, anyway," said Minrah. "And at this rate, you'll ever get me under the sheets."

"On that we are agreed," said Cimozjen, disappointed in spite of his better judgment.

"Ah. An agreement," said Four. "Now that you are done with the requisite arguing, I have a question. When does the man come to repair me?"

The other two stopped. "What?" said Minrah.

"The man. When does he come to repair me? As I said earlier, I have a damaged neck and several severed linkages within my torso."

"There's no one who does that for you now, my friend," said Cimozjen. "Come morning, though, we can find someone."

"Why does he not find me? He always has every other time I have been damaged."

Cimozjen gave him a friendly clap on the shoulder. "That's part of being free, my friend. You get to take care of yourself."

"That's great!"

Minrah laughed. "I don't much think so," she said. "Life was a lot easier when my parents took care of me. I had hardly a care in the world."

"I meant 'great' as in vast and powerful, because this state of being free impacts the entirety of my future existence and requires that I attend to my preservation and restoration in a way that I had not previously been required to do."

Minrah rolled her eyes. "Whatever you say, Four."

❂ ❂ ❂ ❂ ❂ ❂ ❂

In the morning they found an artificer who was able to work on repairing Four. Cimozjen's coin was running a bit low, but the artificer agreed to work in exchange for a promissory note from Cimozjen, drawn against the coffers of the Karrnath Temple of the Oathbound and redeemable from the moneylenders of House Kundarak. Granted, the artificer appended his usual bill with a hefty "runner's fee," but Minrah was nonetheless amazed that someone could garner such valuable services based solely on upon his word. Or, as she put it, "I'm going to have to try that trick."

The artificer expected the work on Four to require the better part of the day, so Cimozjen and Minrah thought it would be a good opportunity for them to go enquire after the Valleau household and see what they might find out with respect to Torval's shoes.

They chanced upon a greengrocer's cart heading out the Galifar Gate to the local farmsteads. It was empty of anything save hay, which the driver had loaded to cushion the more fragile of the produce he intended to buy. With a kind word and a dazzling smile from Minrah, they managed to hitch a ride.

The autumn morning was very crisp and bright. Cimozjen and Minrah sat facing the rear of the wagon, away from the morning sun. The last of the hoarfrost evaporated from the fields around them, coiling wisps of mist demarking the end of its existence. Minrah huddled close to Cimozjen for warmth, and he spread his arm and cloak over her like a protective eagle. The sunshine on Cimozjen's back was warm, but not enough to overcome the chill in the air, and as a result, Minrah kept herself pressed as close against him as possible. At such an intimate distance, the smell of her hair warred with the metallic bite of the nippy fall air, and eventually won.

For a long, quiet time, there was nothing but the rolling of the wheels across the flagstone road and the occasional nicker of the horse, who seemed ill-pleased to be walking into the rising sun. For his part, Cimozjen felt some measure of peace. The trip brought back memories of time spent with his wife decades earlier, when they were both young farmers in the awkward courtship of early adulthood. For a few moments he found himself feeling young again, with an attractive young maiden at his side and a vaguely idyllic future in store, the disorienting love of heady youth stirring within him . . .

Then the whole illusion came crashing down. The woman beside him was hardly a maiden, and her interest in him far lower than the lofty goals of the young Karrn lass of so many years before. Their marriage had been long since consummated, years before the shifting fortunes of the Last War had torn him from his family, his country, and his king. Their promising life together had been destroyed, overrun with slaughter, shame, imprisonment, and the obliteration of an entire nation. He wondered if he would ever see his wife again, if such a thing were even possible anymore.

His conscience told him to loosen his embrace of Minrah, release his grip on her vibrant, feminine, youthful presence . . . and her hold on him. Yet he was traveling to find the man who'd made the shoes in which a good and noble friend had been murdered as a slave, and he appreciated the company. Any company. Especially hers, so unlike anything else he had known since he last saw his wife, though a part of her charisma was the knowledge of how compliant she would be.

His heart knew he should pull away the protective embrace of his arm, but his brain argued against such a measure by using the protective codes of chivalry—he could hardly delight in making the young girl cold this morning—to keep himself in an embrace too intimate for a married man and a young lass who worried his oaths like a terrier with a bone.

Somehow it never crossed his mind that he should just loan her his cloak.

❂ ❂ ❂ ❂ ❂ ❂ ❂

An hour before midday, they passed through the wooden gate and entered the Valleau fields. Cimozjen paced his steps with his pole, and Minrah had one arm slipped through his elbow.

"We're here," said Cimozjen as he shut and barred the wooden gate behind them.

"Let's hope our luck holds," said Minrah.

"Luck has nothing to do with it. Our being here is not the result of coincidence or chance. It was divine intervention."

"Listen, Cimmer, even if the gods were of a mind to tinker with insignificant gnats like us—which they're not—there's no way you could say that for sure."

"Yes, I can and I do. That was undeniably the effect of their influence. It's an indisputable fact."

"Indisputable?" asked Minrah, crossing her arms. "Then prove it to me."

"You did not notice the beggar's shoes," said Cimozjen. "I did. Noticing them was the reward of the Sovereign Host for my devotion. In appreciation for my lifetime of devotion, the Host trained me to have the generosity to give to the needy, the humility to kneel beside them, and the compassion to look after their condition."

"There. You just said you noticed the shoes yourself, because of your habits."

"Habits given me by the holy teachings of the Sovereign Host. Intervention gets no more divine than that."

"You're annoying," said Minrah.

They found the elder Valleau behind his farmhouse, whetting a cleaver while sitting against the bole of an old apple tree. A large decapitated pig hung by its rear legs from a tree branch, blood draining into a bucket that sat next to its vacant head. Minrah averted her eyes, then opted to wait on the other side of the house while Cimozjen questioned him.

"Good morning, fellow farmer," said Cimozjen as he approached. "I hope I am not disturbing anything."

Valleau looked up from his blade. "You don't look like one," he said.

"Pardon me?"

"You don't look like a farmer."

Cimozjen nodded ruefully. "Thirty years of military service will do that to a person. But I grew up on a farm not unlike this one. My father raised goats—fur, cheese, and meat. They're much hardier than cattle."

"And you sound like a Karrn."

"I am. My father's farm was near Vurgenslye, no more than two bow shots from the banks of the Cyre River."

"Then you can leave," Valleau said.

"Farmer Valleau, I came to ask a simple question regarding your second son's handiwork, if you'll allow me."

The farmer spat. "I don't."

"And to pay you for your answers, if that is the only way I can merit your attention."

The farmer said nothing, which Cimozjen took as encouraging. He pulled out the shoe from his haversack, kneeled a respectful distance away from Valleau, and extended his arm, holding the shoe. "Do I understand that this design here is your son's mark?"

The farmer looked at Cimozjen's extended hand, so he withdrew it, pinned a sovereign under his thumb where it held the shoe, and extended it again.

Seeing the flash of silver, one of the farmer's eyebrows rose. He reached out, took the shoe and the coin, and tested the silver with his teeth. Satisfied, he tucked the coin inside his wide leather belt, then he turned the shoe over in his hands. "This is his mark," he said with a nod.

"That's nice work," said Cimozjen. "A very sturdy shoe, yet I should imagine it to be fairly affordable, since it is simple of construction and plain of decoration."

The farmer shrugged.

"I was hoping that you could tell me what sort of people purchase shoes like this," Cimozjen said.

"Why, did you lose your other one?"

"It belonged to a friend of mine," said Cimozjen.

"No surprise," said the farmer. "The Custodians needed shoes for the prisoners. So I had my boy make them."

"So who buys these shoes now?"

The farmer shrugged. "We stopped making them once the War ended," he said. "No more need."

"So all of these shoes your son made, you sold to the Custodians?"

"S'right."

"But how did you handle that? The Custodians had groups all over the country, did they not?"

The farmer sighed deeply and glared at Cimozjen, making it clear that the interruption, silver or no, was taking too much of his time. "The Custodians had an overseer in Fairhaven, at the temples of the Cathedral of the Heavens. Friar Hannel by name. I brought them all there to him. What he did with them afterwards, I couldn't give a pig's eye." He spat again, and resumed honing his cleaver.

Cimozjen withdrew and rose, then tossed another sovereign onto the ground beside Valleau. "I thank you for your time. You have been far more helpful than I could have hoped."

The farmer nodded but didn't look up.

Cimozjen left, idly wondering whether the farmer wanted to see his headless corpse dangling from his tree.

Chapter
NINETEEN

The day was fine, so they ate a light lunch by the banks of the Aundair River before walking back to Fairhaven, and did not return to the city until the middle of the afternoon. They went straight-away to the artificer, to check up on his progress with rebuilding Four.

"I finished repairing him, yes," said the artificer, "but as for how he is, well, you'll have to answer that yourself."

"What do you mean?" asked Minrah. "You haven't . . . done something to him, have you?"

"I don't think so," said the artificer.

"Where is he?" demanded Cimozjen.

The artificer gestured with his thumb. "In the back room. He's barricaded himself in."

"Oh, good," said Minrah.

"Good?" asked the artificer.

"Never mind," said Minrah. "We'll handle it. He's had a rough life . . . or whatever you call what their kind has."

The artificer directed them to the back of his house and pointed to a closed door. "He's in there. It's only maybe five feet wide and eight deep, but he's in there with his axe, and I can't get him to come out."

Minrah walked up to the door and knocked.

"Go away!" came Four's voice, muffled behind the wood. "I am home!"

"Four, my fine 'forged friend, it's me, Minrah."

Silence, then, "You may come in."

"If it's all the same to you, Four, I'd rather you came out. Please?"

"Why?"

"Because I want to see you. And because if I come in, you might think I was breaking into your home to fight you. And if that happened, that would be bad for me."

"That makes sense," said Four. They heard shuffling noises, and after a moment the door opened. Slowly.

"Everything's safe, Four, you can come out," said Minrah. "Cimmer and I are both here."

The warforged cautiously exited the small room.

"We're sorry we left you behind," said Minrah. "We won't do it again."

"That would be   good," said Four.

"So, Four," asked Cimozjen gently, "how do you feel?"

"With my hands."

Minrah giggled, and asked, "Have you been fully repaired?"

Four nodded. "Everything is working normally."

"Hmph," said Cimozjen. "Puts you one up on me."

"I am glad you two are back with me," said Four.

"Come then," said Minrah. "Let's go."

"Are we going back to the Dragon's Flagons?" asked Four.

"No," said Cimozjen. "I think I need to avoid that place for a while. We need to get to the Cathedral. Then we'll go back to our lodgings and plan our next move."

The Cathedral of the Heavens stood proud against the night sky, illuminated from below by a celestial radiance that fell upon it from nowhere, a divine miracle that was supported by hourly devotions from a hundred pious acolytes.

However, the three visitors were not heading for the temple proper, but toward a complex of rooms in the long, pillared building that ringed the temple on three sides, framing the so-called outer courtyard.

The crest of the Custodians of the Fire and Forge stood atop a wrought-iron pillar standing outside a sizable and elegantly carved double door. Next to the door a cut-glass window glowed, a faint but warm light coming from within.

Cimozjen opened the door, ushering Minrah and Four inside before following.

Within, a tonsured silver-haired monk, having weight in far greater abundance than height, sat at a ledger. A candelabrum sat on the table beside him, and a quill pen hovered magically over the paper, awaiting his next instruction. He looked up at the trio, squinting through a monocle that seemed to be thicker than it was wide.

"M-may I help you?" he asked in a coarse voice. He twitched his head around as if he could not see any of them, sending waves shuddering through the flaccid folds of flesh about his neck.

"I certainly hope so, brother. You are called Hannel, are you not? I am Cimozjen Hellekanus of Karrnath, escort of the holy church, bound by oath to the lifelong service of Dol Dorn, Master of Might and Father of Fortitude. I am here to enquire after the services your brotherhood rendered to the crown in the War, if I may."

"Bound by oath, eh?" He gestured Cimozjen closer with two pudgy hands. "Mm. Come here, that I may take a look at you."

Gesturing Minrah and Four to remain, Cimozjen walked over and stood at the table across from the old monk, who leaned forward as far as his frame would allow. He worked his mouth as he studied Hellekanus's face, sending ripples along his sagging jowl with each movement.

"Mm, yes," Hannel said, "yes, you have the aura of the Sovereign Host about you, though only they know what kinds of necromantic heresy some of your Karrn brethren are up to. Of what do you wish to enquire this evening?"

"Brother, I understand that your order had among them those called the Custodians?"

"Yes, we did, mm, we do still, that is. They're an old tradition, seeking to build up the very souls of the fallen and craft them into—mm—beautiful objects. They tend to those criminals that the crown believes could be of menial service to the nation. It's a good work that they do. Mm-hmm. Far better for the country than keeping them in a prison and wasting food on them, like they did in the old days of Galifar. The ones that aren't too dangerous that is. Mm-hmm, thieves, harlots, smugglers, and the like. Make them work. Nothing like ten years mucking the sewer to make someone rethink disobeying the king's own law. Or re-cobbling the street while having children throw rotten food at you all day long. Hah!" Hannel pounded his desk. "I dare say I've helped flagellate a few myself with produce past its prime. Mm."

Cimozjen raised one hand to stop the monk from conversing too far afield. "Truly, the order does a great service to the crown. Now, during the Last War, did the Custodians not also take prisoners from other nations under their care?"

"Yes, we did. Mm, those who were of the right heart about it. By that I mean that some of the prisoners were so hateful that they'd just as soon rip your throat out with their teeth. Mm-hmm. We couldn't do a thing about those ones but throw them into a dungeon pit and toss food down from time to time. But those were mostly the Thranes, what with all their Silver Flame gibberish and talk of holy warfare and bringing the light to Galifar. Those who surrendered honorably were treated honorably."

"Indeed," said Cimozjen. "And I understand that the control of the Custodians was handled through this place?"

"Control?" He shook his head. It looked like a violent squabble between flesh and bone. "No no no no. Communication, my son, that's what we are for. The Keeper of the Divine Wrath must keep oversight over all of his servants, mm-hmm? For the last seven years I have had the honor of serving as the liaison for my order to the Church."

"And before that?"

"Brother Margan was the liaison, mm, Sovereigns rest his soul. I served as his aide and scribe."

"Very good," said Cimozjen. "Tell me then, what happened to the prisoners once the Treaty of Thronehold was signed? How did the brotherhood divest themselves of their charges?"

Hannel leaned back and laced his fingers high upon his pudgy breast. "Queen Aurala commanded that we of the church take every step we could to document how we abided by the terms of the treaty. Every prisoner was to be repatriated. We wanted to ensure we had a clean record, mm, by the Queen's own order."

"Is there a way to tell if a given prisoner was returned to his homeland?"

"Certainly. That is most of what I do these days, you know. I research the missing. Mm, you see, we may not always have kept good track of them while they were on a work detail—there were indeed times when catastrophe or warfare created a disturbance in our duties—but we were very careful when peace came, mm-hmm. Once everyone we had was returned, I've spent my time trying to, mm, clear up any discrepancies."

Cimozjen smiled, a genuine show of hope. "That is wonderful news, for I fear my friend may have slipped through the cracks."

"Indeed? Mm. What can you tell me of him?"

"His name was Torval Ellinger, a soldier of the Iron Band. He was sent to . . . the, um . . ."

"He cut timber at the Areksul garrison," said Minrah.

"Hm? Is someone else there?" asked the friar, flustered.

"I am a friend of Cimozjen's," said Minrah. "I am sorry. I didn't mean to startle you."

"Mm . . . hmm . . . you didn't startle me, young girl, I just didn't see you over there in the shadows. Mm." He looked over his shoulder. "Ourielle, my dear? Would you kindly fetch me the book on the Areksul garrison?"

A creature crawled out from beneath the table at which the monk sat. It seemed a monstrous, misshapen spider at first, with long, thin, fleshy limbs slowly and quietly uncurling, each ending in a delicate, long-fingered hand. Its body was akin to a human's head, naked of hair. The legs sprouted from roughly where the neck should have been. Sparing a brief glance at the visitors, it moved across the floor on its twice-jointed limbs. Its hands made the barest padding noise as they struck the tiles.

"Such a pleasant sound, mm-hmm," said the monk. A tight smile puckered his face. "She likes to be barefoot," he added.

A few minutes later, the creature returned. It moved on three legs, as the fourth held a thin volume in its long-fingered hand, yet its gait was as smooth and noiseless as it had been when it had departed. The creature walked up to the monk and crawled beneath the table once more. The last part of it to be seen was its fourth leg, which deftly placed the book gently by the side of the monk's hand before it, too, disappeared beneath the woodwork.

"Mm. Such a sweet young thing, she is. Always very quiet. Mm." He shooed the quill pen to the side, and it returned obediently to its inkwell. He opened the book and leaned close over the pages, one hand fiddling with his monocle.

The trio waited patiently while the clerk went through the elegant calligraphed pages of the tome. "Here we are, mm-hmm. The list of prisoners from Areksul garrison. Looks like there are a few amendments here already—told you they couldn't write—but . . . hmm . . . yes, there he is. 'Ellinger, Torval, Karrnath, Iron Band.' He was repatriated. Unless, mm, he took ill and died while being sent home."

"Or something of that nature," said Minrah.

"Tell me," said Cimozjen, ignoring her comment, "what exactly was the procedure for repatriating the prisoners?"

"Mm? For the most part, the church arranged for their departure by communicating with those of equal standing in the churches of the other nations. Obviously this was rather more troublesome when dealing with Thrane, mm-hmm, but they finally got enough good sense in their heads to let the remaining faithful handle the exchange, rather than leave it to those myopic sots that overthrew the king."

"Myopic, you say?" asked Minrah.

"Mm?" Hannel glanced up, cast about, and looked in the general direction of Cimozjen. "Yes, mm. Indeed."

"Enough, Minrah," said Cimozjen, raising one hand to cut off any dispute. "Brother, you said 'for the most part.' Was Torval part of that group, or was he handled a different way?"

"Mm. Not him, no," said Hannel, shaking his head and setting his flab to waggling again. "Not according to this annotation. He was to be afforded special treatment."

"Special?"

"The Prelate, Host bless his ailing health, insisted that certain select prisoners be afforded special treatment as suited their station or service."

"Prelate Quardov?" blurted Cimozjen.

"Mm. Yes. His Reverence the High Archdeacon of the Cathedral of the Heavens, Blessed Apostle of the Church of the Sovereign Host, and, mm . . ."

Minrah pulled Cimozjen towards her as Hannel prattled on. "You know him?" asked Minrah quietly.

"Yes, I do," said Cimozjen, lowering his voice so the aging friar couldn't hear. "Or rather, I know of him, and saw him. Near the end of the War he visited the infirmary where I was serving, and asked several pointed questions about me and my disposition, or so one of the hospitalers informed me. He took a long look at me while I worked, and I tell you the truth, there was no warmth in that gaze."

"Sounds like a dangerous man," said Minrah.

"That is the truth of it," said Cimozjen. "As soon as I returned his stare, he averted his eyes and moved on." He scratched his ear and grimaced with the memory. "I thought at the time he was a coward, but a coward with power is a very dangerous man indeed."

Taking a breath, he leaned forward to the monk. "Tell me, Brother Hannel, what was this special dispensation that the Prelate ordered?"

"Mm? Oh, we were to turn the prisoners over to the Holy Escorts Martial."

"Who are they?" asked Minrah.

"They are supposed to stand watch over the property of the church," said Cimozjen, "but really they're more like the personal bodyguard of the highest in the clergy."

"Right you are, mm," said Hannel. "I understand that Escorts Martial delivered the prisoners into the care one of the dragon-marked houses. Mm. Their power and reputation crosses all borders equally, you know, so they'd be best suited to oversee all the prisoners back to their homes. Mm-hmm."

"Which prisoners received this special treatment?"

Hannel leaned back again, drumming his fingers on his pallid cheek. "All of the high-profile ones, you know. We needed to show proper respect, mm. There were plenty. Noble-born commanders and other royalty, of course, and even senior members of the Church of the Silver Flame or the Eldeen druidic sects. Plus we'd taken prisoners from a number of the elite formations. We've had people from the Queen's Swords, the Iron Band, the Green Pantaloons, mm, and the Cyran Storm Cavaliers. We even captured a bone knight once, mm-hmm. I searched the names out personally, you know. I wanted to ensure that all who merited the dispensation were so blessed."

"Which house handled them?"

"Mm?" Hannel shrugged, a gesture that seemed to take far more effort than it was worth. "Once the Escorts Martial turned them over? House Ghallanda, I suppose. Mm. Excellent hospitality would be a good way to see after the well-being of such important personages." He licked his lips and smiled as he patted his stomach.

"You suppose?" pressed Cimozjen. "Why do you not know?"

"Mm? Well, perhaps House Thuranni and their bodyguards might also have been a good choice. Keep them safe amidst an angry crowd."

"Tell me which it was!" snapped Cimozjen.

"Calm down, my son," said Hannel, holding his pudgy hands aloft. "I'm just musing about it. Mm. They didn't tell me about it. The Escorts Martial took care of it all. Our work was done once we delivered the prisoners to them. Mm-hmm. But it didn't really matter which house it was. All that mattered was that they were being taken care of. I just followed his reverence's wishes."

Cimozjen leaned against the table and ran his hands across the back of his neck, rolling his head in annoyance. "You can be sure that that's what a lot of people said at the start of the Last War."

❀ ❀ ❀ ❀ ❀ ❀ ❀

Back in their lodgings, Cimozjen leaned against the window frame and stared out into the night, watching as the last waning sprays of sunset slipped beneath the overhanging clouds. Occasional droplets of rain spattered on the mullioned window, refracting the lights from lanterns and glowstones as the autumn night fell.

"House Ghallanda," muttered Cimozjen. "That makes a malformed sort of sense. They bear the mark of hospitality, and although we hear of the many services they render to highborn nobles, their services would extend as easily to lowborn knaves with money to frivol away."

"The rich poor?" asked Four. "That is incongruous."

"Not at all," said Minrah. "A lot of people profited greatly from the War. The dragonmarked houses, especially. House Deneith supplied mercenaries to all sides, while house Cannith made engines of war like trebuchets and . . . well, you."

"But the dragonmarked houses are all nobles, are they not?" asked Four.

"There were also a lot of smaller families that tried to pull themselves to a higher station," said Minrah. "People who provided weapons, redirected supply trains, or transported goods that were in high demand."

"Arms runners, embezzlers, bandits, and smugglers, in other words," said Cimozjen. "Vagabonds, the lot of them."

"Hoy there, no need to sound so vindictive," said Minrah.

Cimozjen turned his head from the window and looked at her, one questioning eyebrow raised above a piercing gaze.

Minrah dropped her gaze. "Yes, that's how I grew up," she said. "My parents were merchants of Khorvaire, as they put it. They believed in the Galifar kings and the unified kingdom—for that matter, they had lived in it—and so they ignored the borders that the War had drawn." She looked back up, but Cimozjen still had the accusatory gleam in his eye.

"We never sold weapons or anything like that. That wasn't the way Dadda worked. But with the War, sometimes certain commodities could be hard to find, especially the rare and the refined—Zil silk, Karrn paper, Aundairian jewelry and sculpture, Brelish magic, even simple things like black pepper and fragrant oils. There was a lot of money to be made by circumventing the warlords and their so-called borders." She laughed once, a bitter sound tasting of the ashes of Arcadian memories. "I think I've been over most of the continent. Those were good times. Dadda taught me how to read the land, read the weather, and most importantly, read the people.

"And some of the people we dealt with, they were pretty scary. They weren't wandering merchants like us. They were like great spiders in the cities, with a web of spies and hooligans. They were the ones that actually evaded the city watch and the church and the royalty . . . assuming they weren't selling our goods to the royals outright. I never wanted to be one of those carrion crawlers."

She shook her head. "But it's true that some people like that made a lot of money on the War, and if they were of a mind to spend it, they'd be plenty happy to see folks like Four be taken from their cages and made to fight. All the better if it happens in a safe location with Ghallanda food and drink."

Cimozjen looked at the floor and scuffed it with his boot. "House Ghallanda. I'm not sure how we can handle this," he said.

"Look on the bright side," said Minrah. "At least it'll make me a great story."

Chapter
Twenty

Cimozjen breathed deeply and evenly. The faint sound reminded Minrah of the sound of distant surf. She rose from her feigned meditation and went over to kneel next to Four, who sat in a chair in the corner. He held his battle-axe upright, with its hilt resting on the floor.

"Listen, Four," she whispered. "I've been thinking about things, about Jolieni's 'revenge' and all, and I have an idea I want to follow up on. You stay here and watch over Cimmer, will you?"

"You do not wish for me to come with you?"

She shook her head. "I'll be fine. I'm a little worried about him, though. Even though he says he sleeps lightly, I'd be afraid of what may happen if someone from the other night were to sneak in here . . ."

"I would kill them," said Four. "That is what I do."

"And that's just what I need you to keep doing, right?" She smiled. "I'll knock when I get back, so you don't get all excited. Don't forget."

She crept over to their piled belongings and rifled through them until she found a large pouch. It clinked slightly as she picked it up and opened it. She checked its contents, nodded happily, and closed and folded the pouch. She slipped it beneath the waistband of her skirt and quietly left the room.

Huddled within her cloak against the dripping rain, she walked swiftly to the Dragon's Flagons.

It was still open when she arrived, although at that late hour the clientele had thinned to a bare handful. She was relieved to see that Jolieni was still there, burying her hateful demeanor beneath a layer of alcohol.

Minrah ordered a mead and made a point to look at Jolieni whenever the veteran warrior's attention was engaged elsewhere. As soon as Jolieni returned her gaze, Minrah averted her eyes, then waited to begin the cycle again. It only took a few repetitions of the gambit to induce Jolieni to rise from her seat and stalk over to the bar.

"What's your issue?" she demanded.

"Nothing, nothing at all," Minrah said, not looking up from her mead. She drew another swig and waited until Jolieni was just starting to speak again. "I just wanted to see if you were actually as tough as you claim to be. And I think you're probably pretty tough."

Jolieni leaned over, her mouth open but silent as she fought for the right word. She finally squeezed it out. "Probably?"

"I think so, yes," said Minrah nodding.

"That's daring talk from such a little waif of an elf," said Jolieni.

Minrah turned to look at her, eyes surprised. "Is it? I do apologize. That was not my intent. Just trying to be accurate, find out the truth of things. That's all."

Jolieni rested her arms on the bar and leaned closer, her eyes narrowing to dangerous slits. Minrah felt the breath from Jolieni's truncated nose brush her cheek.

"And you think I'm 'probably' tough." Jolieni drew a dagger, long and thin and very sharp, and began cleaning her fingernails. "I think, little one, that you must be quite the fool not to be afraid of me."

"Me?" said Minrah. She laughed. "Of course I'm afraid of you," She tapped her hand intimately on Jolieni's arm. "That is, I would be if I didn't have my friend looking after me."

Jolieni drew back. "You mean that old carthorse you drink with?"

Minrah nodded as she took another drink from her mead. "S'right."

Jolieni laughed, stood, and started to turn away.

Minrah set down her cup, clanking it with just a bit of extra force to ensure Jolieni continued to listen. "He's old all right," she said brightly, "but—pfft!—he was fighting while you were still figuring out the drawstring of the local bumpkin."

Jolieni stiffened then turned her head haughtily back to sneer down at Minrah. "I've killed men half his age and twice his skill," she said.

"I'm sure you have," said Minrah. "Crossbows are like that."

"Crossbows?" flustered Jolieni. "I—"

"Don't fret about it," said Minrah, holding up her hands. "It's not like it matters anyway. The War's over, so if you want to think you could beat him, fine. Doesn't matter to me."

" 'Tis fine to boast so proud and tall / When cow'ring 'hind the ringing wall," said Jolieni.

The Saga of Valiant and Vigilant, isn't that?" said Minrah.

"Well, if your friend hasn't the string to stand by your words . . ."

"You mean a challenge?" asked Minrah. She giggled. "Easy coin." She pulled out Cimozjen's coin pouch, but then tucked it onto her lap again. "But isn't a melee in public proscribed by law here?" She rose and tucked the coin away. "Thank you, no. I'm not going to let you trick me into getting us arrested and pilloried. Won't hear of it."

"We won't," said Jolieni. "There's—"

Minrah covered her ears and began to leave the Flagons. "No, I'm not listening. I don't want to be arrested for this."

"Coward," called Jolieni as Minrah reached the door.

The young elf stiffened, then took a moment to ensure that the smile was completely erased from her face before she turned back around. "Pardon me?"

Jolieni pointed to a stool. "You sit there," she said. "I'll be back within the bell, and we'll see if your carthorse truly has the courage you claim for him." So saying, she swept past Minrah into the night.

❂ ❂ ❂ ❂ ❂ ❂ ❂

Cimozjen stirred as the morning light coaxed him from his sleep. "What's that smell?" he murmured, then he bolted upright. "Fire? Is there a——" He cast about, and his eyes finally settled on Minrah, curled up cross-legged in one of the chairs.

"Since when do you smoke a pipe?" he asked, unnerved.

Minrah giggled. She took a deep draw, then let the smoke out in a series of tiny Os that floated across the room until fading from existence.

"It's a habit I picked up from Dadda. I always smoke a bowl whenever I win."

Cimozjen rubbed his eyes, and coughed. "Win?"

"I have us a trail to the answer to our mystery, and our key into the secret workings of House Ghallanda," she said triumphantly. She pulled a tightly curled piece of parchment from her sleeve. "Take a look at this." She waggled it between her fingers.

Cimozjen grumbled something unintelligible and dragged himself out of bed, wrapping the blanket around him. He waddled over to Minrah, took the parchment, and unrolled it as best he could.

" 'Eighth bell, Corner of Stockade and Braided, gray door in the alley,' " he read.

"It's an invitation," she said with a grin as wide as her ears were long. "All our answers are there."

Cimozjen raised his eyebrows. "I see. And what will we find there?"

"I really haven't a clue." Minrah winked. "My guess is that

we'll get to see what the fights are really like, and hopefully figure out who's behind it, then leave as quickly and quietly as possible. Though you'd likely be best served by bringing your sword and mail, 'cause we're dancing a dangerous line here, and things could get difficult if I'm wrong."

❦ ❦ ❦ ❦ ❦ ❦ ❦

It was well past dark as Cimozjen, Minrah, and Four searched through the fringes of the neighborhood known as the Newall quarter, looking for the address scrawled on their invitation. The rain had eased to a dull drizzle, and both Minrah and Cimozjen huddled in their rain gear. Four remained unfazed by the weather, and carried his battle-axe at the ready.

They finally found their destination—a nondescript door built into the rear of an elegant stone building, an edifice so large that a dozen or more wealthy houses could likely fit inside. A single oil lamp with a reflective dome on top cast light in a circle around the doorway. Heavy drips fell from the building's eaves, splatting in the rain puddles and banging the lamp's protection like a tiny ill-tuned gong.

"Hoy, this is exciting," said Minrah. "And kind of scary."

Cimozjen gave her a quizzical look. "You truly know not what lies in here?"

"Know for a fact? No, I don't. I'm not even completely sure the prisoner fights are held in there, but I think so. I have other suspicions, but they're nothing more than wild flights of fancy. Let's just see what we get into, all right?"

Cimozjen eyed her, then tossed his head in resignation. "And I thought you were merely holding out to be a tease."

She sidled closer as enticingly as she could whilst covered with a rain-drenched cloak. "I may tease the others, Cimmer, but you're the one holding out on me."

Cimozjen ignored the comment, drew a breath, and knocked firmly on the door.

After a few moments a view slit banged open. Two suspicious eyes glared out, darting back and forth between the three. The business end of a crossbow made an appearance as well. It was not pointed directly at them, but it conveyed a threat nonetheless. "What's yer business?" snarled the guard, his voice somewhat muffled by the wooden door.

Cimozjen handed over the paper that Jolieni had given Minrah.

The eyes glanced at the paper, then back at the trio. Then they glared at Four.

"What's that doing here?"

"It's Four," said Cimozjen.

"What?"

"This is Four."

"I don't care what it's for," said the guard. "Get it out of here."

"That's his name," said Cimozjen. "Four."

"I don't care what you named it for," said the guard. Then he added, in a tone that said the concept should be painfully obvious to all, "We don't allow their kind in here. You leave it outside. And away from the door. Makes the other folk nervous."

"I'm sorry, Four," said Minrah.

"Sorry for what?" asked the warforged.

"Sorry that you can't come in."

"I was trying to be funny," said Four. "Is that not what the doorman was doing?"

Minrah sighed. "Sadly, no. And maybe Four isn't such a good name for you after all. But regardless, they won't let you in. You can wait out here, say in that alley across the way there, or you can meet us back at our rooms."

"I will await you here and think about which name might suit me better." He turned to face the disdainful eyes. "Do not fret, doorman, I will remain out of sight."

"Try to stay out of trouble, Four." said Cimozjen.

"Right," added Minrah. "And don't kill anyone who doesn't deserve it."

Four withdrew, and the door opened. Cimozjen entered, followed by Minrah.

"That way," gruffed the guard, pointing to a descending stair. Cimozjen took the stairs, and Minrah started to follow, but the guard stopped her. "You go that way," he said, pointing down a hallway away from the stairs. "We can't have you mingling with them."

Cimozjen stopped and turned. "Pardon me for asking," he said, "but—"

The guard pointed impatiently down the stairwell. "You got questions, git downstairs. They'll tell you everything you need to know." He shoved Minrah toward the hallway as another knock sounded on the door. "Now git moving, girl. I'm busy here."

Thus impelled, Minrah turned to berate the door guard, but curiosity overcame her natural rebellious streak and she did as she had been bidden. The hallway turned a corner and descended a half flight into a common room with several small barred windows along one wall. Behind the windows, Minrah saw several people and a large billboard. No one stood at the windows at the moment, although a scattering of people chatted quietly in clusters about the room. Minrah opted to continue scouting, and slid through the common room to the wider staircase that descended from the other end.

The stairs descended into a large auditorium that seemed as large as the building that rose above. Thick arching pillars served as the roots of the building's foundation. Between the stone pillars, rows of seats overlooked a small clay field, scarred and stained, and sunk ten feet below the closest of the seats. Close to half of the seats were already filled.

"Dark Six," whispered Minrah. "I was more right than I thought."

She ran back up to the common room and dashed over to one of the windows. In the enclosed room behind, a large, lined board proudly displayed—

Match / Challenger / Defender / Odds / Trend

Sepia-colored lines crawled on the board like centipedes, forming and reforming letters and numbers.

There, partway down the list, she saw "Cimozjen Hellekanus" listed. He faced long odds. Seemingly in a trance, Minrah pulled out her pack and began pulling out a long loop of twine.

❦ ❦ ❦ ❦ ❦ ❦ ❦

Cimozjen found himself in a room with as diverse a group of fighters as he could imagine. They ranged in age from arrogant youths too young to have seen action in the War to aged and grizzled veterans who looked like time had treated them far worse than the enemy ever had. The majority of those present seemed to be of his age or up to a decade younger.

Almost every race was present—humans, a dwarf, a smattering of elves, and a sizeable collection of the more aggressive species—and the weapons each carried were as varied as the people themselves. He recognized several faces from the Dragon's Flagons. Many of them talked to each other, boasting, bragging or comparing ideas, making the noise level as loud as that of a packed tavern, and requiring people to raise their voices to communicate.

There was one other door in the room, a large, heavy door eight feet tall and five feet wide. Along the wall beside the door stood a man with a tin whistle and a quillboard and a quartet of solidly built, armored men bearing short pole arms with blunt forked-tipped ends.

Cimozjen turned in a slow circle, trying to get himself oriented, figure out what was going on.

"Haven't seen you before," lisped a hobgoblin, thumping Cimozjen on the shoulder. He had to raise his voice to be heard over the talk. "I'm surprised you don't look more nervous." He held out a hand. "I'm Tholog."

Cimozjen clasped his hand and noted that his grip was steady and strong. "Cimozjen Hellekanus, at your service. Glad to make your acquaintance."

"Who are you up against?"

"I'm sure I do not know," said Cimozjen, still slightly bewildered.

The hobgoblin snuffled, which Cimozjen took to be a laugh. "If you didn't issue a challenge, then it's Traveler's draw for you. Hope it doesn't pair you off with Ripfist or the Black Shield. Either of them, and you're meat."

"Issue a cha—?" Cimozjen narrowed his eyes. "Minrah," he said darkly.

"Minrah? Don't know her. But I'm sure you'll do fine. You've got a warrior's look about you, and you're a lot calmer than most newcomers. Most have a sort of desperate look about them. Or eager, and that's worse."

The noise in the room grew to that of a crashing sea. The hobgoblin looked like he was going to say something else, but just closed his mouth and patted Cimozjen on the shoulder.

The man against the wall consulted his quillboard and raised the whistle to his lips. He piped a clarion and shouted, "Nelter! Let's go!"

A halfling emerged from the corner of the room and swaggered to the door. Tholog nudged Cimozjen and gestured to the small warrior with a smirk. Cimozjen saw that despite the overconfident gait, the halfling was drumming his fingers on his thigh. One of the armored men opened the large door, and even more sound washed in through the opening. It was the sound of cheering. The halfling stalked out the door, and a loud voice boomed out, cutting through the roar and proclaiming, "Nelter Toothrider, challenger!"

The door closed up behind him.

Tholog nudged Cimozjen again, and pointed to a row of benches that ran along the wall that flanked the door. Cimozjen twisted his face to show his lack of understanding, but Tholog walked over and stood on one of the benches, bringing his face up to the level of some small windows set into the wall. Cimozjen followed and climbed up on the bench beside him.

The halfling stood to one side of a beaten-clay arena defensively swinging a tangat, a small, heavy sword with a blade curved marginally less than a scimitar. In his off hand he held a boomerang. His light scale armor glittered in the glow of many lights.

Across the arena, a human stood. He was clad only in worn peasant's garb—a sleeveless tunic, pants that frayed to an end just below his knee, simple leather shoes. He looked like he had scraps of cloth tied about his hands and another scrap tied as a headband. He stood as if awaiting something, swaying slightly, looking about at the crowd. He seemed not to notice Nelter at all.

Tholog nudged Cimozjen, and pointed to the human. "Bad draw," he shouted.

The crowd was roaring, so Cimozjen held up his palms to ask why.

Tholog leaned very close to Cimozjen's ear. "That's Ripfist," he said loudly, enunciating every word carefully. "Need a fast feint, or you die. Watch."

Cimozjen watched as Nelter edged toward the apparently defenseless human along a long arcing path. He waited until his Ripfist had turned his head away, then let fly with his boomerang. The weapon spun in, curving around behind Ripfist, yet as it drew close, the human spun and swatted the weapon aside with his hand. He turned back around, scanning the entire crowd, his brow furrowed in consternation.

"It's strange," yelled Tholog with a grin. "It's like he's always half asleep."

The halfling pulled a small shield from his back and strapped it to his arm. Then he closed in with his shield in front and his tangat concealed behind it. As Nelter drew closer, Ripfist finally seemed to take notice of him, and watched passively as the halfling stepped into striking distance.

Nelter's step grew jittery. Cimozjen saw his feet shuffling with nerves. Then, at once, he pulled his shield aside and thrust with the point of his tangat.

Ripfist reacted with blinding speed. He pushed his hip to the left, barely evading the attack. Then he grabbed Nelter's sword hand with his left hand and twisted it up and over, putting the halfling into a joint lock. With his right, he speared his victim in the esophagus, then released the sword arm.

Choking, Nelter dropped his sword as he reached for his throat. Ripfist smacked his hands on the halfling's ears, rupturing the eardrums, then, with his thumbs, he gouged out the hapless fighter's eyes. With his hands thus firmly gripping both sides of Nelter's skull, he kicked up with his knee and smashed the halfling's nose onto it.

Ripfist shoved Nelter to the ground and vaulted over him, a spinning near-somersault that sent his legs flying through elegant and dangerous arcs. Ripfist quickly spun as if expecting unseen enemies, then grabbed Nelter's chin and head and turned his head completely around, severing the neck.

Nelter flopped face first onto the clay arena. Or, Cimozjen noted, it would have been face first if his head weren't so out of position.

For a moment, a dead silence reigned.

Then the crowd erupted in wild cheering. Ripfist shuffled around, the now-familiar look of consternation on his face.

Tholog slapped Cimozjen across the top of his arm. "Too obvious," he said. "Too slow."

Cimozjen nodded, but not in response to Tholog. He nodded because he finally realized the extent of the fights. As he'd feared, House Ghallanda had never delivered the prisoners commended to their safekeeping. But rather than just pitting prisoners against each other for sport, they allowed headstrong veterans and would-be warriors to challenge them. By keeping the elite warriors from every nation, Ghallanda made the duels a daunting, exciting task, but, with gambling, one that could pay off handsomely if a challenger won.

House Ghallanda, of course, won either way.

Cimozjen studied Ripfist as an unarmed boy gently led the monk from the arena. He looked at his appearance, his rags. He was definitely a prisoner as Torval had been. And while Cimozjen was too late to save his friend, there were still some he could save—Ripfist stood as testimony to that—and he could see to it that whichever members of House Ghallanda had perpetrated this crime against the Code of Galifar faced justice for their heinous deeds.

He smiled coldly. "This should make for a good story, Minrah," he muttered.

He turned away from the window and hopped off the bench. First to the Sentinel Marshals, then to the Crown. And then to post a note to Theyedir once it was all done, thanking him for being an instrumental link in the chain. And finally, back home to the land he loved to resume his search for the woman he loved.

He walked across the room toward the exit. Preoccupied with his thoughts, he abruptly found his way barred by two of the guards, their unusual forked weapons crossed to block the door.

"No one leaves once the arena opens," said the guard. "House laws."

"But I have to—"

"Slop bucket's over there," said the other guard.

"You misunderstand," said Cimozjen, "I was just—"

"No exceptions!" said the first guard, who shoved Cimozjen back into the room.

Cimozjen turned and found that several of the other fighters were looking at him. Then someone grabbed his arm and turned him around. Cimozjen clenched his fist and cocked his arm for a strike, until he saw Tholog looming over him.

"Give it up," the hobgoblin said. He ushered Cimozjen back toward the windows. "The only way out is through the arena. You'll get over your jitters soon enough."

Cimozjen started to say something, but Tholog cut him off. "No one gets to renege on a bet or a challenge. Bad for business. But relax, you'll do fine."

Cimozjen drew a deep breath as the crowd outside applauded

another bloody match. "Six thanks to you, Minrah," he cursed. "But seven thanks to the Host I came fully equipped."

❧ ❧ ❧ ◉ ❧ ❧ ❧

"Cimozjen Hellekanus! Let's go!"

Cimozjen had long since shucked his oilcloth longcoat, folding it neatly and placing it, along with his haversack, in the care of the errand boy. He'd kept his tunic on to conceal his chain mail. His sword was sheathed at his side, and he grabbed his metal-shod staff as he stepped down from the viewing bench. Tholog gave him a friendly punch on the arm and a big lopsided grin.

Grinding his teeth in frustration, Cimozjen presented himself to the man with the whistle. Just as the door began to open, Tholog hustled over. "You drew the Hawk!" he yelled. "Fast, but weak arms!" He made a chopping motion with his hand. "Over the top! Over the top!"

Cimozjen stepped out of the door, and found himself on the clay arena floor. A veritable sea of faces surrounded him, yelling, taunting, fevered for blood.

Twenty-two years earlier:

Cimozjen stared across the battlefield at the Aundairian lines, yelling and banging their shields, massing for a new attack.

Next to him, Torval stirred. "Hey, Mozji," he yelled, whapping Cimozjen on the shoulder. "Take a look at Kraavel's eye!"

Cimozjen stepped around the massive Karrn, staggering slightly from exhaustion. "What about his—wow, that looks painful," he said with an empathetic wince. Kraavel's eyelid puckered inward and a swath of blood and ichors stained his cheek. "What happened?"

"Bah. Six-damned Aundairian arrow took it."

"Do you want me to see if I can do something for it?"

"Naw," said Kraavel with a grimace. "It won't be bothering

me for much longer, anyway." He glanced up at the sun, still a few hours from setting. "I can endure it a while longer."

"But it's your eye," said Cimozjen, concerned.

"Aw, I can see well enough to swing a flail," said Kraavel, "and it looks like we'll not be wanting for targets. Thank you, Mozji, but save your prayers for when it really matters."

Cimozjen gave a long and hearty laugh, a welcome release of stress and tension. "You're a good man, Kraavel, but I think nothing matters any more."

"That's true."

Across the bloody battlefield, the Aundairian army began sounding their horns.

"We'd best get braced," said Torval. "The moorhens are trying to bellows up their courage again."

The Iron Band formed up anew, a thin wall of iron and bone fortified behind a rampart of Aundairian and Karrnathi dead. Their shields shone red, painted with the blood of the fallen, a dire warning to the enemy. They stood tall, defying their exhaustion, and began chicken-calling at the Aundairians—clucks, hoots, and catcalls deprecating the courage of their foes.

Torval glanced at Cimozjen as the Aundairians readied their charge. He grinned. "I suppose there are worse ways to die than standing next to a stinking oat herder like you, Mozji."

"You're a good man, Torval," said Cimozjen. "Truly, it's an honor to spend the rest of my life fighting next to you." He chuckled. "And your chipmunk."

With a yell, the Aundairians charged. The ground shook with their feet, and the air trembled with the noise.

Torval started swinging his flail in preparation. "I'll bet I last longer than you, Mozji," he said.

"Not a goblin's chance," yelled Cimozjen. "We'll fight over it after we kill them all."

Torval grinned. "Fair enough."

Then all was iron, blood, and thunder.

Chapter
Twenty-One

Trapped
Wir, the 25th day of Sypheros, 998

A magically enhanced voice cut through the cheering crowd, "Cimozjen of Karrnath, challenger!"

Cimozjen looked across the arena at his opponent and his heart sank. He wasn't fighting a prisoner, but another warrior. But what did that mean? And what were the rules? Certainly her propensity toward anger and the behavior she'd exhibited in the Dragon's Flagons indicated that she might well fight to the death. He hoped to avoid that. Again he cursed Minrah for failing to give him even the slightest hint of her plan. He vowed he would never blindly trust her again.

He gritted his teeth and looked across the beaten clay as the booming voice spoke once more, saying, "Jolieni the Hawk, five to two!"

Cimozjen steeled himself to the unsavory task, hoping he could get out of this without making a grievous error. He drew his sword, raised it in the Rekkenmark salute, and murmured a quick prayer to Dol Dorn. Holding his staff like a walking stick, he closed in on his opponent.

Jolieni circled, taking elegant sidesteps and holding her slender blade in front of her, drawing small circles. She wore a hauberk of scale mail, and heavily studded leather covered her limbs. Long boots with an iron facing protected her shins, and a skull cap guarded her head, letting her hair flow freely. A disgusted sneer twisted her face beneath her unpleasant nose. Cimozjen was uncertain what exactly she found so repugnant.

Cimozjen closed the gap and struck. Jolieni parried, their swords clashing. Cimozjen struck again and again, testing her defenses and keeping his staff in front to block any counterattacks. After several sparring flurries, it was clear that she was fast, although it also appeared that Tholog might be right about her unimpressive arm strength.

He stepped back and circled, deciding on his best course of action. While an overhand attack was perfectly feasible, it had a greater chance of striking her head and possibly dealing an unintentionally lethal blow, either by cleaving her skullcap or landing at the base of her neck. He did not want to kill her. There was no call for that, no matter how unpleasant her demeanor might be.

Although, he reasoned, he could use his sword to wear her down and then his staff to beat her into submission. Somehow, that idea didn't bother him in the slightest . . . .

❀ ❀ ❀ ❀ ❀ ❀ ❀

Pomindras walked up to the most luxurious box overlooking the arena, a walled-off section with plush high-backed chairs upholstered with satin. A variety of hirelings ringed the box, the guards armed with magical short swords and the servants armed with the best tasty morsels and liqueurs.

Pomindras entered the box unchallenged and stepped over to the largest of the chairs. "You sent for me, my lord?" he asked.

His master glowered at his lieutenant, then pointed to the middle-aged man in the arena. "That man," he said, his voice honed with displeasure. "He was announced as Cimozjen of Karrnath."

"What?" Pomindras lunged to the front of the box and leaned over, gaping at the veteran sparring with Jolieni in the ring. He turned back to his master, pointing. "How—how did he get here?"

"The more salient question is why is he alive? I thought I tasked you to silence him."

Pomindras gritted his teeth. "Several of our people tried to ambush him and his friends, lord, but he sniffed it out. The mage was ham-handed and alerted him. And the Karrn is a skilled armsman. He and his companions killed four and, um, the other two, they barely escaped with their lives." He crossed his arms and turned back to the match. "But why is he here? Do you think he—?"

"I don't know, Pomindras. But I find it more than coincidental he boarded our ship and disrupted our events, then arrives here and participates. In fact, it is disconcerting. He cost me dearly in Throneport, and he has bothered me long enough. He will not return to the streets this evening. And this time, there will be no excuses. Do you understand?"

Pomindras looked at his master again. "I had already assumed as much, lord. I will make arrangements. And we'll find his bed-warmer, too."

"Him first. Haste, lest this fight end too soon. We'll deal with his companion easily enough once we're certain he is taken care of."

"Of course, lord." Pomindras bowed and ran off to attend to his task.

❋ ❋ ❋ ❋ ❋ ❋ ❋

Minrah walked quickly down the rain-slicked alley, hunkering deep in her cloak. She glanced about nervously, afraid someone from House Ghallanda might follow her. Then a dark shape stepped out of the shadows and seized her by the arm. She gasped and collapsed to her knees.

"I did not expect to see you exit this early."

"Four?" Minrah giggled in relief, a stilted, uncomfortable sound. "You scared me to death!"

"It has not yet been even one hour," said Four. He hoisted Minrah to her feet. "I had thought I would be waiting longer. Either that, or I am so used to waiting that I misestimated the time."

"No, I—I couldn't stay. I can't stomach the—the violence. Left before the second . . . second match even started. I waited around in the foyer, but even the sounds of the crowd, well, it all eventually got to be too much. Regardless, we were right about this place. One of the people in the first match was definitely a prisoner, probably both." Then suddenly an eager smile shone across her face. "Oh, and I bet all your wealth on Cimmer to win."

"What does that mean?"

"To you?" asked Minrah. "Nothing. You don't need food or shelter or things like that, so what need do you have for gold? But to me, it means a lot. Listen, I want to get out of the rain and away from this place. Let's go back to the inn and wait for Cimmer. With a little luck, come morning we'll have even more coin."

Four stalked out of the alley, battle-axe at the ready and Minrah trotting beside casting glances to either side. They turned up the street and made their way back to their lodgings as the drizzle continued to fall.

"How do we find this luck?" Four asked as they walked.

"Say again?"

"You said, that with luck, we will have more coins. How do we find some luck?"

"Oh, well, you don't find luck," said Minrah. "You just stumble on it. Or maybe it finds you."

"It sounds dangerous."

Minrah laughed. "No, Four, luck is like a . . . well, it's like magic, or chance, or something like that. But no one can make it happen. It just happens by itself."

"So it is like a god?" asked Four. "Does Cimozjen pray for luck, then?"

Minrah snorted, shaking her head. "Him? That old stallion prays to the Sovereign Host. Bah! They don't care for us at all, you know. They couldn't care less if we thrive or rot. They're nothing more than absentee landlords that leave the souls of their followers wallowing in empty grayness after they die and aren't any use anymore."

"Then why does Cimozjen pray?"

"He hopes that they will deign to favor him with a morsel of their power, so he might survive to serve them another day. He's made himself their slave for nothing in return."

"You do not pray then?" asked Four.

Minrah giggled. "Oh, sometimes I do, when straits are dire. But I don't bow and scrape to the Sovereign Host. My folks did, you know, and look where it got them."

"Where?" said Four, looking around.

Minrah hesitated before answering. "It got them killed," she said darkly. "They knew they were dealing with a dangerous group, so they left me behind, prayed for safety . . . and never returned. Fat lot of good their prayers did them."

"Fat . . . lot . . . of good," said Four.

"That's sarcasm." Minrah sniffed wetly. "I can never forget that day, that betrayal. They were betrayed by the gods they worshipped, and they were betrayed the mercantile slime they were trying to sell to. That's why I swore never to deal in goods, just services. And that's why I'd rather pray to those more likely to help me."

"Who would that be?"

"The Six, Four. They've been thrown out of power by the Sovereign Host, and thence cast in the roles of villains. Consider this. Once there were thirteen dragonmarks, thirteen moons, and thirteen months of the year. That was before the Mark of Death was lost. Now think about this. There are seven gods in the Sovereign Host. Add that to the so-called Dark Six, and you get thirteen, right? So what makes those six gods evil? Why are they evil, but there aren't six evil moons or six evil dragonmarks?

Do you want to know why? Because they're outnumbered, seven to six. The Sovereign Host kicked them out of the pantheon out of greed. That way they'd only have to divide the worship among seven gods instead of thirteen.

"So I figure I'm giving the Dark Six something they care about, which is prayer and worship—at least when they listen to me. So we have an understanding, the Six and I. They give me what I need if they're in the mood, and when they do I'll give them what they need, which is another follower, someone who recognizes who and what they are: those betrayed by their siblings in a grab for power."

"And once you die," asked Four, "they do not leave you in emptiness?"

"I haven't the vaguest idea. But I figure they'll reward those who helped them. It's in their best interests, after all. They need more power to overthrow the Host, so they'll probably train me to be in their army."

"So you would fight on their behalf?"

"Not on a gnome's bet," she said. "I wouldn't risk getting destroyed for that lot. They're just as selfish as the other gods . . . as anyone else, for that matter. Sure, I'd scout for them, but let them fight their own wars. That's what I say. Honestly, why should I risk myself for someone else? I sure can't think of a reason."

Four said nothing, but the rest of the way back to their suite he pondered how much her attitude differed from that of her companion, who remained behind in the building, facing the unknown.

❧ ❧ ❧ ❧ ❧ ❧ ❧

As Cimozjen considered his options, Jolieni leapt to the attack. With her left hand, she flung an object at the ground, which burst with a flash of fire and a loud crack that cut through the crowd noise. Flustered, Cimozjen blinked rapidly and backpedaled, but felt her thrusting sword strike his abdomen.

Jolieni's sword broke a link of his chain and cut through his skin, but the iron held otherwise, turning what could have been a lethal blow into a sharp jab that sent him stumbling. She struck again, a glancing thrust that ran along the links of his chain and tore the side out of his tunic.

Eyes still dazzled by the flash, Cimozjen swung a desperate overhand blow while still backpedaling, his staff hand held high to protect his face. He felt it strike something, so he struck again, but missed her entirely. Just to be safe, he swung upward with the inside edge of his sword, again catching nothing but air. Then at the last moment, he saw her thrusting again. He ducked his head to the side, and her blade traced a deep cut across his left cheekbone and took a cut through the curl of his ear.

Years of training and experience kicked in. Knowing that the thrust had left her extended and open, Cimozjen swung his left arm wide, placing the staff in a position to keep her sword arm out of the battle as long as possible. He stepped in and swung his sword low, striking her a solid blow on the ribs with the hilt of his sword, then swept his staff in, fetching her a blow on the side of the head. He pressed forward, pushing into her to knock her to the ground, but as she fell, she managed to trip him up. He stumbled over her and she kicked at him, sending him to the ground. His sword caught the clay awkwardly and, off balance as he was, he lost his grip as he fell.

He rolled away, clutching his staff, and rose to his feet as fluidly as his aging joints allowed. He blinked several times rapidly, glad that the lingering glare from the flash was fading. He considered unleashing his staff to the fullest, but decided against it, confident that he could still defeat Jolieni without killing her.

Jolieni stood opposite, still holding her sword, but not in the same martial stance she'd been in earlier. She rubbed one eye with the heel of her hand, and then the other with the back of her wrist. Cimozjen wondered whether she was daubing at sweat or tears.

He charged, swinging his staff overhand. She raised her sword to parry, deflecting the swing to her left, but Cimozjen used the shift in momentum to swing the staff around and strike again with the other end. She blocked that swing, and the impact jarred Cimozjen's hands as it drove the sword down. He swung again and again, sweeping the staff around to strike overhand with either end in turn, beating down her defense.

At the last, she abandoned her attempt at defense and lashed at Cimozjen as the metal-shod staff came down. He struck her squarely atop her shoulder, and her blade caught the heel of his hand where it held the staff. Between the wound and the impact, Cimozjen lost his grip on the staff, but his powerful blow drove Jolieni to the ground. With a flick of her sword she spun the staff off her, and it landed close enough to her that any attempt to recover it could be lethal.

Instead, he stepped back and recovered his sword, for he had planned his angle of attack to drive her away from his primary weapon for just that purpose.

She started to rise as he grabbed his sword, so he lunged in and slashed at her ankle. The impact knocked her foot out from under her and set her down, supine. She started to rise again, but he stepped over her, planting one leg firmly on the blade of her sword. He inverted his grip on his sword and held it to her throat, one hand on the hilt and the other flat against the blade to steady it.

The yells and whistles of the crowd, which had been a fairly steady roar, began to pulse.

Cimozjen saw that Jolieni's face was indeed spattered with tears. His heart hesitated with compassion, but then he disciplined himself to end the combat. It was truly the most merciful thing to do. "Yield!" he demanded.

She squeezed her eyes, trying to blink away her tears. "Give me Killien back!"

Cimozjen shook his head.

The pulsing noise became gradually comprehensible. "Kill her!" chanted the crowd. "Kill her! Kill her! Kill her!"

"Rotting bastard!" She kicked at him to free herself, but he pressed the blade to the skin at the base of her neck.

"Yield, for the Host's sake," he shouted. "You fought well, but you've lost! Yield with honor!"

Her mouth worked for a moment, the noise of the crowd sounding like nothing so much as a vile, monstrous heartbeat. She gritted her teeth. "I'm sick of this," she spat, and she shoved at Cimozjen's foot where it stood on her sword. His foot slid down her blade, throwing him off balance.

His sword plunged into her naked neck.

The crowd roared so loudly that Cimozjen couldn't even hear himself scream.

Chapter
Twenty-Two

Minrah awoke from her meditation before dawn. She rose, stretched like a spoiled cat, and sauntered over to the window, her bare feet making no noise as she walked. She pulled the curtain back and gazed at the sky, and her keen elf eyes noted the faintest lightening in the east—a slight warmth that crept beneath the cloud cover, the subtle promise of the coming dawn.

She turned and padded quietly over to Cimozjen's bed, then drew up with a gasp. "Four?" she whispered. She heard the construct shift slightly. "Where is Cimozjen?"

"I presume he is still in the building where we left him."

"I certainly hope not."

"Why not?"

"Well," she said weakly, "because I more or less figured that the fights between folks would, I don't know, just be fights or something. Like wrestling match with swords. He was supposed to teach Jolieni a lesson about swords. No one was supposed to get killed . . ."

"Why would you think that?" asked Four. "I killed countless people in the arena."

"Sure, but you were a prisoner. They didn't care if you lived or died, so having prisoners fight to the death was fine."

"As a prisoner, they owned me. Would they not wish their property to remain undamaged?"

"Yes . . ."

"So if destruction of their own property was acceptable, why would it be unacceptable for non-prisoners to fight to the death?"

"Just . . . because! It's not the way they're supposed to do it!"

"If they had skilled warriors as prisoners, why would they waste them fighting each other, and not free people? And if they wished their slavery to remain unknown, why would they treat any duel differently from any other?"

Minrah tugged at the hem of her jersey, face flustered. "Because that's not what I thought the challenges were all about!" she wailed.

"What evidence or experience did you base your conclusions on?"

Minrah rounded on her companion. "Quiet, Four! We can't waste time thinking about that sort of stuff now! Don't you understand that? There are more important things. We have to find out what happened to Cimmer. If he hasn't come back, then something really dreadful happened, like he got badly injured." Her fury spent, she turned and paced helplessly, twisting her fingers around each other. "Or maybe he's dead. We need to go back and see."

"We cannot do that," said Four. "They will not allow me in the building, so that is a part of the adventuring that I cannot participate in. But we can go back to the door together, if that is your wish, and then you can explore inside some more."

"Without you?" whined Minrah.

"They will not admit me," he said. Then, with his voice altered to imitate the doorman, he added, " 'We do not allow their kind in here. You will have to leave it outside.' "

"Fine," said Minrah. "Let's go."

They wended their way back to the entrance to the arena. The rain had stopped some hours before, and only an occasional drip fell from the eaves overhead. Four concealed himself in the alley, while Minrah hesitantly stepped up and knocked. She waited.

And waited.

With a nervous glance in Four's direction, she knocked again. Waited. Paced, her fingers writhing with impatience and dread. Finally she stopped and turned in Four's direction. "Why won't they answer?"

Four stepped out of the shadows. "Perhaps you are too timid in your knock," he said. "Your muscles and bones are not particularly robust, and are thus ill-suited to making enough noise to attract the attention of the occupants. Permit me to demonstrate."

The construct walked up to the door, battle-axe in hand. He hefted the weapon and slammed the butt end of the weapon hard into the door. *Wham! . . . Wham! . . . Crack!* And with the last blow, the wood of the door partially buckled under the impact. The warforged inspected the dent and the small split on the wood, nodded in satisfaction, then stalked back over to his hiding place, leaving Minrah staring agog after him.

The view slit in the door slammed open. "Hey!" barked a voice. "What in the ashes do you think you're doing?"

Minrah whirled back around, and the eyes in the view slit grew wide. She gathered her frazzled wits and smiled as sweetly as she could, given her mental state. "I'm sorry, what was your question?" she asked, stalling for time.

"You—uh . . . you?" asked the doorman. "Um . . . *you* knocked?"

"Why yes, yes, I did. I . . . had to leave early last night. I wanted to follow up on how things developed."

"Well, um . . . almost everyone's gone, but . . . um . . . wait just a moment." The view slit closed much more gently than it had opened, and after a short time, the door swung wide to admit her.

Minrah stepped in hesitantly, faking a smile that shone bright and warm in contrast to her chilled and fearful heart.

"Ah, Minrah Teamaker," said a gentle voice, "it is you after all." She turned and saw the purser from the betting window. He snapped his fingers once, sending an aide running down the hall, then he reached one hand out to her. She extended her hand and he took it and kissed it gallantly.

He smiled and bobbed his head. "I was beginning to fret about your absence," he said. "The audience departed many bells ago, and you are the only one not to collect her winnings."

"Winnings?"

"Indeed. You fared quite well this day. Your sole wager bore fruit, and I am pleased to give you your harvest. Quite a crop, if I do say so myself." Just as he finished his words with a smarmy smile the aide returned, bearing a pouch and a small piece of paper curled tightly and tied with ribbon. The man turned, took the two items from the aide, and presented them to Minrah.

Amazed, Minrah reached out and took the bag. It sagged over her slender hands, heavy with coin. Her fingers clenched, gripping some of the coins through the coarse cloth. She shifted the bag to one hand and took the proffered curled paper. "What's this?"

"A certificate for the balance of your winnings," came the reply. "We've found that most of our clients like to have the security of a Kundarak-notarized promissory note, but still retain a portion of their winnings in ready coin for various means of immediate celebration." He chuckled.

"Why . . . thank you," said Minrah.

"No, we thank you, dear one, for patronizing our establishment. We do hope that you will choose to return soon."

"How is Cimozjen?"

"Who?"

"The, uh, the person whom I was lucky enough to bet on. The fighter."

"Ah. Obviously, he won, but beyond that I am afraid I do not know."

"But he lived?"

The man shrugged, still wearing his insincere smile. "It is likely, although in fairness I must advance the possibility that he suffered what we call a 'simultaneous finish.' In those rare events, the house pays to the side that the judges deem to have prevailed, the actual results notwithstanding. And I find I must also add that even if I did know his status, it is against house policy for family members or employees to discuss or theorize about the health of any competitors. We must maintain our propriety and neutrality, and cannot be thought to be tampering with the odds by means of idle speculation. I suggest you watch the boards; if his name appears, you may draw your own conclusions."

Minrah nodded, trying not to let her disappointment cross her features. "I see. So . . . when might I be able to come back? I'm not fully acquainted with your schedule."

"The second night hence," said the man with an eager bob of the head. "It's a smaller event, but should provide quality amusement nonetheless. I'll be sure to hold an excellent seat for you."

Minrah smiled as best she could and clutched her winnings to her breast. "I thank you. I shall see you then."

❋ ❋ ❋ ❋ ❋ ❋ ❋

"So is Cimozjen dead?" asked Four. He had started to ask the question just after Minrah had left the building, but at that time she had silenced him with a gesture. She had led Four to several temples, the House Jorasco compound, and the undertaker's, all the while demanding his utter silence.

Back in their lodgings, the warforged reckoned it might safe to try asking the question again.

"No," said Minrah, slouched in her chair. She spoke in a distracted monotone around her thumbnail, which she chewed on as she thought. "I don't believe he's dead. Whoever these people are, they kept Torval alive for years, so I don't think they'd be so clumsy as to let an old warhorse like Cimmer die. Even if he did anger them as he is wont to do."

"So you believe he is captured?"

"Yes, I do. It was pretty clear from the way the customers behaved at the Flagons that the fighters were free to leave after the fights ended, was it not?" She leaned forward and gestured toward the window. "I mean, look at that snub-faced Jolieni. She barged in swinging a bag of coin and crowing about her victory and ready to celebrate. She was letting herself be carried on the emotion of a fresh victory, probably no more than an hour before."

Minrah sagged back into her chair and pulled her legs up. She steepled her hands in front of her face, as she continued. "So if Cimmer suffered nothing more than a light injury, he'd have returned. If he were badly hurt, he would have been taken to a healer's, or he would have healed himself, and again he would have come back. If he were killed in a fair duel, there'd be no reason to hide the body like they did with Torval. So the only reasonable assumption is that he's being held in slavery, just like you were, or his friend Torval. Which is illegal by the Treaty of Thronehold."

"You two released me. I am sure we can do the same for him," said the warforged. "Just tell me what to do."

"I don't know." She sat for a while longer. "If we're to figure out what to do, we need to know for sure who's behind this. Which house it is."

"Is it not House Ghallanda?"

"That was Friar Hannel's guess, but I'm not so sure he's right. I don't put much stake in his read of people, you know what I mean?"

"What does it matter which house, if they are breaking the law?"

"Because it's someone that has some sway with the Sentinel Marshals." Minrah shifted in her chair so she could drape her head across the back and look at the ceiling. "Remember how they released Rophis and Pomindras and kept the others? That means it's someone the Marshals fear, or someone who had some sort of political sway over them. The Marshals have a reputation as being the toughest, most dedicated, law-upholding hunters in Khorvaire. They've got license to operate across the continent, regardless of sovereignty, and they still swear their duties to the Galifar Throne. So whom do they have to be afraid of?"

Four held up his palms in resignation. "I do not know. What houses exist?"

Minrah drew a deep breath, then sat up and swung her legs off the chair. "Let's see," she said, and began ticking the houses off on her fingers. "There's Vadalis, but they deal with animal husbandry and the like. They seem an ill-suited choice to care for and transport prisoners. There's Ghallanda, who has the mark of hospitality. They are as good a choice as any to care for prisoners as they bring them home, and they'd also be interested in putting together an entertaining evening of pit fights."

"I thought you did not like pit fights."

"I'm being sarcastic, Four," she said, rolling her eyes. She drew a deep breath and blew a stray lock out of her face. "Hmm. House Kundarak, well, they're deep into their lending and coin-counting. Would they support gambling? Sure, if there's money to be made. But transporting prisoners? No. I just can't see them guarding something they can't lock in a vault. Then there's Jorasco, but their house code would not allow them to participate in what we've seen here. They are required to render aid and succor."

"Might not they send fighters against each other, then heal them afterwards?" asked Four.

"It's conceivable, Four, but we should start with likely. While someone in the Jorasco family might possibly do something like this, it goes counter to the house's charter, and if it were ever found out, the whole house would suffer."

"I see."

"Sivis. They have the mark of scribing. I doubt they'd take the job, and I damned sure know that no one would trust gnomes to transport prisoners back home. Those crafty little leeches would wring every piece of information out of them. House Cannith— they're the ones who made you and the other warforged—not only is this not their strength, but they're no longer unified. If one branch of House Cannith tried to transport prisoners, the others would try to assassinate the lot of them, just to make the first side look bad.

"Orien runs the lightning rail. I could see them being called on to transport prisoners, because the lines stretch all across Khorvaire. Lyrandar is another possibility. They have the airships, which would be a natural means of transporting prisoners quickly, and without the traceability that the lightning rail has. But I can't see any compelling reason for either house to fail to transport someone. They stake their reputations on safe deliveries, after all."

She paused, drumming her fingers. "With their mercenaries, Deneith has probably the best capability of safeguarding people, plus they rigidly hold to their neutrality in matters of state. But as with Orien and Lyrandar, their dependability is paramount to them. If someone hires mercenaries, they need to be certain those mercenaries will show up.

"Who else?" she asked, pulling her index finger down. "That's nine. I'm missing four more. Ah. Medani. Theirs is the Warning Guild. They'd be another good bet for keeping people safe, and less obtrusively than Deneith. And I suppose that their powers of detection might make their covert fight nights a little safer for them. But again, when the prisoners didn't show up, that'd be a black mark on their reputation. And there's Phiarlan and Thuranni, the shadow guilds. But they're spies, so again, I can't see anyone trusting them with prisoners any more than they'd trust the gnomes.

"That leaves . . . um . . . House Tharashk. I'd suspect their Finders Guild would be better suited to finding prisoners than transporting them. So where does that leave us?"

Four shifted. "You indicated that Ghallanda would be the most likely to create an arena, Lyrandar and Orien would be the most likely to transport, and Deneith and Medani would provide the most protection. That seems to give us little information."

Minrah rose and started pacing. "Well, let's see. Ghallanda is a halfling house based in Gatherhold."

"In my time, I did not take note of any halflings. Those who unlocked my home or repaired me afterwards were always humans."

Minrah stopped her pacing. "Always?"

"Always."

She started pacing again. "Come to think of it, everyone that I can remember at the wagers window was a human, too. And so was the door guard. So that narrows things down, now doesn't it?"

"So which houses are human?"

"For starters, Orien is a human house." She stopped pacing at the window and looked out at the streets below. "And it's based in Passage. Now that is curious, is it not?"

"I do not know," said Four. "What do you see out there?"

She turned and sat on the windowsill. "Passage is a city south-west of here. So we have a human house—and humans were the ones who handled you as a prisoner—and it has its prime estate right here in Aundair. The arena we saw in Karrnath—where we found you—was on an Aundairian merchant ship. And that explains why the Sentinel Marshals were so circumspect. House Orien holds Queen Aurala's ear, I'm sure, and more important, they could deny the Sentinel Marshals access to the lightning rail, which would greatly impede their work." She smacked her fist into her palm. "Now we know what we're up against. And if we can convince House Lyrandar to provide assistance to the Sentinel Marshals—maybe free passage on their airships or something— then the Marshals can make a move against House Orien without fearing the cost to their mobility. The Marshals uphold the law, Lyrandar gets to see their rival take a punishing hit, and we get to spring Cimozjen from their grasp."

"That sounds good to me," said Four. "But how will we get the attention of a dragonmarked house?"

Minrah spun, smiled, and produced her quill pen.

Cimozjen returned slowly and painfully to consciousness. His every joint ached, several muscles twitched and spasmed, and raw sores itched at several places across his skin.

He tried to remember what had happened. He'd been having dreams, nightmares of a treacherous cloudburst, being jolted, flashes of lightning coursing through his body as he tried to attack the armored thunderheads. His sword falling to earth from nerveless hands.

With a grimace, he forced his eyes to open. At first he saw nothing, then as his brain oriented to the dim light he began to take in his surroundings.

He lay on a pallet, clad in his shirt, chain hauberk, pants, and boots. The links of the chain mail, pressed against his naked flesh, were very uncomfortable.

With a grunt, he forced himself to sit up. His head ached. The pallet bed lay in a small room empty of furniture. His sword and staff leaned against the corner by the door. He noted no other ornamentation, although his eyes registered something amiss.

He lurched to his feet. The blood drained from his brain and he teetered on the verge of passing out. Drawing on his training, he forced himself to retain consciousness, putting all his effort into willing his mind to focus. He swayed for a moment more, and then lurched and put his hand against the wall for support.

His head pounded, and every time he moved in the slightest, it felt like a load of bricks shifted around in his brainpan. He ran one hand across the back of his neck, stretching. It did little good.

He leaned against the wall for a moment, breathing heavily, and came to the conclusion that being semi-delirious with his weapons in hand was probably safer for him than being semi-delirious unarmed. With heavy, limping strides he shuffled his way to his sword and staff, accompanied the sound of metal rattling across stone. He paused. Looked down. He saw a cuff of iron around one ankle, fastened by a long chain to a stone set in the center of the floor.

He stumbled toward his weapons, only to be reined in at the last moment by the manacle, his fingers a mere foot from the grip of his only defense. His hand flew to the small of his back, only to find that his dagger, too, was missing. He looked at the door and finally realized what his subconscious mind had noted all along. The door had no latch.

He was trapped in a cell.

And then it all came back to him—killing Jolieni, being ushered from the field blinded by his tears, then being attacked by the guards with their blunt forked spears that wracked him with agony every time they touched him. He'd fought, pain and fear and anguish driving him on, but he wasn't even sure if he'd managed to land a blow on any of them.

Now he understood the burning pains he felt. He ran his hand down his tunic and found a small charred hole situated over one of his burns. Whatever elemental magic was imbedded within those cleft polearms, his chain mail had done nothing to protect his body from it.

Slowly he peeled off his tunic, and then his chain hauberk. It grated across his wounded ear, eliciting a hiss of pain. He let the armor fall to the floor. It half covered his foot.

Caged.

Just like Torval had been, he was certain of that. Caged and forced to fight in the arena for the amusement of others. The promise of repatriation twisted into a never-ending nightmare of mortal combats for the benefit of the heartless.

He turned around and surveyed his room anew. A bucket sat against one wall, a second lay across from it. Slop and food, he assumed. The walls were of windowless stone. There was nowhere even to sit but the pallet. No decoration of any sort, save the words "Ajiuss Aeyliros" scratched into one wall. He presumed it was a name. Either that, or an elven epithet.

Torval had suffered for years like this. Two long years of

brutality. Cimozjen looked about. With his belt, he could probably figure out a way to hang himself, deny his captors the satisfaction of any further entertainment from him.

But if he were to do that, he would fail in his sworn goal. His friend Torval would remain unavenged, and his own last act would be one of defeat. He wouldn't even be dying for anything, just dying against something he did not want to endure. Just like Jolieni, with her bitter face and her pointless suicide that he knew would haunt his nights for months.

No, he had to hold on. He had to play his part and wait. He had an advantage that Torval didn't. He had friends on the outside who knew his situation. Four hadn't been allowed into the building, and hopefully Minrah had escaped their clutches as well. She was clever. All he had to do was wait until they figured out a way to set him free. Which, he admitted, might take weeks, even months.

In the meantime, he had to survive, and, to the best of his ability, avoid any more killing. He was here to free his fellow prisoners, not to murder them. And the other warriors, the ones who opted for this dangerous sport, they probably did not know that people like him were held in bondage.

For him to survive, though, he'd have to fight. He'd have to cause needless pain on people who knew not the extent of what they were doing or, worse yet, shared in his cruel fate. He'd have to do the bidding of his captors, or at least appear to be doing so . . . if there was truly any difference.

He hated the feeling of being trapped. He'd had the feeling before, prior to being captured, and it had not ended well then, either. At least this time he had a better inkling of what he needed to do to get out of the situation. Somehow he had to keep winning . . . without killing his opponents.

If he could help it.

He hung his head.

And there, thanks be to the Host, he saw his holy symbol still dangling about his neck. With a grim half smile, he grasped it in his right hand. And for the first time in twenty-two long years, he prayed for his own healing without a trace of guilt.

❧ ❧ ❧ ❧ ❧ ❧ ❧

Pomindras snarled and tore the broadsheet from the pillar where it had been tacked. Ignoring the shouts of the other commoners nearby, he quickly folded it up and stormed away.

His fury propelled him to the walled compound that served as his family's residences and halls of business. Guards opened the door for him that he might not have to break stride. His heavy boots clomped up the central stairway and down to the end of the wood-floored hallways until at last he reached the grand suite that overlooked the serene Aundair River.

He was admitted immediately.

A large, gilded desk polished to a mirror sheen dominated the room. Behind that desk sat a large overstuffed chair, so grand in design that it nearly rivaled a throne. At the moment, that throne showed its back to the door, turned as it was to face the panoramic windows that had been opened at the rear of the room. The view out the windows showed the dawn unfolding on the cityscape below and the countryside across the river.

Pomindras stepped into the suite and around the desk, stopping near the huge chair. He bowed to his master. "Something I think you should see, lord Rophis," he said.

Rophis neither turned his head nor answered, but simply held out one hand.

Pomindras placed the broadsheet in his grasp, saying, "About halfway down, lord."

Rophis unfolded the broadsheet and read.

Bound by Iron
A True Adventure in Betrayal, Murder,
and One Man's Quest for Vengeance

Part the First

Scribed by Minrah Penwright, Who Has Seen All that Has Transpired and Swears to Its Veracity

This is a tale of sacrifice and loss, blood and woe, betrayal and redemption; and you, dear readers, may yet play a part in the final act in which, we all fervently hope, shall at last be had the wrathful vengeance for illicit wrongs done to untold innocents guilty of no crime other than wishing to be returned home after the armistice that concluded the Last War.

Our story, dear readers, begins some seventeen days prior to this, in the city of Korth, near the harbor on the left bank of the Karrn River . . .

Chapter
TWENTY-THREE

The Dragon's Trail

Sul, the 1st day of Aryth, 998

It was incongruous. If she were so meaningless, if she were the small insect she felt she was, why then should her heart pound so hard that she feared it might rattle the walls?

Minrah sat at the edge of a large, uncomfortable chair placed in the middle of a large, inhospitable room devoid of any other furniture. Exquisitely carved Eldeen darkwood paneling with delicate molding covered the walls. The immaculate floors were of polished pearlescent stone that seemed to glow with a gentle light, there being no other apparent explanation for the illumination in the room. Huge shields adorned with the Lyrandar family crest—the coiling tentacles of a kraken grasping at a perfect pearl—hung at the four corners of the room, and she was certain that the tentacles actually moved whenever she wasn't looking at them. Even the frilled draperies strung along the ceiling were coiled and arranged to resemble the grasping, suction-cupped limbs. She wondered if they'd come to life were she to make some grievous error.

The chair was large enough that her feet didn't quite reach the floor, which was itself unnerving. It made her feel even more like a child. Her toes tapped together and she pulled on her fingers, alternating hands obsessively.

"Is that a spell you are casting?" asked Four, peering over the back of the chair to watch her fidgeting hands.

"I wish it were," said Minrah. "I'm just nervous. It took us almost two days to get this appointment, and I hope I didn't shoot wild."

"In my consideration, you presented your arguments quite well."

"We'll see."

They waited some more in the large, empty, silent room.

"I hate this," said Minrah.

"Hate what?"

"Waiting."

"We have not been waiting long," said Four.

"Not long? I'll bet it's been a bell, maybe two."

"Yes."

"That's a long time!"

"You have never truly had to wait," said Four. "I find the lack of stimulus to be peaceful."

Minrah shifted to sneer at the warforged. "So you're saying my talking is disrupting your relaxation?"

"Yes."

She turned away and curled up in the chair. "Well, I am sooo sorry."

Minrah waited some more, stewing. The knowledge that Four was settling back into a pleasant nothingness did nothing to improve her mood.

Finally, with the loud click of a heavy latch, the double doors at the far end of the room opened, admitting the Lyrandar representative Minrah had spoken to earlier. Minrah heard Four stiffen behind her, but thankfully he made no aggressive moves.

"We have reviewed your tale, Minrah," said the Lyrandar.

"It's not a tale. It's all true, and I saw it with my own eyes."

The Lyrandar held up one hand. "Permit me to rephrase. We

have inspected the publications of the *Chronicle* for the twenty-seventh through today, and reviewed your contributions thereto. However, we find nothing in there that would justify opening hostilities between ourselves and another dragonmarked house, especially one as powerful and influential as Orien."

Minrah sniffed and leaned forward, her hands on her knees and her elbows out confrontationally. "If you had listened to me, you'd have noticed that I did not ask you to do anything hostile to anyone. All I asked was that you provide benevolence and consideration for the Sentinel Marshals should House Orien decide to curtail their support. Which I expect they will do after the Marshals put an end to this ongoing travesty. In fact, the only thing stopping the Marshals from giving the Oriens a hard law-enforcing kick in the groin is fear of losing the mobility that Orien support grants them without something of equal value being provided by another means."

The Lyrandar smiled. "We heard you the first time, Minrah. However, we wanted to ensure that you heard yourself. You have not asked us to initiate hostilities, nor will we. However, we will be more than happy to render whatsoever aid or assistance the Sentinel Marshals might require, and out of respect for the Code of Galifar, to do so without recompense. And if this should help us both to remove our individual obstacles, so much the better."

He bowed shallowly and gestured to the door behind Minrah. "I believe our audience is concluded. The guards will escort you out." He smiled blandly. "We thank you for your time and attention in this matter, Minrah, and look forward to more installments of your prose."

❖ ❖ ❖ ❖ ❖ ❖ ❖

Unseen hands—presumably magical—unlatched the shackle that held Cimozjen away from his equipment. After three days of waiting, marking time in a cell with no human contact, he presumed he was to fight again. He assumed they'd made him wait in solitude for so long in an attempt to break his spirit, but they had failed. He had his patron god, and somewhere out there he had his friends, so he did not feel isolated.

Cimozjen wondered what would happen to him were he to refuse to prepare to fight, or to enter the arena. All the answers he came up with were short and brutal, and diminished his chances of finding justice for Torval, let alone the other prisoners.

He donned his armor. He wished he had a helm, but he'd not worn one into the building, thinking that secrecy was of the greatest import. He stepped over to his weapons, checked the edge of his sword and, satisfied, girded himself with his belt and scabbard. He picked up his staff, checked it thoroughly, and saw that it had not been tampered with. So much the better. Finally he picked up his dagger, held it for a long moment, and sheathed it.

Cimozjen genuflected, murmuring a long, soulful prayer to the Sovereign Host for their guidance and protection, and to Dol Dorn that he might have both strength to prevail and mercy not to kill.

Then he waited, occasionally stretching out to try to limber up his aging limbs.

After a short while, he felt the floor shift beneath him, a ripple passing through the earth as though his cell itself was crawling. Perhaps, he mused, it is.

The undulating sensation passed, and then his door opened. He saw a short passage, no more than three feet long. At the other end, another door swung open, and the sound of a hooting, whistling crowd washed in. He walked through the doors to his next appointment.

He stepped into the arena. The crowd applauded as a voice intoned, "Eager to return to the ring following his brutal murder of Jolieni the Hawk, hungry for more blood, Cimozjen Hellekanus, the Killer from Karrnath—defender!"

Across from Cimozjen, a second door opened. Tholog sauntered out, holding a huge warhammer slung over his shoulder. "And, with strength to match his opponent's ruthlessness, Tholog, the Full-Hammer Hobgoblin! Odds are level—one to one!"

Cimozjen winced as he saw Tholog's weapon. With light weapons, it was possible to pull a blow to inflict less damage, potentially sparing a life. With a massive hammer, the inertia was difficult if not impossible to overcome, thus each strike had a greater chance of being the last.

The hobgoblin smiled as he approached but stopped just out of weapon's reach. "I had to find out," he said, shouting to be heard over the crowd. "You fought well against Jolieni."

Cimozjen gave a slight bow. "I am flattered," he said. "But if you will please indulge me, grant me a moment to survey the arena before we start. I had no chance to do so last time."

The hobgoblin spread his arms graciously. "As you wish," he lisped, his protruding teeth mutating his sibilants. "Meeting you is my only appointment this evening—save perhaps healing a few cuts and bruises after I defeat you."

Cimozjen stepped back several paces—no sense in presenting too tempting a target—then looked about the theater. Rising tiers of seating circled the arena walls, ranging from simple stone benches to ornate upholstered chairs.

Then his eyes fell upon a face he recognized—Pomindras, who'd commanded the *Silver Cygnet* as well as ambushed him in the streets of Fairhaven. He stood at the edge of a luxury seating area, which was cordoned off from the rest of the crowd by a festooned wall that rose to about four feet.

The timbre of the cheers and yells from the crowd started to take an impatient turn.

Cimozjen turned his head away before was caught staring, then walked back to face Tholog. "Who is that man? The bald and bearded one standing by the expensive seats."

Tholog stole a glance out of the corner of his eye. "Him? No one knows his name. No one I know, anyway. We call him the Black Shield. That's how he's announced when he fights. Speaking of which, Killer from Karrnath, I put my money on winning, not slaying. You seemed decent enough, so I thought I'd give you a chance to survive, hmm?" He readied his warhammer.

"Your money?"

"Of course. You think I do this for fun? It is, sure—I like whacking people with Pounder here—but the pay isn't enough. So I place a bet on myself whenever I walk the clay."

"Pay?"

The crowd started to hiss and whistle their annoyance.

Tholog looked at him funny. "Yes. Why, did you get shorted?" He chuckled. "If so, you need a pounding for being a buffoon."

Cimozjen planted his staff on the clay, but did not draw his sword. Instead, he placed his hand on his hip. "You know that I'm being held against my will."

"Quit talking." Tholog shifted his grip and moved his weapon into an attack position. "The crowd's getting restless."

"I've not left this building since I fought Jolieni. They've kept me in a cage."

"They what?"

"They imprisoned a friend of mine since the end of the War, making him fight," said Cimozjen. "Wore peasant's garb and an iron armband. He died two weeks ago. That's why I'm here. Now they have me." He studied Tholog's reaction. "Minrah. Remember that name. Minrah. She's at the guesthouse on Chandlers Street near the lightning rail station. Find her and tell her I'm here."

Tholog shook his head. "No . . . no. You can't be telling the truth."

The crowd's displeasure grew louder, more insistent.

"Minrah! Remember it! She knows not where I am!"

"Don't lie. This is all volunteer. You knew what we were getting into just as much as I did."

"Do you distrust me? Look at my right boot. Look at the marks the shackles made."

Tholog glanced down.

Cimozjen struck, whipping the dagger from the small of his back, flipping it in his hand, and plunging it with a back-handed stab into the nape of Tholog's neck.

Tholog's eyes bulged. He dropped his hammer and clawed at the wound as blood spurted forth.

Cimozjen forced him to the ground, not a difficult proposition as the hobgoblin was quickly bleeding to death. Eyes glaring, Cimozjen leaned his face right into the hobgoblin's. Tholog's eyes rolled back in his head.

Cimozjen hunkered over the body for a few moments. The crowd went silent, wondering if he were smothering the hobgoblin or possibly working other atrocities with his dagger. At last he straightened up and shoved Tholog away. He wiped off his dagger, stropping it several times on Tholog's sleeve, then wiped the blood from his fingers on the material as well.

He stood and raised his arms to the crowd in acknowledgement of his victory, holding his red-stained hands aloft. He took a bow, his bloody holy symbol swinging like a pendulum and his dagger glinting in the light. He retired to his cage to the hissing and catcalls of hundreds of angry spectators.

      ❧ ❧ ❧ ❧ ❧ ❧ ❧ ❧

Rophis the Winemonger wrenched a leg from the magebred turkey that sat steaming in the center of the table. He tore some of the meat from the bone with his teeth, breathed in and out to cool it a little with the passing air, then gobbled it like an alligator.

The Blinking Hippo was an experiment, a Ghallanda eatery supplied with magebred animals of every sort from the best breeders of House Vadalis. Odd animals they were, like this turkey with four fat legs, but very tasty indeed. They promised to deliver a six-foot long rack of ribs for him next week.

He was looking forward to it. Life had turned very, very good.

The door to the private dining room opened, and a familiar figure stepped in.

"Pomindras!" said Rophis around the half-chewed chunk of turkey that was still in his mouth. "Come! Sit!"

He patted the back of the empty chair at his right hand. Rophis had held the chair open for him, a gesture of appreciation for his assistance in capturing the damnable paladin who'd disrupted the operation of the *Silver Cygnet* in Thronehold and just as swiftly had galvanized the house's clientele as the most hated man in the arena. After they'd debarked from the *Fire Flight*, Pomindras had been excluded from the table as punishment for allowing the troublesome Karrn to board the *Silver Cygnet* in the first place, but Rophis was a forgiving man, happy to reward those who overcame their own failures. Rebuke and reward. It was a powerful combination to bend people to his will.

Pomindras came around the table and sat down, his pleasure evident. He placed a sheaf of high-quality Karrn paper to the side.

Rophis gestured with his mangled turkey leg. "Try some." He bit off another large, greasy mouthful and chewed, rolling his eyes back in pleasure. He followed with a hearty swill from his large mug of stout. "Mm. Wonderful."

Pomindras did as he'd been bidden, cutting off a large chunk of breast, though truly it required no measure of loyalty or obedience to sample the savory bird.

Rophis smacked his lips and waved one hand vaguely. "Glad to have you here at last, Pomindras. You may begin."

Pomindras set down his knife, wiped his hands and took up the papers. "Attendance continues to grow, lord, at roughly the same pace. Wagers have risen more rapidly, as have participants, and despite a few setbacks, we are profiting well." He switched to another page. "I've been keeping my eye on several potential candidates who may be valuable additions. However, Alain—you remember him, the albino lad?—we've confirmed that he's in touch with the gnomes, so I've arranged a special event for his benefit."

Rophis chuckled. "Excellent. Monsters are always a good draw. Tell me, what sort is it?"

Pomindras smiled. "I'd rather it remained a surprise, lord. Trust me, though, it's a good one."

Rophis looked aslant at Pomindras, then laughed. "A surprise, eh? Pomindras, that sounds like—"

The door to the private dining room opened, and an unfamiliar figure stepped in.

"You have the wrong room," growled Pomindras.

"Oh, no, I do not," said the small elf gaily. She winked at Pomindras. "In fact, as soon as I saw your bald little head bobbing on in, I knew I'd find myself in the absolute right room." She blew a kiss to Rophis. "How are you faring, O winemonger son of Raanel?"

Rophis leaned to his right, an incredulous twist to his lip. "I know that face. Who is she, Pomindras?"

"You wound me," said the elf, clutching her heart with melodramatic anguish. "On board the *Silver Cygnet*, you said I was a lovely creature with a radiant face, and now you don't remember me?" She sighed and sagged against the doorframe. "But that's fine, because I remember you, and now, thanks to the *Chronicle*, the whole of Khorvaire will soon know what you're doing."

"Now I remember you," said Rophis. "You're the Karrn's bit of sleeve lace. And you're our mysterious narrator, too?"

Minrah curtsied. "Indeed I am. And now you're holding my friend. Cimozjen, in case you've forgotten. Let him go before nightfall, or I'm calling the Marshals down on you."

Rophis stared at her blankly. "The Marshals."

"That's right," said Minrah. "The Sentinel Marshals. So you might want to give me the answers I want before they wring them from your tortured body."

"Pfft!" snorted Rophis. "Empty threats." He waved a turkey leg. "Pomindras, deal with her."

Pomindras stepped around the table. His hand went to his belt, but of course House Ghallanda had required him to surrender his sword upon entry into the Blinking Hippo. So instead he flexed his arms and cocked one meaty fist by his shoulder. "All right, youngster . . ." he said.

The elf slid back and pushed the door open a bit wider. A large warforged stepped through the door and adopted a protective stance.

"This is Four," said the elf.

Pomindras swaggered a little as he approached. "It's for . . . what?"

"This," said the warforged. He threw a fast punch from the waist, catching Pomindras right below the ribs. Pomindras doubled over, gasping for breath, and he staggered and fell to the floor, pulling a chair over on top of himself.

"Seeing as you have markedly little hospitality," said the elf, "we'll be on your way. Free Cimozjen by sundown. I'm giving you one last chance."

The two of them departed, and the warforged pulled the door closed behind them.

"More than I'll give you," muttered Pomindras. He rose and set the chair upright again. "I'll fetch some others and we'll—"

"You'll do nothing," said Rophis waving him off with the bone. "Not yet. Ambush her in the streets, and the chronicles will hear of it. That would be bad, because it makes her story all the more compelling. We need a way to eliminate her without adding to her influence, and —" He stopped in mid-gesture, then a jaded smile slowly spread across his face.

"Sit," he said.

Pomindras sat. "What's your plan, lord?"

"We'll send her an invitation that she won't be able to resist," he said. Then he returned his attention to his turkey leg.

Chapter
Twenty-Four

Lying to the Authorities
Mol, the 2nd day of Aryth, 998

Do I know how to work a crowd, or don't I?" Minrah smiled as she saw the people assembled around the latest edition of *The Korranberg Chronicle*, where it was plastered to a large, blank wall. The top of the broadsheet featured the fourth installment of her story, and was the subject of much animated discussion.

"If you wanted an angry crowd, you have succeeded," said Four.

"Indeed I have. Now that we have the crowd behind us—or at least behind the thought of righteous revenge—we need to talk with the Sentinel Marshals."

"I do not understand. If you are relying on the Sentinel Marshals, why do you want the crowd excited?"

"Two reasons. The first is so that the Marshals feel the pressure. If they know that every face they meet on the street wants to see Torval avenged, they're more likely to help. That way they're less likely to pull some limpid sort of trick like they did at Thronehold, leaving the guilty to go free."

"And what is the second reason?"

"I want the crowd personally involved. There's nothing like a lynch mob to get a job done right. Once the crowd realizes they're a part of the story, that they're involved with history as it's being written, they'll get the revenge they all want, laws and Marshals notwithstanding."

Four considered this. "Might not there be some casualties, if an angry mob were to attack the Marshals and House Orien?"

"Most assuredly," said Minrah. "And that makes for an even more exciting story. We just have to make sure we keep ourselves safe. Come, Four. We're off to see the Marshals."

❖ ❖ ❖ ❖ ❖ ❖ ❖

Cimozjen woke up with a groan. His head ached, an ugly taste had encamped in his mouth, and when he opened his eyes the world looked fuzzy.

He lay on his pallet bed, clothed and armored and very stiff. He'd been there for a while. He remembered defeating Tholog and, as he hadn't wanted to face the guards with their electrified spears again, walking out of the arena with his weapons in hand. He'd gone back into his cage like a trained animal.

Cimozjen forced himself to sit up. There in the corner were his staff and his sword, just as he remembered leaving them, and just out of his reach. With a grunt, he leaned forward, resting his elbows on his knees. What had happened next?

Next he'd . . . woken up.

They had done something to him.

He put his hand to the small of his back. His dagger was gone.

He stood up and shuffled his way across his cell as far as the chain would let him. There, on the ground by his other weapons, was his dagger. That was why they had struck him unconscious. Somehow they'd known he hadn't given up his third weapon, and some house wizard had felled him like a tree. He shuffled back over to his pallet bed and sat heavily. He turned his hands over and looked at them.

They wanted him unarmed.

But why? One obvious answer was that he could kill himself with his dagger. Still, he could probably commit suicide by hanging himself with his belt or ankle chain, or by starving himself, or even just by falling on his sword in the arena.

Then he remembered Torval. Torval had used a sharp object to cut into his skin and create a scar. Perhaps they didn't want that to happen again.

Cimozjen pushed up his sleeve and looked at his bare forearm. What kind of message was Torval trying to send?

He traced his fingers along his skin. S . . . I . . . And then he realized: it's wasn't an I. It was an L. Torval had been writing Slave, but something had stopped him from completing it.

He looked up, at the three weapons that lay in the corner, just out of his reach.

No wonder.

❂ ❂ ❂ ❂ ❂ ❂ ❂

Minrah and Four walked across town to the outpost of the Sentinel Marshals, located in a corner tower of one of the Aundairian government buildings along with the speaking stone station operated by House Sivis and the Kundarak Banking Guild—an above-ground service desk for their subterranean operations.

Inside, the Sentinel Marshal outpost was actually welcoming. While well furnished, it had neither the pomp of royalty nor the ostentatious hubris of the dragonmarked houses. The power it projected was quiet, much like, it was told, had been the case with the early kings of Galifar. The dark wood had been warmly polished to have a deep luster reminiscent of coals burning on a winter night. Papers were posted about containing splendid renditions of wanted criminals, some of them created with magical glamers that seemed as true to life as one could possibly want. A map of Khorvaire dominated one wall, peppered with tiny flags and pins, and opposite that hung a detailed map of the streets of Fairhaven, likewise peppered with little colored flags and notes.

A clerk sat at a high desk, scribing gear all about him. He looked at Minrah as she and Four entered the room, his fingers laced at the edge of his desk.

"Good morning to the both of you. Do you have a criminal complaint, or are you seeking some other service?"

Minrah smiled as she walked over. The desk was just a tad too high for her to peer over, so she slipped to the side. It also helped her flirting to stand closer to her target. "It's rather more complicated than that," she said, gazing at him from the corner of her eye as she feigned timidity.

"Indeed? How may I be of service?"

"My name's Minrah Hunter," she said with just a trace of coyness. "And you are . . . ?"

"Sorn d'Deneith, at your service."

Minrah's fluttered her eyes and faced him more fully. "I'm sorry, Sorn . . . ?"

"Of House Deneith," he said. "My apologies if it wasn't clear. Sometimes that double 'D' comes out sounding like a stutter."

"Deneith. Right," said Minrah. She tried to force her smile back, but her furrowed brow smothered it as a thunderhead stops the sunshine. "House Deneith. But I thought . . . aren't the Sentinel Marshals an . . . independent . . . force?"

"Of course we are. It's part of our charter, just like the Blademarks Guild and the—"

"And the Defender's Guild. Right." Her expression went from anxious to vacuously sunny in an instant. "That's why I'm here. I was looking to hire a bodyguard. Would that be possible?"

"I'm sorry, miss," said the clerk. "That's not what we do in this office. We only handle criminal investigations here. Contracts for the Defenders Guild are handled through the main House Deneith enclave."

"Was I mistaken?" gasped Minrah. "I am so sorry."

"Not a worry. It can be a little confusing sometimes. We

Marshals keep ourselves physically separate from the rest of the house to help maintain our neutrality. If you'd like, I can give you directions."

"That won't be necessary. I know where I'm going."

"No problem, young miss," said the clerk with a respectful nod of the head. "Happens all the time. Truly."

Minrah left quickly, grabbing Four's arm as she departed. She dragged him behind her until they had exited the tower, walked half a block, and then ducked in an alley. No sooner were they out of sight than Minrah leaned against the wall, trembling, squealed a high-pitched cry and grabbed at her hair with clawed hands.

"Are you ailing?" asked Four.

"Yes!" said Minrah. "I am so stupid!"

"Ah. Your brain is damaged, then?"

"Four," said Minrah, "don't you see? All this time we've been looking at who might have sway over the Marshals, but who has more sway than *their own people?* House Orien isn't behind this! It's House Deneith!"

"But you said they were rigidly neutral and true to their pledge, and would not want to risk their reputation."

"Obviously, I didn't think it through all the way. But it all makes sense now. Who's better to take control of soldiers than soldiers, who's more likely to promote fighting than mercenaries, and who's less likely to hold to the law than sellswords? No wonder Rophis was so unruffled when I threatened him with the Marshals raiding his gambling arena. Just think about it. The Sentinel Marshals are one arm of the house, and they always uphold the law and vanquish the wrongdoer . . . unless doing so crosses their own! They can't very well cut the purse that pays them, can they? That's why the Marshals let Pomindras and Rophis go free on Thronehold, Four. They were letting members of their own house off the hook." She snorted. "Meanwhile, the people they hired or duped—the passengers, and that Kundarak moneycounter—they get arrested and prosecuted for their part in the slave trade."

"Great!"

Minrah looked up at him, confused and disgusted. "What?"

"That is great. Great as in large, ominous, and far-reaching."

Minrah placed her face in her hands. "We really need to work on your language skills."

"You have said that before," said Four, "but you never follow up with lessons." He paused, and seeing no response was forthcoming, asked, "So what is our next step?"

Minrah rubbed her face, then looked to the steely autumn sky. "Since we can't go to the law, we go to the power." She stood erect, brushed her hair back, and regained her composure. "We go to the crown. Queen Aurala will be ill-pleased to hear that people are being enslaved in her fair land."

Striding out the other end of the alley, she spoke to Four over her shoulder. "Let me be realistic," she said. "We're not going to see her. We'll see some low-ranking administrators that will be ill-pleased on her behalf. But on the bright side, maybe they'll have some magic for us, something we can use to our advantage."

❦ ❦ ❦ ◉ ❦ ❦ ❦

The view slit slammed shut. And, after a moment, the bland gray door opened to admit Tholog into the front rooms of the arena. He nodded to the door guard and went down the passageway to the right, thinking about how all door guards seemed to like to slam view slits.

He entered the booking area, walked up to one of the barred wickets, and rapped his knuckle on the wooden counter. "Seneschal!" he called, lisping the sibilants.

The only person within the booking room was an older human, checking ledgers. He looked up. "Ah, yes, may we help you . . . ?"

"Tholog."

"Yes, that's right, Tholog." The seneschal rose and walked slowly over, touching one finger to the side of his nose. "Didn't we pay out against you last night?"

Tholog rubbed a hand self-consciously on the bandage over the base of his neck, where a wound, a good two fingers wide but merely skin-deep, marked the place where Cimozjen had stabbed him. "Uh, yes, you did," he growled bitterly, "and that's what I'm here for. I want to issue a challenge."

"Looking for revenge, are we?"

"No," said Tholog. "I'm still too weak for that. I lost a lot of blood. If I stand up too quickly, the darkness takes me."

The seneschal leaned forward, hands clasped together over his heart. "Was the wound serious?"

"It should have been fatal. Cursed Karrn cheated me!" spat the hobgoblin. "Distracted me with talk of honor, then stabbed me in the neck as I was thinking. I cannot leave him unpunished. I want my vengeance now, but I don't know when I'll be strong enough to return."

"That is a pity," said the seneschal, looking truly compassionate. "You've been doing so well for us. And for yourself, of course. How is it then that we can help you?"

"I have someone I'd like to use as a stand-in for my revenge. I've found another fighter who'd be well suited to the arena, and I hope to make some money backing him with my wagers before everyone else figures out how good he is."

"Do tell us of him."

Tholog rubbed his wound again. "He's a bugbear, mercenary from Darguun, and he's a tough one, eager for a scrap."

"Bugbear?" asked the seneschal. "I don't believe we've ever seen one of them in our establishment."

Tholog shrugged, then winced and clutched at his wound again. "I can't speak for the whole race, but this one is pretty much the same height and build as a front-line warforged. Thank the Host for his fur, because he wears pretty much nothing but his armor. Saw him at a drunken brawl across town the other night. Took down several with nothing but his teeth and claws. When he was done, I hied off with him before the watch showed up. No sense in wasting a good warrior in the dungeons, right?"

The seneschal wrung his hands. "The creature sounds impressive indeed," he said, "and the novelty could be good for business. You are aware that we do not normally allow third-party challenges, but since you were treated so unfairly in the previous fight, and since you've provided such good results for us over the last year, I suppose I will endorse your invitation. It's too late to add anyone to the lists for tonight, but I can put your champion in for the morrow, if you'd like."

"Thank you. Please pair him off against . . . grrh, I can't remember his name. You know who I mean."

The seneschal smiled. "Cimozjen, the Killer from Karrnath. I know him well. He's already drawn quite a bit of betting activity for us. I am sure this match will do well for all of us."

"Good." Tholog put a small pouch on the counter. "Put this on Cimozjen . . . to die."

❂ ❂ ❂ ❂ ❂ ❂ ❂

"The man no one dares challenge, fighting by lot, Cimozjen Hellekanus, the Killer from Karrnath, defender!" boomed the voice.

Cimozjen ignored the boos and catcalls from the crowd. It was safe for cowards to berate a warrior when safely ensconced in the seats above the arena. He also tried to ignore the pangs of hunger that plagued his stomach, for the rations he'd been given since his capture were not quite enough to sate his appetite. No wonder Torval had looked so thin.

Instead of attending to distractions internal or external, Cimozjen prayed that Dol Dorn would allow him to prevail in this combat without taking a life.

Across the way, the door opened. Within was a shadowy shape, and, from his vantage point, Cimozjen could see that it had been contained within a large crate. He wondered how many others had watched Four step out of a crate just like that.

"And, by special request," boomed the voice, "a new creature enters the arena! We've managed to procure, at great expense and at the risk of losing our immortal souls in the Karrnathi bureaucracy, a real Karrnathi zombie!"

The crowd cheered.

"Who will it be, people? Which vile spawn will prevail, the living or the dead? Cimozjen favored, four to one!"

Four to one, thought Cimozjen, with no small sense of pride. Pretty good odds. I wonder what Four's odds were like.

The zombie stalked out of its crate, and suddenly Cimozjen had the answer. The roaring crowd. The lone voice, cutting through the noise, calling the odds, dragging out the pronouncement to stoke the excitement. Four to one. Ffourrr-to-oooonne! It was the noise the warforged had imitated for them. How suitable that it had served as the seed for his name.

The zombie closed like a seasoned warrior, its legs in a wide, well balanced stance. It kept its center of gravity low, and held its shield and sword to the sides, ready for action. No mortal could maintain such an aggressive stance for long without tiring. It was one of the advantages the zombie had. That, and the zombie couldn't bleed to death.

Its eyes glowed with a malevolent fire, a glint as of the gaze of Khyber himself. They shone starkly against its leathery skin, blackened and desiccated by the alchemical reagents that helped give it motility. It bared its teeth and began to close.

Giving ground to buy time, Cimozjen watched the undead creature, studying its armor, the tatters of its uniform, and the cut of its facial features. Well, he thought, at least it's no one I know.

He also realized that Dol Dorn had answered his prayer. Only one life was at risk this evening.

Chapter
Twenty-Five

As Minrah opened the door to the Dragon's Flagons, the hot, noisy air gushed out into the chill autumn evening. She took a step back, wondering if that was what war was like—sticky, loud, surrounded by violent people who smelled of sweat and other things best left unmentioned. She steeled her resolve—made possible by the fact that Four entered in front of her—and plowed her way into the thick atmosphere.

As they had discussed, Four went and stood in the corner. Aside from making him feel comfortable, it also gave him the best view of the tavern and kept him out of harm's way. Minrah stood beside him for a while, watching the business.

"Do my eyes deceive, or are the thugs swarming more than on other nights?"

"There are more people here," said Four. "Almost half again as many as the most we have previously seen."

"Something's going on," said Minrah. "Well, that will possibly allow me to complete my task a tad more readily. Now to find my target. Keep an ear angled for me, Four. Or whatever you have that hears sounds."

As crowded as it was, Minrah was forced to move among the patrons to find the person she was after. And, after being jostled, cursed at, mocked, lewdly propositioned, and doused with a spilled tankard nigh full of cheap ale, she at last found the person she sought.

"Boniam," she said with a smile far sunnier than her heart truly was. "Would you . . . permit me to sit at your table?"

He gestured grandly to the empty seat with his mug. "Why wouldn't I?"

Minrah sat demurely. "Well . . . I don't see Jolieni here tonight . . ."

He canted his head in acknowledgement. "Indeed. And we won't be seeing her here again, more's the pity."

"I was afraid you'd say that," said Minrah with a compassionate look. "What . . . precisely happened?"

Boniam gave her a strange look. "Your friend killed her, didn't you know?"

Minrah gaped.

"That's not entirely accurate, I suppose," he said. "Rather Jolieni used your friend to kill herself. He tried to get her to yield."

"I—I'm so sorry," said Minrah.

"It happens," said Boniam. "As a soldier, you accept that. And with her, the way her heart was burning, it was bound to happen sooner than later. In fact, it may have been the best thing for her, to end it all quickly, rather than get eaten up from within with your own blood poisoning your soul and killing you a day at a time."

"But—but she was your—"

"She was an acquaintance," said Boniam. He took another swig. "We were helping her out, but she didn't let anyone get close to her."

"Oh. Well. There it is, then." Minrah struggled for words. "Um . . . how are you faring?"

"I've been better," he said.

"Really? What news?"

"Took a sword to the bowels," he said, grinning ruefully. "Thought I was destined for Dolurrh, make no doubt, but the healer got to me in time. So now I am indebted for several hundred sovereigns, and I'll be working that off."

"Several *hundred* . . ."

"And well worth it, believe you me," said Boniam. "I can't tell you what it feels like. The warmth—you can feel the warmth of your own insides on your hands, but at the same time you feel the cold of the world inside you . . . it's just . . . well, I'd rather be working off a debt to a healer than any of the other results I can think of, even if it does take a couple years or more. I'd double my debt if I could get that memory out of my head."

"So you're working off your debt by . . . ?"

"By fighting in the ring, of course." He smiled sheepishly. "I just hope I don't get eviscerated again, or I could spend the rest of my life in that circle of clay of a debtor's prison. To better fortune!" He raised his mug in salute. "And how is it by you, fair one?"

"Better than many, and envied by most," she said. "I've won a fair haul with a canny wager, so I've more than enough crowns to keep me in wine."

"Wonderful news!" said Boniam. "Next round's on you!" He drained his mug and slammed it on the table. "So what's the word? I haven't seen you here in several days, thought maybe you'd moved on."

Minrah leaned forward, her chin resting on her interlaced fingers. She gazed raptly at Boniam, searching his face. "Really? Our absence was a surprise?"

Boniam pushed out his lower lip and shrugged. "I guess maybe not. At least no more so than you showing up here in the first place. Doesn't really seem like your kind of place. But the Karrn seemed at home."

Minrah's gaze flicked from one of his eyes to the other and back. "So are you interested in me, or not?"

"Who wouldn't be? You're a very pretty thing, especially for an elf." His faced flushed. "That's not what I meant."

"You mean you're not attracted to me?"

"No, I am. I mean, um, ah, my tastes usually run to bigger, more robust women than your typical elf. Besides, you seemed like you were attached to that Karrn. But I don't have anything against elves in general. Spent too much time fighting alongside them to have any problems with them, that is."

Minrah feigned a pout. "And here I thought you were interested in me personally. Consider the other night, you came and sat with us, and you were asking all sorts of questions. Where we were from, what we did . . ."

"Oh, that? This one gentleman—one of them that owns the arena, I think, at least he's rich enough to—he was asking after you, that's all. Wanted to know more about you so he could invite you to dinner or sponsor your man in the ring or something." Boniam shrugged again. "He asked me to find out for him, because this isn't his sort of place."

"Oh, then I guess it was a coincidence," she said. She managed to signal one of the serving girls to bring Boniam another drink.

"What was?"

"We were ambushed that very night," said Minrah, matter-of-factly. "Assaulted by a small band of brigands as we walked home."

Boniam reared back, then his temper took hold. "Filthy goat-whelps!" he slammed his fist on the table. "One thing I can't stand, it's them who beat up weak folks for fun or purses! Uh, no offense."

Minrah giggled. "Don't fret your words," she said. "I know I don't cut a terribly frightening profile. But my friends were plenty big enough."

"Do tell."

Minrah described the events of the battle as well as she could remember them, which was not overmuch, considering she'd spent most of her time hiding her face. As she recounted the tale, she looked intently at Boniam's face, but saw not a flicker of recognition or duplicity in his expression, just a righteous indignation at robbery and those who make it their profession, and a cold glee to hear the fate of those that had perished. And, judging him to be concerned with the brutalities of war rather than the subtleties of deception, she decided he was truly ignorant of his role in the events.

Boniam's next drink arrived, and Minrah flipped a copper crown onto the serving girl's tray.

"Oh, hey, you don't need to be paying for my drink," he said. "I only spoke in jest."

"It's not a problem in the slightest," said Minrah. "As I said, I've done well."

Boniam winced. "You should probably be saving it to pay for healing, though," he said. "Seeing what happened to your friend last night, I don't think it's very kind of you to spend it so freely. Unless the two of you aren't involved any more . . ." A vague, confused look of hope crossed his features.

"What happened?"

"You didn't hear?" He grimaced. "Folks say he got the business end of a broadsword the other night, fighting one of his zombie countrymen. Cut him up good before he put a dagger in its brain."

Minrah gaped. "Oh my word," she said, putting a hand to her mouth. "I hope he can hold up. I knew we were running out of time."

"Time for what?"

"When's the next, um, fighting thing at the arena?"

"Tomorrow night. Should be plenty of time to hire a hospitaler mage." He glanced around the tavern at the other warriors. "And I'd suggest you do so. Looks like we'll have a full slate."

Minrah sucked on her lips for a moment, her troubled eyes darting around the table. At last she made up her mind. "Boniam, you seem like a decent man," she said. "Direct, honest."

"Thank you."

"Have you ever broken someone's trust?"

"Of course not."

"Have you ever told someone a secret told to you in confidence?"

"No. Uh, well, not since I was a child." He shrugged. "There was a time I didn't know better, but not since I became an adult."

Minrah stared into his eyes. "Never?"

He thought for a moment. "No, I never have," he said plainly. "Why?"

Minrah grimly blew a stray hair out of her face and signaled for more drinks. "Because I'm about to tell you the terrible truth."

● ● ● ◉ ◉ ● ● ●

The next day was bitterly cold and windy, but Minrah did not spend it waiting in their suite. Four followed her around the entire city as she wandered aimlessly, unable to sit still for more than a few moments.

Sunset found them sitting at a roadside table in a small courtyard. Minrah picked at some food that had long gone cold in the wind.

Four looked at the small potion in his hand, a colored glass bottle sealed with wax that bore the Aundairian royal sigil. The clerk had said it was magic.

"What am I to do with this?" he asked.

"Four, just—!" She held up one hand, seemingly cutting off her own tirade. She growled. "I'll tell you when it's time, got it? In the meantime, just be quiet and let me think!"

"Why are you so unsettled?" asked Four. "Your visit with the Aundairian authorities went well, did it not? They said they would launch a raid at our discretion. And Cimozjen is still alive, is he not?"

Minrah sagged, then looked up and smiled wanly. She tossed her fork to her plate. "It's the waiting, Four. I'd hate to see it all slip away at the last moment. There's a lot that could go wrong, but so much that could go right. I just want everything to turn out." She stood and wrapped her cloak around her. "I'm just anxious, that's all."

She walked down the street toward the riverside.

Four followed, wondering if she were concerned more for Cimozjen, or for the story she'd been writing.

　 ❋ ❋ ❋ ◉ ❋ ❋ ❋

"Cimozjen the Black, the Killer from Karrnath, defender!" bellowed the barker, his arcanely amplified voice cutting through the ambient noise. At the heels of the introduction rose a rash of hisses, catcalls, and even the occasional supportive cheer.

Cimozjen didn't care. Let the crowd think what they wanted to think. If he made a name for himself in the arena, be that name honored or infamous, it would only make it easier for Minrah or Four to find him and set him free.

He stalked into the arena, holding himself proudly. Even as a gladiator and a slave, he was determined to uphold the honor of the Iron Band and to win every fight that came his way. Only through survival could he possibly make his holy retribution for his fallen brother, and only through survival could he continue to defy those who held him against his will.

Freedom. The first thing he'd do would be to get a decent meal. The gruel they fed him tasted like the underside of a hard-ridden saddle.

He wore his chain mail, padded beneath by his tunic. He wasn't sure why they let him keep it. He still didn't have a helm, nor did he think they'd ever give him one. He had his sword in hand, his staff in his off hand, and his dagger concealed at his back.

And he had a seven-day growth of stubble across his chin, slowly forming itself into a beard. He did not relish the thought of using his sword—or worse yet, his heirloom dagger—as a razor, but his other options were slim.

He pulled his attention back to the present, shoving away thoughts of food and hygiene. He had someone to fight. And, unfortunately, someone he might have to kill. He knew that, given his nickname and the reputation he'd backed into, anyone he faced would be unlikely to give him any mercy.

A bugbear entered the far side of the arena, holding a massive double-bitted battle-axe. The creature was large, six feet tall, covered with a coarse dark-brown fur. Large goblinoid ears propped out to each side. The one on the right had a pair of silver hoops run through two piercings, the one on the left was tattooed with a pair of runes or symbols that Cimozjen couldn't read at that distance. It had small eyes that seemed to glow with anger. Its muzzle was pronounced and powerful, reminiscent of the bear for which the species had been nicknamed untold ages ago. It wore a breechclout and a pair of heavy leather straps crossed across its breast, but no other clothing or armor.

Cimozjen closed the gap, sizing the creature up. It likewise stepped closer, walking upright rather than using the bandy-legged gait Cimozjen had expected.

Cimozjen stopped. He cocked his head, inspecting the bugbear's features more closely. He smiled. "You have experience in the arena, I see," he said, raising his voice to be heard above the crowd.

The beast raised his axe and spun it about its haft, then stretched its arms out to the side. "Silence!" it bellowed in its gravelly voice, and the crowd obeyed. "Cimozjen Hellekanus," the beast continued, shouting. "I bring a message to you from Tholog. He remembers your deeds in this ring, and tonight he wishes to see you die."

The crowd roared.

Cimozjen lunged with his sword, aiming straight for the heart.

* * * * * * *

"What was that?" yelled Rophis, leaning forward in his plush chair.

"I haven't the slightest," said Pomindras, seated beside him. "I'd swear he was going to skewer that beast just like he did the hobgoblin. He didn't miss at that range, did he?"

"Of course not," said Rophis. "The impact pushed the bugbear back. Their breastbones must be tougher than we think."

"Bad luck to him, then," said Pomindras. He gestured to the side. "More wine!"

Rophis looked askance at him for just a moment.

"I want to enjoy this," said Pomindras. He took the proffered goblet and took a long sip. He sighed contentedly. "As much as I can, for as long as he lasts."

Rophis settled back into his chair, clapping with appreciation as Cimozjen got inside the bugbear's reach and the two combatants clenched for a moment like wrestlers. It looked like the bugbear was trying to bite Cimozjen's ear off. Then the bugbear threw Cimozjen aside and took to the offensive.

Rophis leaned toward Pomindras. "My friend," he said, not taking his eyes off the combat, "I don't know whether or not I hate the man any more. He caused us problems, it is true, but he is so entertaining to watch. And his callous attitude has drawn out the crowd."

"Drawn out their crowns, you mean," said Pomindras. "He makes us a lot of money on wagers."

Rophis laughed. "You're right. He may be the best thing that's ever happened to us." He turned his head. "More wine!"

❧ ❧ ❧ ◉ ❧ ❧ ❧

Cimozjen stumbled and fell, then rolled quickly out of the way as the bugbear's axe came down. It bit deeply into the arena surface, spraying Cimozjen with small bits of clay. He rolled further away and regained his feet, panting heavily.

The crowd groaned and cheered at his escape.

He wiped one hand across his upper lip, locked eyes with the bugbear, and said, "Well, at least we're making a good show of it. I doubt anyone expected you to last this long."

"It is now time for you to die!" yelled the bugbear.

"Think so?" panted Cimozjen. "Last I checked, I had a say in that decision." He staggered momentarily, then lunged to the attack. He jabbed his staff at the bugbear's eyes to distract him, and swung his sword in a low, rising forehand slash, aiming for the hip. He connected right below the crest of the hip. His arm jarred with the impact, but the bugbear showed no sign that he even recognized that he had been struck.

The bugbear swatted Cimozjen's staff from his sweaty hand. It fell to the clay at Cimozjen's feet.

Cimozjen stumbled forward with his momentum, but the bugbear backpedaled and used the butt end of his two-handed axe to get underneath Cimozjen's forearm. With a strong flip of his muscular arms, he pushed Cimozjen's sword arm into the air, and then he swung crossways with his axe, striking the blade at the pommel and stripping it from Cimozjen's hand. The sword twirled through the air for about ten yards. It landed point first into the clay, digging a divot before flipping over and landing.

Cimozjen looked at his numb hand. "Blessed Host, that hurt," he said.

He feinted for his sword. The bugbear swung at his back to fell him as he ran, but he ducked under the whistling blade and doubled back for his staff.

He snatched it up and ran to the center of the arena. The bugbear cagily stayed between him and his sword. Cimozjen shifted his staff to his left hand and drew his dagger from the small of his back. "Here we go," he muttered.

The bugbear closed, his large hands twisting on the haft of his weapon.

With an efficient little flip of the wrist, Cimozjen reversed his grip in the dagger, holding it point-down for a quick slash-and-plunge. He lashed out, aiming to slash across the front of the bugbear's throat, then reverse direction and stick the blade in behind the beast's jugular, but in that split second the bugbear's powerful hand let go of his axe and seized Cimozjen's wrist in a grip like iron.

Cimozjen's eyes went wide. With his left hand, he struck the bugbear about the head and shoulders, but the angle was all wrong, and the blows, while loud, availed him not.

The bugbear twisted Cimozjen's wrist over, then he dropped his axe and pried the blade from the Karrn's hand. He turned his shoulder and used his weight to drive Cimozjen to the ground.

With his staff, Cimozjen tried to strike the bugbear the harder, but lying on his back robbed his blows of power. The bugbear shifted his grip and grabbed Cimozjen by the throat, using his knees and elbows to keep him pinned. Cimozjen drew up his right hand and clenched it over his heart. "No! Please!" he screamed. His terrified voice sounded alien to his ears.

"It is time for you to pray to the Host," said the bugbear. The creature glanced down and saw the small hole in Cimozjen's chain shirt where Jolieni's blade had nearly skewered him. He maneuvered Cimozjen's dagger into position. Cimozjen struck the bugbear again and again with the staff in his left hand, but despite his fear, he knew he could not do enough damage to stop the blade.

Murmuring a frantic prayer for salvation, Cimozjen felt his own blade pierce his skin, then slide into his chest.

◉ ◉ ◉ ◉ ◉ ◉ ◉

"Ooohhhhh," said Rophis with mock pity as the bugbear drove the dagger into Cimozjen's chest up to the hilt. He poured out the rest of his wine on the floor, spattering the stone with red. "I guess that's that."

Twenty-two years earlier:

Cimozjen fought the return of consciousness. He fought against the rising awareness of pain, the disorientation that muddled his brain, the stench that assailed his nose, but he had to yield before the persistent awakening.

He opened his eyes, and found himself face to face with a dead man, open blank eyes staring through him into eternity. Is that me? he thought. Then he saw the small dragonhawk emblem on the front of the man's helmet, and he remembered him. He remembered seeing that look on the man's face as Cimozjen's dagger slipped between the plates of his mail and into his heart, the look of surprise, dismay, betrayal, defeat. His mind began to piece things back together, unfolding the memories of the last stand of the Iron Band.

He moaned softly, an indulgence he granted himself, an admission of the aches that held his body and by no means a plea for help. How he'd managed to remain alive, he had no idea. Perhaps he had been struck across the helmet, or perhaps a horse had knocked both him and his final victim down. It mattered little. He was alive.

Slowly he raised his head. Viewed from the ground, the battlefield was an endless badlands of broken armor and broken bodies, the only vegetation the blades and spears that rose from the carnage where they had been planted. Overhead, the sky grew gradually darker as the sun sank toward the horizon.

"Mozji . . ." said a voice, so weakly it was almost a whimper.

Cimozjen turned his head to see Kraavel lying some five feet away, clutching a wad of bloody cloths to his abdomen just below the ribs, pressing it tight with both hands. His face was ashen and drawn.

"Mozji," he gasped, "it won't stop bleeding. Heal me."

Cimozjen turned his head to scan the area. A few Aundairian litter crews worked the battlefield, looking for the injured. Nearby, a pair of desultory spearman stalked about, searching the field. As Cimozjen watched, they stopped. One of them nudged something with his boot, then the other plunged his spear downward. A hand briefly shot up from the ground, then fell limp. The Aundairians continued their hunt, drawing closer to where the two Karrns lay. Dread seized Cimozjen's heart.

He looked back to Kraavel. "Lie still!" he whispered. "Play dead!" Cimozjen clutched his holy symbol, concealed beneath his body, with his right hand.

"But Mozji," pleaded Kraavel, "the bleeding, it—"

"Let them pass by, and then I'll heal you! Just hold on for a few moments!" He didn't mention—couldn't admit, not aloud—that he feared the Aundairians might stab him as he lay there, and he wanted to save his healing for himself, just in case. He didn't want to die, not here, not like that, not stabbed to death while feigning to be a corpse. He felt the fear, he felt the dishonor, and he was ashamed.

"Mozji, I'm so cold . . ."

"Hsst!"

Cimozjen lay still, one eye peering through the crook of his dead foe's arm to watch the progress of the Aundairian spearmen. He steeled his mind, bracing himself to feel a stab wound, willing himself not to react to the pain, preparing his soul to pray for his healing even as the cruel blade was withdrawn from his torso. Concealed beneath his prone body, the telltale glow of his holy symbol would not be noticed, and he might survive the encounter.

The Aundairians moved past, never closer than thirty paces to one side. Cimozjen heard them talking quietly, their accented words a strange murmur in the settling evening.

After they passed, after the tension eased from his joints and limbs, Cimozjen began to move, carefully, quietly. He found his dirk still embedded in the chest of his foe and gripped it, then crawled stealthily over to where Kraavel lay.

"Hsst! Kraavel!" he whispered. "They're gone!" He pushed Kraavel over to get a better look at the wound, but his friend lay limp. His undamaged eye was dilated, staring nowhere. His half-open lips looked faintly blue.

As the sun set over the last battlefield of the Iron Band, Cimozjen stared into the face of his friend, abandoned by an act of cowardice to die a cold and lonely death.

"I am so sorry, my friend," he whispered. "Please forgive me." He began to weep, silently. "And I swear, never, ever again."

Chapter
TWENTY-SIX

Pomindras rose. "Lord, I should be going. I'm due on the clay shortly."

"You enjoy that, don't you?" asked Rophis, slurping away the last of his wine. "Who is it this time?"

"Some stiff-necked youngster who wants my shield," he said as he carefully hefted his prize possession by the straps and slung it over his back. The gold rim shone beautifully, while the black boss remained as black as midnight. "He challenged me, can you believe it? Bah. Odds are as long as I've seen them, but I'll still chain myself up, just in case the lad gets a lucky strike in."

"Pomindras, while you're down there, sign that bugbear up with the family. I liked his style."

"If you insist, lord," he said. He picked up his sword by the scabbard and trotted to the stairwell that led to the arena.

● ● ● ◉ ● ● ●

The bugbear looked around. A sea of faces—yelling, cheering, clapping—surrounded him. It was a new experience. He looked down at the thin blade in his hand. It was so small compared to his great axe, but in the right hands, just as deadly. Perhaps even deadlier. It was all so confusing, the noise, the dealings, everything but the arena. For a moment, he wished he were home.

One of the doors to the arena opened and a trio of workers stepped out, unarmed and dressed in simple peasants' attire. They walked over to Cimozjen's body. One hand was still clenched over his heart, and the other still tightly held to his staff. Blood trickled down the links of chain mail to form a small pool on the clay.

One of the workers continued to walk across the plaza to pick up Cimozjen's sword. The other two moved to recover his body. They each grabbed one heel and started pulling, and as they dragged him across the field, friction slowly drove his arms over his head. It almost looked like he was cheering another victory.

"Hey," said the trailing worker, the sword slung easily over his shoulder. "He ain't lettin' go of his stick!" He chuckled a little at the oddity.

One of the other workers called back to him over his shoulder, saying, "That's why it's called a 'death grip.' He'll drop it soon enough."

They dragged Cimozjen's body out of the arena. The third worker trailed close behind with the sword, and as he grabbed the latch to close the door behind him, he noticed that the bugbear had followed them. "Hey," he said. "You're supposed to go out that other door." He pointed across the arena with his empty hand, then started to close the door.

The bugbear reached out and grabbed the edge of the door.

"Hey!" yelled the worker. He raised his voice and spoke more slowly. "Go to that door. Understand? Not here. There." He pointed again. "That door. Go. This door, no!" He took a moment to turn to his companions. "Hey. Did you hear that? I rhymed!"

The bugbear yanked the door open and stepped in.

"Hey!" yelled the worker. "I said the other door!"

The bugbear closed the door behind him.

"Now look, you nit-brained—"

The bugbear kneed the man as hard as he could in the gut. The worker gagged with the impact, nigh to vomiting, and doubled over, whereupon the bugbear slammed one heavy fist onto his back just between his shoulders.

Cimozjen jerked into motion. Still clutching the staff tightly in his hand, he lanced it like a spear at one of the people dragging him and smacked him at the base of the skull. Stunned, the man let go of Cimozjen's leg. The other turned. Surprised to see the corpse moving in such an animated way, he also dropped Cimozjen's foot in surprise.

Cimozjen, in an awkward position at best, nonetheless swung his staff to strike the worker on the knee, temporarily hobbling him.

The bugbear leaped over Cimozjen and grabbed the two startled workers. They clearly had no fighting experience, and in a few swift breaths the bugbear had them both pinned beneath his burly arms. He squeezed the air from them until they both went limp, then banged their heads together a few times for good measure.

The bugbear turned to see Cimozjen had regained his feet. "That was easy," he said.

Cimozjen laughed darkly. "For you, maybe, but I was the one that got stabbed."

"I have been damaged many times."

"That's true," said Cimozjen, "but I think it feels different to creatures like us, Four." He picked up his sword. "Got my knife?"

Four handed Cimozjen his blade, then looked at his extended arm. "How do I get rid of this fur?" he said. "I do not like it. It is not me."

"It's just a visual illusion, Four. Your body still feels the same beneath it. It'll wear off sooner or later. I hope." Cimozjen sniffed and looked around. "So how do we get out of here?"

"We do not," answered Four.

❀ ❀ ❀ ❀ ❀ ❀ ❀

"What is going on?" said Rophis. "If they need to fight, put them in the pit!"

He stood and turned to find the source of the ruckus that had seized an entire section of seats somewhere off to his right.

There, near the entrance, it seemed a number of the audience had broken into a brawl. He strode toward the disturbance, waving several house guards to follow. Curiously, the crowd seemed to be evading the mischief, instead of feeding it.

But then he saw two unexpected things that put everything into perspective.

He saw the hobgoblin that Cimozjen had bested three days previous, and beside him the lad who owed them a few years in the arena after his evisceration. And he saw the rich blue tabards of the Aundairian soldiery.

They were forcing their way in to the arena, arresting as many people as they could and driving the rest before them like cattle. The two turncoat pit fighters were gesturing in Rophis's direction, searching the crowd for familiar faces.

Then the hobgoblin locked eyes with him.

Damn my height! thought Rophis. He turned, shielded his face as best he could, and grabbed one of the guards nearest him. "Destroy the evidence!" he ordered. "Now!"

He turned and began pushing his way through the audience, hoping that he could effect his escape before panic seized the crowd—or at least before the Aundairians captured him.

❀ ❀ ❀ ❀ ❀ ❀ ❀

Pomindras moved swiftly through the passageways beneath the audience's seating, heading around the curve of the arena for the fighters' exit. He muttered to himself, wondering why Rophis would want to contract a bugbear when they were as unreliable as a goblin and as smelly as a Karrnathi zombie.

Thus preoccupied, he did not notice that someone was waiting for him as he entered one of the open areas that dotted the outside of the arena.

Four, still clad in the last fading vestiges of the illusory bugbear trappings, stepped out and swung his battle-axe at Pomindras, aiming squarely at the ebon shield that covered his back, intending to cleave it in two—and, with the same powerful blow, Pomindras' spine.

Somehow the impact was dramatically off; The blow rocked Pomindras's shield and sent him tumbling, yet at the same time it cracked the haft of Four's weapon, and the shield remained unmarred.

Pomindras turned his fall into a roll and came up quickly. He grabbed the hilt of his sword and slung the scabbard to the side, baring the blade. Alarm and confusion held his face for just a moment, until he saw Four and Cimozjen. "You," he said, looking at Cimozjen. "Alive? How?"

He turned his gaze to Four and narrowed his eyes. "A glamer? You infiltrated us!" He backed up toward the hallway behind him, looking to narrow the area he had to defend. "That whole fight was mocked? That was a piece of work. I thought he really stabbed you to death."

"In truth, he almost did," said Cimozjen. "I prayed for healing as he withdrew the blade. That's why he had to kill me with my knife instead of his axe. We needed his body to block your view of it. I used the same trick to spare Tholog a few days ago."

Pomindras shucked his shield around and gripped it. It wasn't as maneuverable as it would have been if he'd had it properly strapped, but it was more serviceable than nothing. "Too clever by half," he said, "but you're still not getting out of here alive." He started backing quickly down the hallway.

Cimozjen chased after him. Four remained where he was, inspecting the odd angle at which his weapon had cracked.

Pomindras backpedaled, then turned to run.

"Coward," said Cimozjen. "I'll gladly see you dead with your sole wound to the back."

Pomindras sneered. "Bravely spoken for someone with armor," he said.

"I have naught but a staff for a shield," said Cimozjen. "You're well rested and perhaps ten years younger than I, yet you show the courage of a pock-marked adolescent and the honor of a febrile kobold. You attacked me in the streets with five others, yet fled the field ere your sword tasted the air. Go. Run. Get help. We'll see whether the dawn still bears tales of honor for the ring fighter called the Black Shield. That is you, correct? Or are you just his shield boy?"

"I had to flee earlier, because you had me outnumbered. Damn cowardly thugs." Pomindras gave a lopsided smile. "But in this hallway, there's just room enough for you and me. Unless you're going to make your pet warforged to do your work for you."

Cimozjen called back, saying "Four, Pomindras is mine. Cover my back."

"There is something you should know," said Four. "My axe cracked the wrong way. I have no explanation for it."

"It'll have to wait until later, Four," said Cimozjen. "I have someone here who wants to kill me, and I'd rather not indulge him."

Pomindras worked his arm into his shield straps. "I thought I'd missed the pleasure of killing you, but you've just made it all the sweeter." He dropped into a combat stance.

Cimozjen gave the Rekkenmark salute then readied himself, metal-shod staff angled backward and sword leveled for a thrust.

Pomindras took a low, wide stance and closed on Cimozjen crabwise. Seeing this, Cimozjen considered trying to wear the man down. A series of powerful overhand strikes on the shield would stress the knee, slowing him and forcing him to change his stance. Unfortunately, it would also take time and make a lot of noise, both of which would increase the chance of reinforcements coming. Instead, Cimozjen thought to go straight for the kill.

With a low feint at the leg combined with a sweeping upward follow-through, Cimozjen could draw his attention low, and possibly also draw his shield down. A surprise cut to the head with the inside edge could be telling, especially since Pomindras wore no helmet.

Pomindras jumped forward, swinging his shield in front of him to conceal his attack, then yanked it aside and thrust with his sword. The attack was low, to Cimozjen's surprise. He was caught raising his sword to parry, and was unable to reverse his momentum. Pomindras's lunge caught Cimozjen in the joint of his hip. The blade hit hard, and with a flash of sparks several links of Cimozjen's chain mail shattered and flew about the corridor. The blade bit into Cimozjen's skin and scraped painfully across his hip bone.

Cimozjen gasped in pain as the sundered links skittered across the flagstone floor. His brow furrowed. "An enchanted blade?"

Pomindras chuckled.

Cimozjen took to the attack, executing his planned chop at the leading leg. Partway through the swing he rolled his wrist and changed the angle of attack upward, leading with the inside edge of the sword, aiming for Pomindras's ear. But either Cimozjen was too old and slow, or Pomindras had seen the trick many times in the arena, because he ducked out of the way and raised his shield.

Cimozjen saw an actinic flash, felt a jarring bolt flash through his body, thumping painfully at his forearm and his knees. He felt the point of his sword dig into something, and he nearly lost his grip.

But there'd been no crash of metal.

Cimozjen stepped back, shaken and unnerved, his sword held out defensively. Pomindras slapped his shield upward at Cimozjen's weapon. As soon as the gold rim of his shield contacted Cimozjen's arm, another flash and charge of numbness blasted through him. Between the shock and the impact, he lost his grip on his sword, and he saw it fall from his fingers.

It didn't slide across the boss of Pomindras's shield. Rather it fell in, quickly becoming obscured by shadow and vanishing from sight altogether.

"Oops," said Pomindras in amusement.

And as his foe moved the shield to the side, Cimozjen finally understood what made the shield so impenetrably black. It was a ring of gold-colored metal . . . encircling *nothing*.

Cimozjen retreated a few steps, shook his hand to restore feeling, and gripped his staff tightly, the bottom end toward Pomindras, the upper end held behind his ear. He slid his right hand to find the proper place.

Seeing Cimozjen disarmed gave Pomindras new confidence. He closed quickly, circling his sword in a taunting sort of manner. "Now I rip apart your chain mail piece by piece, Karrn." He lunged, a lightning move that slipped past Cimozjen's parry, carved a terrible slice into his arm, and sheared half of his chain sleeve away.

Sundered links of chain tinkled down the hall.

"And if you think your little stick is going to stop me—"

Cimozjen surged forward, raising the staff for an overhand swat. Pomindras raised his shield. Then with his thumb Cimozjen flipped a tiny switch embedded in the staff and a long, thin blade speared out of one metal-shod end, shattering the small piece of clay that camouflaged the hole. Instead of continuing his overhand attack, Cimozjen put his weight into plunging the spear downward, driving it completely through Pomindras's foot just forward of the ankle.

Pomindras screamed and staggered, unable to move the injured foot.

"Oops," said Cimozjen with a glower.

He yanked the spear to the side, pulling Pomindras's leg to the side before the blade plowed through the flesh between the tarsal bones, slicing Pomindras's foot lengthwise.

Pomindras fell, scraping down the walls as he scrabbled for traction, gasping in pain.

Seeing an opening, Cimozjen thrust with his spear at

Pomindras's unprotected torso. Pomindras cried out, shock and pain taking command of his every action. Cimozjen plunged his spear again and again, until he was certain that the son of Deneith would scream no more.

Chapter
Twenty-Seven

The Quiet Touch of Death
Wir, the 4th day of Aryth, 998

That is a lot of weapons," said Four.

Cimozjen shrugged. "It's an armory for House Deneith. I'm not too surprised." He scratched his head and began to poke around. "I wonder where the boy stashed my longcoat. I hope they kept it rather than sell it. I paid a lot of coin for that thing."

"Cimmer! You're alive!" Minrah bounded into the room and leaped into his arms. She snuggled into him, squeezing him as tightly as her small arms would allow.

Cimozjen hugged her back, laughing with relief, but also very aware of every nuance of her proximity, including the way her delicate fingers shifted their position on his back. She sighed contentedly, and the sound was as soft and beautiful as a summer brook.

"I'm so glad you're safe," she murmured, burrowing her head into his sweaty tunic.

"I would not let myself be defeated, not here," he said.

"So how'd you like my plan?" she asked brightly, looking up at him with open, vulnerable, delighted eyes. "That was my idea. Pretty clever, huh?"

Cimozjen half-shrugged. "I guessed at it pretty quickly."

"Guessed?" asked Minrah. She backed up, affronted, hands on hips. "He was supposed to whisper it to you! Why didn't you tell him, Four?"

Cimozjen intervened. "It was so loud in the ring," he said. "We could hardly talk to each other. But the 'SI' tattoo on his ear was a good idea, and Four dropped a few pretty good hints, as good as he could while shouting. But just to be safe, I jabbed him right here." He rapped a knuckle on Four's hammered-iron chest piece, which showed a new scratch across it. "I had to make sure it was no trick, and I figured if it was Four in disguise, I'd scratch his armor. If not, I'd draw blood."

"That was a dangerous maneuver," said Four. "I reacted on reflex. It was too similar to the other times I spent . . . out there. For a moment, I was engaged to kill you, but then I remembered your face in the tavern, and how I diverted my axe—"

"Let's not travel any further down that road, shall we?" said Cimozjen. "We both survived, and Minrah brought Aurala's army at the right time."

"We timed it."

"You did?"

"Yes," said Four. "I saw the signal and told you it was time to end the fight."

"My companions," said Cimozjen with a gracious bow, "I am impressed."

"So what's this?" asked Minrah, reaching for the ebon shield that leaned against a stool next to Cimozjen. A spark flashed brightly, and she yanked her hand back. "Ow! Filth! What's that evil trick?" she snapped, clutching her arm to her breast.

Cimozjen looked over his shoulder at the shield slung there. "A farewell gift to me from the late unlamented Pomindras, erstwhile commander of the *Silver Cygnet*." He picked it up and held it by the straps with the inside facing Minrah. "Observe. On this side, a more or less normal wooden shield with arm straps. But on the other"—he turned it around—"a fiendishly clever device. The gold

ring around the edge emits a potent electric shock. And the center
. . . it's just not there."

"What do you mean?"

"It's nonexistent. Try to touch it. Go on, I've done it myself. So
long as you avoid the ring, you'll come to no harm."

Minrah reached out tentatively with her other arm. She brushed
her fingers at the black boss. "That's odd," she said. She reached
closer. Closer. "There's . . ."

"Nothing," said Cimozjen, peering over the rim of the shield.
"And from my perspective it looks as though your hand is reaching
into the shield up to your wrist."

Minrah yanked her hand out, studied her fingers, then leaned
forward carefully and reached in again, well past her elbow. "How
far does it go?"

"I've no idea at all," said Cimozjen. "It may well go forever. It
swallowed my sword, and I doubt I'll ever get it back. Unless you
want to crawl in and try to find it for me . . ."

"Buy yourself a new one," said Minrah, pulling her arm out.

"I'll make sure I'm armed before you drag me through another
one of your wild plans," he said with a chuckle.

"I'm sorry if it was hard on you, but we didn't have much time
left."

"What do you mean?" asked Cimozjen.

Minrah pulled out an envelope from her bag. "Take a look at
this. Two days ago Rophis delivered an invitation for me to come
see him at the Deneith enclave tomorrow. It even includes a guarantee of safe passage, notarized by House Sivis."

"Why would he want to meet with you?" asked Cimozjen. He
took the paper.

"I don't know," said Minrah, "but I figured that boded ill for
you. I got it the day after I confronted him and demanded your
release."

Cimozjen handed the paper back to Minrah. "Hold for a
moment," he said, espying an Aundairian officer walk toward the
trio.

"Excuse me, Minrah Penwright?" said the officer as he closed. He nodded to Cimozjen and Four in turn. "Pardon the intrusion, my good men. Minrah, I thought you should know that we have completed our search of the premises."

"And . . . ?"

"While we have found several caged beasts, we have not uncovered any direct evidence of enslavement. Certainly nothing that would withstand the Code of Galifar. Yet . . . that is, perhaps you should accompany me."

"Captain," said Minrah, "this is Cimozjen Hellekanus, the man whose saga I told to you. He was held against his will. And this is Four, whom they enslaved from the time he was created until a week or two ago when we freed him."

The captain glanced at them again. "Pleased to make your acquaintances. You should accompany us as well."

Cimozjen and Four grabbed their gear. The captain led them through the chambers and hallways beneath the arena until they came to a long corridor with a dozen open archways all along one wall.

The captain gestured them forward. "This is what we found," he said.

Cimozjen moved down the hall, peering into the open doors. "Yes, this is the sort of room I was kept in. Pallet bed, buckets for food and slop . . . but I see no manacles. How could they . . ." His words drifted off as he became aware of the weight of the shield upon his back. Manacles could easily have been unlocked from their footing and dumped into the shield, or into something like it, never to be seen again. He sighed heavily.

He inspected the door, and noted the lack of an interior latch. "There was such a door on my room, but it led not into the hallway, but almost straight into the arena."

"That's impossible," said the captain. "We've checked every exit from the arena. They all lead to hallways or common rooms."

"Magic," said Minrah. She was standing in a doorway, running her hands up and down the frame. "Runes carved into the frame, but every frame has been marred. I'll wager that a mage could ensorcel these, connecting them to the arena. That way, the only places prisoners could go would be straight from their pen to the arena and back."

"There's more," said the captain, and he gestured down the hall.

Cimozjen walked slowly along, following the captain's direction. Two more doors, and he saw what the captain meant. A body lay in the middle of the room in a pool of blood, his face crushed by a spiked instrument.

Cimozjen kneeled down beside the body and placed his fingers on the man's throat. There was no pulse, but the skin had not yet gone fully cold. "They killed them."

"Yes, they did," said the captain. "And they did a thorough job. We can't identify him by his features, and he has nothing on him to indicate his name or allegiance."

Cimozjen moved to the next archway. "And another."

"And more down the hall. Worse yet, there's a whole room with crates that contain nothing but wrecked warforged just a little further on."

Cimozjen shook his head. "They killed them all," he said, his voice thick with emotion. "Killed them so they'd not tell you they were being held prisoner."

"You know that, and I know that," said the captain. "But the Code of Galifar treats these as simple murders. We could perhaps try a diviner or a necromancer, but that's expensive and the results they can get are spotty at best. And we have hundreds of potential murderers that we've arrested, and who knows how many more got away?"

"I saved not even a one of them. They all died."

"Not the one in the last cell," said the captain. "You should take a look."

Cimozjen walked to the last opening and peered in cautiously. There, in the center of the room, stood a man dressed in worn peasant's clothing. He looked at Cimozjen, not a flicker of recognition in his eye.

"Ripfist!" blurted Cimozjen.

"What?" said Minrah. "Who?"

"They call him Ripfist," called Cimozjen over his shoulder. "He's . . . he's had monastic training of some sort. A combat monk."

"A monk?" asked Minrah. "Is he Aundairian?" She scooted quickly down the hall, shielding her eyes from the corpses that lay in the rooms.

Cimozjen looked in his eyes. The man had a glassy stare, deep behind which moved a semblance of consciousness, like the shadow of a leviathan stirring at the bottom of a calm, still lake. "I doubt if he even knows any more," said Cimozjen.

He moved slowly, subserviently into the room. Ripfist watched him with awareness, but no interest. Cimozjen moved closer, and saw that his hair was a tangled mess on one side of his head. He leaned closer and blew gently, moving a shock of hair enough to see a large jagged scar on the side of his scalp near the front.

He heard Minrah pad into the room behind him and gasp.

"He appears to have taken a nasty blow to the head," said Cimozjen. "Be careful, though, he still has all his deadly instincts, and there's no way to tell what might ignite his fury."

Minrah moved closer and sat on the floor. Cimozjen backed away to the door so as not to crowd Ripfist. Four was walking down the hall to see as well, and Cimozjen gestured for him to remain where he was.

Minrah leaned forward and patted the ground. "Come and sit, please. Can we talk?"

"Talk . . ." said Ripfist blankly.

"Yes, talk." She patted the ground again and smiled. "Will you come and sit? Come!"

"Sit," said Ripfist. His brow clouded for a moment. Slowly, uncertainly, he lowered himself to the floor, sitting on his heels with his hands resting on his thighs.

"My name is Minrah," she said. She spoke gently, as though to a shy child. "Do you remember your name?"

"No, I . . . I do—" he tried to say something else, but the words wouldn't come out of his mouth. He scrunched up his face in anger and frustration, and looked about the room. It seemed he was almost ready to cry.

"That's just fine," said Minrah. "Don't you worry your head."

Ripfist raised one hand to his scar. "My . . . my head, it . . ." He looked at Minrah and licked his lips. "Sit," he said with a tentative smile.

"That's right," said Minrah. "We're sitting together, you and I. It's very nice, isn't it?"

The smile flickered about his lips again, but never reached his eyes.

"Are you from Aundair? You sound like you are. You have a lovely accent."

"Aundair," he echoed, and a genuine warm smile crossed his face.

Minrah looked over her shoulder. "This could be too good to be true, Cimmer. An Aundairian monk? Grouped with the other elites, like Torval? If he's a member of that secret society, why, the gnomes would—"

"What secret society?" asked Cimozjen quietly.

"I told you about it before, Cimmer," said Minrah. "Some sort of secret assassin's cult or something that the gnomes wanted to know more about. They said it was called the Quiet Touch, and they—"

"The Quiet Touch," said Ripfist. His brow furrowed. He leaned forward and gripped Minrah's knee.

"Yes, that's right," said Minrah. "The Quiet Touch. You know about it?" She placed her hand gently over his. "Were you one of the Quiet Touch?"

"The Quiet Touch," said Ripfist, pride and confidence making an appearance in his tone even as his eyes darted about. He squeezed Minrah's knee warmly.

"That's right," she said. "The Quiet Touch. Can you tell me anything, anything at all? What do you remember?"

Confusion clouded Ripfist's face. He dropped his hand from her knee and looked around. "Wh—where . . ."

"You've been a prisoner," said Minrah. "Do you understand? You were captured, but we—"

Ripfist shook his head, scared. "No capture."

"Easy, everything's fine now," said Minrah compassionately. "You were captured, they held you prisoner, but—"

Comprehension flooded his eyes, and he speared Minrah with the intensity of his gaze. "Death before capture," he said urgently. In one fluid motion he reached his right arm behind his head, looked left, grabbed his chin, and yanked his head around, breaking his neck with a grotesque snap. His body flailed once and he flopped to the floor, his right arm pumping through the same yanking motion over and over.

Minrah shrieked, scooting herself backward on hands and feet, unable to tear her eyes from the terrible spectacle. Cimozjen moved to intercept her, grab her, hold her, but she kept trying to crawl away. At last he turned his body to shield her eyes, and pressed her to his chest, holding her tightly, and her screams dissolved into sobs.

He found himself kissing her head in an effort to calm her and stopped himself, relieved that she seemed not to notice.

With one last look at the twitching body, he picked her up and carried her from the room.

Chapter
Twenty-Eight

Parting
Zor, the 5th day of Aryth, 998

Where's your shield, Cimmer?"

"It had 'Pomindras Lasker d'Deneith' carved on the inside. I thought it particularly foolish to bring it along."

Minrah, Four, and Cimozjen walked through the streets of Aundair, heading for the House Deneith enclave. The winds of the previous day had blown through, driving away the last of the rain clouds, and the cobbles glistened in the morning sun.

Four had replaced his battle-axe with a nearly identical one from the Deneith armory. He carried his weapon slung over one shoulder, a relaxed posture that both of the others noted but refrained from mentioning.

Cimozjen had Pomindras's sword at his waist and his family dagger at his back, but had not worn his chain mail, for fear that the swishing sound of the links would cause them difficulties.

"So what is this about?" asked Four.

"I really don't know," said Minrah. "But it seemed best to take Rophis up on his invitation if we're going to get any real answers."

"I hope we are not making a mistake," said the warforged.

"So do I," said Cimozjen. "Unfortunately, there is only one way to find out. If we hide ourselves away, I'll always feel Torval peering over my shoulder."

The Deneith compound was a small city block of buildings that enclosed a gated courtyard. Each of the buildings was built with the solid architecture of a fortification, made of square-cut stone so keenly carved and fitted that no mortar had been necessary. The monolithic walls were broken only by narrow windows ideal for defensive archery fire, and crenellations ran along the rooftop. Thick wrought-iron fencing stretched from building to building, each vertical bar capped by a vicious dragonshard-embedded spearhead that continually gave off wisps of smoke, hinting at cruel magical enhancement.

"Well," said Minrah, "we're here. Let's get this over with."

They walked up to a smaller structure at one end of the compound. It was the only building they could see that had an exterior door in it, a heavy double door easily tall and wide enough to fit a covered wagon. A large statue of a chimera stood watch over the gate, its heads turned in each direction. Two guards stood outside, armed and armored. They wore the livery of House Deneith—yellow and green tabards with sharply cut angles—as well as very bored expressions.

After a moment's hesitation to gather her composure, Minrah walked up to the guards with a businesslike stride, Cimozjen and Four just behind her. She flipped her hand in a supercilious gesture, snapping her paper open at one of the guards. He started slightly at the suddenness of the gesture, then reached out and took the proffered parchment.

"Appointment to see Lord Rophis d'Deneith, have you?" he said.

"Yes, we have," said Minrah, stressing the word *we* ever so slightly.

"This says nothing of additional guests," said the guard. "You may proceed. Alone."

"It says nothing against additional guests, either," said Minrah. "These are my bodyguards."

"They are not allowed in."

Minrah scoffed. "Is your mighty house afraid of them?"

"Not at all. I assure you that our compound is the safest area in all of Fairhaven."

"And that just fills me to the brim with confidence," said Minrah. "I mean, House Deneith looks veritably under siege here. She picked up a rock and threw it through the fence.

"Hey, watch it!" yelled a house servant walking across the court with a load of foodstuffs.

"Your courtyard isn't even properly warded," said Minrah, "and there are those who would see me murdered." Her voice continued to rise in volume as her rant gained momentum. "Does House Deneith guarantee my safety against sling stones, missiles, and bolts of lightning while my bodyguards idle outside? And what if your house has been infiltrated, as has been recently suggested by the whispers on the street? What then? I demand my noble right to have my bodyguards accompany me, or by the gods you yourself can escort me and explain your actions to Lord Rophis personally," she finished with a shout.

"My lady, I will be more than happy to escort you personally to your appointment," said the guard, stiffening. He adjusted his scabbard and rested his hand on the hilt of his sword. Then he nodded politely. "Along with your bodyguards, of course. I've no wish to offend the guests of the family."

He led the trio through the gatehouse, across the flagstone courtyard, and into the grandest of the compound's buildings.

"This is some lobby," whispered Minrah as they entered.

Cimozjen glanced about at the polished marble floors, veined with gold. The exquisite magewrought illustrations of famous Deneith generals, animated and ensconced in free-floating gem-studded frames. And the massive chandelier, wrought of platinum and boasting well over a hundred magical glowlamps. "You speak the truth," he said choking back his anger. "It is almost blindingly so. And it has been paid for by the blood of a hundred years of mercenaries that the house has sent to battle."

They walked up a grand staircase to a short but elegant hall, carpeted in plush gold trimmed with green. The guard escorted them to a pair of doors artistically carved with the crest of House Deneith. Two more guards flanked the door, unarmored, but wearing extravagant silken uniforms with a herringbone patterns of swords embroidered in silver thread.

Their escort displayed the paper, and the two guards each rapped on their door in perfect unison, then unlatched the doors and swung them open, revealing an opulent room with six chairs and two end tables. The back wall was well stocked with a bewildering variety of wines, brandies, cognacs, and other spirits, as well as an extensive supply of glasses in all shapes and sizes.

"Wait here," said their escort. "Lord Rophis will be with you in a moment. I trust your bodyguards know not to touch anything."

The doors closed behind them with a nearly inaudible click.

"You heard the man," said Minrah, imperiously flitting her hand. "Behave yourselves." She walked briskly over the liquor board, grabbed a big glass, opened the first bottle that came to hand, and dumped it into the glass until it was nearly full. "Luckily, he didn't include me in that sentiment." She took a deep swig while pacing the room, and Cimozjen noticed that her nerves were causing the surface of the liquid to tremble.

A few minutes later, another door in the room opened, and Rophis d'Deneith walked in. "It's grossly uncultured to fill a snifter that full, Minrah," he said. As he crossed the room, he stuttered slightly in his walk. "Well. I most certainly did not expect my guest to have brought anyone else . . . let alone you, Cimozjen Hellekanus." He smacked his lips in annoyance. "No matter. I will deal with you presently."

Rophis walked over to the bar, took down a tall, thin glass, and poured himself a drink of something slightly bubbly, pale lavender in color. He swirled it in his glass, turning it at an angle to inspect it, then swirled it some more and held it to his nose. "You have to dispense with roughly half of the bubbles before drinking," he said to no one in particular. "Otherwise it's a little too full of bite." He swirled it a little longer, then took a sip, and smiled broadly. "Perfect."

He walked over to one of the chairs and sat, took another sip from his drink, then set his glass on the end table. "Sit," he said with a gesture. "We've supped together, no need to be so stiffly formal. Although I would appreciate it if you sent your Cannith conscript out of the room."

"His name is Four," said Cimozjen.

"Ah." Rophis picked up his glass and took another sip. "How quaint."

"I remember you," said Four.

"Do you? Well, I'll have to take your word for it." He looked back at Cimozjen and held up his empty hand in resigned apology. "They all look the same to me." He took another sip. "But if you've gone and named it, that means you're attached, and not likely to send it out." He sucked on his teeth for a moment. Then he looked at Minrah and patted the back of the chair next to him. "Sit," he said again.

"I'll stand, thank you," said Minrah. But she did walk closer and rest her arms on the back of the chair opposite Rophis.

Rophis set his glass back down. "I have been following your serial with quite some interest," he said. " 'Bound by Iron,' I believe you titled it? It's quite good. You have talent, Minrah."

"Thank you," said Minrah. "It's almost completed. But as a surety against anything ill befalling me before the morrow—I hope you'll understand that I've lost much of my confidence in your sense of justice—I have the final installments in the hands of a reliable messenger, who will deliver them to the *Korranberg Chronicle* in the morning if I do not return."

"Why, Minrah, whatever have I done to lose your trust?" said Rophis.

"Lied about your Karrn roots, for starters," said Minrah. She took a deep draw from her snifter. "On the *Silver Cygnet*, you swore to be Aundairian in order to hide your heritage, and with it your ties to House Deneith. Or how about using Boniam to find out about us, and then having Pomindras ambush us? Kidnapping sweet old Cimmer and making him fight? Keeping Four in a cage for two years? And if that's not enough, I'll bet I can come up with a few others."

Rophis held up his hands. "I must grant you those points as valid," he said, "but if you had not boarded the wrong ship, I would have not had to resort to dissimulation. You were allowed to board because he was a warrior, and he looked as if he'd come to participate. Initially, I was excited to have such a grizzled, capable veteran aboard our ship. I quickly found out that that was not the case, but it was too late. You had paid your fare, and we of the Deneith are raised never, ever to break a covenant. We were wrong to have allowed you aboard. If I could have one mistake to undo, it would have been that one. I would have left you on the dock."

"Don't feign such charity," said Minrah. "You only wish that because then your secrets would still be safe."

"Indeed, that is true," said Rophis, "and I wish them still to remain unrevealed, which is why I invited you here today."

"What do you mean?" asked Minrah.

"As I said, I've been reading your work. It's a story that needs a thrilling ending. Thus, while I could have you assassinated to protect my secrets, doing so would be wasteful of your talent, cruel to your readers, and ultimately would cause your publisher gnomes to start sniffing around your trail, which would make me most disconcerted. So rather than take that course, I have a mutually beneficial proposal."

He reached inside his surcoat and pulled out a folded piece of parchment from a hidden pocket. He leaned forward and handed it to Minrah, who took it suspiciously.

"I have had some of my best minds working on this since the day you stopped in at the Blinking Hippo," he said. "May I present to you an alternate ending for your story, one that suits your needs as a scribe, and my needs as a leader of this house."

He leaned back and picked up his glass again. "You'll find the salient points there. Naturally, we want you to rewrite it in your own particular style."

Minrah opened the parchment and scanned it. She blinked several times. "This is good," she said. She took another healthy sip from her glass.

"And I think the use of bitter Cyrans as the villains will evoke a better response from your readership."

"Minrah," said Cimozjen, "you're not seriously considering this, are you?"

"Of course she is," said Rophis wearily. "It's a better ending than the truth, and instead of angering a dragonmarked house, she gains favor in one." He turned to speak to Minrah again. "Such favor that we would be pleased to forward any suitable new stories for you to immortalize. Naturally, such assignments would be for pay—wages that we would remit in addition to your monthly stipend."

"Monthly stipend?" asked Minrah.

"Seven galifars a month, if that suits your lifestyle. We want you to be able to focus on your art."

Minrah sprayed her drink. "S-seven?" She giggled. "No more odd jobs . . ."

"Minrah!" said Cimozjen. "You cannot do this!"

"Can't? I have to, Cimmer! This is seven gold a month! Do you have any idea how little I've lived on? This is a lot! And this is without doing anything! He said stories are extra! I could just . . . write! Anything I want!"

"You'll be publishing a lie!"

"So?" asked Minrah, her hands held wide. "That's what writers do. We make stuff up for a living to entertain the crowd. Do you think the commoners care if it's true or not? Of course they don't. Look at the theater. Do you think even a tenth of the plays are based on anything real? No!"

"Do you not see what he's trying to do? He's trying to corrupt you, poison your soul, purchase your freedom one month at a time. Each month you take their blood money is one more braid in the rope with which they bind you!"

"They can't bind me," said Minrah, "because they're not making me do this."

"You misunderstand, Minrah. You're binding yourself *for* them!"

"You don't get it, do you?" Minrah shouted. "They're not making me do anything! *I'm* making *them* do this by the power of *my* pen! Mine!"

Cimozjen fought for words, but he saw that Minrah had been bought. He tried one last gambit. "What about Torval? Are you going to let him lie unavenged?"

"I was clear from the start, Cimmer, that you were in it for the revenge, and I was in it for the story. You yourself said I was only chasing ink, so don't get all huffy now." She folded the parchment and put it in her pouch. "At least I got what I was after. I got my story, and it's a good one. But you . . . well, Torval is still dead, and by pursuing it, you made them kill the other prisoners they held, too. You've gotten nothing, Cimmer. You've gotten less than nothing. You even know who's responsible now, but do you think you can stop a dragonmarked house? You and Four? Not a kobold's chance. There's no way you can stop it, Cimmer. At least I'm smart enough to profit from it." She turned to Rophis. "If I can pick up my stipend the first day of each month at any Deneith enclave, you have yourself a deal."

"Done," said Rophis with a smile. "The charter is already prepared. It will be given you when you depart." He swirled the liquid in his glass, and drained the last of it with a happy sigh.

"Now I know you, Minrah," said Cimozjen. "I understand why you despise my oaths, and why you are proud of your ability to lie."

"You don't know me at all, Cimmer. You can't see a thing through your eyes, because they look at the gods as goals, and they don't see the real world at all. I see the world as it is."

"I see clearly. But I also keep a vision of the world as it ought to be. And that includes you, Minrah."

Minrah sneered at him. "Preach all you want. I have a story

to write. And it no longer includes you. Too bad, though." She licked her teeth and waggled her eyebrows. "You'll never know what you missed."

" 'Lo, thou shall know them by their words. Their own tongue shall reveal them, for they shall laud their sins, and their depravity they shall exalt, but thy virtue shall they mock as folly.' "

Minrah made a rude gesture at Cimozjen, then turned and left the room.

Rophis chuckled. "It looks like the information the gnomes gave us on her was well worth the price." He rose and poured himself another drink. "Will you join me?" he asked, swirling his glass. "I thought not." He walked back over to his chair and sat. "You're a strong man, Cimozjen Hellekanus, and a fearsome foe. But she's right, you know."

"Right?" asked Cimozjen. "Right about what?"

"There's nothing that someone even as determined as you can do to stop a dragonmarked house, or even to stop the arena."

Cimozjen shrugged and scratched the back of his head. "Let me be honest, Rophis," he said. "What has me most confused was how this started. It ill fits the reputation of House Deneith."

"No, it's definitely out of step for us," said Rophis. "We—I, that is, for although the germ of the idea was unintentionally handed to me, I must give myself the full credit for brilliantly developing it and nurturing it to its present state—we were selected to deliver the most important of the prisoners home. By important I mean the elite of the enemy armies, the most dangerous generals, and the upper crust of the nobles . . . and Prelate Quardov made it as clear as he could that he would be most pleased if those people never quite made it back home. It seemed a reasonable suggestion. So I made similar overtures to the other nations, and they also found the idea of value. And lo, the day after the end of the Last War I had a sizeable stable of experienced veteran fighters, none of whom were to be repatriated."

He took a sip of his drink to wet his throat. "At the same time, the nations were starting to stand down their armies. Thousands of veterans and, better yet, those who'd stood guard for years and never gone to war, all were turned loose with nothing to do. So I thought to bring the two together. Slowly but surely I eliminate the people entrusted to our . . . how shall I say, 'hospitality,' and I get to evaluate the former soldiers. The novices died. The very best, we recruited into our mercenaries. If they refused, we arranged for them to fight one of our best prisoners. And no matter what happened, we made money by means of gambling."

"Ah," said Cimozjen. "Death by commercial enterprise."

"I suppose you could put it that way. But what is a mercenary house other than commercial killing?" He took another sip. "With my plan, I recruit away the very best of everyone's armies, deaths erode away their manpower, and my house even gets gambling revenues. Over time, my enclave grows richer, and eventually there will be no army with any experience left in Khorvaire . . . but ours." He spread his hands helplessly. "You see how brilliant it is?"

"I must admit, it has a vile beauty to its completeness," said Cimozjen.

"I do not understand," said Four. "I never fought in the War. Why was I used?"

Rophis waved a hand dismissively. "Please, there were plenty of your kind still warm from the forges at war's end. No one wanted your kind any more, so the Canniths gave us a good price the day before emancipation. Now be a good little whoreforged and shut your jawbone."

He set his glass on the end table and drummed his fingers twice on the polished wood. "As I said, I was not expecting to see you here today, but I hope I have shown myself to be hospitable. I am also forgiving. You fought quite well in the arena, Cimozjen Hellekanus. You are a valuable warrior, and I would be most pleased were you to choose to join one of my house's mercenary companies. I do believe you'd have command potential, and your wages would reflect that."

"I want the arena combats to end," said Cimozjen. "That would be a suitable step toward justice for Torval."

Rophis leaned forward. "Weren't you listening?" he said reasonably. "Why do you think I told you all that I have? To show you that you cannot win. You cannot stop me or my plan. We have enough momentum now that we can continue the fights without the prisoners. Even if you were to bring everything I said to the chronicles, no one would believe you in the face of Minrah's story. Plus, as I warned a few moments ago, you'd earn the wrath of a dragonmarked house, and that leads to a short and painful life."

Cimozjen curled his lips into a snarl. "Then I shall kill you to and put an end to this."

Rophis sagged, rubbing his forehead with one hand. "Your anger is blinding you. You can't stop it. I can't even stop it now, and I started the damned thing! The arena has been running for two years here in Aundair, a year in Sharn, and as you may have deduced, I recently introduced it to Korth. The wheels are well in motion, and it is far too late to stop the cart. Within five years, arenas will be in operation across the continent, and in ten years, I'm sure we'll be able to operate in the open."

Cimozjen's hand twisted on the hilt of his sword. "If I cannot stop the arena, at least I can get revenge on you for the pointlessness of Torval's death. Arm yourself."

Rophis sighed, clapped his hands on his knees, and stood. "You still don't grasp this, do you? This is has nothing to do with you personally, or even with your friend. But perhaps you can understand that your friend did not have the pointless death that Quardov and others like him wanted. I made sure of that. His fighting gave other veterans like him something to do. His fighting helped build my house. In fact, you yourself helped further my goals in the arena. By so rapidly becoming such a hated fighter, you increased attendance and gambling income. My house made a lot from you and your friend, whatever his name was."

Cimozjen drew his sword.

Rophis shook his head. "I was afraid you'd feel that way. But according to Minrah's writings, you're an oathbound, aren't you?"

He walked over to Cimozjen and turned his back, his hands clasped placidly in front of him. "Go ahead, my fellow Karrn. I am unarmed. My back is turned. I cannot stop you. Strike me down."

There was a short silence, the only audible sound that of Cimozjen's breathing.

Rophis chuckled. "You can't stop the arena, Cimozjen. You can't even kill me, the one man you hate most. You may as well just leave and go home."

"You're right," said Cimozjen. He lowered his head. "I cannot kill you."

❖ ❖ ❖ ◉ ❖ ❖ ❖

Cimozjen and Four backed out of the receiving room, bowed, and closed the doors quietly behind them. The door guards on either side scowled, but Cimozjen touched his brow in deference and said, "We know the way out."

Nonetheless, one of the door guards escorted them down the hall to the stairs and across the lobby of the building.

The pair walked across the courtyard toward the gatehouse.

"I just realized something," said Four.

"What's that?"

"Do you remember the coins that the strange people gave me when they took me out of my home?"

"How could I forget?" said Cimozjen. "They sent you off with several hundred in mixed coinage dangling from a burlap bag around your neck. What of it?"

"Minrah bet them all on your victory in the arena the first night."

"Did she?" Cimozjen snorted derisively. "At least she bet on the winning side."

"She did," said Four. "But she never gave me back my coins."

"She kept—argh, I tell you the truth, Four, we are the better for her absence."

Four looked at his hands for a moment, then curled them into fists. "I wish to have a new name now," he said.

"Oh? What would that be?"

"Free."

Cimozjen smiled wistfully and clapped the warforged on the shoulder. "It's a good name, all things considered."

They passed through the gatehouse and into the city's streets. Cimozjen paused, unsure which way to go now that his crusade of the last few weeks had so abruptly ended.

"Pah! Some bodyguards you are," called one of the gate guards. "Your patron left a good while ago."

"She decided to contract with your house, instead," said Cimozjen.

"Hullo, warforged," called the other guard, "I thought you had a battle-axe when you came in."

"I did," he said. "I left it with Rophis."

HEIRS OF ASH

RICH WULF

The Legacy . . . an invention of unimaginable power. Rumors say it could save the world—or destroy it. The hunt is on.

Book 1
VOYAGE OF THE MOURNING DAWN

Book 2
FLIGHT OF THE DYING SUN
February 2007

Book 3
RISE OF THE SEVENTH MOON
November 2007

BLADE OF THE FLAME

TIM WAGGONER

Once an assassin. Now a man of faith. One man searching for peace in a land that knows only blood.

Book 1
THIEVES OF BLOOD

Book 2
FORGE OF THE MINDSLAYERS
March 2007

Book 3
SEA OF DEATH
February 2008

THE LANTERNLIGHT FILES

PARKER DEWOLF

A man on the run. A city on the watch. Magic on the loose.

Book 1
THE LEFT HAND OF DEATH
July 2007

Book 2
WHEN NIGHT FALLS
March 2008

Book 3
DEATH COMES EASY
December 2008

RAVENLOFT
the covenant

RAVENLOFT'S LORDS OF DARKNESS HAVE ALWAYS WAITED FOR THE UNWARY TO FIND THEM.

Six classic tales of horror set in the RAVENLOFT world have returned to print in all-new editions.

From the autocratic vampire who wrote the memoirs found in *I, Strahd* to the demon lord and his son whose story is told in *Tapestry of Dark Souls*, some of the finest horror characters created by some of the most influential authors of horror and dark fantasy have found their way to RAVENLOFT, to be trapped there forever.

LAURELL K. HAMILTON
Death Of A Darklord

CHRISTIE GOLDEN
Vampire Of The Mists

P.N. ELROD
I, Strahd: The Memoirs Of A Vampire

ANDRIA CARDARELLE
To Sleep With Evil
March 2007

ELAINE BERGSTROM
Tapestry of Dark Souls
June 2007

TANYA HUFF
Scholar of Decay
October 2007